Wilhelmina

Lori J. Bridges-Hahn

First Edition: 2025
Editor: The Book Nook Editorial & Proofreading Service
Cover Design: Ruth Anna Evans Designs
Formatting: KII Formatting
Author Photo: Pottinger Photography (Cincinnati, Ohio)
Published by: Lori J. Bridges-Hahn via Amazon KDP & IngramSpark

ISBN:
9798992864014 – Paperback

For Doug:

Thank you for your undying encouragement and support.
I love you.

For Lil:

I miss your laughter, your hugs, and your stories of the ghost you named Wilhelmina, who constantly hid or moved your belongings. Perhaps this book tells Wilhelmina's story, and she can now rest in peace with you at her side.
You left us too soon, Lil.

Part 1: Charlotte

Strength. Independence. Resilience.

CHAPTER ONE

July 1990

Cold. So very cold.

A whisper of rain brushed Charlotte's goose-pimpled skin, forcing her eyes to flutter open. Although a warm breeze grazed her cheek, blowing a lock of hair across her face, she shivered against the chill. Thunder rolled in the distance, so far away she barely heard it, while the sun waged a war against dark clouds as it crested the horizon, the dismal gray skies winning the battle. The rain became heavier, pelting her face, arms and legs, and fog rose around her.

Where am I?

Charlotte jolted upright, blinking rapidly and glancing around. She found herself at the top of a stone stairway meandering up a slight incline from the street below. Tall lampposts lined the street, casting an eerie orange light on a dilapidated English Tudor house resting several yards away. Thick ivy hugged the stucco structure and covered most of the windows like stiff linen drapes. Cedar framed the leaded glass panes, and on the third floor, one lone window faced the street.

Aging trees and unkempt bushes towered over the cobblestone walkways encircling the house. To the left, the path led to a spacious covered porch dwarfed by a massive stone fireplace, its chimney rising majestically above the roof. Charlotte leaned back, her gaze aimed high. Five additional chimneys jutted from the rooftop and her lips parted in awe. To the right, the walkway leading to the rear of the house was covered in weeds pushing up between the stones. Farther to the right sat a carriage house, long since converted into a four-car garage. Charlotte scanned the steps where she was sitting. Many were cracked and others had large chunks missing.

Charlotte rose to her feet, wincing at a stabbing pain in her knee, then ran her hand over the trail of dried blood ending at her lower shin. The scrape to her knee wasn't nearly as disconcerting as not knowing how—or when—it happened.

Charlotte turned away from the house intent on running, but a hand touched her shoulder. Shivering, she whirled around—but no one was there. It must have been the wind caressing her skin.

Curiosity winning out over fear, Charlotte clenched her hands into tight fists and slowly approached the porch. A short flight of stairs led to an ornate, cherrywood door flanked by stained glass sidelights. She watched as a shaky hand reached for the doorknob— her own hand. Just as her fingers touched the knob, something passed through her body. Goosebumps once again rose on her skin, and a slight pain rushed through her fingers, past her wrist and up her arm. Her spine tingled as if something was crawling down her back.

It didn't make sense to her. How could she get an electrical shock from a doorknob on an abandoned house? No, it didn't make sense, but it *did* scare her enough that she fled from the porch, taking the stone stairs two at a time until she reached the bottom, where she found her car waiting at the curb. After fumbling in the pockets of her denim shorts, she pulled out a set of keys and fingered through them until finding the one for her car. She unlocked the door, hands still shaking, and slid in behind the steering wheel.

Charlotte inserted the key in the ignition, closed her eyes, and rested her head on the steering wheel.

Take deep breaths, Charlotte.

When her heartbeat finally slowed, Charlotte stole one last glance at the house. The grass was overgrown; the house completely dark inside. But then something appeared in the third-floor window. Or someone.

What was that?

She scrunched her eyes closed, shook her head, and looked again. The rain slowed to a drizzle as the sun rose and cast just enough light through the fog for Charlotte to make out someone in the window—a woman with blond hair falling just below her chin. Charlotte blinked again but the woman was gone. She must be imagining things … or maybe it was just the fog.

Trembling, Charlotte started the engine. She had no idea where she was and had never been to this part of Cincinnati before. Not that she remembered, anyway. And yet, that house—and the woman in the window—seemed strangely familiar.

What day was it? How long had she been on those steps? And how did she get there?

Charlotte reached for the car phone resting on the console between the seats when an open map on the floor caught her eye. A circle had been drawn in red ink on one small area of the map. She picked it up and examined it. The circle surrounded Glenmary Drive in Clifton Heights. Dropping the map on the seat, she then checked her driver's side mirror and pulled out into the street. She paused at the corner long enough to check the street sign, confirming she was indeed on Glenmary Drive.

The needle on the dashboard hung dangerously close to E, and she sighed before weaving through the neighborhood. After reaching the main road, she spotted a gas station and pulled in next to the pumps. She searched for her purse and found it tucked on the floor behind the passenger seat, but instead of rummaging for her wallet, she yanked out her checkbook and flipped it open to the calendar. Her hands became clammy, and her skin grew damp.

July 10, 1990. Tuesday. Six o'clock in the morning.

She had lost nine hours this time.

CHAPTER TWO

February 1985

Charlotte Schmidt threw her head back as an exuberant, booming laugh escaped her lips. The sound resonated through the crowded tavern. Several people turned their heads toward Charlotte when she doubled over near the bar and held her sides, as if she might burst open at any moment. These strangers smiled, some even chuckled, although the only two people who knew the cause of the laugh were Charlotte and her friend, Mindy Brown.

Wiping away the tears streaming down her face, Charlotte gasped. "That's the craziest idea I've ever heard, Mindy! No way am I going to one of those matchmaking companies. Can you just imagine me bumbling my way through the video? I'd make a damn fool of myself, and you know it. And don't try to change my mind. I don't care how long it's been since I've been out with a guy!"

"What are you so afraid of?" Mindy sighed deeply. "You've got nothing to lose. You know that's how I met Caleb and look how that worked out. You need to find someone new!" Mindy and Caleb had married two years ago and had just bought their first house, hoping to fill it with children soon.

"It's just not for me, Min. Besides, you met Caleb when you went in to record your video and he was there in the waiting room. You never even submitted your application because you two started talking and hit it off from the get-go. I don't think that will happen to me. Look, maybe I'm just not meant to have that someone special in my life." Turning to the bartender, Charlotte held up two fingers. "Two more whiskey sours, please."

They sat in silence for a moment, sipping their drinks. Music poured from the jukebox in the corner. In the distance, billiard balls knocked together. *Snap, snap!* Charlotte glanced into the mirror behind the bar and caught the reflection of a tall, sandy-haired man standing at the entrance as he casually slung his coat over his shoulder. His eyes darted around the room until they met hers in the mirror. Charlotte quickly looked away, but he was already strolling in her direction.

No, no, no, she thought. *Not today. Not now. Not ever.*

She hung her head as he stopped directly behind her. Still reeling from a difficult breakup six months ago, Charlotte was not ready to date and had no interest in finding someone new.

"Excuse me, miss," he said, his voice warm and buttery. "I believe your purse fell to the floor a moment ago."

Charlotte glanced down at the floor, where her purse was in fact toppled on its side. She started to reach for it, but he touched her arm, and she stiffened. Her spine prickled and goosebumps rose on her flesh.

"Allow me," he said. As he handed her the purse, he continued, "I'm Richard. And you are?"

Charlotte's gaze flashed quickly to Mindy, then she rolled her eyes, and spun on the stool to face him. "Not interested," Charlotte said with an icy tone.

"C'mon, Charlotte, be nice. After all, he saved you from losing your purse." Mindy stuck out her hand. "I'm Mindy, and this is Charlotte. You said your name is … Richard?"

"Yes, Richard Palmer. Nice to meet you, Mindy and Charlotte." Richard turned slightly to address Charlotte. "I was captivated by that boisterous laugh you just let out. Must've been quite a joke."

"Uh-huh," Charlotte muttered. She tossed her blond bangs out of her eyes. "And it was a private conversation, so if you'll just move along, please. Thank you for telling me about my purse."

"You're quite welcome. Maybe we'll meet again soon."

"Not likely."

"Charlotte!" Mindy exclaimed. Facing Richard, she said, "I apologize for my friend here, Richard. She hasn't been on a date in months and she's a bit touchy. Thanks again for retrieving her purse."

Richard nodded slightly, flashed a smile in Charlotte's direction, and strode into the billiards room.

"Really, Mindy, did you have to be so damn nice to that guy? Geez!"

"Well, you certainly could've been more pleasant. Gosh, Charlotte, he could be a really nice guy and you just blew him off like yesterday's news!"

"Look, Min, how many times do we have to have this conversation? I am *not* going to find a guy on a dating site and I'm certainly not going to go out with some dude I met in a bar. End of story. Can we just move on and forget about my love life? It doesn't always have to be the topic of our conversations, you know! Besides, I'm just not ready to date again. Honestly, I'm enjoying the single life."

"Sure, Char, whatever you say."

After finishing their drinks, the two friends drove separately to a nearby movie theater, bought their tickets and popcorn, and settled in Theater Number Two for *Places in the Heart.*

Charlotte found it hard to concentrate on the movie, and her thoughts began to wander.

Maybe Mindy is right. Maybe I just need to be more adventurous, meet someone new and exciting. My life has been so dull. Sheesh, listen to me. I'm actually considering applying with a dating company. C'mon, Charlotte, get a grip.

But Charlotte couldn't stop thinking about her life, her childhood, her family.

Charlotte Marie was born on April 29, 1955, to Albert and Elizabeth Schmidt. Albert was the first of his German family to be born in America, and grew up speaking both German and English. He majored in business and accounting at the University of Cincinnati and worked as a waiter at local restaurants throughout college. Shortly after graduation, Albert landed a position with the local Internal Revenue Service in Cincinnati and worked there until January 1943, when he was drafted into the United States Army and sent to combat in Germany and France.

On June 6, 1944—also known as D-Day—Albert was hit by mortar shells at Normandy Beach and lost his right leg below the knee. He spent three weeks in a French hospital and was sent home to Cincinnati, where he was admitted to the Veterans Administration Hospital. During his five-month stay, he met Elizabeth Harper, one of his nurses. He fell in love the first time he saw her.

Albert could never fully explain, to himself or anyone else, what it was about Elizabeth that made him fall so deeply in love. Perhaps it was her gentle touch when changing his dressing, her genuine smile when she woke him every morning in the hospital, her easy laughter at his pathetic attempt at jokes. Or was it her chocolate hair, her crystal blue eyes, and her bright red lips?

In October, the physicians fitted Albert with a prosthetic leg. It was a damn heavy thing, made of wood and leather, and he bristled every morning when Elizabeth tried to attach it to his knee. He would often slip into his native language, hollering *"Ach nein!"* whenever Elizabeth or one of the other nurses retrieved the prosthesis from the bedside cabinet.

The doctor came in one late November morning to discharge Albert and inform him that it was time to return to his home. What would he do? Albert's mouth became dry, throat constricting, and he felt sick to his stomach. Through each rapid breath, Albert blinked back the pooling tears and wrinkled his brow.

Fisting his hands on the sheets, Albert met the doctor's gaze. "But … where shall I go?"

"I don't understand," the doctor replied. "Do you not have family here?"

"Ach, nein. Ahh, no, I do not. My parents died many years ago. I have no home here." Albert shut his eyes, holding back tears. *Why am I about to cry? What is wrong with me?*

"I see," the doctor said. "We will have patient services stop in to see you. They will be able to find a place for you to stay until you can find employment and save enough for a place of your own. I'll arrange for someone to see you today. You will be discharged in a few days, I'm afraid."

Elizabeth comforted Albert over the next few days. "We've sent many veterans to Templeton, Mister Schmidt. No need to worry. It's a nice place to live."

"*Ach*, Nurse Elizabeth, please call me Albert. And I'm not so worried about Templeton. I've heard good things from the other nurses and doctors."

"Then what is it, Mister Schmi …? I mean, Albert?"

"I … I do not know how to say it. *Du wirst mir fehlin*, my dear Elizabeth. *Du wirst mir fehlin*." Albert's voice cracked, and his eyes became bright and shiny with fresh tears.

"I'm sorry, Mister … Albert. I don't understand German."

"I fear saying it to you. But, *ach*, I must. I will miss you."

Patting his hand, Elizabeth cooed, "Ahh, Albert, and I will miss you. You will be fine, and I'm sure you will continue to recover."

"Dare I ask if I may see you again?"

"Yes, you can stop by the hospital anytime. I would welcome your visit."

"*Ach, nein.* I mean to say, may I take you out for coffee? Or a meal?"

Elizabeth's face reddened and she lowered her eyes, endearing her to Albert even more. "I … I'm not sure, Albert. Perhaps. I don't know, though."

Despite Elizabeth's hesitation, she and Albert did indeed meet for coffee just two weeks later. The following week, it was lunch. By the end of December, they were meeting for dinner twice a week. Albert had landed a position with a prestigious accounting firm, Doyle & Barclay, at the beginning of December, and was saving his wages for an apartment. Elizabeth lived at home with her parents, and Albert would ride the streetcars to her home, where they could walk to nearby cafes and shops.

Elizabeth's parents were strict disciplinarians who insisted on a long-term relationship before Albert was permitted to propose. But propose he did and nearly three years later, on May 9, 1948, Albert and Elizabeth were married. By this time Albert had risen to the stature of junior partner with Doyle & Barclay, and Elizabeth continued nursing at the hospital. They moved into a large two-bedroom apartment and spent their evenings together listening to the radio, reading, or talking. Their life together was happy and filled with love.

Sadly, Elizabeth miscarried their first child in 1950 and their second in 1952. But in 1955, Elizabeth happily carried their third and only child to term, and their beautiful daughter Charlotte was born.

Albert found a small three-bedroom house in St. Bernard, a suburb of Cincinnati, where Charlotte made friends and went to school. Their standard of living was modest but comfortable. They bought their first television set in 1957 and a car in 1958. Elizabeth quit working when Charlotte was born, and never returned to nursing. In 1966, they moved to Fairfield, north of Cincinnati, and lived there until Charlotte graduated from college in 1977.

Charlotte dated a few boys throughout high school. A pretty, hazel-eyed blonde, she became a cheerleader, was elected class president, was homecoming queen and prom queen during her senior year, and graduated at the top of her class.

Mindy and Charlotte met in college and shared a dorm room for four years. They became friends quickly, soon considering the other as a sister, and were rarely apart. Their years at the University of Cincinnati were spent studying, dating, going to sorority and fraternity parties, and drinking beer. Mindy became a veterinarian technician. Caleb Brown had just graduated from the police academy when he and Mindy met at the matchmaking company. Charlotte took an immediate liking to him. He and Mindy never made Charlotte feel like the third wheel, and she was elated when they announced their engagement.

Like her father, Charlotte majored in business and accounting. In 1977, a small, family-owned accounting firm in Hamilton recruited Charlotte directly out of college. Then in 1984, Charlotte landed a position with the city of Hamilton as the Assistant Finance Director.

Charlotte had no siblings or cousins to play with during her childhood. In fact, as she sat in the dark movie theater reflecting, she couldn't remember ever seeing photos of her father's parents and had never been told much about them. She vaguely recalled their names—Oskar and Wilhelmina Schmidt. They had both been born in Germany, although they never met until after they migrated to Cincinnati, where they both worked in the local meat packing plant.

Charlotte vaguely remembered bits and pieces of their history: her grandfather died in 1925 at a mere thirty-four years old; her grandmother remarried but died just ten years after Oskar, leaving their son, Albert, to be raised by his stepfather. Beyond that, Charlotte's parents never spoke of Wilhelmina or Oskar. She didn't even know the name of her father's stepfather.

Her mother's parents lived in Cincinnati and doted on their only grandchild with loving affection. But they died when Charlotte was five, tragically killed in a bus accident.

Charlotte met Robert Miller at a company picnic in 1978; he was her boss's younger brother. They began dating right away and moved in together within six months. Charlotte was happy and very much in love. They talked about getting married someday. Robert was attentive and loving ... until he wasn't. Shortly after the sixth anniversary of their first date, Charlotte found Robert in their bed with his secretary.

Charlotte realized she had allowed Robert to manipulate her throughout their relationship, and somewhere along the way, she had lost her sense of self. Now, finding independence for the first time since college, she loved being able to do whatever she wanted, whenever she wanted. And, despite Mindy's feeble attempts at setting her up with someone, Charlotte was simply not ready to date again.

"Hey, you! Are you awake?" Mindy interrupted Charlotte's thoughts. "What did you think of the movie? Or did you even stay awake for it?"

"Uhh, to be honest, I couldn't really pay attention to it. I'm sorry, Min, I'm just not sleeping well, and I guess I dozed off," she lied.

They donned their coats and headed toward the lobby.

"Char, maybe you should ask your doctor to prescribe something to help you sleep," Mindy suggested, tossing the empty popcorn bucket into a trash can. "You've been complaining about insomnia for ages."

"Probably a good idea. Hey, I'll make it up to you, okay? That new movie, *Witness*, is coming out in a couple weeks and I really want to see it. My treat, okay?"

"Sounds great. You know how much I want to see it, too." Mindy glanced outside and said, "Guess we better get outta here. Looks like the snow is getting deep."

Charlotte and Mindy hugged their goodbyes in the parking lot and drove their separate ways home. Charlotte tossed and turned in her bed, unable to calm her mind. Questions kept running through her mind. Questions about her grandparents.

Who were they? Why didn't Papa ever talk about them?

The last thing Charlotte remembered before finally falling asleep was the time on the clock: three-thirty in the morning. Another sleepless night.

CHAPTER THREE

March 1985

Charlotte stood in line at the movie theater concession stand, a jacket draped over one arm, as she tried to decide between popcorn or a soft pretzel. She crinkled her brow, eyeing the oversized Hershey bar and large box of Raisinets, but her hips told her otherwise. Besides, it wasn't a good idea to have anything with caffeine right now. Thanks to her new prescription of Melatodrol, she finally slept well the night before, and certainly didn't want to adversely affect her ability to sleep later.

"Earth to Charlotte," said Mindy. Narrowing her eyes as she poked Charlotte's arm, Mindy grumbled, "Hey, are you paying any attention to me?"

"I'm sorry, Min. I was just lost in thought."

"You've been spacey a lot lately. Are you still not sleeping?"

"Actually, I started a new prescription just last night to help me sleep. I didn't wake up until the alarm went off this morning. I just have a lot on my mind. The auditors will be at my office in two weeks, and I have a boatload of files I need to prepare for them before they show up. You know how I hate these quarterly audits."

"Yeah, I know. So, wanna share a popcorn tonight?"

"Sure, but I really just want chocolate." Charlotte's lips pulled up into a small smile as she chuckled.

"Well, so do I, but we both know better, don't we? I'll pay for the popcorn since you bought the movie tickets. I'm really excited about this one. You know how obsessed I am with Harrison Ford, and I heard this was a great movie."

Another laugh escaped Charlotte's lips. "I bet you'll be so horny after two hours of Harrison Ford that Caleb won't have a chance later tonight!"

Both girls snickered as they stepped up to the counter. After ordering their popcorn and drinks, they turned to head toward the theater when Charlotte suddenly came face-to-chest with a tall man.

"Oh my gosh, I'm so sorry!" she cried. "Did I spill anything on you?" Looking up, she met brilliant green eyes framed by smile lines. He grinned widely as he reached out to steady Charlotte.

"No, I'm fine. Are you okay?" He touched her elbow, sending a cold shiver through her body.

"Y-Yes, I'm fine. I-I'm sorry, have we met before?"

"We have, actually. A few weeks ago at Bar None." Glancing at Mindy, he nodded. "You're Mindy, I believe and you," he said as his gaze turned back to Charlotte, "are Charlotte. Did I get it right, or is it the other way around? I'm so bad with names."

Mindy interjected, "Yes, you got it. And your name is, wait a minute, I'll remember. Randy? No, that's not right. Richard?"

Richard lightly tapped the tip of Mindy's nose. "Ding, ding, ding! On the nose! So, ladies, what movie are you seeing? I'm here for that new Ford movie myself."

"So are we," Mindy said. "Why don't you join us? We'll wait for you over there." Mindy tipped her head toward the entrance of the first theater room.

"Sounds lovely. I'll just order something and be right with you."

Charlotte quickly walked away, handed her ticket to the attendant, and stood outside the theater doors, waiting for Mindy to catch up.

"Damn it, Min, why did you ask him to join us? This is girls' night, after all!"

"Look, Char, this is twice now that we've run into this guy. I think the stars are aligning, trying to tell you something. You need to live a little, try something new. You never do anything just for the hell of it. Besides, I think he's charming. And certainly good looking. Did you see how green his eyes are? Mmmmmm."

"Stop it, Min. I don't find him charming at all. Disarming, yes, Charming, no. Look, he's heading over here, so just drop it, okay?"

Charlotte led Mindy and Richard into the theater, with the intent of seating Mindy between herself and this man who sent the crawlies up her spine. Much to her dismay, Mindy stepped past her and plopped into a seat, leaving Charlotte to sit next to Richard.

No, no, no! This cannot be happening. I do NOT want to be near this guy!

"So, Richard," Mindy asked, "what do you do for a living?"

"I'm a pharmacist here in Fairfield. How about the two of you?"

"Oh, I'm just a vet tech, but Charlotte here is a big shot executive with the city of Hamilton. She's a brain, especially with numbers." Mindy nudged Charlotte's arm with her elbow, eyes widening. "Tell him, Char."

Heat crawling into her cheeks, Charlotte swallowed and said, "Stop it, Min. I'm not a big shot." She shot a furtive look in Richard's direction. "I'm just the assistant finance director. No big deal."

"Well, it sounds fascinating to me. Much more interesting than counting pills all day long." Richard laughed—a hearty, full-bodied laugh that filled the empty theater.

As more people filed into the theater, the three continued to chat—or, rather, Mindy and Richard chatted. Charlotte said very little as she squirmed in her seat, trying not to bump knees or elbows with Richard. The lights soon dimmed, and the previews of upcoming movies began playing on the screen.

Moments later, Richard touched Charlotte's arm, again sending a cold chill throughout her body. His lips brushed her right ear. "I've got some Raisinets and a Hershey bar. Would you like some?" he whispered.

That's really weird, Charlotte thought. She whispered back, "Umm, no thanks. I'm trying to be good. Oh, it looks like the previews are over. The movie must be starting."

She turned in her seat, slightly away from Richard, and grabbed her bottle of water from the cup holder between her seat and Mindy's. Charlotte narrowed her eyes at her friend and mouthed, "I'm so mad at you," and then focused on the screen.

As they were walking out of the theater two hours later, Richard pushed the door open and gently placed his hand on the small of Charlotte's back, guiding her through the door. Charlotte walked through quickly, followed by Mindy who was flashing her prettiest smile at Richard.

Why do I feel cold every time this guy touches me? Stomach acid churned inside Charlotte's gut. She just wanted to say goodnight and make it home as quickly as possible. There was something about this stranger, this strange man, this 'Richard' that she just didn't like.

"Well, ladies, it was a pleasure running into you again and thank you for allowing me to share the movie with you. Excellent flick. Ford should get an Academy award for that one."

"I completely agree," Mindy beamed. "But then again, I'm a Harrison Ford fan."

Charlotte sighed. "More like a fanatic, Min. Look, it's late and I'm tired. I'm going to head home."

Mindy nodded at Charlotte. "Okay, good ni—"

"Sorry, Mindy. Don't mean to interrupt. Say, Charlotte, any chance you'll agree to dinner with me? Please say yes. I'd love to get to know you more."

"Uh, no, thank you. I'm very busy at work right now with auditors." Charlotte leaned in to hug her friend. "Love you, Min. I'll see you at the pet adoption event on Saturday. Call me this week to remind me what time I need to be there. Goodnight."

With a curt nod to Richard, Charlotte practically ran to her car. She managed to get her key into the lock, hands shaking, and opened the door before climbing in. Breathing heavily, she locked the door and started the car. The air had turned quite chilly, so she turned the dial on the dashboard to Heat, pulled out of the parking space, and headed home.

Charlotte slept well that night, thanks to the Melatodrol, but her sleep was fraught with dreams that made no sense. Not dreams, really, but rather a shadowy, ghost-like image of a woman's face, a young woman with chin-length blond hair. She wore no smile, no expression at all, really. Her eyes were sad. Charlotte didn't recognize the woman whatsoever—and yet, she seemed familiar to her.

March was having a hard time deciding whether to come in like the proverbial lion or the lamb. Just last week, the air had turned cold and breezy. Today, though, was warm and sunny. Charlotte stepped out of her apartment building, drank in the heat of the sun, and headed to her car. A short ten-minute drive took her to the local SICSA—Society for the Improvement of Conditions of Stray Animals—for the pet adoption event. Mindy had conned Charlotte into volunteering for the event five years earlier, and she was hooked. She loved playing with the kittens and puppies, and it gave her great joy to see them adopted into loving families.

Pulling into the lot next to the SICSA building, Charlotte parked and quickly made her way to the welcome tent where Mindy was busy going over an application with a young couple.

"Hey, Char," Mindy said, looking up from the table. "I'll be with you in a minute to show you where you'll be stationed this year."

"Take your time, Min. I'll just go take a look at the puppies." Charlotte aimed for a tent several yards away. The delighted giggles of the children brought a smile to her lips. They held and played with the dogs, excitement bright in their eyes. *This is what it's all about,* she thought. *Someday, I'll give my children a dog or cat, or both. Someday. Guess I need to get married first."*

Her thoughts were interrupted by Mindy tapping her on the shoulder. "Ready to get started, Char?"

"Sure. Lead the way."

A few hours later, Charlotte headed inside to make more copies of the adoption application. After grabbing a bottle of water from the refrigerator, she quickly began programming the copier to collate and staple. She brought the water bottle to her lips as she eyed a nearby bulletin board and read the notices. She made a mental note of the date for the next adoption event and, lost in her thoughts, she jumped at the sound of footsteps behind her. The temperature in the room suddenly dropped, and Charlotte's heart pounded.

"Charlotte? Is that you?"

Nearly spitting out the gulp of water she had just taken, she spun around to meet emerald eyes sparkling above the man's wide smile. Charlotte swallowed the water, put a hand to her heart, and took a step back, gasping for air. "My gosh, I didn't hear the door. This old copier is so loud. Umm, do I know you?" As soon as the words were out of her mouth, vague recognition settled in.

"Yes, well, somewhat. I'm Richard. We bumped into each other at the movie theater last week. It's so good to see you again. I was just out driving when I passed by and thought I'd check it out. I'm thinking of getting a cat for my mother."

Charlotte's mind raced back to last weekend. Yes, she remembered this man. She remembered how overly charming he was, as if he were trying too hard. She also remembered the chills he sent up and down her spine every time he touched her.

What in the hell is he doing HERE?

"Oh, yes, I do remember. Umm, a cat? Yes, we have several cats. Do you want a kitten or an older cat? We have all ages today. You'll have to complete an application. My friend Mindy can help you with that." She was talking too fast.

"Great, thank you. Let's get started, shall we?"

"I have to take these copies out to Mindy anyway. They're almost done." As if on cue, the copier stapled the last set of papers and droned into silence. "Well, guess they're done. Just follow me."

Richard quickly stepped in front of Charlotte, leading the way to the door, and held it open for her. As she passed by, he placed a hand lightly on the small of her back, pushing the door open farther with his other hand. Once again, icy tendrils crawled up her spine, leaving behind visible goosebumps.

Outside, a breeze had picked up and the air seemed significantly cooler than earlier. It must have been the sudden change in weather that had made her shiver, not Richard's touch.

I'm probably just imagining things, she told herself.

Charlotte and Richard took their places in line at the welcome table behind an elderly man with a cane, who was just finishing up his application. Charlotte absently touched Richard's arm, fingers tingling, as she stepped up to the table.

"Hey, Min. This is Richard. Remember? From the movies?"

"Oh, yes, wow! Hi, Richard. Fancy seeing you here!"

"Hello, Mindy. Nice to see you again, too."

"Richard is here to possibly find a cat for his mother." Charlotte handed Mindy the applications she had just copied.

Mindy set the pile down, took one stapled set of papers from the top and gave them to Richard, along with a pen.

"I'm going to go back to filling water bowls while you take care of this. Okay, Min?" Charlotte wanted to get away as fast as she could.

"Sure, Char. Thanks."

Charlotte rushed back into the building and headed to the kitchen. She began filling water bowls and placing them on a rolling cart. She was deliberately taking her time, hoping Richard would be gone before she went outside again. She checked her watch. Thirty minutes had passed. Surely, Richard had finished the application and left by now. At least she hoped so.

Just as Charlotte neared the rear door, it swung open so suddenly she had to jerk the cart back to avoid a collision, sloshing water onto the floor.

"Oh, so sorry, Charlotte. Let me help you clean that up!" Richard immediately went in search of something to wipe up the water and returned with paper towels from the kitchen. They both knelt and began to sop the water off the floor. Charlotte leaned forward too far and lost her balance. Richard's hand shot out, catching her by the elbow.

"Steady, there. Don't want you falling and hurting yourself, now do we?" That voice was so velvety ... and yet frosty at the same time.

Charlotte's heart thumped away inside her chest. Her cheeks grew warm and the hairs on the back of her neck stood at attention.

"N-No ... umm, n-n-no, we don't. I'm ... I'm sorry. I guess I got a little dizzy for a moment. I didn't get much sleep this week, thanks to work. I'm prob ... probably just tired." She pulled her elbow out of Richard's grasp and stood. "I'm fine now, really. Thank you for helping with the water."

Charlotte returned the cart to the kitchen, refilled most of the bowls, and headed back outdoors. Richard was waiting for her at the back door, which he opened for her. She passed by him quickly, aiming for the tents with the animals. She lowered her head, hoping to give the impression she was merely concentrating on the job, but inside, she was nauseated.

Richard followed her to the dog tent and helped her set the water bowls on the ground.

"Honestly, I appreciate your help, but I'm fine. I can do this," she said.

"I'm sure you can, but since it's my fault you spilled the water, I'm obligated to help you set these out."

They worked in silence for the next few minutes, setting bowls out under the tents and returning the cart to the kitchen. Charlotte darted her eyes about, trying to think of what to do, what to say. She was about to dash to the ladies' room when Richard turned toward the door.

"I've got to go. I'm about to be late for work. I left my application with Mindy and am hoping to have a cat for Mother in a week or so. Thanks for helping me with that."

"I didn't do anything really." Charlotte licked her dry lips. "Good luck. I hope it works out for you … er … for your mother."

Richard left, and before the door even slammed shut, Charlotte ran to the ladies' room, threw herself into a stall, and engaged the lock. She slid down the wall and held her head between her knees, willing the nausea to stop. Several minutes later she emerged feeling somewhat calmer but apprehensive.

What if he's still out there? Outside, waiting for me? Damnit, who IS this man, anyway? Why does he keep showing up?

Charlotte and Mindy took in an early dinner after the event. Mindy prattled on about her job, how the event went, all the great people she met who wanted to adopt a pet, so on and so on—but Charlotte barely heard a word. They finished their meals and hugged their goodbyes in the parking lot.

That night, Charlotte lay sleepless on her bed, sweating. She checked the thermostat: sixty-eight degrees. *Why am I sweating?* After grabbing a book from the nightstand, she climbed back into bed and made several feeble attempts at reading. She fell asleep with the book on her stomach.

Charlotte's dreams were vague and gray. She remembered fog, an old run-down house, and a woman's face. *That* woman again. The same face from her other dreams. The same blond hair, the green eyes. Like emeralds. *Emerald eyes.*

The image faded, and Charlotte slept, dreamless, until morning.

CHAPTER FOUR

Late March 1985

Exhausted from a grueling week with auditors, preparing payroll, and too many meetings for her liking, Charlotte stood at the grocery store meat counter on a Friday evening trying to decide between a pork chop or steak for her dinner. Opting for a steak meant baking a potato, which would take an hour. She could just make mashed potatoes with the pork chop, but that would require peeling the potatoes. The cooking would be faster, but the prep would not be as easy as a baked potato.

Or I could just get another frozen meal and call it a day, she thought. *Better yet, maybe I'll just eat ice cream again.*

Charlotte was still pondering her dinner dilemma when a familiar voice came from behind. A tingle traveled down her spine.

"Charlotte! Well, I never thought I'd run into you again, let alone here at the grocery store!"

It was Richard … again. His emerald eyes flashed, and his smile widened to reveal pearly white teeth. His sandy hair was freshly cut, not a strand out of place. He was clean-shaven and sported black trousers, a white shirt, and a red, black, and white striped tie. His black Oxfords shone like glass and were free of scuffs or scratches. His black leather jacket hugged him tightly, revealing strong shoulders and a broad chest.

Perfect. Everything about him was perfect. So why did Charlotte freeze up every time he was near? Why did he make her feel so strange, so cold?

"Oh, hello … Richard?" Charlotte looked around, trying to figure out a way to escape the store.

"I see you're looking at those steaks. They don't look very appetizing, now, do they?"

With a small chuckle, Charlotte replied, "No, they really don't. I'm about to opt for ice cream for dinner instead."

"Now, that would be a shame. A pretty girl like you, home alone, eating ice cream on a Friday night? Surely you have someone special coming over later?" Richard grinned and winked mischievously.

"No, no, I don't. It's been a hard week at work. I just want to get something to eat and curl up with a good book."

"Another shame. Look, none of this food looks all that great to me either. I know this great steak place nearby. Please join me. You can meet me there. Just dinner. My treat."

Charlotte closed her eyes for a moment, trying unsuccessfully to find some excuse to decline. She couldn't get Mindy's voice out of her head. *"You need to live a little. Try something new."*

Snapping her eyes open, she heard herself say, "Yes, all right. I guess one dinner can't hurt. What's the name of the restaurant? I might know it."

"Oh, wonderful! It's A Touch of Steak over on Nilles Road."

"Yes, I do know that. Well, to be honest, I've never eaten there, but I do know where it is. Meet you there, then?"

"Lovely. I'm looking forward to dining with you, Charlotte."

They parted ways and drove separately to the restaurant. Being a Friday night, it was quite crowded with an hour long wait, so they took seats at the bar and ordered drinks. Their conversation consisted of small talk: how cold and windy early March was, the audits that Charlotte endured at work, where they went to school—typical "first-date" chatter. Charlotte sighed internally; she had no intention of ever considering this a date.

"What's your family like, Charlotte?" Richard asked. "Any brothers or sisters.?"

"No, I'm an only child. My father is 100 percent German but was born here in Cincinnati. He fought in World War II for the U.S. He lost part of his leg at Normandy Beach and met my mother here at the VA Hospital during his recuperation. Mama was a nurse there. She had two miscarriages before I was born. Papa's parents died long before I was even a glimmer in his eye, but I spent a lot of time with

Mama's parents when I was little. I was their only grandchild, so they tended to spoil me a bit. They both died in a car accident when I was five. Papa just recently retired, and he and Mama are traveling the world."

Charlotte smiled as she recalled happy memories. "What about you, Richard? Do you have family in the area?"

"My father, Charles, was adopted. His birthmother was not married, and her family forced her to give him up. He lived in an orphanage for several years before his parents, Anthony and Caroline Palmer, adopted him. They also adopted two more children, my Aunt Marjorie and Uncle Jim. Dad was an engineer with General Electric and Mom was a secretary, until I came into the picture. She never worked after that. I have no brothers or sisters, but I do have eight cousins, three from Marjorie and five from Jim. We lived within three miles of each other throughout my entire childhood, so we all went to the same schools and played together all the time. It was a happy childhood. Dad didn't know much about his real parents, only that his father was a doctor. He knew nothing about his mother, though. And my mother, Margaret, was an only child like me, so no aunts and uncles or cousins on that side."

"Have you ever thought about doing any research to find out about your father's parents, or do you not really care about that?" Charlotte had always wondered if adopted children wanted to find their birth parents. She hoped to adopt a child of her own someday.

Richard shrugged and told Charlotte, "Oh, for the most part, I don't care. But I do have some curiosity. I've never really considered doing the research, though. Seems like an awful lot of work just to get information on people who gave up my dad. Dad always considered his adoptive parents as his real parents and never thought twice about it. They moved to Florida some years back and are just enjoying retirement. Dad adored them."

"Are they still alive? Your parents, I mean."

"Dad died three years ago. Cancer. Mom is still alive, but she's starting to get dementia and is living alone, for now. Some days, she doesn't remember me at all. Other days, she does. The doctors thought having a pet would help her. That's why I wanted to adopt the cat.

"My Aunt Marjorie and Uncle Brian moved to Florida last year, about an hour from my grandparents. Their kids are scattered all over the globe. Uncle Jim and his wife Marsha live in Arizona now. A few of my cousins live here in the Cincinnati area, and others live out of state. We're not as close as we were growing up. I miss the closeness, but they're all married, have children, and lives of their own, you know? Not much time in their schedules for their boring, unmarried cousin."

Richard laughed.

His laugh is so bold and animated. He seems like a happy, well-adjusted man. And now that I really look at him, Min is right. He IS quite good looking. Those eyes ... so captivating.

Charlotte and Richard talked all the way through dinner. For dessert, he ordered a New York cheesecake; she, a decadent chocolate mousse. Charlotte found it somewhat alarming that she suddenly seemed to feel very comfortable with Richard. As long as he didn't touch her, sending those icy feelings through her body, he was quite magnetic and pleasant to be around.

They left the restaurant moments before closing time, Charlotte's hand resting gently in the crook of Richard's arm. He held the door for her and walked her to her car. For the first time, she didn't feel tingles or shivers or iciness at his touch.

"I'd love to see you again, Charlotte. You're quite beautiful ... and not just on the outside. May I have your phone number?"

Charlotte averted her eyes, licked her lips, and began picking at her fingernails. She had to admit that the evening was enjoyable. Their conversation came easily, and their laughter felt natural. But she wasn't sure she should see him again.

Still, she saw herself handing him a pen from inside her car, heard herself rattling off her phone number. She looked up to tell him goodnight as his warm, moist lips pressed against her cheek.

"I had a lovely time tonight, Charlotte. Thank you. I'll call you soon. Drive home safely."

"Goodnight, Richard, and thank you for dinner. I had a nice time, also."

After arriving home moments later, Charlotte enjoyed a refreshing, hot shower, climbed into bed, popped the Melatodrol into her mouth with a swallow of water, and turned out the light. She lay there for a few minutes, reflecting on the evening's events. She *did* enjoy her time with Richard. Yes, maybe Mindy was right. Maybe fate had stepped in. Maybe she was meant to meet Richard. Maybe …

Charlotte fell asleep even before the next "maybe" came to mind.

CHAPTER FIVE

June 1985 to Early 1990

Charlotte and Richard were virtually inseparable over the next few months. They went to movies, restaurants, and baseball games. On many country drives they would stop at antique shops or ice cream parlors. Mindy and Caleb joined them on their outings now and then, but they were alone most of the time. Regardless of where they were, their hands were always clasped, they gazed into each other's eyes frequently, and they laughed. Oh, how they laughed.

Richard's mother moved to Arizona soon after he and Charlotte began dating. Margaret's dementia was worsening, and Richard wasn't comfortable with her living alone any longer, so her brother-in-law Jim and his wife Marsha took her into their home. Charlotte didn't even know she had left Ohio until several days later. She questioned Richard one night about the sudden move.

"I just don't understand why you didn't at least let me come to the airport to meet your mother and see her off, Richard!" Charlotte complained.

"Look, Charlotte, things were so hectic with selling Mom's furniture and packing her clothes, I just didn't even think about having you come to the airport with us. What difference does it make, anyway? Mom wouldn't have understood who you were and certainly won't ever remember you."

The exasperation and fatigue in Richard's voice came out loud and clear, so Charlotte decided to drop the subject, thinking perhaps she would suggest a trip to Arizona when Richard wasn't so exhausted and worried about his mother.

Richard charmed his way into Charlotte's heart. She didn't know when it happened, or how, but Charlotte fell in love. He would send flowers to her office or, better still, show up at her door with a bouquet in hand. She received romantic cards and love letters in the mail. He would surprise her with trinkets—a pair of pearl earrings or a diamond bracelet. For her thirtieth birthday in April, he presented her with an authentic, hand-carved German music box, explaining it was a family heirloom, and he very much wanted her to have it. Charlotte protested that it was too soon for such a gift, but he wore her down quickly. She gave in, accepting the gift with a faint smile.

Richard would come inside the City of Fairfield's main building whenever he took her to lunch, and she would watch through her office window as he charmed the secretaries and clerks. Laughter would roll through the building like distant thunder. Richard had a natural ease with people, never at a loss for words and always complimenting everyone he met. On many occasions, Charlotte's co-workers commented on how kind Richard was and that she was the luckiest girl on the planet.

One evening in early June, Charlotte was particularly quiet at dinner. She picked at her food as she sat in silence while Richard talked about his day.

"Charley, something's wrong. You've barely touched your dinner, and I know you aren't really listening to anything I'm saying. What is it, honey?" Richard took her hand from across the table, and stroked the back of it with his thumb. "Did something happen at work? Or … Oh, gosh, please don't tell me something happened to your parents on their trip!" Charlotte's parents had been traveling through Europe since April.

Shaking her head to clear the fog in her brain, Charlotte said, "No, Richard, nothing happened at work. And Mama and Papa are fine. In fact, they called today from Italy and said they're having a wonderful time."

"Then, what is it, Charley?" Richard had started using the nickname on their fourth date, and as much as she didn't care for it, she could not convince him to stop using it.

"My lease is up on my apartment, but the rent is going up so much I'm contemplating looking for a new place. My raise this year was bare minimum. Not nearly enough to cover the increased rent. I just hate moving, and this is not a good time to be looking at apartments. You know this is budget season at work and I'm so busy, sometimes I just can't see straight."

"Then move in with me. I've been asking you for two months. Now's the time, Charley."

"I don't know, Richard, it's just so soon. Are you sure we're ready?"

"Of course, I'm sure. I knew it the moment I first saw you."

"I'll have to think about it. I just don't want us to move too fast."

In spite of her apprehension, Charlotte found herself spending every moment of her spare time boxing up her belongings. Richard had hired a moving company and tried to convince Charlotte to let them do all the packing, but she felt uncomfortable having strangers going through her closets, drawers and cabinets, so she insisted on doing the packing herself. Her apartment was small; she didn't have a lot of furniture, very few pictures, and only a few pieces of cookware. With so few possessions, it only took her a couple of weeks to finish the job.

Richard also insisted on sleeping over the night before Charlotte's move, saying this way he would already be there to ensure the movers arrived on time and everything went smoothly. He refused to take no for an answer, so Charlotte gave in. She had wanted to spend her last night on her own by herself, but Richard became agitated when they talked about it again a few days before the move, and hearing the exasperation in his voice, she agreed to let him spend the night.

They had pizza delivered and sat on the couch, eating their food in silence. Afterward, they loaded Charlotte's clothes into Richard's car and took them to his townhouse ten miles away. He grabbed his overnight bag, already packed with his toothbrush and a change of clothes, and they headed back to Charlotte's apartment. Charlotte dozed in the passenger seat during the drive.

Charlotte checked her watch when they arrived, and realizing it was already after ten o'clock, she said to Richard, "Let's take a quick look around to be sure we have everything packed, but I'm exhausted and just want to shower and go to sleep, if that's okay with you."

"Of course, Charley. You need your rest. Tomorrow will be a big day."

Richard was fast asleep when she emerged from the shower. Charlotte donned her pajamas, climbed into bed next to him, and turned off the bedside lamp. She stared at the ceiling as her eyes adjusted to the dark. She yawned and closed her eyes. Thoughts invaded her mind like pieces of a jigsaw puzzle strewn across a table. She couldn't focus on any one thought for more than a moment, couldn't settle her mind. She turned to her side, back-to-back with Richard, and closed her eyes again … but she still failed to rest her mind.

She thought of the first time she saw Richard at the bar and how her skin seemed to crawl whenever he touched her. Charlotte recalled their first dinner at the steak restaurant, how they had talked so easily with each other. In her mind's eye, she saw the bouquets of flowers lining her office window and filing cabinets. She saw the earrings and the bracelet he had given her. Small tokens of his affection, given far too early in their relationship.

Charlotte adjusted her pillow and, feeling chilly, drew the covers over her shoulder. A vision of the music box Richard had given her came into view behind her closed lids. The base was round and made of wood stained in a dark walnut. The lid, held closed with a brass clasp, displayed a Bavarian church modeled after the Theatine Church in Munich, complete with two domed towers. Small figurines of children clad in lederhosen surrounded the building. As Charlotte pictured the music box, she could hear it playing "*Alle Vögel sind schon da*," a German folk song signifying the arrival of spring.

Charlotte drifted off to sleep with the tune still playing in her mind.

"Surprise, Charley!" Richard exclaimed. Charlotte was bent over a pile of financial documents when he burst into her office unannounced.

"What are you doing here, Richard? It's only ten o'clock." Charlotte sighed heavily, annoyed with Richard for interrupting her during work.

"I have a surprise for you, honey. I've been chosen to represent the pharmacy at a convention in Vegas next month. All expenses paid. I want you to come with me."

"Richard, you know I'm very busy right now. I'm not sure I could take the time off."

"It's only three days, Charlotte. Surely, they can spare you for three days. C'mon, it'll be fun. You can relax all day at the pool or do some gambling while I'm at the convention. I'll give you cash to use. We'll be together for dinner every night. Look, I heard there's a new dance show at the Riviera that's supposed to be fabulous. *Splash*, I think it's called."

Richard rounded Charlotte's desk and pulled her to her feet. "Let's go ask Marian now if you can take some time off. I've got to book the flights today, Charley."

Charlotte ran a hand through her long hair as she took a step back. "Richard, please, I just …"

"I don't want to hear another no from you, Charlotte. You've been working too many long hours, and you need to have some fun. We haven't been out of the house in ages." Richard pulled Charlotte closer and guided her out of her office and down the hall to her boss's door.

Three weeks later, Charlotte and Richard boarded a plane and headed for Las Vegas. They checked into a luxurious suite at Caesars Palace on the Strip, where Charlotte unpacked her suitcases before drawing back the curtains to reveal a view of the Fountain of the Gods below. Decorated in calming tones, the room included a separate dining area, living room and wet bar. Passing the king-sized bed, Charlotte stuck her head into the bathroom complete with double sinks, a large walk-in shower, and a whirlpool tub. Two plush robes hung from hooks on the wall next to the shower.

I'm surprised the pharmacy could afford such an expensive room, Charlotte thought. Shrugging it off, she said to Richard, "Wow, this place is amazing."

"It is. Hey, let's go down and gamble away some of our money before we head out to dinner."

For the next three days Charlotte tanned by the pool, visited the spa for a massage and manicure/pedicure, learned to play craps in the casino, and slept. At night she and Richard frequented the most elegant and expensive restaurants, walked the Strip, and took in two shows.

Richard let himself into their room on the third afternoon, the convention having just ended, to find Charlotte soaking in the tub. He quickly threw off his clothes and joined her. They made love for the next two hours, breathlessly lying back on the bed, sweating and satisfied.

Soon, Richard threw his legs over the edge of the bed, sat up, and checked his watch.

"We better get quick showers and dress for dinner. We've got reservations at seven, and I still have a couple things I want to see tonight before we leave in the morning."

At the restaurant, Richard ordered steak and lobster for two and a bottle of their best champagne. He caressed Charlotte's hand and gazed into her eyes while they chatted. A flaming bananas Foster appeared tableside just as they finished the champagne.

They walked hand in hand along the Strip, chatting about the wonderful food and fun they had. Charlotte had to admit that she did, indeed, have fun and got some much-needed rest. Feeling a bit dizzy, Charlotte threaded her hand through Richard's arm and leaned on him for support as they strolled.

"I think I had moo tuch to drink." Charlotte giggled.

Richard threw his head back and laughed loudly. Charlotte pinched his arm and whispered, "Shh … people will stare!"

"My dear, Charley, let them stare. We're having a great time. Don't spoil it with your worries about what people will think."

"But—"

"Not another word, dear Charley. I have a surprise for you."

"Ooooh, what ith it?" Charlotte leaned her head against his shoulder, the world spinning around them.

"You'll just have to wait and see."

Richard led her around a corner. A pearl white stretch limousine was idling at the curb, shimmering softly in the moonlight. The chauffeur, clad in a black suit with a crisp, white shirt and black tie, was leaning on the back panel of the vehicle. He spotted the couple and quickly opened the rear door, offering his hand to Charlotte to help her inside.

Her mouth fell open as she sat on the plush leather seats. The interior of the limo sported wooden panel accents, a well-stocked mini bar centered between the two bench seats facing each other, and a panoramic sunroof revealing a starlit sky. Richard snuggled in next to Charlotte as he grabbed two goblets and a bottle of champagne from the bar.

As Richard poured the bubbly golden liquid into the goblets, the chauffeur took his place behind the wheel. Neon ambient lighting flickered on, accompanied by soft music.

"My name is Manuel. Are you both comfortable, sir?" the chauffeur asked.

"Yes, quite. We're ready to go, Manuel," Richard replied as he handed a goblet to Charlotte.

Charlotte's heart raced as she sipped the champagne. It tickled her nose and she giggled.

"Richard, I'm … I just don't know what to thay. I'm overwhelmed. Thith limo …it's … Honestly, I'm at a loth for words!" A fluttery sensation spread through Charlotte's stomach but quickly faded as Richard laughed heartily.

"I knew you'd be surprised. Here, drink up. I have more surprises in store for you." Richard poured more champagne into her glass.

Charlotte watched in awe as they passed resorts, restaurants and casinos. The lights of the MGM Grand and Circus Circus shone brightly, revealing throngs of people on the sidewalks. They rolled down the windows of the limo, and music emanated from the casinos as they passed.

They drained their champagne goblets, refilled them, and drained them again as the car meandered along the Strip to their destination—one still unknown to Charlotte.

"Tho ... Where are we going, Rithard?" Charlotte's earlier tipsiness was gaining momentum. She touched her forehead. "I'm drinking thoo much. Feeling … uhhh …"

Richard responded by pouring more champagne into her goblet. "You're fine, Charley. Have fun. Let loose. We're almost there."

Against her better judgment Charlotte sipped more champagne. She closed her eyes against the bright lights blurring past, and her head tipped back and forth, heavy and pounding. *I've got to stop drinking,* she told herself. *I'm dizzy ... so dizzy.*

Her body eased sideways as the car turned, and she opened her eyes. The chauffeur steered them into a parking lot and into a space next to a building. He put the gear into Park and hopped out of the limo. Charlotte was about to ask Richard again where they were when the chauffeur opened her door and extended his hand.

"Go on, Charley. Get out," Richard said.

She exited the limo, followed closely by Richard. He took her elbow, thanked the chauffeur, and led Charlotte to the front of the building. She stumbled on a loose brick, but Richard quickly steadied her as he chuckled softly. She raised her head to look at him, but the sign on the large, white building grabbed her attention— Graceland Wedding Chapel. They stepped through the arched doorway and were greeted by a middle-aged woman seated behind a desk on the left.

"Welcome to the world-famous Graceland Wedding Chapel, the oldest chapel in Las Vegas. We are the original—often imitated but never duplicated! You are a lovely couple. How may we help you?" The woman beamed.

"Hello, and thank you," Richard said. "I'm Richard Palmer. We spoke earlier today. I trust all the arrangements have been made so that we can be married right away."

"Yes, of course," replied the woman.

"Wait, wha ... what?!" Charlotte cried. "Did you thay ... married?" Charlotte swung her head back and forth, the champagne wreaking havoc on her speech.

"Yes, darling Charley! Married! That's my surprise." Richard dropped to one knee, pulled a small velvet box from the pocket of his slacks, and said, "I love you, Charlotte Marie Schmidt, and want to spend the rest of my life with you. Will you marry me?"

Richard opened the box, revealing a rather large, sparkling diamond ring.

"I ... I just don't know what to thay," Charlotte stammered. "I never expected—"

"I know you didn't. That's what makes it a surprise, silly girl. Marry me!" Richard flashed a brilliant smile.

"Yeth, yeth, I'll marry you." Tears formed in Charlotte's eyes as Richard took her hand and slipped the ring onto her finger.

Turning to the woman behind the desk, Richard asked, "What do we need to do now?"

"Just complete this form and both of you sign it. You'll pay after the ceremony." The woman handed a single sheet of paper to Richard.

Richard completed the form while Charlotte swayed next to him. She tried to make sense of what was happening. Her head was still pounding from too much alcohol. She felt like she was in a dream and couldn't wake up.

"Here, Charley, you sign the form on this line," Richard said as he handed her a pen. She signed the form and gazed into Richard's eyes. *Those blazing green eyes. Oh, how I love those eyes.*

"Perfect," said the woman as she nodded toward a row of chairs lining the opposite wall. "Just have a seat for a moment. Elvis will be right with you to begin the ceremony."

"Thank you." Richard guided Charlotte to the chairs. She nearly missed the seat, but Richard held firmly to her hands to keep her from tumbling to the floor.

The next twenty minutes flew past in a whirlwind of arrangements. A man pinned a boutonniere onto Richard's jacket lapel, someone shoved a bouquet into Charlotte's hands, and the woman who had greeted them brushed Charlotte's long blond locks.

Richard disappeared down the hall and into the chapel just as Elvis walked into the reception area and placed Charlotte's hand in the crook of his arm. Music began to play from inside the chapel as Elvis led Charlotte through the doors. Several rows of small white pews lined the aisle leading to the altar, where Richard and Elvis number two stood waiting. A tall, elderly man in white robes stood behind a white podium, and an arched stained-glass window rose high on the wall behind him.

Elvis number two began to sing "Love Me Tender" as Elvis number one guided Charlotte slowly down the aisle. As the song ended, the elderly man announced, "Dearly Beloved, we are gathered here …"

Charlotte heard the man's voice but later could not recall anything he said. She had a vague memory of Richard taking her hand, someone handing her a silver band which she placed on Richard's finger, and then another ring slipped onto her finger. She recalled hearing Elvis number one singing the "Hawaiian Wedding Song" out of key before Richard's lips pressed into hers.

"I now pronounce you man and wife. Congratulations, Mr. and Mrs. Palmer!" the elderly man declared. "Please pay Carol at the desk as you leave."

The first few years of marriage brought joy and bliss to Charlotte's life—and fun. She and Richard booked a Caribbean cruise shortly after their wedding, followed by trips to Mexico and Alaska the following years. They dined out nearly every night, took in movies, danced at local clubs, and attended concerts. They enjoyed Sunday dinners at Charlotte's parents' home, watching sports on television all afternoon, and talking. Albert and Elizabeth found Richard warm, caring, and charming.

Mindy and Caleb had their first child, a daughter, the year after Charlotte married Richard. The second daughter arrived two years later, and a son two years after that. Charlotte rarely saw Mindy these days and missed their friendship. She knew Mindy was busy raising her children and no longer had time for their girls' nights out, but Charlotte still ached for the closeness they once shared. She had crocheted blankets for the first two children and began working on another blanket for their son.

She wanted a child of her own. Maybe she just wanted to fill the void left by losing her best friend. Maybe she wanted something or someone new to love. Early in their marriage, Charlotte asked Richard if they could adopt a kitten or puppy, but he refused emphatically, saying they didn't have time to care for a pet with their work schedules. Besides, he told her, he wanted to travel with her, and "some damn animal" would only tie them down.

In October 1989, Charlotte arrived home from work to find an urgent message from her mother on the answering machine. Her father had suffered a stroke and was rushed to the VA Hospital, where he was admitted to the ICU in critical condition. Charlotte scribbled a brief note for Richard and rushed out.

Albert remained in the hospital for nearly a month before being released to the VA Rehabilitation Center, where he underwent physical therapy for several weeks before going home. By Christmas he was able to use a walker but still could not talk much. When he did speak, his words were disjointed and slurred. Elizabeth's health was declining while she cared for her husband, causing Charlotte's concern to rise.

"Mama," Charlotte said one day while lunching with her parents, "why don't you take a nap for a few hours while I watch Papa. I have nothing planned for today and you really need to get some rest. You're just doing far too much."

"Oh, darling, yes, thank you so much," Elizabeth said. She hugged Charlotte and headed for her room.

"Okay, Papa, what shall we do?" Charlotte looked around the room, found the box of alphabet blocks, and carried it to the TV stand sitting in front of her father. "Let's go over our letters today, okay, Papa?"

Albert blinked at Charlotte and gave her a half smile, the left side of his mouth drooping slightly. Hot tears stung Charlotte's eyes. She turned her head away from her father, wiping the tears from her cheeks.

They worked with the blocks for a few moments, Charlotte encouraging him with each letter—"Here, Papa, this is an S, like for sharp, silver, sunny, or Schmidt—your last name," or maybe, "Look, Papa, here's a C, like for cat, color, or Charlotte. That's me."

Albert's eyes traveled to each block as Charlotte placed them in front of him, but then his gaze would drift and he'd stare blankly at a spot on the wall behind her.

"Okay, let's try something a little different." Charlotte placed blocks on the table to form the word "C A T" and pointed to each letter. "This is a C and this is an A and this one is a T. All together, they spell cat. Can you say cat, Papa?

Albert opened his mouth, licked his lips, and muttered, "C ... Ca ... Ca ... Cat."

"Yes, Papa! Yes, that's it! That's great! Let's try another one. Let's see ... Okay, yes, this one is B, and here's an O, and here's a Y. Let's sound them out." Charlotte pointed to the B block and said, "Ba, Ba, Ba. That's the B." Pointing next to the O block and then the Y block, she sounded both letters out as before.

"Now, Papa, can you put them all together? Let's try, okay? Ba, Ooo, Eee. Ba-oy. Boy. You try it now!"

"Ba ... ba ...," Albert began. He looked into Charlotte's eyes and swallowed before trying again. "Ba ... boy."

"Very good, Papa. Now, let me look here for some other blocks. Oh, yes, this will be a good one." Charlotte grabbed four new blocks from the box and sounded them out as she placed them on the stand. "This is a W and this is an I. This one here is an L and here's a D. Can you sound them out with me?"

Together, Albert and Charlotte sounded out the letters, one by one, until he was able to say them by himself. He reached up with his right hand and touched the W and the I and the L. He clumsily pushed them together and grunted. "Wil .... Wil ..."

"Wild, Papa. The word is wild."

"N ... N ... Nooooo." Albert's voice cracked and strained as he spoke. "Wil ... Wil ... Wilhel ... Wilhelmina!"

"What, Papa? What are you saying? Who's Wilhelmina?"

"Mmm ... Mmm ... My moth ... mother. Sss ... Sss ... Save mmm ... mmm ... my mother!" Tears were streaming from Albert's eyes as he struggled to explain. "Sss ... Sss ... Save Wilhel ... Wilhel ... Wilhelmina." Albert flung his right arm off the table, sending the blocks crashing to the floor.

"Papa, it's okay. I-I just don't understand. Save your mother? But she died so many years ago, Papa. How can I save her?"

"Sss ... Sss ... Save her. It ... It ... It wasn ... wasn't her. Ple ... Please, Char ... sss ... save her."

Albert's head dropped back onto the headrest of his chair, and he closed his eyes as if shutting out the world around him. He fell into a deep sleep, so Charlotte moved the TV stand to one side and activated the chair's motor so her father could recline. She tiptoed to her parents' bedroom to check on her mother, who was just waking up.

Charlotte told Elizabeth about what had just happened and fired a barrage of questions at her. "Who is Wilhelmina, Mama? What did he mean when he told me to 'save her'?"

Elizabeth closed her eyes, took a deep breath, and said, "Wilhelmina is your grandmother, honey. Your father's mother. She came to Cincinnati in 1916. She worked for a few years and then married and had your father. But a few years later, a terrible thing happened."

"What, Mama? What happened?"

"Oh, Charlotte. I suppose we should've told you all this years ago, and I wish I could tell you more now, but your father so rarely spoke of his parents. I just don't know much myself."

"Know what? Please, tell me."

"Honey, your grandmother, Wilhelmina, committed a terrible crime. She murdered several men."

"WHAT?!" Charlotte cried. "I … I don't even know what to say. My grandmother was a serial killer? I just … I just don't believe it. But what did Papa mean when he told me 'it wasn't her'? And what happened to her?"

Elizabeth's shoulders sagged as she whispered, "I don't know, Charlotte. I honestly don't know. Your father refused to talk about her."

CHAPTER SIX

July 10, 1990

The rain that pelted Charlotte's skin just moments ago as she ran away from that old house now came down in torrential sheets. Her wipers flew across the windshield as she squinted to see the lines on the road. Her grip tightened on the steering wheel, breaths growing quick and short, and her muscles twitched with every passing mile.

She checked the clock on the dashboard, and a wave of nausea rolled through her stomach. *Oh, please, let me get home before Richard wakes up. Please, time, slow down!* Charlotte checked her side and rear-view mirrors over and over, fearing she would lose her way. She began second-guessing the route she had chosen to get home. Images flooded her mind of Richard standing before her, eyes blazing with anger, as he questioned her about where she had been all night.

A sigh of relief escaped Charlotte's lips as she exited the expressway and turned onto the road to her neighborhood. *Just a few more turns, Charlotte, and you'll be home. Maybe, just maybe before he wakes up.*

Moments later she turned into the apartment complex and steered her way through the asphalt parking lot to their townhouse. Charlotte put the car in Park, turned off the ignition, and sat with her head on the wheel, taking deep, calming breaths and fighting to hold back tears. Outside the car the rain slowed to a drizzle.

It's now or never, Charlotte.

She shoved the map into the glove compartment, grabbed her purse, and exited the car. Charlotte ran the short distance to her townhouse, unlocked and slowly opened the door. Darkness greeted her from inside. Charlotte bent down to remove her shoes before stepping over the threshold, then gently closed and locked the door behind her. She placed her purse on the entryway table, dropped her keys in a tabletop tray, and put her shoes on the rack below the table.

On tiptoes, Charlotte aimed for the stairs, biting her lip. One little creak and she'd wake him. She gingerly placed a foot on the first step and held her breath. She took another step up and released a breath. Then another step, and another, and another until she reached the landing at the top of the stairs. Turning left, she then quickly bypassed the bedroom and headed straight for the bathroom. There she tossed her damp clothes into the hamper, started the water in the shower and brushed her teeth. Charlotte stood under the hot water for several minutes as her thoughts drifted back, back to the previous evening, back to that house where she had awakened just an hour ago.

Come on, Charlotte, think. What's the last thing you remember from last night? I'd just finished the dinner dishes and sat down on the couch to watch a movie. I couldn't keep my eyes open. Did I fall asleep on the couch? But then what? And how did I get all the way into Cincinnati without even remembering it? And that house ... so old and run down. I wonder how long it's been empty. Okay, face it, Charlotte. That house creeped you out. And what did I see in that window?

I must be going crazy. This is the third time I've fallen asleep and woken up in a strange place. What the hell is happening to me? Why do I keep waking up doing strange things? Oh, dear God, I must be losing my mind.

Charlotte stepped from the shower, toweled dry, and donned her robe. She ran a comb through her wet hair, checked to be sure her eyes weren't red from crying, and turned to leave the bathroom when the door suddenly swung open.

Charlotte jumped back a step and let out a small scream. "Oh my gosh, Richard, you startled me!" she said.

"I'm sorry. I didn't realize you were in here. I thought maybe you were still on the couch asleep," Richard said. "And good morning, by the way." He chuckled softly.

"Goo ... Good morning, honey. I'm sorry I fell asleep on the couch again last night. I guess I'm just so tired from work these days.

I didn't even wake up to take my Melatodrol. Umm, Richard, do you have time to chat while I get ready for work? I need to talk with you about something."

"Is it urgent, Charley? I need to be at the pharmacy early today. Besides, it's already 7:15. If you don't hurry, you'll be late for work again."

"Oh, wow, I didn't even know what time it was. I just jumped in the shower and never checked the clock. Yes, yes, honey, it can wait until tonight, but I do want to talk with you. What time will you be home for dinner?"

"I should be home by six tonight. I'm going to jump in the shower now. I'll see you tonight, sweetheart." Richard planted a light kiss on Charlotte's cheek, removed his robe, and stepped into the shower.

Charlotte dressed quickly, grabbed her makeup bag, and practically ran down the stairs. She retrieved her purse and keys, and headed out. At work, she went to the lunchroom and poured a cup of coffee, then headed to her office where she began to apply her makeup before her co-workers arrived.

After lunch Charlotte crossed the hall to Human Resources and stuck her head in the manager's office. "Hey, Jenny, do you have a few minutes?" A large pile of file folders occupied half of Jenny's desk, and Charlotte raised her brows. "Or are you super busy right now?"

"No, Charlotte, I've got some time. What's up?" Jenny Compton was in her forties with short brown hair, warm brown eyes, and an even-tempered personality. She and Charlotte often had lunch together and had a good working rapport.

Closing the door as she entered the office, Charlotte said, "Well, umm, we have a mental health benefit with our insurance, right?"

"Yes, but …" Jenny furrowed her brows, eyeing Charlotte. "Is everything okay?"

"Well, for the most part, yes. Okay, so I've had trouble sleeping for about five years now, and I take ten milligrams of Melatodrol every night. But ever since my father's stroke a few months ago, I've been experiencing some"—Charlotte folded her hands together and swallowed—"anxiety, maybe? Or depression? I don't know. I'm falling asleep watching TV, or even here at work, and then I don't feel rested when I *do* sleep in my bed. I don't know. I think I'm just overwhelmed between work and my father and keeping up with the housework. And I've been wanting to talk with Richard about starting a family, but something always seems to get in the way, and it just gets put on a back burner. I thought maybe I just need someone to talk with about everything, someone who can give me an objective viewpoint. So, I wondered if we have a psychologist or someone on our insurance who I could see."

Jenny reached across the desk and patted Charlotte's hand. "Yes, Charlotte, we do. Let me find it here." Jenny searched through a drawer and pulled a folder out. "Yes, here we are. We have two doctors you could see, a man or a woman. Do you have a preference?"

"Yes, yes, I'd like to see a woman, please."

"Okay. Her name is Linda Roberts. I'll just jot down her phone number and address for you. And, Charlotte, anytime you want to talk with me, I'm also available."

Taking the piece of paper, Charlotte said, "Thank you, Jenny. I'll keep that in mind. Thanks for your time."

Dinner was ready the moment Richard walked through the door that evening, the table formally set, complete with glasses of water with lemon, and crystal goblets filled with red wine. Charlotte stood next to her chair at one end of the dining room table, waiting for Richard to take his seat at the other end. She couldn't remember the last time they had eaten in a restaurant; it might have been over a year ago when they took their last vacation to Florida.

"Hello, honey," Charlotte said. "Dinner's all ready. How was your day?"

"Hi. It was just another day. I do have another pharmacists' convention coming up in a couple of months." Richard took his seat, placing his linen napkin on his lap while Charlotte lit the candles in the center of the table. "Considering your father's health, you probably won't want to join me this time."

Charlotte opened her mouth to point out that a few days away from the real world might do her some good, but immediately clamped her mouth shut, not wanting to anger Richard tonight. She had waited all day to talk with him, and she needed him in a pleasant frame of mind.

"Yes, you're probably right," she said. Charlotte began spooning food out of the serving dishes onto Richard's plate. "I really don't want to be far away from Papa right now."

Charlotte finished filling Richard's plate while he sipped his wine. She began piling food onto her plate when the oven timer beeped in the kitchen.

"Oh, goodness, honey, I almost forgot the rolls. I'll get them now."

When Charlotte returned to the dining room and took her seat, Richard asked, "What was it you wanted to talk about, Charlotte?" He took a bite of the chuck roast and sopped his potatoes in gravy. "This is good."

"Well, I was going to wait until after dinner, but …"

"Nonsense, we can talk while we eat. Go ahead, Charlotte."

Oh dear, Charlotte thought, *he only uses my given name when he's upset or angry with me. Or when he really doesn't want to talk with me.*

She closed her eyes as she took a bite of food, stalling for time while she planned her words. She took a sip of water and peered across the room at Richard, who was concentrating on his food, head down rather than meeting her gaze. Moments later, Richard said, "Charlotte? Are you going to tell me what you wanted to talk about or not?"

"Oh, yes, I'm s-s-s-sorry, honey. I just wanted to take a few bites first. Umm, well, you know I've been having problems sleeping lately. I fall asleep on the couch while we watch television, and I've even fallen asleep at work a few times. You remember I told you I woke up cooking one night, and then another time, I was on the couch crocheting that blanket?"

"Yeah. Melatodrol can cause people to sleepwalk. I told you that. You might want to have your dosage decreased."

"I know. I just keep forgetting to call my doctor. But …" Charlotte licked her lips and looked down at her plate. Raising her gaze to meet Richard's eyes, she said, "Remember I told you about waking up at that abandoned factory once? And then the time I woke up in the laundry room at Good Samaritan Hospital?"

Richard dropped his fork on his plate and rolled his eyes. "Where is this leading, Charlotte? Surely, you don't believe you really woke up in those places, do you?"

"Please, Richard, let me finish."

"All right, then, go ahead. But, as I've told you before, it's pointless."

Charlotte slumped, but not enough for Richard to notice, and placed her fork on her plate. "I wish you would believe me about this. Richard, last night I fell asleep on the couch, but I woke up outside an old abandoned house down in Cincinnati. I didn't even know where I was until I checked a map. I was in Clifton Heights, not far from the university. I'd never been there before, Richard, and it terrified me! How can I be driving to all these places while I'm asleep? And why those places? Really, honey, I'm scared!"

"Look, Charlotte, I've told you before, and I guess I have to say it again—the medicine you take for sleep is having an adverse effect on you. You're sleepwalking. And as for those times you *say* you woke up at, what was it? A factory? In a hospital? And now some old house? Come on, Charlotte, I've been here every time you had one of these episodes, and I'm telling you, you have never left this house. You've always been in our bed or on the couch, sound asleep. You're having very lucid dreams, Charlotte, and nothing more. And I don't see why you keep bringing this up! Now, may we finish our dinner in peace?"

"But Rich—"

"Now, that's enough," Richard snarled. "All you need to do is have your dosage lowered or go off the medicine completely. I'm not going to tell you this again. Now just do it!"

Richard threw his napkin onto his plate as he shoved his chair away from the table, the metal feet of the chair scraping the wood floor.

"I'm going to bed. Please run the dishwasher tonight. You forgot last night, and I'm sure it will be full with tonight's dishes. Goodnight, Charlotte," Richard muttered as he stormed from the room and up the stairs.

When he was out of sight, Charlotte pushed her plate away, dropped her head onto her arms, and began to cry. Her breathing erratic, she tried to silence her sobs. The last thing she needed was Richard returning. She held her stomach, forced her breaths to slow, and wiped her tear-stained cheeks. Feeling somewhat calmer, Charlotte cleared the table and loaded the dishwasher. She reached for the light switch but suddenly stopped.

Run the dishwasher, Charlotte. She had almost forgotten again.

Not wanting another showdown with Richard, Charlotte curled up on the couch and turned on the TV.

I don't care what Richard says. I was not *dreaming about those places. I was there! Tomorrow I'm calling Dr. Roberts. I've got to find out what is happening to me.*

She was asleep within minutes.

CHAPTER SEVEN

August 1990

Charlotte breathed deeply as she stood outside Dr. Roberts's office. *Now or never,* she told herself as she opened the door and stepped in. Several plush chairs lined three walls situated around small coffee tables bearing magazines and newspapers. To her left was a sliding glass window; a young man, looking to be in his twenties, sat at the counter behind the window, which he opened as Charlotte drew near.

"Hello," he said and smiled. "How can I help you?"

"Charlotte Palmer to see Dr. Roberts. I'm a little early."

"That's fine. I'm Bill," he said as he handed her a clipboard with forms attached. "Please fill out these forms while you wait and bring them back to me when you're done. There are cups of pens on the tables."

"Okay, thank you," Charlotte replied. She took a seat, fetched a pen, and began completing the forms. Just as she finished signing them, the door to the interior offices opened.

"Mrs. Palmer, Dr. Roberts is ready for you. Please follow me," Bill instructed.

Charlotte followed Bill to a small office decorated in warm tones. A large plush couch sat along one wall, flanked by an armchair. Across the room, situated at a window, was a desk that held a phone, calendar, pens, and a stack of files. As Charlotte turned to take a seat on the couch, she handed the clipboard to Bill, who then left the room and closed the door behind him.

Butterflies fluttered inside Charlotte's stomach while she waited. She licked her lips, shut her eyes, and sat on her hands to keep from biting her nails. The door opened moments later, and Dr. Roberts strode into the room holding a file and sat behind her desk.

"Hello, Mrs. Palmer. I'm Dr. Roberts. I've looked over your intake forms and see you have trouble sleeping and you've had a few episodes of sleepwalking."

"Yes, that's correct," Charlotte rasped and cleared her throat, bringing her hands together on her lap. She was taken aback by the doctor's abruptness but kept silent. *It's probably just my nerves.*

"I'd like to start by getting to know a little about you," Dr. Roberts stated as she walked to the armchair and sat. "May I start by calling you Charlotte?"

"Yes, that's fine."

"Great. What do you do for a living, Charlotte?"

"I'm the assistant finance director for the city of Hamilton."

"That must be an interesting job."

"Yes, it's challenging and rewarding. But it's also very stressful."

"I'm sure it is. Tell me about yourself. I'd like to know about your childhood, where you grew up, your hobbies or other interests."

"Well, I was born in the St. Bernard area of Cincinnati, but my parents moved us to Fairfield when I was eleven. I've lived there ever since. I got married five years ago. Richard and I live in a townhouse. Umm, let's see. What else? We don't have any pets or children. The first few years after we married, we traveled quite a bit and ate out nearly every night. We used to go dancing, to concerts, movies, that sort of thing. We also used to go hiking in some of the local parks, and once we went to the Smoky Mountains and hiked several trails there."

"You said, 'used to.' Don't you do any of those things anymore?"

"Well, our last vacation was to Florida over a year ago. After that, Richard started working more and more hours. He's a pharmacist. And my job, as we've already said, is very stressful. I'm in line to be promoted to the finance director position when my boss retires in a couple of years. But, to answer your question, we very rarely eat out anymore or go anywhere. Richard decided he wanted home-cooked meals. I used to read a lot and crochet, but I don't do much of either anymore. I'm still working on a baby blanket for a friend. The sad thing is, her son was born two months ago and I'm not even halfway done with the blanket. Between my job and all the housework, I just don't have much time these days."

"Does Richard help with the household chores?"

"Not much, really. He will do his own laundry, though. He's very particular about how his clothes are washed. But I do the lion's share of the work around the house."

"I see that you take ten milligrams of Melatodrol nightly to help you sleep. How long have you been on that dosage?"

"I started taking five milligrams about five years ago but increased to ten several months ago after my father had a stroke."

"I'm sorry to hear about your father, Charlotte. How is he doing now?"

"He's finally home. He was in the hospital for several weeks and then in a rehab facility for a couple of months. He's walking much better and starting to talk more. Mama says she talks to him quite a bit, but every time I visit him, he doesn't have much to say and what he *does* say doesn't make any sense."

"How so?"

"Well, all he ever says when he sees me is his mother's name, or he'll say 'save her.' Mama and I don't understand what he's trying to tell me. His mother died in 1935."

"I see. So, between work, your household responsibilities, and your father's health, it seems you are under an exorbitant amount of stress. Do you believe that is contributing to your problems sleeping?"

"It probably is. But the fact that I'm not sleeping well, or that I fall asleep on the couch, and … and … I've even fallen asleep at work—anyway, those things don't bother me as much as the sleepwalking. But sleepwalking isn't the only problem. There's m-m-more." Charlotte choked back a sob as tears formed in the corners of her eyes.

"Take your time, Charlotte. We'll get you through this."

"Thank you," Charlotte whispered. She swallowed hard. "I woke up once at two in the morning cooking breakfast. I mean, *really* cooking breakfast! I had bacon frying and was scrambling eggs when I woke up. And another time, I woke up in the middle of the night sitting on the couch crocheting the baby blanket. I have no memory of getting out of bed or even what time I fell asleep. But—"Charlotte flexed her hands into fists and shut her eyes. "I'm sorry, Dr. Roberts. My mouth is so dry. Could I bother you for a glass of water?"

"Of course." Dr. Roberts walked to the water cooler, grabbed a paper cup, and filled it. Handing the cup to Charlotte, she said, "Here you go. Please proceed when you feel ready."

"Thank you," Charlotte said. She took several sips of the water before setting the cup on the table in front of her. "Recently, Dr. Roberts, some very odd things have happened. While I was asleep, I mean."

"Whenever you're ready." Dr. Roberts's voice was gentle and comforting.

Charlotte felt at ease, in spite of her earlier apprehension, and somehow knew she could be completely open with the doctor. "It was late January. I took my sleeping pill and went to sleep around ten. But I woke up sitting in my car in a parking lot next to a large brick building. It was pitch dark outside and I couldn't see much. There were no lights on in the building, none in the parking lot, and no streetlights. I got out of my car and walked around the corner of the building to see if I could figure out where I was. I still couldn't see anything, so I went back to my car and got a flashlight out of the glove compartment. A giant clock hung above the door. It was dingy. Many of the numbers were missing and both hands were gone. Below the clock were letters hung on the building, but some of those were also missing. The only ones still hanging were K, A and S.

"I flashed the light all over the building and across the street. The area was run down, buildings were decaying, and some were partially torn down. Empty lots littered the street. There were no cars, no traffic whatsoever. The windows on the building where I stood were boarded up. Well, most of them anyway. Some had broken pieces of glass. Some had no glass at all. It looked to be about four stories high. I walked back to my car and noticed several old smokestacks on a building several hundred yards away. And then … Oh, this is going to sound crazy."

"Go ahead. You won't get any judgment from me. You're safe here."

"Thank you. As I was looking across the parking lot at another building with those stacks, I thought I saw a woman in a long dress, down to her ankles, and wearing an apron. It was a full, white apron, with smudges down the front. A black hairnet held her hair tightly around her skull. She was walking toward me, and then she was gone. Right then, I felt very cold, even though I had on flannel pajamas, a heavy winter coat, and gloves. I got into my car and took the gloves off. My hands were icy. I started the car and cranked the heat up. I sat there for several minutes, I really don't know how long, trying to get warm. Then I drove home, and even though it took me half an hour or more, I could never get warm. I looked at the clock on my dashboard when I pulled into my parking space. It was one o'clock in the morning. Just like with the sleepwalking, I had no memory of ever leaving my house, much less driving! I was terrified, Dr. Roberts!"

"What happened when you got home?"

"I crawled back into bed and tried to sleep. Richard never woke up. Doctor Roberts, the really scary part about it was … was …" A lump formed in her throat, and Charlotte blinked back more tears.

"It's okay, Charlotte. No need to hurry."

Sniffling, Charlotte continued, "When I told Richard about it the next morning, he said I never left the bed, never left the house. He insisted that it was just a dream. But, Doctor, it *felt* so real! I knew it was real, but he was adamant that it wasn't. The more I tried to talk with him about it, the angrier he got. Then there were two other times that I woke up in strange places. One was the laundry room of Good Samaritan Hospital. The other was outside an old, abandoned house in Clifton Heights. Each time, Richard told me I never left home and was merely dreaming. I thought … I think … I-I think I'm going insane!"

Dr. Roberts checked her watch and said, "Rest assured, Charlotte, you are not going insane. I would like to explore this further, but I'm afraid we are almost out of time today. I'd like to see you again in two weeks. There's something I want you to consider trying."

"What's that, Doctor?"

"I've started some hypnosis therapy with a few patients who have memory loss, and it seems to work most of the time. I'd like you to consider going under hypnosis to see if we can draw out more about what happened to you while you were blacked out. It's perfectly safe, I assure you. We don't have to start right away, only when you're ready. I would like to have you tell me more next time about the other two incidents, however."

"Okay. I'll give it some thought. About trying hypnosis, I mean. Thank you very much."

"You're welcome. Please schedule the next appointment with Bill before you leave." Dr. Roberts rose and extended her hand. Charlotte took the doctor's hand, receiving a warm handshake in return.

"Hello, Charlotte. Please have a seat on the couch. I'll be right with you." Dr. Roberts jotted a few notes, closed the file before picking it up, moved to the armchair, and took a seat.

"How has this past week been for you, Charlotte? Any trouble sleeping?" Dr. Roberts clicked her pen as she crossed her legs.

"I've slept well, for the most part. What I mean is, I haven't woken up in any strange places or doing anything. I've had a recurring dream, however. Nearly every night."

"Can you tell me about it?"

"Yes. It's the same thing every time. Just a woman's face. She's young, it seems, but she's dressed as a much older woman would dress. I'm not making much sense. Let me try to explain. Her hair is blond and is cut just below her chin. It's a little curly on the ends, like mine. She's wearing a black dress with white lace on the collar and cuffs of her long sleeves. A silver cross hangs around her neck. Her mouth is moving. I think she's talking, but the dreams never have sound. I have no idea what she's saying. And then it all fades away in a mist."

Dr. Roberts looked up from her notepad. "And you just started having this dream recently?

"Well, no …" Charlotte bit her lip and glanced around the room. As her eyes drifted back to meet Dr. Roberts, she said, "The first time I had it was right after a visit with my father. The first time he tried to say her name and told me to 'save her.'"

"I see. Let's table this for now. I'd like you to tell me about the other times you woke up in unfamiliar locations. Before you begin, would you like some water?"

"Yes, yes, that would be helpful." Hands pressed against her abdomen, Charlotte waited as Dr. Roberts retrieved the water and brought it to the table in front of the couch. Charlotte leaned over, taking the cup, and took a few sips.

"Ready, then?" Dr. Roberts picked up her pen and notepad.

"Yes. Let's see, the first time was the factory. I'm trying to remember ... The second time was at the hospital. I had fallen asleep on the couch again, like I seem to do so often. I don't know, I just can't seem to stay awake very long after dinner. I sit down to watch TV with Richard or read a book, and I'm out in minutes. Okay, I'm sorry, I got off topic there. Where was I?

"Oh yes, anyway, I'd fallen asleep at around eleven that night. The local news was just coming on, but that's the last thing I remembered until I woke up. I was sitting in a chair near a door. When I'd cleared my head and fully woke up, I saw I was in some sort of laundry room. Not like in a house, but a very large room with dozens of industrial-sized washers and dryers along three walls. Several metal tables were placed end to end in rows in the middle of the room. Some of the tables were piled high with folded bed sheets and blankets, and others held blue gowns. You know, like the gowns patients wear. On the floor near the washers were several large bins on wheels. I got up and crossed the room to look inside the bins. They were full of dirty sheets, towels, and more gowns.

"No one else was in the room, but the washers and dryers were running. I stood there for a few minutes, trying to remember but everything was a blank. I only remembered being on the couch and then waking up in that laundry room. I turned to leave and saw something in the glass of the washer door. It was a woman's face. Her blond hair was styled short to frame her round face. She was saying something I couldn't hear.

"I quickly left the room and started down a long hallway, when I slipped on the tile floor. Dr. Roberts, I was once again in my PJs, but this time, I didn't have on shoes or a coat. I was wearing my old, ratty slippers and a sweater! I began to sweat, and goosebumps crawled up my arms. I remember feeling very cold. I felt my hands. They were icy. Just like at the factory in January, but since this was April and I was indoors, I didn't understand why my hands were so cold.

"I practically ran down that hallway, turned a corner onto another long hallway, and kept going until I found a bank of elevators. I wasn't sure which floor I was on, but I pressed 1 and came out to another hallway. I looked around and saw an exit sign, so I headed in that direction until I found the main entrance to the hospital. I passed a welcome desk. No one was stationed there, but a pile of pamphlets caught my eye. It was then I saw I was at Good Samaritan Hospital. I'd never been in this hospital before. I didn't even know where it was located.

"I continued to shiver and felt like spiders were racing up and down my spine, so I left through the revolving door to find a parking lot nearby. I reached into the pockets of my sweater, hoping, oh I was hoping. And I did land on my keys. Now all I had to do was find my car. I have a fairly new car with a remote key, so I pressed the engine start and sure enough, several yards away, my car lights flashed. I ran to the car, unlocked the door, and got in. As soon as I put the key into the ignition, I turned on the overhead light to check my watch. It was two o'clock in the morning! I retrieved a map from the glove compartment and plotted out my route home. I was panicking, terrified of what was happening to me, but I took deep breaths and tried to calm down enough to drive. I got home about forty-five minutes later."

"What happened when you got home?"

"Well, I was afraid to climb into bed and wake Richard. He always gets so upset if I rouse him in the middle of the night. The TV was still on in the living room, so I went back to the couch where I had fallen asleep. I grabbed the throw off the back of the couch and laid down. I couldn't get my mind to rest. I couldn't stop shivering, either. I eventually fell asleep and was awakened the next morning by Richard, who was shaking me and yelling my name. I was late for work that day. It wasn't the first time I'd been late due to lack of sleep."

Dr. Roberts remained silent while she wrote on her notepad. Charlotte drank more water, got up from the couch to refill her cup, and sat back down before Dr. Roberts looked up.

"Okay, Charlotte. Can you tell me about the third time you woke up in this manner? And have there been any other times this has happened?"

"No, it's only happened the three times. And each time afterward, I've had that same dream for three or four nights in a row."

"Okay. You said the first time, at the factory, was in January, correct?"

"Yes."

"And the time at the hospital was in April. When was the last time this happened?"

"Just recently. In July. It's what prompted me to call you. As I told you before, every time this happened to me, I talked with Richard about it, but he was so unyielding that I had just been dreaming, that I'd never left the house, that I honestly thought I was starting to lose my mind. I didn't know if it was an adverse side effect of the Melatodrol, so I did have my dosage reduced back to five milligrams after the first time, you know, the factory. But then it happened again at the hospital and again in July at the house. That's when I knew I had to talk with someone about this. Richard's been no help at all."

Charlotte paused for a moment, fighting to hold back fresh tears, while Dr. Roberts made notes in the file. *Richard and I used to be so great together. He was so loving and gentle, and romantic. But this past year or so ... I wonder what changed?*

"Okay, Charlotte, you may proceed. You said the last time was at ... where? A house? Tell me about that."

Charlotte cleared her throat, scrunched her eyes closed for a moment, and inhaled deeply. She told Dr. Roberts about the house ... the Tudor house in Clifton Heights where she had awakened in July. She told the doctor about feeling a hand on her shoulder, about the fog, the disrepair of the house itself. And she told her about seeing the woman in the upstairs window.

"Oh my gosh, Dr. Roberts! I just realized something!" Charlotte's hands shook, nearly spilling the cup of water she was holding.

"What, Charlotte?"

"The woman in my dreams, the blond woman. It's the same woman I saw at the factory! And … And in the hospital laundry room. It's the same woman in the window at that house! Oh my gosh. That's … That's … I just don't know. Isn't that odd?"

"It might not be that odd, Charlotte. Have you given any more thought to trying hypnosis? I wonder if it might help you tie all these incidents together. Maybe give you some answers as to what these places mean or who the woman is."

"Well, umm, okay, maybe that *would* be a good idea. I've got to figure out what all this means."

"Great, then we'll try it at your next appointment," Dr. Roberts said as she glanced at her watch and rose to her feet. "Our time is up for today, Charlotte. Schedule with Bill again and rest assured, we will figure all this out for you. You take care, and I'll see you in two weeks."

"Thank you, Doctor. I will."

Charlotte drove back to work white-knuckled and still shaking.

CHAPTER EIGHT

September 1990

"I want you to lie on the couch, Charlotte. Get comfortable," Dr. Roberts instructed in a soothing, near-whisper. "Now close your eyes. Picture your toes in your mind. I want you to relax your toes and your feet. Now think about the muscles in your calves. Let them go slack and relax them, too. Imagine a place that gives you a sense of peace … serenity. What are you picturing, Charlotte?"

"The mountains," she murmured. "The Smoky Mountains."

"Good. Now picture yourself lying in a meadow in the mountains. Relax your knees, your thighs, your hips. Allow the calm to wash over your body like the mountain breezes. Relax your arms, your shoulders, your neck. Now let your jaw muscles soften, your cheeks, your forehead. Your entire body is at rest, Charlotte, your muscles are loose. You are sleepy and completely relaxed. How do you feel, Charlotte?"

"Mmm … peaceful," Charlotte moaned.

"Good, good. Keep your body at rest. Sink into the couch. Let it wrap around you like a warm embrace. You're safe here. You are in complete control of this time. Now I'm going to give you a word that will wake you up, and when you do, you will remember everything you've seen or heard. That word is 'peaceful.' What is the word to wake you up, Charlotte?"

Charlotte licked her lips. "Peaceful."

"Okay, now take yourself back to the factory. You saw part of a sign, the company name perhaps. Remember how dark and cold it was that night in January. What do you see?"

"I see a huge brick building next to the parking lot, close to the street. Farther from the lot are more buildings, smaller, but they have several smokestacks. Some are falling apart. The large building has an old clock above the door. Numbers are missing. There's a sign under the clock with missing letters. I see the letters … K, A, and S. It looks like two letters were between the A and S. Wait, now I can see a faint outline of the letters that were once there. K … A … H …I'm trying to see … N … S. K-A-H-N-S. Kahn's. I'm looking closer at the clock. Yes! I see it! There's a faded painting of a hot dog on the clock. Oh my! This is the old Kahn's factory! They made hot dogs and pork roasts and … it's a meat processing plant! But I don't understand why …"

"Calm, Charlotte, stay calm. Relax your mind and your body. Don't try to understand why you're there just yet. Just tell me what you see. Go back to that factory, Charlotte. What do you see?"

"A woman. There's a woman walking toward me from the building with the stacks. She's wearing a dress that hangs almost to her ankles. Her shoes are clunky with low heels. I think they were called Oxfords. Over her dress, she's wearing a full-body white apron, but there are dark smudges all over it. She has short blond hair. I can see her eyes now. They are green, like emeralds. She's opening her mouth to say something to me. No, wait! Please come back! I'm looking all around me, but the woman is gone."

Charlotte tossed and turned on the couch while she spoke. Droplets of sweat formed on her brow. She swallowed and licked her lips.

"Please, come back! I couldn't hear what you said! Oh, please …!"

"Charlotte, I want you to relax your mind now. Take a deep breath. I'm going to wake you up. On the count of three, I'm going to give you the wake word. One … Two … Three … Peaceful."

Charlotte opened her eyes and turned her head to peer at Dr. Roberts. She started to sit up, but Dr. Roberts touched her shoulder.

"Give yourself a minute, Charlotte. Take deep breaths."

Moments later, Charlotte sat upright and drank some water.

"Do you remember what you saw, Charlotte?"

"Yes, I was at the old Kahn's factory. I saw the woman again, but this time, I could see she had blond hair and green eyes. Her eyes were like emeralds." *Like emeralds,* she thought.

"Do you know who the woman was?"

"No, but she was dressed like … from a long time ago. Ankle-length dress and industrial shoes. Could that have been the 1920s or 30s?"

"Perhaps," said Dr. Roberts. "I think you've had enough for today, Charlotte. I don't want to overtax you. See me again in two weeks."

Charlotte sat cross-legged while finishing the baby blanket for Mindy's son, a light rain falling outside and plinking against the windows. A greeting card, box and wrapping paper took up the space next to her on the couch. Stevie Nicks and Fleetwood Mac sang to her from the CD player speakers as she worked. She sewed in the last end of yarn, looked at the clock on the far wall, and quickly folded the blanket. Charlotte smiled as she carefully placed the blanket in the box and covered it with tissue paper. She then wrapped the box, attached a bow and grabbed a pen to write something on the card. Mindy and Caleb were due to arrive any minute.

As if on cue, the doorbell rang just as Charlotte sealed the envelope with the card inside and attached it with tape to the box. She set the box on the table and sprinted to the door. She hadn't seen her best friend since a few days after Timmy was born—nearly four months ago. Life had gotten in the way, it seemed, and she and Mindy rarely saw each other. When they did, it was without Richard, who complained about Mindy's whining daughters, now four and two.

Charlotte threw open the door and chaos began as the three adults hugged and laughed. Two little girls, Stephanie and Jenny, jumped up and down, squealing and shouting with glee, "Auntie Char, Auntie Char!"

Charlotte knelt to take both girls into her arms. "Oh, my sweet girls, I've missed you both so much. And just look how big you've gotten!" Her eyes darted to Mindy, sparkling as they dampened with tears.

"They've missed you, too, Char." She sniffled. "And so have I."

"Same, Min. Gosh, guys, why are we all just standing here at the door? Come in, come in!"

Mindy's eyes shot around the room as she tilted her head toward the stairs. "Umm, is he home?"

"Richard? No, he's working at the pharmacy today. He won't be home for hours."

"Good. He's so impatient with the girls," Caleb said as he picked up the portable car seat carrying the baby, and strolled to the couch.

"I know," Charlotte said. "I'm sorry."

"Nonsense, Char," Mindy replied. "Nothing for you to be sorry about. You can't *make* Richard like children, now can you?"

Charlotte opened her mouth, but then snapped it shut immediately. She wanted so much to tell her friend about Richard's refusal to start a family or even talk with her about it. *Not today, Charlotte,* she thought. *Best leave it alone for now.*

The three friends talked for several minutes before Mindy and Caleb opened their present. Caleb wrapped the new blanket around Timmy and handed him to Charlotte to hold. Stephanie and Jenny sat on the floor playing with their dolls.

"I'll be back. I just need to warm up a bottle." Caleb eased up from the couch, but not before winking at Mindy and patting her on the shoulder.

As soon as Caleb disappeared into the kitchen, Mindy turned toward Charlotte. "Okay, Char, what's going on in your life? And I don't want to hear about work. I want to hear about *you.* You look exhausted, by the way. And I don't mean that to sound mean." Mindy squeezed Charlotte's hand.

"I know you don't, Min." Charlotte stole a look toward the kitchen, hoping Caleb wasn't about to return to the living room. She wanted a few minutes alone with her friend. "I'm not sure what to tell you, Min. Work *has* been stressful. I've got my hands full around the house, too. I've been having some problems sleeping."

"You're still on that med, aren't you? Isn't that helping anymore?"

"Yes, I'm still on it. It's not so much that I'm *not* sleeping. It's the dreams I'm having."

"What do you mean? Like, nightmares?"

"I suppose you could call it that. A few days after Papa's stroke last January, I started having a dream of just a woman's face. She is talking to me, but I can't hear anything she's saying."

"Ooo, this sounds intriguing." Mindy leaned in, eyes sparkling.

"Yeah, well, I guess you could call it that. It's kinda creepy, if you ask me. Anyway, that's not all. Richard says I'm just having lucid dreams, but they seem *so* real, Min. And I'm falling asleep early in the evening, right after dinner. I've even nodded off at work a few times. My boss is not too thrilled with me these days."

Charlotte caressed Timmy's cheek and, glancing away from Mindy, saw Caleb stroll into the room.

"Sorry to interrupt. The bottle's just about ready. Here, Charlotte, let me take the baby." Caleb took the infant and headed back to the kitchen.

"Tell me about these dreams, Char."

"Well, it started out I was sleepwalking and …"

"What?! Sleepwalking? Like, here in the house?" Mindy's eyes widened with worry.

"Ah huh. I woke up one morning, cooking. I was frying bacon and scrambling eggs! And then I woke up another time sitting right here on the couch, crocheting that blanket. I checked it over the next day—not one incorrect stitch, Min! But there's more, and I'm not sure if I should even tell you. You'll probably agree with Richard and not believe me."

"C'mon, Char. You know me better than that. Tell me. Don't worry about Caleb. He's going to feed Timmy his bottle out in the kitchen, so he won't interrupt us."

For the next twenty minutes, Charlotte told Mindy about waking up at the factory and the hospital and the house, about seeing the psychologist, and about starting hypnosis therapy. Mindy listened intently, holding Charlotte's hand, caressing her arm now and then, and never interrupting. Charlotte told her about the first words her Papa had said to her after his stroke, the words about saving his mother. She told Mindy everything—except she didn't. She couldn't bring herself to tell Mindy how Richard had become distant and demanding, how he insisted on her doing all the cooking, cleaning, grocery shopping, and other household chores.

"And that's really about it, Min," Charlotte said. "Richard doesn't believe I really woke up in those places. He says I never left the house. Min, I thought I was losing my mind. I mean, I'm under so much pressure right now, and then those weird, silent dreams, and then waking up in places I've never been to before. And Richard saying I was here the whole time. So that's when I went to see Dr. Roberts."

"Wow, Char, that's a lot. I mean, a *lot*! I don't even know what to say about those dreams and waking up in those places, but I hope the hypnosis helps you figure it out. You know how I love a good mystery. I hope you'll keep me in the loop." Mindy bit her bottom lip in excitement.

Charlotte laughed, but it was hesitant, nervous. Nothing like the way she used to laugh before she met Richard. "Yeah, yeah, Min, I'll keep you in the loop. Gosh, I miss this. We just never have any time together anymore."

"I know, but three kids don't allow for any time for myself. Hey! I have a great idea!" Mindy's face lit up with excitement.

"I'm almost afraid to ask," Charlotte groaned.

"No, seriously, hear me out. I was working on a family tree and planning to have it embroidered, so I wanted to research my family history. I don't know if you knew this, but the Mormon church created a genealogy database a few years ago and now, with computers becoming so popular, there's a program you can buy. Well, not *you*. I've actually already bought it. It's on disks, and they go right into the computer, and I can search just about any name. It helps to know birthdates and places, but wow, we could put your father's name in and see if it gives us any information about his mother."

Mindy was unstoppable. She convincingly persuaded Charlotte to write down her father's birthdate and anything she knew about her grandparents. Charlotte told her she only knew their names were Oskar and Wilhelmina Schmidt, that they were both from Germany but met in Cincinnati.

Charlotte leaned back, throwing her head against the couch. "Min, I just don't see the point in—"

"Now there you go again. Always practical. It'll be fun, Char. I'll put in the information and let's just see if we can find out anything about your grandparents. Your parents never talked about them, and now your father is telling you to 'save her'? There's got to be something there. You know how much I love this kind of stuff. I'll do all the work, I promise. And if I find something, I'll print it out for you, or you can come to the house and look for yourself. Deal?"

Charlotte rolled her eyes and chuckled. "Okay, Mindy, deal. You're such a nut!"

"I know, but you love me!" Mindy pulled Charlotte into a bear hug and laughed loudly. Releasing her friend, she called out to the kitchen, "Hey, Caleb. It's getting late. We better get going." Turning to Charlotte, she said, "Sorry we have to fly but my folks are coming over tonight for dinner. I'm going to start on this research tomorrow. Oh, I'm so excited about this! A mystery to solve!"

Mindy and Caleb gathered up their belongings and children, hugged Charlotte at the door, and headed home.

I wonder if Mindy is right about Papa's parents. I wonder if there really is some mystery to solve. Why else would Papa never talk about them?

CHAPTER NINE

October 1990

Charlotte's eyes grew heavy, her body slack. The sound of Dr. Roberts's soft, soothing voice flooded her ears. Images flitted across her closed eyelids as the doctor whispered instructions—the woman appeared to her clad in a white button-down blouse and black skirt, the silver cross glinting on her neck.

"Concentrate on sounds now, Charlotte. Block everything else out of your mind and just listen. Listen to the woman speaking to you. What is she saying?"

"I ... I don't know. I still can't hear her," Charlotte breathed.

"Slowly, Charlotte, focus. Focus on the woman's words."

"Ye ... Yes, I think I can hear her now. Wait, I ... I don't understand."

"What is she saying to you, Charlotte?"

"She's saying ..." Charlotte swallowed hard. "She's saying 'I didn't do it.' Nothing else. Just 'I didn't do it.'" Charlotte began fisting her hands at her sides and moving her head from side to side.

"Okay, Charlotte, relax. You're calm, at rest. Nothing can harm you. You're safe. Relax, Charlotte, relax. Try to talk to her now. Anything that comes to mind."

"Umm, I don ... Oh, okay. Umm, yes. She's looking into my eyes. Oh goodness, she has such beautiful green eyes. Yes, I'll ask her ... I'll ask ..." Charlotte unclenched her fists and squirmed on the couch. "I'll ask her ... Who are you?"

The woman in her vision reached a hand toward Charlotte, who jumped slightly as soft fingers grazed her cheek.

The woman whispered, "I'm your grandmother. My name is Wilhelmina."

Charlotte began writhing on the couch, flailing her arms wildly. Dr. Roberts dropped her notepad and yelled, "You'll wake up now, Charlotte. One … Two … Three … Peaceful!"

Charlotte bolted upright, eyes wide. Her face turned ashen; her palms dampened with sweat.

"What is it, Charlotte, what did she say?"

"She … She … She said she's my grandmother. She's Wilhelmina!"

Mindy and Charlotte stared at the computer screen, neither speaking. Charlotte absently rubbed her arms as she slumped in the chair. Mindy sat shaking her head, opening her mouth to speak, and then closing it again. Time stopped.

The phone jangled loudly on the desk beside the computer, and both girls jumped, hands on their chests. Mindy reached for the phone and said, "Hello?"

Moments later, she returned the handle to its cradle and turned to Charlotte. "It was just Caleb letting me know he's picking up dinner for tonight. He'll be home soon."

Charlotte nodded and turned her gaze back to the screen. "I … uhh … I don't … What does this mean?"

"Let's look it over again, Char. You know, to make sure we didn't miss anything." Pointing to a small box on the screen, Mindy said, "See, this is your father, Albert Schmidt. It shows he was born in 1920 here in Cincinnati. So, we know that information is right."

Mindy's finger trailed upward on the screen. "And here's your father's parents, Oskar and Wilhelmina Schmidt. Oskar was born in Berlin, Germany in 1890, and Wilhelmina was born in Munich in 1900."

Mindy moved the mouse and clicked on Oskar's name. "This brings up more information about Oskar. It shows he immigrated to America in 1917 and began working at Kahn's Meats the same year. Looks like he died on March 4, 1925. Gosh, he was only thirty-four years old, Char.

"Let's go back and click on Wilhelmina's name. Look here. Her full name was Wilhelmina Marie Heinrich. Marie. That's where you got *your* middle name from! Wilhelmina appears to have been born in 1900 to Klaus and Brigitta Heinrich. Oh, gosh, look at this. She had five brothers. Seems she was the youngest *and* the only girl. Let's keep scrolling."

They discovered that Wilhelmina remarried a few months after Oskar died but, after a couple more hours of research, they hit a dead end. Their necks were aching and eyes watering from staring at the computer screen for so long.

"Look, Char, I think that's about all we can find here. I think we need to take a trip to the library. Are you free tomorrow?"

"Sure. Let's meet for lunch first, okay? I haven't been to Casper's in a while. Say, 11:30?"

"Sounds like a plan. See you tomorrow!"

A few days later, seated at Charlotte's dining room table, she and Mindy began poring over the books and copies of newspapers they had borrowed from the library. Each had a pencil and legal pad to jot down notes as they read the information.

"Oh my God, Charlotte! You've got to see this!" Mindy gazed at Charlotte with wide eyes. "You won't believe what I just found!"

Charlotte walked around the table and took a seat next to her friend. She took the pad from Mindy and scanned her notes, then grabbed the newspaper laying open in front of Mindy and compared the information on it.

Their eyes met. Mindy covered her mouth with a hand as she began shaking her head slowly back and forth. Charlotte's chin quivered and she rose from the table so suddenly she knocked the chair over onto the floor.

"N-N-No, Mindy. This can't be true! It … It just *can't*!" Charlotte ran around the table, heading for the living room. She didn't know where to go or what to do; she only knew she needed to run away, away from that newspaper, those notes, her family history.

At the doorway to the living room, she paused and turned to face her friend. Mindy was staring at her blankly, continuously licking her lips and rubbing her legs.

"Char ... I ... Oh my God!" Mindy's eyes widened as she averted her gaze toward something behind Charlotte.

Charlotte turned quickly, immediately finding herself face-to-chest with Richard.

"Oh ... I-I'm s-sorry, Rich-Richard," she sputtered.

"Charley, you're absolutely white as a ghost. What's wrong?" Richard grabbed Charlotte by the shoulders, steadying her as she teetered backward.

She shook her head and squirmed in his grasp, but she could not wrench herself from his hands. Richard's gaze shot to Mindy and then to the table. He released his wife and strode closer to the table, picking up one of the legal pads. He scanned it quickly, sighed deeply, and looked up at Charlotte.

Without looking at Mindy, he growled, "Mindy, I think you better leave."

"N-N-No, Richard, I want to stay," Mindy squeaked.

Richard scowled at Mindy. "Leave," he snarled.

Mindy glanced at Charlotte, eyes soft with concern.

"It's ... It's okay, Min. I'll be fine. Go on home," she croaked as she stepped toward her friend and took her by the elbow, leading her to the door. "I'll call you later."

Mindy grabbed her purse from the couch as they passed and said, "But—"

"Mindy, it would be best if you do as I've asked. You need to leave—*now*!" Richard's eyes flared with anger.

Charlotte shut the door behind Mindy, and she slowly turned to face Richard.

"Sit down, Charlotte. We have some things to discuss."

Part 2: Wilhelmina

Resolute Protector. A Desire to Protect.

CHAPTER TEN

May 1915

Fifteen-year-old Wilhelmina Marie Heinrich lay in her bed in the dark listening for the voices of her parents or brothers. When she was certain everyone was fast asleep in their own rooms, she felt around on her bedside table for a match, then carefully lit the gas lamp resting on the table and got out of bed. She removed her nightgown, donned her prettiest dress, and ran a brush through her long blond hair before dimming the flame in the lamp and tiptoeing to the window.

Opening the sash, she suddenly stopped as it creaked, her ears perked. She took deep breaths, slowly pushing the window open, and climbed through to the porch roof. Wilhelmina had begun sneaking out of the house when she was eight. She would roam the streets of her neighborhood, pretending to be a princess from days past wandering through the woods or a village near her castle. Sometimes she would merely lie on the damp grass in her backyard and gaze at the stars. As she grew older, she would sneak off to meet a boy or go to the local theater to watch the vaudeville show that, earlier that evening, her parents had forbidden her to see.

This May night was cool, the skies gray with heavy clouds. Shivering and wishing she had grabbed her shawl, Wilhelmina expertly navigated the roof, shimmied down the flower-covered trellis, and landed effortlessly on the thick grass. She scanned the dark house, ensuring no one inside had awoken to discover her escape, before running through the yard to the street behind her parents' house. In a black touring car around the corner, her friends waited, all ready for the frat party near Ludwig Maximilian University in the heart of Munich. There, Wilhelmina's rebellious nature emerged. She danced and laughed, drank beer, and sang songs with the other partygoers. Wilhelmina had her first kiss at one of these parties when she was just thirteen. She made out with many boys over the next few years, enjoying the dangerous aspects of going against her parents' rules. She allowed the boys to fondle her budding breasts and stick their tongues in her mouth. She especially enjoyed making them stop, knowing it made them angry and disappointed.

The youngest of six children, Wilhelmina was born at the turn of the century to pious Lutherans, Klaus and Brigitta Heinrich. Hers was a life of luxury, privilege, and social prominence. An executive with a renowned Munich bank, Klaus earned a substantial income and provided amply for his family. Every Sunday they attended St. Luke's Church, known to them as Lukaskirche, on the banks of the Isar River. Klaus and Brigitta were strict parents who instituted daily devotionals within their household, consisting of prayers and reading the Bible. Although they did allow a few works of fiction, most of their books covered religion and education. On Klaus's insistence, the entire family learned multiple languages, including Italian, Spanish, and English.

The only daughter and her mother's favorite, Wilhelmina was spoiled and given a wide berth. She had a sweet smile and pleasant mood when she had her own way. Whenever she was told 'no' or reprimanded, her temper rose steadily like a slow-burning fire. The usually peaceful Heinrich household would erupt with Wilhelmina's shouts and tantrums until her exasperated parents would give up and allow Wilhelmina to once again have whatever she wanted.

Wilhelmina's five brothers ranged in age from sixteen to twenty-four; the oldest three were fighting in the Great War—two in Africa and one in Bulgaria. Wilhelm, the oldest, was in medical school when he was drafted into the German federal defense forces in September 1914. Twin twenty-year-old brothers, Alfred and Albert, were attending Ludwig Maximilian University when they went to war in November 1914. Only Wilhelm and Alfred returned unscathed from the four-year conflict. In March 1915, Albert was killed at the Battle of Verdun, where bitter fighting continued for most of that year. Eighteen-year-old Karl, sixteen-year-old Hans, and

Wilhelmina studied at Munich's notable Nymphenburger Schulen Gymnasium and Realschule, a private school with a comprehensive curriculum focusing on academic excellence. The boys were expected to become doctors or lawyers or bankers like their father. Wilhelmina was expected to be a teacher or nurse, get married, and have children.

Popular with the boys, Wilhelmina had few girlfriends and confided in none. They were envious of her natural good looks, wavy blond hair, and dark green eyes. Most of the girls at school despised the way she shamelessly flirted and would whisper behind her back that she was "loose." They called her a "hure" to her face. The name-calling only fueled the fire inside Wilhelmina; she squared her shoulders and lifted her head, nose in the air, as she strutted past the other girls in the school hallways.

Contrary to the rumors the students spread throughout her school and neighborhood, Wilhelmina was a virgin. As a child, she saw boys and girls kissing in the park and wondered how it felt. She taught herself how to kiss using a hand mirror. She would stand outside the door to her brothers' room, eavesdropping on their conversations about the girls they made out with. One night she heard Wilhelm telling his brothers that "it felt good when I put it in her." Wilhelmina did not understand what Wilhelm meant.

One morning twelve-year-old Wilhelmina let out a shrill scream from the bathroom. "Mama," she cried. "Mama, I'm bleeding!" Her mother sprinted up the stairs and threw open the bathroom door to find Wilhelmina standing naked in the empty tub with blood trickling down her legs.

"What is it, Mama? Why am I bleeding?" Wilhelmina's wide eyes filled with tears as she reached out to her mother with shaking hands. "Mmm … Mama?"

"*Ach mein Schatz,*" Brigitta whispered as she wrapped her arms around her daughter. "Oh, my darling, let me help you."

Brigitta helped Wilhelmina out of the tub, grabbing a towel to dry her off. She then opened a nearby cabinet, and hauled out a belt and a thick cloth pad. She showed Wilhelmina how to attach the pad to the belt and then where to place the belt around her hips so that the pad rested between Wilhelmina's legs. She then wrapped her daughter in a robe and guided Wilhelmina to her bedroom. While she dressed for school, her mother told her about menstruation and that it meant that Wilhelmina was becoming a woman and could have children. Brigitta never explained to her daughter how a woman becomes pregnant—only telling her that a husband would touch his wife in her "private places" and then lie on top of her. Brigitta instructed Wilhelmina to be careful around boys who "only want one thing." She had no idea what that "one thing" was, but she wondered if it was what Wilhelm had told his brothers.

In the three years since she started having her periods, Wilhelmina learned how to smile coyishly at the boys, how to bat her eyes, and to flirt. She sewed her own clothes, discarding her traditional Gibson-style gowns, styling the dresses in the new silhouettes becoming popular around the globe—a slim dress line faded quickly around 1915 to a wider, flared line. Dress lengths rose to the mid-calf. Numerous arguments ensued between Wilhelmina and her parents, who felt strongly that women should never show any part of their legs, not even a glimpse of skin allowed. Brigitta took to her bed with a raging headache when Wilhelmina modeled a new dress for her, one with a lower neckline that revealed her collarbone. She no longer purchased light pastel materials, but opted for heavier tones like blue, green, purple, and brown in patterns of plaid, thin vertical stripes and gingham. She embellished her new dresses with large bows, white collars, and ruffles. Every item of clothing Wilhelmina made was with one goal in mind: to attract the boys.

Wilhelmina performed another act of rebellion against her parents' strict rules and religious beliefs. Just days after sneaking out of the house for the frat party, she locked herself in the upstairs bathroom, scissors in hand, and cut her long locks into a bob. Her lustrous golden waves, once cascading down her back, now lay on the black and white tiles at her feet. She then applied color to her cheeks, eyelids, and lips from her mother's rouge pots. Taking a step back, Wilhelmina admired her reflection in the mirror above the pedestal sink. She began to twirl around the room, imagining she was at a party dancing with the most handsome men.

A loud pounding on the door startled Wilhelmina from her daydream.

"Open up, Wilhelmina!" shouted her brother Karl from the other side of the door. "I must get ready for the debutante ball!" Karl continued beating on the door until Wilhelmina reluctantly unlocked it. Karl burst into the room and suddenly stopped, eyeing his sister standing before him.

"It's about time … Wait a minute!" Karl's eyes grew wide as his mouth dropped open. "What in the world have you done? Mama and Papa are not going to be happy with this." He turned toward the stairs.

"Wait, please, Karl." Wilhelmina grabbed her brother's arm, her heartbeat racing in her chest. "Please, let me show them later, after they take you to the ball. Please, please, don't tell them yet."

"Oh, all right. You always can persuade me to not tell Mama and Papa about the things you do, can't you, *Schwesterlein*? Don't fret, Willy, I won't tell. But you better make sure they are in a good mood when you *do* show them. Oh boy, I am glad I won't be here!"

Karl stayed true to his word and did not tell Klaus or Brigitta what his sister had done. Later that night, though, the house rebounded with Wilhelmina's indignant shouts, her father's rage and her mother's sobs. In the end, the Heinrichs gave up their argument, hoping their daughter was merely going through a phase and would allow her hair to grow long again over the next few months. But Wilhelmina was determined to do whatever she wanted, and she always got her way.

Curled in a fetal position, hands on her stomach, Wilhelmina lay on her bed writhing, tears streaming down her face. Pain blazed in her abdomen like a thousand stabbing knives. Fear, as she had never known before, swept over her, even greater than her fear of dying when her periods first began three years ago.

"Oh, God, please make it stop," she pleaded to her empty bedroom. "Make. It. Stop!"

Another wave of white, hot lightning struck her body, so intense she let out an ear-piercing, blood-curdling scream. Moments later her mother rushed into the room to find her daughter crumpled on the floor next to her bed. Brigitta dropped to her knees and embraced her daughter, rocking her like an infant.

"My darling daughter, what is the matter?" Brigitta wiped the tears from Wilhelmina's face and peered intently into her eyes.

"Ma-Mama, it hurts so bad. Please m-m-make it stop." Wilhelmina whimpered.

"What hurts, baby girl?"

"My stomach. Here," Wilhelmina said, pointing to her lower stomach. "Hurts so bad, Mama."

"Come, darling, try to get up." Brigitta helped her daughter to her feet and onto the bed. "Now lie down while I get the aspirin." She drew the blankets over Wilhelmina's body before turning to retrieve the medicine.

It took two doses and four hours for Wilhelmina's pain to subside just enough to emerge from her bedroom. She walked slowly down the stairs and into the parlor, taking a seat on the settee. Brigitta looked up from her embroidery and lowered the hoop onto her lap. Her hand covered her mouth as she stifled back a cry.

Wilhelmina's ghost-white skin glistened with sweat. Despite the mild August temperatures, she shivered and grabbed the shawl from the back of the settee, wrapping it around her shoulders. Her teeth chattered as she drew her legs up close to her body.

"S-S-So cold, Mama."

Brigitta set her embroidery on the stand next to her chair and stood. "I will call the doctor. We will get you some help, my child."

Several minutes later, Brigitta returned to the parlor with a lap blanket in hand, which she placed over Wilhelmina, now curled into a ball on the settee.

"Not to worry, my child," she whispered. "You will see Dr. Konig next week."

CHAPTER ELEVEN

September 1915

Wilhelmina sat next to her mother in the doctor's examination room, her knee bobbing up and down while she chewed her fingernails. A healthy girl, she had rarely been to see the family physician and, unlike her brothers, had managed to avoid the typical childhood maladies of chickenpox, measles, or the mumps. This would mark the first time she would ever see a gynecologist. Her stomach roiled as she struggled to slow her breathing. Time seemed to stand still, yet the rhythmic ticking of the wall clock thundered in her head. She wanted to run away and was about to rise from her chair when the door swung open. Dr. Johann Konig strode into the room.

A tall, well-built man with tousled brown hair going gray at the temples gazed at Wilhelmina with steel blue eyes hidden behind rimmed glasses. It was a handsome face with its straight nose, high cheekbones, and prominent chin. The doctor sported a tailored suit and tie, covered by a white cotton lab coat. A stethoscope hung around his neck. Dimples appeared on both cheeks as he smiled widely at Brigitta and Wilhelmina.

"Hallo, Frau Heinrich. It is good to see you again," Dr. Konig said as he took a seat. "And this must be Wilhelmina." He stretched his arm out, shook Brigitta's hand, and turned to Wilhelmina. He extended his hand to her, but she lowered her eyes to the floor, removed her fingers from her mouth and pushed both hands beneath her thighs.

"Do not be afraid, Miss. All will be well." His voice was soft and soothing but did nothing to allay Wilhelmina's growing fear. Turning again to Brigitta, Dr. Konig continued, "I understand Miss

Wilhelmina has experienced extreme pain with her menstrual cycle. Is that correct?"

"Yes, Doctor, that is correct. She was doubled over with the pain a week ago and was sweating but complaining of being cold. I gave her aspirin, but it did not seem to help much." Brigitta pulled Wilhelmina's left hand out from under her thigh and held onto it.

"I see. And when did you start having your cycle, Miss?"

Wilhelmina raised her eyes slowly to meet the doctor's gaze. "I-I don-don't ..." she began as she wrenched her hand from her mother's grasp and pushed it back under her thigh.

"Wilhelmina is anxious about this visit, Dr. Konig. It is her first," Brigitta explained. "She began having her cycles three years ago, when she was twelve. They have never been as heavy as this last one, and this is the first time she has suffered such pain."

Dr. Konig retrieved a pen and pad of paper from a nearby table and scribbled on the paper before turning back to Wilhelmina and her mother. "I will need to do a full examination. Frau Heinrich, I will ask you to wait in the other room. My nurse will be in to help Miss Wilhelmina undress."

"Thank you, Doctor," Brigitta said as she rose from her chair.

"N-No, M-Mama! Please, don't leave me!" Wilhelmina jumped to her feet and grabbed her mother's arm, panic flooding her eyes with fresh tears.

"Wilhelmina, darling, I must leave. The doctor cannot examine you with me in the room. You will be okay. I promise." Brigitta grabbed her daughter's hands and led her back to the chair. "You just do everything the nurse and Dr. Konig tell you to do. I'll be right outside." With that, Brigitta turned and left the exam room, followed closely by the doctor.

Alone in the room, Wilhelmina recalled how her mother often told her to never let anyone touch her "secret places." She had heard other girls whispering in the new indoor restrooms at school. Something about having a "cold" object inserted inside them at the doctor's office, about the doctor feeling their breasts, and pushing on their stomach. On the drive here today, Brigitta talked about Dr. Konig being one of the best gynecologists in Munich and rambled on about his qualifications, although Wilhelmina heard nothing but a drone that sounded vaguely like her mother's voice. Now, as she waited for the nurse to come in, her eyes darted to the walls where diplomas and certificates hung in wood frames and touted the doctor's credentials. She swallowed as she tried to calm her nerves and convince herself she was in good hands. Still, her pulse raced, and her head spun.

Moments later, Wilhelmina found herself sitting on the edge of the examination table in a robe, opened in the front, covering her naked body. She had a dim memory of a woman coming into the room and helping her remove her dress and underclothes and handing her the robe. She remembered stepping on a low stool and climbing onto the table. The nurse spoke to her, maybe even smiled—but it all seemed like a dream to her now.

The sudden opening of the door made Wilhelmina nearly jump out of her skin. She pulled the robe tighter around her body. The doctor's footsteps reverberated in Wilhelmina's ears as he drew closer.

"Now, Miss, I'm going to need you to lie back on the table," he said. She leaned backward until she met the cold table beneath her and squeezed her eyes shut. "That's a good girl."

She fisted her hands at the sound of clinking metal. One … two … three clicks. Then the doctor's warm hands touched her left foot and raised her leg, placing her foot in the cold, metal stirrup. He repeated the movement with her right foot. She instinctively clapped her knees together, keeping her legs tightly closed.

"You are almost through school now, are you not, Miss Wilhelmina?" His voice was a mere murmur, as soft as a soothing balm spreading over her frayed nerves.

Why is he asking me about school at a time like this?

She felt his hands spread her knees apart and fought against the motion. "Dear Wilhelmina, I will need you to open your legs. Do not worry, it will be over in a moment. You are doing fine."

Wilhelmina gradually opened her eyelids to find the doctor seated at the end of the table, peering between her legs.

Oh, God, no! This isn't right!" And she quickly squeezed her eyes shut.

"I am going to insert a tool into your vagina, Miss Wilhelmina. You will feel pressure. I use this to examine your cervix. I will be as gentle as possible, Kindchen."

Wrestling against her trepidation, Wilhelmina opened her eyes again, licked her lips, and said, "Wha … What is a cervix?"

The doctor's gaze shot up to her. He cleared his throat, sweat beading on his forehead, and asked her, "My dear, you do not know? Ach, what a shame you have not been properly taught. Your cervix is located at the top of your vagina. It is the opening to your uterus. Do you know what that is, child?"

Wilhelmina shook her head from side to side.

The doctor sighed. "The uterus is where you would carry a baby. Until then, it is where blood gathers, and once a month, that blood is expelled from your body. That is your monthly menstrual cycle. Attached to your uterus, on either side, are Fallopian tubes and ovaries. Your ovaries hold very tiny eggs, so tiny that we cannot see them with the naked eye. Those eggs leave the ovaries once a month, followed by the blood. When you have intercourse with a man, an egg can be fertilized by his sperm and that creates a baby. Do you understand?"

Wilhelmina nodded, unable to find her voice, although she understood very little of what the doctor was saying.

"Now, I will insert the speculum. Just lie still."

She flinched when his hand grazed her inner thigh, his fingers moving down and touching her most private areas. And then something cold pushed slowly inside. She turned her head to the side, tears dropping from her eyes to the table beneath.

"You're doing fine, Miss Wilhelmina. You are such a pretty girl. You probably have many boyfriends. Such pretty green eyes and a sweet smile. Yes, you are a very pretty girl. You remind me of my wife."

Wilhelmina felt the icy metal inside her and wanted to run away. How could her mother allow this to happen to her? She glanced at the end of the table. Dr. Konig held a magnifying glass in one hand and looked through it.

"You … You are married?" It had never occurred to Wilhelmina that this man would have a normal life. She wondered if he had children, if he had daughters.

"Ach, no, pretty girl, my wife died a few years ago."

"Oh … I-I am so sorry. I didn't mean—"

"It is fine, young Miss. You did not know. There, now. We are all done."

Wilhelmina stared at the ceiling, gritting her teeth, as the doctor removed the speculum.

"Let me help you up, Miss. The nurse will be in to help you dress and then I will be back in to talk with you and your mother." Dr. Konig helped Wilhelmina to a sitting position and left the room.

Moments later the nurse reappeared and helped her dress. She gave her a belt and pad, much like the ones Wilhelmina wore when she had her periods, and instructed her to wear a sanitary napkin for a few days as there "may be some slight bleeding."

Alone again in the room, Wilhelmina fought back her tears. Everything her mother told her about not allowing anyone to touch her flooded her mind. She felt violated. And yet, she also felt a sense of calm washing over her. The doctor had been kind and gentle. She wiped the tears from her face just as her mother walked into the room, followed by Dr. Konig.

Yes, he is a kind man. And handsome. I think … I think I like him.

"Come sit in the chair, Miss Wilhelmina, next to your mother," Dr. Konig said.

Brigitta grasped Wilhelmina's hand as they both sat.

"I believe you have a condition called endometriosis. Yes, I know, that is a very large word. Allow me to explain. Women have tissue that lines the uterus. You remember I told you what the uterus is?"

Wilhelmina nodded.

"Good. With this condition, this endometriosis, sometimes the tissue grows outside of the uterus, which causes extreme pain and often heavy bleeding. I believe it will go away as you get a bit older. I will give you a prescription for laudanum for the pain. Take it only if you have symptoms again with your next cycle." Turning to Brigitta, Dr. Konig handed her a slip of paper and said, "I trust you have an apothecary near your home where you can pick up this prescription?"

"Yes, Doctor, we do. Thank you," Brigitta said as she took the paper.

"Good, good. Now, young Miss, you may also use warm compresses on your stomach to help alleviate the pain. And I would like to see you two weeks following your next cycle. I will examine you again to see how you are progressing."

Brigitta withdrew several paper bills from her purse and handed them to Dr. Konig. "Thank you again, Dr. Konig. We will see you next month."

✆

Belting her new hip-length trench coat around her, Wilhelmina climbed the stairs to the open-air top level of the tram. A chilly October breeze swept past as she held her hat in place atop her head. She had chosen to wear one of her finest Callot Souers dresses, although she knew with certainty that Dr. Konig would never see her in it. The dress, influenced by the popular Orientalism of the day, consisted of two parts: a thin underdress of beige cotton served as an opaque slip beneath a transparent net overlay embroidered with gold, pink and copper sequins. The intricate over-layer was a bold style-setter with a variety of complicated filigrees and motifs. A wide, black silk belt accentuated the Empire waistline. Wilhelmina's toque hat, which she now grasped in her lap (having given up on the increasing wind), displayed silk floral sprays which she had applied to the raised brim.

Wilhelmina fidgeted in her seat as she traveled alone to her appointment with Dr. Konig, frequently checking her dress, her shoes, or her hair. Her mother had a previous commitment and could not accompany her today. Wilhelmina was frightened when her mother first told her she would have to go alone, but as the day grew nearer, her fear melted into eager anticipation. She recalled how kind he had been ... and how handsome.

At the doctor's office, Wilhelmina carefully draped her dress over the chair, covering her undergarments, coat, and hat. She donned the cotton robe and positioned herself at the end of the examination table. She closed her eyes and imagined herself lying on a blanket with a handsome, dark-haired man, drinking wine and laughing. She could almost feel his lips on hers as she pictured the passionate kiss they shared. She rose to her feet and fled through the field, giggling as he chased her around a large tree. They fell together on the blanket, lips meeting again, tongues touching, his hands roaming over her curves—

The door opened, and footsteps tapped across the tile floor. Wilhelmina's eyes shot open as Dr. Konig closed the door behind him. Butterflies flitted in her stomach. She clasped her hands together, surprised by the sweat on her palms.

"*Guten morgen*, Miss Wilhelmina." His voice was like butter, soft and velvety. "And how have you been doing since we last met?"

"I …" Wilhelmina's voice sounded like a mouse squeaking behind the walls. She cleared her throat and began again. "I-I've been well."

"And your last cycle, how was it?" Dr. Konig was all business, taking a seat opposite her, pen and paper in hand.

"It was … It was, umm, heavy. Some pain. Not nearly as bad as before."

"Did the laudanum help? And the warm compresses?"

"Yes, yes, they did. Thank you." Wilhelmina's mind raced, struggling with what to say, struggling with her daydream of just moments ago. *Ahh, he is very handsome.* She tried to push the thought away but could not take her eyes away from his. *Blue, like the sea. Mmm, the calm sea.* She felt at ease, peaceful, in the doctor's presence. Courage overswept her, and she batted her eyes before lowering her gaze, a coy smile on her lips.

"Good, good," he was saying. "I will examine you again. You remember the last time? It did not hurt much, Miss?"

"N-N-No, it did not." Wilhelmina leaned back. Dr. Konig placed a hand at the small of her back, helping her to lie on the table. Then she heard the familiar clicking of metal and knew he would touch her legs next, placing her feet in the stirrups.

"Just relax, Miss Wilhelmina. You may rest your feet here," he said as he moved her feet into place. "I will need to examine you more thoroughly this time."

Dr. Konig rose from his chair and moved to her side. He gradually opened her robe, revealing her ample breasts.

"Ahh, yes, you are becoming a woman, young Miss Wilhelmina, and as your physician, I must ensure you are ready for marriage. First, I will examine your breasts. Not to worry, it is a new procedure to ensure you have no malformations. You may close your eyes if you like. Good girl. Such a pretty girl."

His hands slid over her breasts, squeezing each one rhythmically. His fingers drew circles around her nipples. She sucked in air and scrunched her eyelids even tighter as her nipples grew hard beneath the doctor's touch.

"Mmm, yes, pretty Miss. Very fine breasts, very fine," Dr. Konig whispered.

A tiny pain shot through her as he pinched both nipples. She writhed on the table, wanting to run, yet giving in to the sensations flooding her body. Something warm, something wet, grazed over one nipple, so she opened her eyes. The doctor's head was lowered as he stroked her nipple with his tongue. She squirmed, but he held her arms against her body in a strong grip. She could not sit up. The doctor leaned over and began running his tongue over the other nipple, and her back arched involuntarily.

What is happening to me? This is wrong, so wrong. But, oh my G ... Oh my, it feels so good.

The doctor raised to his full height and said, "Keep your eyes closed, pretty Wilhelmina. I must examine your vagina now."

The sound of his shoes tapped away, and then his hands were on her knees, parting her legs. She knew he would be inserting that tool, that instrument again, and braced herself for the cold metal pushing inside.

But something was different. Something *was* being pushed inside her, but it was not cold at all. And it wasn't metal. It ... It ... Wilhelmina could not determine what was sliding into her, and, afraid to look, she dared not open her eyes. This wasn't anything like the last time with the speculum. The speculum may have filled her, but it didn't move while the doctor looked through his magnifying glass.

But this, whatever this was, was moving!

It glided into her slowly and then out again and back in, this time slightly faster with more pressure. The movement continued for several minutes, this *thing* pushing in and out of her. She instinctively tightened around it, her muscles squeezing it.

What is this? Wilhelmina screamed inside her head.

"Mmm … Mmm, yes, yes, you are a woman now, Miss Wilhelmina. Mmm, yesss …" The doctor's moans grew steadier with each push inside.

Wilhelmina gripped the sides of the table, raised her head, and slowly opened her eyes. Her mouth dropped open as her eyes grew wide. Dr. Konig's head was back as if he were looking at the ceiling, but his eyes were closed. He was licking his lips. Wilhelmina's gaze dropped to between her legs. The doctor's slacks hung loosely around his thighs, and he was moving his hips back and forth. With each of his movements, the *thing*, whatever it was, thrust deeper inside. She tried to slide away, but he caught her hips, holding her in place.

"Just another moment—ohh, so close. So good. So good, my beautiful Anya," Dr. Konig muttered.

Pain shot through Wilhelmina's stomach. *But who is Anya?* Something was pounding inside her vagina. She looked again just as he pulled slightly out. For a brief second, she did not understand what was happening, but then as the doctor forced it back inside, realization struck.

"P-P-Please," she croaked. "Please, s-s-stop."

But the doctor ignored Wilhelmina's pleas and, instead, began thrusting into her harder, faster, his moans growing louder with each push. Wilhelmina clapped her eyes shut again and covered her mouth to stifle her screams. The pain subsided but something else was happening. Her legs and body began to shudder, building in intensity with each of the doctor's thrusts. She could not stop writhing and shaking. She could not control the feelings rushing throughout her body.

Then the doctor released a muffled scream, and inside something warm filled her, then she was empty. It was over.

Wilhelmina wrapped the robe around her body and locked her knees together. Hot tears flooded her eyes and poured down her cheeks, their saltiness coating her lips. She was too afraid to open her eyes.

"We are done for today, Miss An ... Miss Wilhelmina. Yes, you are fine. You are a woman now, and we will hope you have no further problems with your cycles. You may have some slight bleeding today, but I will not need to see you again for another year. I have another appointment soon, so you will pay the nurse when she comes in. Good day, Miss Wilhelmina."

When the door closed, she opened her eyes, sat up, and sobbed into her hands. Voices came from the other side of the door—probably the doctor speaking with the nurse—and Wilhelmina knew she had to get out of there. She rolled off the exam table, scrambled for her clothes, and dressed quickly. She was adjusting her coat just as the nurse came into the room.

"All ready to go, Miss Heinrich?" she asked.

Wilhelmina only nodded and handed money to the nurse.

"Thank you. Good day, Miss."

Wilhelmina fled from the room, down the hall, and out the door to the street. Looking around, she spotted a waiting tram near the corner and took off at a run. She paid the toll and sank into a seat on the lower level. Tingling crawled up the back of her neck as she rode home. She touched her hot cheeks, her gaze darting to the other passengers. She was sure they were all looking at her, knowing what she had just done, but everyone was lost in their own thoughts, reading newspapers or talking with their children. No one paid attention to Wilhelmina.

At home she ran up the stairs and locked herself inside her bedroom. Luckily, her brothers were still at school and her parents were not at home. Wilhelmina quickly undressed, donned her bathrobe, and slipped out of her room and across the hall to the bathroom. There she lay listless in a hot bath until the water turned cold. It did nothing to drown out her sorrow and shame. How could she accept what had happened?

Wilhelmina told no one.

Chapter Twelve

Early December 1915

"Wilhelmina Marie Heinrich!" Brigitta's shrill voice carried from the bottom of the stairs into the bathroom, where Wilhelmina sat on the cold floor leaning her head on the toilet. "Get down here right *now!*"

Oh, Mama, not now, Wilhelmina thought. *I'm so sick. Please, Mama, stop screaming. I've been so good lately!*

Wilhelmina's behavior changed exponentially since that day last fall at Dr. Konig's office. With each passing week, she grew more and more distant from her few friends at school and even stopped sneaking out of the house at night. She picked at her food, rarely participated in family outings, and locked herself in her bedroom, often reading, sleeping, or crying.

Her mother yelling from the first floor frightened her, and she wanted to hide in her bedroom. But Wilhelmina knew better than to disobey her parents and pulled herself off the floor. She stopped to look in the mirror above the sink, straightened her hair, and ran a cloth under the cold water from the tap. She blotted her face, sighed deeply, and left the bathroom.

Brigitta was standing at the foot of the stairs, arms crossed, tapping her toe. "Do not take all day, daughter. I must speak with you before you go to school. Now, hurry up." She turned and stomped into the parlor.

Wilhelmina's feet dragged on the stairs and across the wood floor of the hallway. She stopped dead at the doorway to the parlor, flinching at the sight of her mother's face. Brigitta's lips pursed, her eyes sent fiery daggers toward Wilhelmina, and her toe tapped incessantly, just as it had moments before. Pointing to the settee, she growled, "Sit."

Clutching at the silver cross hanging around her neck, Wilhelmina trudged into the room and plopped onto the settee.

"Mama, I'm so sick, please don't make me go to school today."

"You will not be going to school today, believe me. Sick again, are you? And how many days is it now, daughter?"

A sour taste filled Wilhelmina's mouth, which she unwillingly swallowed. "I-I don't know, Mama? Fifteen days? Maybe twenty? I don't know. Oh, please, Mama, can I just go back to bed?"

"No, you may not. So, you've been vomiting for fifteen days. Perhaps more. Daughter, you have a very serious problem … *and* you have a confession to make." Brigitta sat next to her daughter, taking her hands between her own.

"I-I don't know what you mean, Mama."

"Dear daughter, how long has it been since you had your last cycle? Do not lie to me."

"M-M-My cycle? But what does that have to do—"

"Tell me."

Wilhelmina wrenched her hands from her mother's grasp and began wringing them in her lap. Biting her lip, she rubbed her fingers on the cross pendant and diverted her eyes from her mother's imploring stare."M-Mama—"

"Tell me *now*, Wilhelmina!" Brigitta's chin jutted outward, eyes narrowing.

"I-I think my last cycle was October. But Mama—"

"Stop right there, young lady. I want no questions, no excuses. I already knew when you had your last cycle, dear daughter. Did it never occur to you that I would notice the lack of soiled cloths each month? No," she said, raising a hand, "do not speak. You will listen.

"So, you haven't had a cycle in three months, and you've been vomiting nearly every morning for nearly one month. Daughter, you are with ch-child!" Brigitta rose from the settee and rushed across the room to the window, turning her back to her daughter. "I am ashamed of you!"

"I-I'm sorry, Mama. I don't know how … or when—"

Brigitta turned, facing her daughter, crossed her arms over her chest, gritted her teeth, and rasped, "Who is it?"

"What? Who is …? I do not know what you mean, Mama."

"Who is the father, Wilhelmina?"

Wilhelmina rose from the settee and took two steps toward her mother, who raised her hand. Wilhelmina stopped where she stood.

"I have already sent word to your father. He will be home momentarily. It is best if you tell me now, before he arrives."

"M-Mama, I just do not know."

"You do not know," Brigitta replied flatly. "How can you claim to not know, young lady? Have you been with so many that you do not know which one did this to you?" Brigitta's eyes flared like flames. "Do not lie to me. I want to know right now. Who is the father?"

"Mama, I promise, I do not understand. I do not know!"

Brigitta closed in on her daughter and shook her by the shoulders. *"Tell me!"* she screamed. "When did you have intercourse?"

Nausea built in Wilhelmina's belly, her knees going weak. She fell to the floor in a heap of tears at her mother's feet. "Oh, Mama, it was … it was…" She wailed. "It was … I think it was Dr. Konig!"

Brigitta took a shaky step back, hand to her heart, eyes bulging in disbelief. She dropped to her knees and tipped her daughter's face up by the chin. Her eyes wildly searched Wilhelmina's. "W-What are you saying, daughter?" she choked.

"My … My last visit with … with him," Wilhelmina whispered. "He said he had to be sure I was a woman, that I was ready for marriage. And then he did things to me. I … Oh, Mama, I didn't know how to stop him. I begged him to stop, but he wouldn't. And then he called me …" She sucked in air. "He called me 'Anya.'"

Brigitta embraced her daughter, drawing her into her chest, and began to shed silent tears. "Oh, my darling daughter, my baby girl. Oh, whatever shall we do?"

The two sat crumpled on the floor, their bodies shaking, their sobs uncontrollable. After several minutes, Wilhelmina dried her tears and pulled away.

"Mama, please help me."

Brigitta wiped away her own tears, sighed, and said, "I will try, daughter, but your father's punishment will be harsh. Gather yourself together, daughter, and wait in your bedroom. I will speak with your father first. But hurry now, he will be home soon."

Wilhelmina pushed to her feet, briefly gazed into her mother's eyes, and fled up the stairs to her room. She paced the floor, biting her fingernails, terrified of her father's wrath. Klaus Heinrich had always been a strict parent, enforcing rigid rules and high expectations within his household. His wife never disagreed with him on any matter, at least not in the presence of their children. Brigitta was obedient and subservient to Klaus, always putting his needs first. The children were granted very little playtime when they were young; when they weren't completing the assigned chores, they were studying the many educational volumes in their father's library, or listening to their mother read stories from the Bible. They were each taught the utmost in manners at a very early age, and never interrupted adults in the midst of conversation. The boys never seemed to stray from the rules laid down by their parents (or they just didn't get caught), while Wilhelmina was the rebellious one.

When the Heinrich sons misbehaved, they were often sent outdoors to break off a large twig from one of the many sycamore or English oak trees scattered throughout the backyard and then return it to their father, who would then lash at their bare legs with the stick. Klaus would line up his other children in the front yard to watch him whip the unruly child with the twig; the neighbors were witness to these disciplinary measures as well. Wilhelmina, however, was never made to bring her father a twig. Klaus would oversee Brigitta delivering their daughter's punishments. Brigitta would raise Wilhelmina's skirts and spank her buttocks with an old wooden spoon she kept for such occasions.

Although Wilhelmina was by far the most rebellious and unruly of the six Heinrich children, she also received the fewest spankings. She had her brothers, Karl and Albert, wrapped around her finger and they would frequently take the blame for whatever Wilhelmina had broken, or sweet-talk their parents into being lenient with their sister. But Karl was in Berlin at Humboldt University preparing to study law, and Albert had died in the Great War nearly a year ago. Wilhelm and Alfred were still fighting in the war, and Hans was too involved in his final year of high school to pay much attention to his sister. Wilhelmina no longer had an advocate. Flopping face down on her bed, she reached deep inside herself to find the courage to face her father, fresh tears filling her eyes.

Wilhelmina woke with a start at the sound of someone rapping on her bedroom door. Bright sunshine sneaked through a gap in the drapes, casting a dusty ray of light into the room. She rubbed her eyes and rose from the bed, glancing down at her wrinkled dress. She smoothed it as best she could as the rapping became a relentless pounding that filled her head until her very eyes ached. She checked the cuckoo clock on the far wall; she had been asleep for nearly three hours.

"Wilhelmina, open this door! Your father is ready to speak with you!" Brigitta's sharp tone snapped Wilhelmina to attention, so she sped across the room and flung the door open.

"Brush your hair, daughter, and come downstairs straight away," her mother instructed. "Your father will speak to you, and then he must return to the bank. Do not dawdle."

A wave of nausea swept over Wilhelmina, but she steeled against it and did as her mother instructed. When she entered the parlor, her father was peering out the window.

Without turning, he growled, "Sit, Wilhelmina."

She took a seat on the chair opposite her mother.

The room became deathly silent, other than the booming sound of a ticking clock. Wilhelmina knew it was the grandfather clock just outside the door in the hallway, but each tick hammered inside her head.

Several minutes went by before her father spoke, but when he did, he kept his back to her, staring out the window. "You will go to America to live with your Uncle Otto and Aunt Frieda in Cincinnati. I will send the necessary telegrams and letters, and you will leave as soon as I receive word back from my brother," Klaus spoke in a bitter tone, a tone he had never used when dealing with his daughter. And he sounded tired … very tired. "You will remain in Amer … America." His voice cracked. "This is my decision, and you are to obey. Do you understand?"

Klaus turned to Wilhelmina, who sat with hands folded in her lap while nodding her head. She did not speak and dared not protest. Klaus Heinrich's decisions were unchangeable. She tried to meet his gazes, but when their eyes locked, he turned away.

"You will begin packing your things immediately. Take everything you need and want. I will book your passage on the train to Copenhagen. From there you will sail to New York. You will not return to Germany."

"But, Papa, it wasn't my f—"

"Enough!" Klaus shouted. "My decision is final. You have shamed me. You have shamed our family name. I should have seen the signs—sneaking out of your room at night, flirting with the boys at school—but in my eyes, you were still my little girl. Your behavior the past few years has led you to…to this predicament, Wilhelmina. Because of your sin and filthy conduct, you are no longer my daughter."

Brigitta stifled a mournful cry from across the room, even moved to embrace Wilhelmina, but Klaus shot her a firm look, so she eased back, wringing her hands. She, too, had to obey her husband's decisions, no matter what.

Wilhelmina turned to her mother, but finding no comfort there, she ran from the room and up the stairs, weeping loudly. Klaus crossed the room to the hallway and turned to look at his wife.

"I am sorry, dear Brigitta. We have no other choice. She must be taught humility and chastity."

"But …" Brigitta squeaked. She cleared her throat and said, "But, dear husband, what about Dr. Konig? Will you speak with him?"

"I shall phone him this afternoon when I return to the bank. Now, wife, busy yourself with your usual household tasks. You may help Wilhelmina pack her things if you like. I will make all the travel arrangements for her to leave as soon as possible. Now, I must return to work. I will see you at supper."

And with that, he donned his coat, scarf, and hat, and strode out the front door and down the walk to take the tram downtown. He made the necessary travel arrangements—Wilhelmina would take the train to Hamburg where she would cross the Baltic Sea on a ferry to Copenhagen. There she would board the SS Frederick VIII passenger ship that would sail to New York City in America. The trip would take nearly twenty days. In a moment of sentiment for his only daughter, Klaus booked first-class accommodations throughout the trip. In New York his brother Otto would meet her, and they would travel together to Cincinnati, Ohio, where he lived with his wife.

Everything was set in place, with one exception. Klaus was unable to speak face-to-face with Dr. Konig to confront him about what he had done to Wilhelmina. They had a brash conversation over the phone, and Dr. Konig hung up on Klaus. When Klaus called the doctor's office again the following day to arrange a meeting, the nurse informed him that Dr. Konig closed the practice abruptly, stating he was leaving Germany. She did not know where he had gone. Klaus had to gather his resolve and give the problem to God. He increased his family's study of the Bible, demanding his children become even more chaste and righteous than ever before.

The next few weeks passed quickly for Wilhelmina, too quickly. She was not allowed to go to school and was forbidden to leave the house at all. Her parents watched her every move. Her mother was gentle and loving, yet her father never looked directly at her or spoke a single word to her.

On a snowy, bitterly cold day in early January, Wilhelmina hugged her brothers, Karl and Hans, and said goodbye. Brigitta kissed her daughter's cheek and wrapped her scarf tightly around Wilhelmina's neck, instructing her to write as soon as she was settled in Cincinnati. Klaus was not at home when Wilhelmina left. She rode the tram to the train station alone.

She kept to herself on the entire trip to America, speaking to few people. Wilhelmina never returned to Germany, and never saw her brothers or parents again.

CHAPTER THIRTEEN

January 1916

Wilhelmina's trip was an arduous one. First-class accommodations were inadequate, thanks to the ongoing war. Her sleeping cabin on the train to Hamburg was damp and drafty, despite the steam heat piped into the cabin from the locomotive boiler. Her threadbare blanket did not provide enough warmth, so she slept fully clothed, often wrapping her heaviest coat around her body before climbing into bed.

Germany was faced with food shortages due to Allied naval blockades during the war, making rations meager. Train passengers were served simple meals such as soups, stews and sandwiches. Bread, cheese, tea, coffee and water were readily available, but Wilhelmina's appetite was poor during the first leg of her trip. Her morning sickness was subsiding, although she did have a few days where she was so overcome by nausea that she would remain in her sleeping quarters the entire day.

The trip to Hamburg took seven days, by which time Wilhelmina had developed a runny nose and cough. Upon arrival, passengers were taken to a smaller train that delivered them to Puttgarden where the train drove inside a ferry, taking them across the Baltic Sea to Rødby, Denmark. There, Wilhelmina boarded yet another train to Copenhagen where she would then board a bus for a forty-minute drive to the harbor.

Nearly eight days after leaving home, Wilhelmina arrived at the harbor in Copenhagen to board the SS Frederick VIII. It was one of the most notable passenger ships operated by the Scandinavian-American Line, offering exquisitely furnished staterooms and suites. Skilled chefs prepared superb cuisine, and passengers enjoyed moving pictures, concerts and a shipboard magazine for their entertainment. Wilhelmina, however, did not participate in any of the ship amenities.

The ship set sail shortly after noon on a rainy day in mid-January and the journey was still quite difficult for Wilhelmina. Her nausea returned in full force, and the cold settled into her chest, which burned with every cough. She remained in her suite for much of the trip, having soups and hot tea delivered. When she did emerge from the room, it would be with the sole purpose of hailing a porter to deliver messages to the telegraph room. During her ten days aboard the ship, Wilhelmina sent seven telegraphs home to her family. She received no messages in return.

Midway through the trip, Wilhelmina asked for the ship doctor. He pressed the cold stethoscope to her chest and back, listening to her lungs. Diagnosing her with acute bronchitis, he advised her to drink herbal teas with honey, continue eating clear soups, and get plenty of rest. He told her to stay in her cabin as much as possible because many other passengers were suffering with cholera, typhus, or measles.

Throughout her illness Wilhelmina took to reading her Bible for hours on end, rarely putting it down. She pored over the passages of the New Testament repeatedly, memorizing the parables and stories of God's love. On one of the few days she felt well enough to leave her suite, she sought out the ship chaplain. She found solace in his soothing voice and confessed her sin of fornication to him, convinced she alone was at fault. On her knees she lit a candle in the chapel and prayed for forgiveness. Wilhelmina reflected on her life, and with much remorse, accepted her behavior as deplorable. She knew she deserved her father's punishment, and her heart filled with anguish.

When she arrived at Ellis Island, dark circles lined her eyes which had once shone bright with exuberance and gaiety but were now as dull as the grayish feldgrau color of her brothers' army uniforms. Her cough and the burning in her chest had subsided somewhat, but she was gaunt despite being five months pregnant. Her collarbone was greatly defined, her wrists tiny, her fingers too thin to wear any of her rings. Having isolated herself in her cabin, however, she managed to avoid the diseases that ran rampant throughout the ship.

While disembarking, Wilhelmina leaned heavily on the arm of one of the ship maids, who also carried a large valise under one arm. Three porters hefted Wilhelmina's wooden trunk from the belly of the ship and followed her into the large brick building just steps away from the docks. Inside, the officials closely inspected her trunk and valise as she handed her travel papers to a bald, rotund man sitting behind a scuffed wooden desk.

"Name, miss?" he barked without looking up from Wilhelmina's paperwork.

"Wilhelmina Marie Heinrich," she replied dully.

"Spell it, please," he groaned. Wilhelmina spelled her entire name for him.

"Place and date of birth."

"Munich, Germany, January 10, 1900."

"You arrived on the SS Frederick today?"

"Yes, sir."

"What is your destination?"

"Err …" She struggled to recall the city. "Oh, yes, Cincinnati. In Ohio."

"Are you traveling with anyone?

"No, sir, I am alone. My uncle is to meet me at … err … Central Railroad Station."

"Fine, fine. Your papers are in order. Proceed down the hall to the third door on the left. Good day."

"Thank you," Wilhelmina whispered. She glanced around the crowded room. Well over two hundred first- and second-class passengers from the ship filled the area. Spotting the porters guarding her trunk, she trudged over to let them know where she would be going next. They nodded and told her they would remain where they were.

She opened the 'third door on the left' to a room jammed with women from the ship. Her eyes darted about, but it was too crowded—she could not determine where to go.

"Go to de corner. There is a nurse at de desk. She will sign you in," said a middle-aged woman leaning on the wall to Wilhelmina's right.

"Oh, yes, yes, thank you very much." Wilhelmina weaved her way through the crowd until she nearly bumped into the desk. There, the nurse asked her name, and Wilhelmina again spelled it out, adding the place and date of her birth and her destination. The nurse handed Wilhelmina a piece of paper and told her to wait until she was called.

Weaving her way back through the maze, she located the woman who had spoken to her moments before. The room was hot, making it difficult to breathe. Someone opened a window, which only blew in frigid air. A wave of nausea coursed through Wilhelmina, and she quickly covered her mouth, hoping she would not vomit.

"Ach, young miss, you are not well?" the woman asked.

Wilhelmina shook her head, and through her fingers, she croaked, "With child. Feel sick."

"Ach, you poor thing. Let's find you a seat."

The woman disappeared into the throng, returning to grab Wilhelmina's elbow and guide her to a seat kindly offered by a young girl.

"Thank you. Very nice of you to help me," Wilhelmina rasped.

The morning dragged into late afternoon as one by one, women would follow a nurse into another room while other women left through the main door. The room was nearly empty when Wilhelmina's name was called. She followed a nurse into a large room, and a sudden burst of heat raced through her, bringing beads of sweat to her cheeks and forehead. Spots flashed before her eyes. She wanted to scream, to yell, to run away, but no sound came from her throat; her feet were like lead, and Wilhelmina was frozen where she stood.

"Now calm down, sugar, nothing to be afraid of. The doctor is just going to examine you. We have to make sure you do not have any lice, now, don't we?" The nurse's lips formed a thin smile, yet she looked on warily, as if regarding Wilhelmina with an air of distaste.

Pointing, the nurse directed Wilhelmina to a row of women next to the wall where men in lab coats were looking in their eyes, noses, mouths, and ears. She took her place in line, watching with narrowed eyes as the doctors moved closer and closer. Clasping her hands together, she shifted nervously from one foot to the other. A young man with dark hair and glasses stepped up to her, and she shuddered, licking her lips and averting her gaze toward the floor. His voice sounded distant, as if traveling through a tunnel, as he instructed her to open her mouth. She rapidly blinked when the doctor shone a bright light into her eyes. Wilhelmina was vaguely aware of the doctor's movements, and yet she felt removed from her own body, as if watching the examination from across the room. She saw her own hand raising to give the paper to the doctor, watched him scribble something on it and hand it back, but it all seemed like a dream.

She found herself following the line of women into yet another room, where they removed their clothing and were inspected by female nurses. She jumped at the sound of a nurse speaking to her, telling her to undress, and began shaking her head vehemently. She struggled to catch her breath.

"Ahh, ahh ... p-p-please, n-n-no." Wilhelmina whimpered.

The nurse caressed Wilhelmina's arms and touched her cheek. "It is all right, miss. We will not hurt you. Try to remain calm. It is an easy examination and will be over soon."

Wilhelmina took deep, slow breaths as the nurse unbuttoned her dress while speaking softly and helping her to relax. The nurse looked up and down Wilhelmina's body, under her arms, around her thighs, and up her back.

"You see, miss, it is over. You have no lice and no sign of tuberculosis. You may dress and wait over there," the nurse said, pointing to the far wall.

Moments later, Wilhelmina emerged from the building to face the setting sun. Followed by the porters carrying her trunk and the maid holding her arm and valise, she made her way to the docks where she showed her papers to an attendant. He scanned them quickly, handed them back to Wilhelmina, and instructed her to take the ramp onto the ferry. She found a seat inside, and the porters and maid sat her belongings at her feet before departing the ferry. Within the hour she once again sought the assistance of the ferry attendants to carry her trunk and valise into the terminal of the Central Railroad of New Jersey.

Inside the terminal, she took in the waiting room where passengers were crammed into every available space. She knew her uncle was scheduled to meet her here and accompany her on the train to Cincinnati, but she could not see over the heads of the people filling the room; there were hundreds.

She turned to one of the attendants holding her trunk. "Please," she implored, "I cannot see over these people. I am looking for my uncle Otto. He is supposed to meet me here. Can you help me?"

The attendant searched the room until he spotted an elderly man holding a sign with a name written on it.

"Miss, is your name Heinrich?"

"Yes, yes, it is."

"I believe I see your uncle. If you'll follow me." He hoisted one end of the trunk and led Wilhelmina and her entourage through the crowd to the exit door, where her Uncle Otto was indeed waiting for her.

Wilhelmina and Otto secured rooms at a motel near the terminal and ate a light supper in silence before turning in for the night. They boarded the train early the following morning, locating plush seats in the first-class car. During the nine-hour trip, they enjoyed a meal of roast beef with mustard sauce in the dining car. Wilhelmina snoozed off and on, unable to find a comfortable position in her seat. Luckily, the weather was mild, even warm, allowing Wilhelmina to shed her heavy coat. Giving up on trying to sleep, she retrieved her Bible from the valise stored under her seat and began to read.

"Ach, you are reading the gospel of Luke, I see," Otto said. "Very good, very good."

"Yes, Uncle. May I ask you a question?"

"Of course."

"Do you and Aunt Frieda attend church?"

"Ach, yes, we attend the First Lutheran Church near our home. You will be attending with us."

Wilhelmina merely nodded and, seeing Otto close his eyes for a nap, returned to her reading. While he slept, though, Wilhelmina could not help but study his face. He was much older than her father, with a full head of silver hair and moustache to match. Her father didn't speak of his brother often; Otto had left home when he was only twenty-five, shortly after marrying Frieda. Economic instability and limited job prospects in Germany at that time drove many to seek better opportunities in America.

A carpenter, Otto landed a job with a prestigious construction company in Cincinnati in 1880 and set to work building houses. Within a few years he built a house for he and his wife in the Over-the-Rhine District of Cincinnati, which served as home to many German immigrants. Otto and Frieda lived comfortably for many years until he fell from a girder while working on a house. Having suffered a debilitating back injury, he was forced to retire. He and Frieda eventually sold their home and moved into a small two-bedroom apartment in a five-story brick building in the same neighborhood.

Wilhelmina wondered if her aunt and uncle had any children. She turned to Otto to see if he was awake so she could ask, but he was sleeping soundly. She shifted her position and allowed her eyes to shut, finally drifting off to sleep.

The screeching of the train wheels slowing to a stop jolted Wilhelmina awake. The conductor strode down the aisle, shouting, "Pittsburgh! Pittsburgh!" Wilhelmina jostled her uncle, who gazed at her with drowsy blue eyes.

"We are in Pitt ... Pittsburgh, Uncle. Is this where we get off?"

Otto yawned and stretched his arms above his head. "Hmm, yes, yes, we must change trains here. Gather your things, Wilhelmina."

Moments later they stepped off the train into warm evening sunlight shining off the black train cars. They headed into the depot followed by three tall, young men carrying the trunk. Wilhelmina took a seat on one of the many benches along the wall while Otto stood in line to purchase their tickets for Cincinnati. The men sat Wilhelmina's trunk at her feet, next to her valise. Otto's small suitcase occupied the seat next to her. While she waited for her uncle to return, Wilhelmina glanced around the crowded depot.

The terra cotta walls, resembling brownstone, were topped with gold-inlayed arches stretching the entire length of the building. The ceiling was constructed of glass panes surrounded by metal framework. The sound of heels clicking on the shiny marble floors reverberated in Wilhelmina's ears as men, women and children rushed to and fro.

Otto returned after weaving through the crowd. "We'll leave in two hours. I've secured two berths in one of the sleeper cars." He set his suitcase on the floor and took the seat next to his niece.

They sat in silence until they heard the announcement for "Cincinnati, now boarding." Otto hailed an attendant, pointing out the trunk, and he and Wilhelmina walked outside to board the train.

Wilhelmina stood on the platform, eyes glued to the men who stored her trunk on a car farther down the track. Lost in thought, she jumped when Otto touched her elbow.

"Time to board," he grumbled. Her uncle was a man of few words so how would she ever manage living with him?

Inside, they found their sleeping berths and stowed their luggage inside before heading to the dining car. They sat at a table covered with a crisp white cloth. The spotless silverware flanked gleaming white China plates holding neatly folded silk napkins. They scanned the menu and placed their orders with the waiter; Otto ordered the filet of sole with vegetables while Wilhelmina selected the lamb chops and baked potato. After dinner, they made their way to the parlor car where luxurious settees and chairs welcomed them. They found seats and settled in to read a magazine or newspaper.

At nine o'clock, Otto looked up from his newspaper and said, "Best be off to bed now, Wilhelmina. The train arrives in Cincinnati quite early in the morning." Wilhelmina rose, set the magazine aside, and headed for the door. Noting that Otto was not following, she turned around. "Uncle Otto, are you coming?"

"No, I will be along later. Sleep well."

Yes, definitely a man of few words. I hope it is easier to talk with Aunt Frieda.

After locating a dressing room so she could change into a nightgown, Wilhelmina lowered herself onto the berth cot, fluffed her pillow, and drifted off to sleep. She was warm and comfortable, no longer experiencing the feverish shivers during her travels across Germany and on the ship.

It was dark outside her window the next morning when someone shook her and called her name. She opened her eyes, finding her uncle bending close by, his hand on her shoulder.

"Time to wake up, Wilhelmina. We will arrive soon. Hurry and change. And wear your coat today. It is likely to be quite chilly outside."

After securing a horse-drawn wagon to carry Wilhelmina's large trunk to Otto's home in Over-the-Rhine, they walked three blocks to the nearest streetcar. They exited the car on Race Street after a short thirty-minute ride and walked two more blocks to Otto's tenement building. The only conversation between the two since arriving at the train station was Otto informing Wilhelmina that her trunk would arrive later that day.

Wilhelmina scanned the street, happy to see it bustling with people as day began to break. Men and women rushed to catch trams, some going in and out of small grocery stores and shops or purchasing fresh produce from wagons parked on the sidewalks. This area of town was named by early German immigrants in the early 1880s, who humorously referred to the nearby Miami and Erie Canal as "The Rhine."

The tenement building itself was a five-story brick with a limestone façade. Monumental cast-iron cornices adorned the rooftop, and limestone boldly framed the paired windows. A densely populated neighborhood, Over-the-Rhine comprised narrow streets and tightly packed buildings. Families lived in small apartments with limited privacy. Many immigrants faced poverty as they struggled to find work. Most of the tenement buildings lacked indoor plumbing, and shared outhouses were scattered along the alleyways.

The district, known locally as OTR, became synonymous with brewing; the most well-known breweries were the Jackson Brewery, Christian Moerlein, and John Kauffman. Many beer gardens, like Wielert's, served as popular gathering spots in the area. Cincinnatians regarded OTR as the city's premier entertainment capital, proudly boasting Cincinnati's Music Hall just two blocks from Otto and Frieda's residence. Completed in 1878, this iconic Venetian Gothic structure was home to the Cincinnati Ballet as well as the Symphony Orchestra, Cincinnati Opera, and the May Festival Chorus.

Directly across the street from Music Hall sat Washington Park, a popular gathering place for residents and visitors alike. Its green spaces, fountains and pathways provided a respite from the rush of Cincinnati streets. Just a few blocks north on Race Street, Findlay Market served as the city's most well-known public market with merchants selling meat, fish, poultry, produce, flowers, cheeses, deli foods, and other ethnic foods. The market often hosted outdoor vendors and street performers during warmer months.

Wilhelmina instantly liked the neighborhood. Having been overly sheltered at home in Germany her entire life—all of sixteen years—she was eager to walk these streets and meet new people. Excitement swept over her, and she smiled for the first time in months.

"Come, come, Wilhelmina. Let's get you inside out of this chilly air," Otto said, interrupting Wilhelmina's thoughts.

"Yes, Uncle," she replied as she followed him into the building and up a narrow stairway to the third floor.

Otto rapped on the door to Number 3C and called out, "Frieda, we are home!"

The sound of Frieda's slippered feet padded across the hardwood floor, and she swung the door open wide. "Oh, dear Otto, you have arrived at last!" Offering her cheek to Otto, she then spotted Wilhelmina behind him, ushered them inside, and said, "Come in, child, come in. You look positively exhausted. Take off your coat and sit over there by the heater. Oh, I am so happy you arrived safely and are finally here. Otto, take Wilhelmina's valise to her bedroom.

That's a dear child, yes, you just rest there and get warm. I will make you some breakfast."

The living area of the apartment was small, with only two upholstered chairs, a small loveseat, and two small end tables near the chairs. To the right of the door, a miniscule kitchen and square dining table with four wood chairs filled the remaining space. To the left, a hallway led to two bedrooms.

Wilhelmina crossed the room and flopped onto one of the chairs near the large heating unit that stood near the window. Frieda rushed over, spread a thick blanket over Wilhelmina's lap, then took her coat and hung it on a mirrored coat rack near the door. Otto emerged from the hallway dressed in heavy wool trousers held up by black suspenders, a collarless white shirt, and sturdy boots. He donned his coat and cap and strode into the kitchen where Frieda was prattling about preparing breakfast.

"Ach, Otto, you must eat some breakfast before you go." Frieda knitted her eyebrows together, frowning at her husband.

"No, no, wife, I must not be late today. I have already lost a week's wages. I will be home for supper." And with that, Otto kissed his wife on the cheek, turned and left the apartment without acknowledging Wilhelmina with a goodbye or even a nod in her direction.

"Ach, that man. Stubborn as a mule, he is," Frieda mumbled to the closed door. "No matter," she said cheerily to Wilhelmina, "we will have a nice talk while we eat. No, no, dear, you stay where you are, get your rest. Oh dear, you must be exhausted!"

"Yes, yes, I am quite tired."

"We can chat while I cook, unless you prefer to lie down for a while?"

"No, thank you, though, Aunt Fr-Frieda. I'll stay here if that is all right."

"Yes, of course. Let's see, here, what would you like to eat? I have sausages, goetta, a few eggs, and some bread. Oh, I'll just whip something up for you. A hot meal will do you good."

"Wh-What is goetta, Aunt Frieda? I've never heard of it."

"Ahh, well, it is made of leftover pork and beef. I season it with rosemary and thyme, at least when I can get them at the market, and add oats. Times are hard these days, you see, and I must do everything I can to stretch our food supplies. Otto works long hours at the factory, but he sees the doctor quite often, so we watch our money closely."

"Is he ill?" It had never occurred to her that her uncle wasn't in good health. He said so little on their trip, but he did complain now and then about being uncomfortable in his seat on the train.

"Ach, no, no. He was a carpenter and built houses many years ago, but he fell and hurt his back. He quit working after that for a time. Oh my, that was, what? About fifteen years ago now. My, my, how time just seems to rush by." Frieda stared off, not looking at anything in particular, including her niece, but at something Wilhelmina could not see. "Ahh, but my mind wanders back to those days. We had a lovely house a few blocks from here that your uncle built but he was out of work for several years after the fall, so we had to sell the house and moved in here a few years ago. Then he was able to take the job at the Kahn's."

"I'm sorry, what is Kahn's?"

"Ach, I forget you are new to Cincinnati. Kahn's is a meat packing factory. They package pork and ground beef, and your uncle makes the hot dogs."

"Oh, dear. I'm afraid I don't know what that is either." Smiling, Wilhelmina sighed. She enjoyed listening to her aunt talk and welcomed the change from the formidable silence she had endured with her uncle.

"Ahh, well, it is a frankfurter, my dear!" Frieda chuckled softly. "But, here in America, they are small, and we put them in rolls called buns. Hmm, I have some here somewhere. Oh, yes, here they are!"

Frieda reached into a basket and pulled out a long roll to show Wilhelmina. "We cut it down the middle, here, you see? And then we put the hot dog in it. Your uncle likes to put onions and sauerkraut on his, but I like mine with mustard. They are really quite good."

While she cooked, Frieda chattered on about Otto's job and the many shops and markets nearby. She told her niece that, for many years, she was a nurse in the children's ward at a nearby hospital and dreamt of the day she would become a mother, but that dream never came to be; she and Otto had no children. This made Frieda very sad, but she devoted herself to the children she cared for at the hospital and found joy in helping them get well.

"Come on over to the table, dear, breakfast is ready," Frieda said several minutes later. "Here you go, some nice eggs and goetta for you. Do you like sugar in your tea?"

Wilhelmina rose from her chair and walked the few short steps to the dining table. Biting into her eggs, she nodded to her aunt, who then set the sugar bowl on the table. Frieda placed a spoon next to the sugar bowl and sat opposite her niece. Silence fell between them while they ate, but Wilhelmina felt at ease with her aunt; the words came easy, unlike with her Uncle Otto.

While Frieda washed the dishes, which Wilhelmina insisted on drying, Wilhelmina asked her aunt, "Do you still work at the hospital, Aunt Frieda?"

"Ahh, no, I am too old for those long hours. But I do still help some of the neighbors from time to time when they are sick or have a small injury. It is good work, and many of them give me potatoes, flour, or sugar in return. What do you want to do when you are grown, Wilhelmina?"

Carefully drying a teacup, Wilhelmina glanced at the ceiling for a moment. "I … I don't know, Aunt Frieda. I've never given it much thought. Papa always said I should be a teacher, but that does not sound interesting to me. I guess I just thought I would marry early, like Mama did."

"Well, you still have time to decide. You are young, yet. In the meantime, I can teach you a few things about nursing and perhaps you can help me with some of the neighbors until you return to school."

"School?" Wilhelmina's eyes widened, and her hands froze on a wet teacup. "I-I guess I didn't realize I would be going back to school. You see, Papa didn't give me much money and, well, the only thing he told me before I left Germany was that I would have to earn my own money."

"Ahh, well, your Papa is a strict man indeed. But you should consider returning to school. There's not much work for a girl your age, but I suppose you might be able to work at Kahn's also. We will discuss it with Otto when the time comes. Now, dear, I know you are very tired. I will show you to your room. You get some sleep."

Wilhelmina gladly followed her aunt into a sparsely furnished room with very little light. A thin, worn curtain hung from the window, but the bed was covered in soft, warm blankets. Frieda closed the door as she left, leaving Wilhelmina alone to change into a nightgown. She thought briefly about putting her clothes away in the small dresser in the corner but, yawning, changed her mind. She climbed onto the bed and quickly pulled up the blankets. This room had no heater by the window, and it was rather chilly. Soon, she drifted off to sleep—the restful, deep sleep she had needed for months.

Chapter Fourteen

May 1916

Wilhelmina settled into life in America with ease. She filled her days with sewing, learning to cook, and reading. Grateful for Otto's long absences while he was at work, she sought out her aunt for advice and comfort, finding it easy to talk with her. Frieda was a kind, gentle woman, much like Wilhelmina's mother, and she offered her niece a strong shoulder upon which to cry.

During the first few weeks, Wilhelmina strolled along the sidewalks of the neighborhood admiring the architecture of Music Hall, peering into shop windows, or buying apples from a street vendor. Her strolls took her to Washington Park quite often, where she would sit on a bench beneath a tall oak and read her Bible. On Sunday mornings she would walk several blocks with her aunt and uncle to the Trinity Lutheran Church, and they would sing hymns accompanied by a grand pipe organ. As her pregnancy progressed, she found it increasingly difficult to participate in many of the liturgical aspects of the worship—the frequent kneeling and standing were burdensome to her swollen ankles and aching back.

When she entered her seventh month of pregnancy, Otto told her she would no longer be permitted to venture out of the apartment. This caused Wilhelmina's temper to rise, and she protested her uncle's decree. "I do not understand, Uncle!" she yelled. "It is so beautiful outside, and you will not allow me to enjoy it?"

"You will lower your voice, young lady. Now sit down!" Otto's face reddened as he paced back and forth. Turning to Wilhelmina, now slumped on the loveseat, he sighed deeply, clenched his jaw, and said, "It is not proper for you to show yourself now. You are … You are too far along to be seen in public."

"But—" she whined.

"Enough! You are to stay indoors until the child is born. That is my final word!" Otto glanced at his wife and stormed down the hall to his bedroom, slamming the door behind him.

Frieda rushed over to her niece and dropped to her knees. "Dear niece, please do not argue with your uncle. This is the way it must be. It is simply not proper to show yourself now, especially since you are not …"

"Not married? Is that what you were going to say?" Wilhelmina's chin trembled as she searched her aunt's eyes.

"I'm sorry, child," Frieda said as she wrapped her arms around Wilhelmina. "Please try to understand. You don't have much longer now and afterward you will be able to enjoy the summer weather. Be patient, dear."

Wilhelmina closed her eyes and sighed. Maybe her aunt was right. Soon she would go on walks with her child to the park. She imagined people stopping to fawn over the baby. She saw herself pretending to be modest about her child's beauty, pride swelling inside her chest.

"Now, Wilhelmina, you must be off to bed." Frieda's words brought Wilhelmina back to reality with a start. "Be sure to say your prayers, dear."

Wilhelmina stared at the crucifix on the wall behind her aunt, and with a half-hearted shrug she rose from the loveseat and muttered, "Yes, ma'am. Goodnight, Aunt Frieda." She stepped around her aunt, still kneeling on the floor, and rushed to her room. She changed into her nightgown and slipped back down the hall and out the door to use the bathroom shared by the third-floor tenants. Frieda was no longer in the living room when Wilhelmina returned. Assuming she had also gone to bed, Wilhelmina grabbed an apple from the bowl on the table and tiptoed to her own room.

Balmy spring breezes blew in a hot, sticky summer, and for Wilhelmina, the days blurred past with nothing interesting to do. Devoid of other books in the apartment, her only reading material besides the newspaper or the occasional magazine was her Bible. By early July she grew restless, itching to be outdoors. She found it harder and harder to concentrate on her reading.

Ach! I've read these same stories a hundred times already! I am SO bored! I hope this blasted baby comes soon so I can get outside!

Wilhelmina held her impatience inside, not daring to show her temper to Otto again. Like his brother, Klaus, Otto was strict and his word final. Often when he arrived home from work, Wilhelmina would be staring out the window to the street below. He'd sigh, as if understanding her loneliness. But in the eyes of the Heinrich family, she needed discipline, and no man bearing that name would allow anyone to catch a glimpse of weakness. Their father hadn't raised them that way. And so, instead of coddling her, Otto would pick up the newspaper and settle into a chair while Frieda cooked dinner, their silence speaking volumes, increasing the tension between them.

Beads of sweat dripped from Wilhelmina's forehead onto the pillow beneath her. She threw the damp sheet off her body and reached for her fan. It was useless. It wasn't even noon, yet it was sweltering in her bedroom. The curtains hung lifelessly at her open window. She turned painstakingly onto her side, trying to find a comfortable position. It was also useless. Struggling to sit upright on the edge of the bed, she cringed at a sharp pain low in her belly, very much like the terrible cramps she had—when was that?—nearly a year ago. It was because of those very pains that she went to Dr. Konig. Wilhelmina shook her head, trying to erase the memory.

Wilhelmina rose slowly from the bed, every movement worsening the pain. She slipped her dressing gown over her shoulders before opening her door and stepping into the hallway. Low voices floated down the hall.

Otto and Frieda must have company. Maybe I should try to dress.

Before she could turn around to return to her room, Frieda spotted her from the living room and called to her, "Come on in, dear. We are just about to have lunch."

"But I am not dressed, Aunt Frie ... Oww!" Wilhelmina's scream brought Frieda racing down the hallway, and she found her niece doubled over. "What is it, dear? What is wrong?"

"P-Pain. So much pain," Wilhelmina squeaked.

"Let me look at you, child. Where is the pain?"

Wilhelmina pointed to her stomach. "Hurts ..."

"Child, when did these pains start?"

"I-I don't know. An hour ago, maybe. Ohh ..." Wilhelmina straightened, rubbing her back. "My back has been aching since early this morning."

"Okay, dear. Was the pain you just had, was it sharp?"

"Y-Yes. It was the first one like that, Aunt Frieda."

"Not to worry, dear child," she soothed as she took Wilhelmina's elbow. She turned her head toward the living room and called, "Marta, come and help me get Wilhelmina back to bed. I believe she is going into labor!"

Marta and Friederich Wagner lived across the hall from Otto and Frieda and attended the Lutheran church with them every Sunday. Marta rushed to Wilhelmina's side and helped Frieda get her back into bed.

"I will bring you cool water, dear. Marta will stay with you." Frieda sped out of the room, closing the door behind her.

Frieda returned moments later with the water, and Marta helped Wilhelmina take a few sips. Frieda said, "I sent Otto to fetch the midwife. She lives two blocks away." Several minutes later—which seemed like hours to Wilhelmina—Otto returned and rapped lightly on the bedroom door.

Frieda patted her niece's hand and turned to leave. "I'll be right back dear. I must speak with your uncle," she said. As soon as she closed the door behind her, she turned faced Otto. "Where is Gertrude?"

"Ach, wife, she was not at home. I went to every door in her building until someone was finally able to tell me she had gone to deliver another baby. But that was hours ago, and they expected her to return soon. I wrote a note and left it at her door."

"Ahh, well, we will just have to hope this baby doesn't come too fast."

"How is she doing?" Otto said as he leaned in closer to his wife, his brows furrowed.

"She is fine. I believe her pains just started. It could be hours before we need Gertrude. In the meantime, we must keep her cool. It is so hot today, and her room is positively stifling!"

Frieda and Marta spent the afternoon taking turns caring for Wilhelmina. They kept a basin of cool water nearby, dipped washcloths into it, and wiped down Wilhelmina's forehead, arms and legs to keep her cool. Otto busied himself boiling water to sterilize scissors and additional cloths needed for the delivery. He located the local iceman, purchased a block of ice, and with Friederich's help, he chipped away at the block so Wilhelmina could suck on pieces of ice.

The walls of Wilhelmina's bedroom seemed to radiate with the July heat as the afternoon lingered into evening. The air within the entire apartment hung heavy, suffocating not only Wilhelmina, but her four caregivers as well. The ladies unbuttoned the tops of their dresses and fanned themselves frequently as beads of sweat ran into rivulets down their skin. The men stripped to their undershirts. Wet patches formed under their arms, around their necklines, and on their backs. Wilhelmina's thin nightgown clung to her body. Outside, the streets were silent as people retreated indoors, taking cover from the blazing sun.

Marta and Friederich left them at supper time but promised to return to the midwife's apartment in hopes she was home and could come to Wilhelmina's side. As darkness set in, a loud knock sounded on their door. Otto opened it and ushered Gertrude inside. After checking in on Wilhelmina, she ordered Otto and Frieda to take their baths and be off to bed.

Nighttime brought a smattering of relief as a breeze floated in through the window, causing the curtains to gently sway. Thunder rolled in the distance, and just after midnight, a welcome rain drenched the streets and sidewalks, bringing cooler temperatures with it. Wilhelmina drifted in and out of sleep for most of the night until the pains increased and grew closer together. She clenched the damp sheets as she struggled to stifle her screams.

The first light of day peeked between the neighborhood buildings shortly after six o'clock, and Wilhelmina screamed again, leaning back against the bed.

The midwife nodded at Frieda and said, "Okay, Miss Wilhelmina, give us a push. Make it a big one. Come on, now, you can do it."

Wilhelmina mustered all her strength and, groaning, pushed as hard as she could.

"Good girl!" cried Gertrude. "I've got the baby's head. Now dear, I need one more push from you to get the shoulders out. Take a deep breath … and then push!"

Wilhelmina sucked in a large breath of air, leaned forward and bared down, grunting for what seemed like an eternity. The pain was nearly unbearable, but soon Gertrude cried out, "Yes, I've got him! You have a baby boy!"

Frieda lowered Wilhelmina to the bed and wiped her face with a cool cloth, then handed the sterile scissors to Gertrude. Wilhelmina closed her eyes, squeezing back tears. A moment later, she heard the smack of flesh on flesh, and the baby began to cry. She opened her eyes as Gertrude wrapped the baby in a towel while wiping off his face and arms. She then laid the baby on Wilhelmina's breast.

Wilhelmina held the crying infant as she scanned her aunt's face. Her lips parted, but no words escaped. She wrestled with conflicting emotions stirring inside. Anger and hatred filled her heart—anger at the man who created this child, anger at her father for sending her away, anger and hatred for this tiny child. The baby's eyes flitted open, and he met her gaze, evoking a new emotion. Dare she love this child?

Frieda and Gertrude stood in the corner, their whispers barely reaching Wilhelmina's ears. What were they talking about? Just when she went to ask, the child stopped crying and wrapped a tiny hand around Wilhelmina's finger. She was taken aback by the tear that escaped her eye and trickled down her cheek.

"Rest, child," her aunt said as she strode to Wilhelmina's bedside. "We must take the child now, to bathe him." Frieda took the baby from her niece's arms and left the room.

Gertrude prattled on and on while cleaning Wilhelmina and removing the towels placed beneath her hours ago. She hummed softly as she worked, reminding Wilhelmina of the lullabies her mother sang to her many years ago. Soon Wilhelmina closed her eyes, and a vision of her mother came into view, her sweet voice lulling Wilhelmina to sleep.

When she awoke, bright sunlight flooded the room with the same oppressive stickiness from the day before. Throwing off her sheets, Wilhelmina went to sit upright but flopped back onto the bed in defeat. The apartment was eerily silent.

What day is it? she thought. *Umm ... Monday. Uncle Otto must be at work but where is Frieda? And ...*

She jolted upright, wincing with pain at the sudden movement. Wilhelmina darted her gaze about the room as she gradually worked her legs over the edge of the bed, her feet landing on the cool wooden floor.

Where is the baby? Why is it so quiet?

She attempted to stand, but her legs were like jelly, unable to hold her weight. She dropped back onto the bed, panic settling deep in her stomach.

She hollered, "Aunt Frieda? Is anyone home?" More silence greeted her.

I've got to get out of this room. Come on now, Wilhelmina, stand.

She pushed off the bed and rose to her feet. Her shoulders slumped as she bent slightly at the waist, reaching out to catch the wall, and leaned on it for support. She slid one foot forward, then the other, until she reached the door. She cracked it open it and called out, "Aunt Frieda," but no one responded. Gingerly, she shuffled down the short hallway into the living room. Glancing around, she found the place empty. She was all alone.

Wilhelmina took a deep breath and tightly scrunched her eyes shut. Opening them, she reached for the end table to her right and balanced herself before taking another step. She reached the loveseat and, holding onto its arm, worked her way to the seat and sunk into it, breathless. She rested her head on the back of the loveseat and closed her eyes.

Where is Aunt Frieda? And the baby? Why don't I hear the baby?

The creaking of the apartment door brought Wilhelmina out of her reverie. Her eyes flew open to find Frieda quietly closing the door, her back to her niece. Frieda turned, and startled to see Wilhelmina, jumped back a step.

"Oh, my dear"—she panted—"you frightened me! What are you doing out of bed, child? You should be resting."

"I woke up, and no one answered when I called. Where were you, Aunt Frieda? And ... And ... where is the baby?"

"Now, dear, not to worry. The baby is with Gertrude. You were sleeping so soundly, and the baby needed food, so Gertrude took him to a wetnurse. Now, you rest there for a moment while I change your bedclothes, and then it's back to bed for you, young lady."

"I *am* very tired, but I'm hungry, too. Is there anything to eat?"

"Yes, dear, we have some bratwurst and cheese. I'll make you a plate, and you can eat while I make your bed."

Moments later Wilhelmina turned herself gently on the loveseat, stretching her legs out in front of her, and munched on the food. Frieda also brought her a glass of cold lemonade, which Wilhelmina downed greedily.

Back in her freshly cleaned bed, Wilhelmina reached for her Bible and began to read, but sleep overtook her and soon she was back home in Germany, running through the lush grass behind her home, playing with her brothers. She skipped and jumped but fell over a rock and landed hard on her back. Her brother, Wilhelm, was shaking her, yelling at her, asking if she was all right.

"I'm all right, Wilhelm, stop shaking me," she said, annoyed. It wasn't her brother at all but, rather, Frieda looming over her. "Oh! Aunt Frieda, is ... is everything all right?"

"Yes, yes, dear. It's just late, and you need to eat. Can you manage to walk again?"

"Yes, oh, yes ... of course."

Frieda helped Wilhelmina into her dressing gown and supported her as they walked, arm in arm, down the hall to the dining area, where Otto was already seated at the table. He acknowledged his niece with a slight nod as she took her seat. Frieda began carrying dishes from the kitchen to the table, making several trips before she sat opposite Otto, folded her hands, and bowed her head.

Otto led them in a prayer before Frieda dished food onto his plate. She took Wilhelmina's plate and piled food on top before getting her own. They ate in silence for a few minutes until Wilhelmina suddenly stopped chewing.

"Uncle Otto, Aunt Frieda … umm … wh …" her voice cracked.

"What is it, dear?" Frieda said.

"Is the … the baby still with the … what did you call it? The … The wetnurse?"

"Eat, dear. You need your strength. We will talk about the baby after dinner. Now, don't argue," Frieda said as Wilhelmina opened her mouth to protest. "Do as I say and eat, dear."

Wilhelmina picked at her food, her mind scrambling to make sense of what was happening. Why were Frieda and Otto being so mysterious?

She rose from her chair and said, "I must use the water closet."

"Do you need any help, dear?" Frieda asked.

"No, I'll manage."

Wilhelmina trudged out of the apartment and down the hall to the bathroom, where she shut and locked the door with shaking hands. Her heart pounded wildly in her chest. She sat on the toilet, feeling faint, as dark spots floated in her vision. Unable to think clearly, Wilhelmina shook her head, her mind racing through the day's events, as an overwhelming sense of dread rose from her fluttering stomach, up through her chest, and out her mouth. She wailed loudly, rocking back and forth on the toilet, suddenly terrified to return to the apartment.

What has happened to my baby?

"WHAT DO YOU MEAN, YOU TOOK HIM AWAY? WHERE IS MY BABY?" Wilhelmina stood facing her Uncle Otto, her face red, hands clenched at her sides.

"Sit down, young lady. You will not shout at me in that way. Do you hear me?" Otto yelled back, jaw tense.

"Please, dear, do as your uncle says. Sit. Calm down," Frieda implored.

"*Calm down*? You want me to *calm down*? Someone better tell me what's going on right now!" Wilhelmina swayed; luckily, the chair was directly behind her as she fell into it. She hugged herself and began rocking as she had done moments before in the bathroom.

Frieda rushed over, knelt at her feet, and clasped Wilhelmina's hand between her own.

"Shh, dear child, shh. Please listen. Your uncle will explain."

Otto strode over and took the chair opposite Wilhelmina.

"Get up, wife. She does not need to be babied now." Otto spoke carefully, his voice like rocks grinding together. Frieda stood, scurried to the loveseat, and sat with her hands clasped together in her lap, head bowed.

"Wilhelmina," Otto began, teeth clenched, breathing in, breathing out. "It was your father's wish—no, his demand—that the child be taken away."

Wilhelmina leaned forward in her chair and cried, "My fa—"

"No, do not interrupt me. You will listen and remain quiet. Your father wrote to me before you arrived, instructing me to take the child to the orphanage. You were not to see the child when he was born, but unfortunately, I was not at home to make sure of it. Gertrude was wrong to allow you to hold the baby. It was never our intent to allow you to keep him. Your father further instructed that you are to enroll in school in the fall and finish your education. After that you will likely need to work to earn your own money. There will be no further discussion and no argument from you. This is how it will be. You are also to continue attending church with us, and you will learn to control your temper and become an obedient woman. Someday you will marry and be a faithful and obedient wife."

"But—" Wilhelmina whispered.

"I said *no*! You will not argue with me about this matter. This is your father's decree, and you will obey. Now, off to bed with you."

Wilhelmina glanced at her aunt, whose head was still bowed, not willing to meet her niece's eyes. Frieda remained where she sat as Wilhelmina rose from her chair and shuffled out of the living room and down the hall to her bedroom. She slammed the door shut and threw herself onto her bed in a puddle of tears.

Chapter Fifteen

November 1918

After ten hours on her feet, labeling packages of pork, bratwursts, and hot dogs, Wilhelmina stepped through the door onto the sidewalk in front of Kahn's Meat Packing Factory. Darkened clouds littered the skies overhead as the sun dropped below the horizon and cold raindrops splattered her hat and coat. She had no umbrella as she walked two blocks to the streetcar stop and was drenched by the time she arrived.

She climbed wearily into the car, paid the five-cent fare, and found a seat near the back. When she first started working at Kahn's, she rode the streetcars with her Uncle Otto, who worked in the slaughtering and processing department, but he recently switched to the night shift, so now she rode to and from work alone.

The car was crowded today with workers from Kahn's and other nearby factories. A few passengers chatted with one another in whispered tones. Many others held newspapers open in front of their faces, reading the day's events. Wilhelmina removed her hat, glanced to her left, and gasped when she read the headline.

WORLD WAR OVER; ARMISTICE SIGNED

The young man sitting next to her gazed over. "Are you all right, Miss?" he said.

"Yes, yes," she replied, pointing to the newspaper in his hands. "What does this mean?"

The man's eyes moved to where Wilhelmina was pointing and back to her. "Ach, it is a peace treaty. The fighting stopped earlier today."

Wilhelmina shut her dampening eyes and sucked in a breath of air. "Over ...?" she whispered. A lone tear trickled down her cheek as she bit her trembling bottom lip.

The man patted Wilhelmina's hand and said, "There, there, it is good news. Do you have family fighting?"

Wilhelmina nodded before opening her eyes and meeting his gaze. His eyes were like melted chocolate—warm and comforting. He was a handsome man with a square jaw, straight nose, and prominent cheekbones. His skin was pale, like porcelain gently touched by velvety pink roses. His hair, a shade darker than his eyes and mostly hidden beneath a fedora, was neatly trimmed and accompanied by sideburns. Since she was seated next to him, it was hard to determine his height, but his shoulders appeared broad beneath the overcoat he sported.

"Yes—" Wilhelmina choked.

"I am sorry, Miss. I am deaf in my left ear. May we switch places so I can hear you better?"

"Oh! Yes, of course!" The two stood, and as she suspected, Wilhelmina's five-foot-three frame barely reached the man's shoulders. He stepped around her, and they both sat, Wilhelmina now on his right side.

"Please, continue, Miss. You were about to tell me about ... about family you have fighting in the war?"

"Yes, I have two brothers fighting for Germany. Wilhelm is now twenty-seven and Alfred is twenty-three. We los ..." Wilhelmina swallowed, trying to find the words. "We lost Albert in 1915. He and Alfred were twins."

"Ach, I am so sorry, Miss. Your family, they are all still in Germany?"

"Yes, I am the only one here in America. Well, except my aunt and uncle. I live with them. I have two other brothers, Karl and Hans. They were lucky and did not have to join the army. Karl is only twenty and Hans, nineteen. I have not seen them since ... since 1916. Do you, sir, have any family fighting?"

"Ach, no, I only have sisters, both older than me. And I was not sent to the war because of my hearing problem. I left Germany just a year ago. What brought you to America, if I may ask?"

"Oh, well, it is a very long story and I'm sure one that would bore you. Oh, my goodness! Here we are talking about our families, and I haven't even introduced myself. I am so sorry! My name is Wilhelmina Heinrich."

"Such a pretty name, for a very pretty young lady. And I am Oskar Schmidt. Pleased to meet you," he said, smiling as he extended his hand and grasped Wilhelmina's into a friendly handshake. "Which factory do you work in, Miss Heinrich?"

"Kahn's. And you?"

"Ahh, I work there as well. I have never seen you there. Have you been working long?"

"Oh, no, I started work last month. I just graduated high school a few months ago. I work in the packaging area."

"I see. Where did you go to school?"

"Old St. Mary's parish school. I was only there two years. I didn't arrive in America until late March in 1916, so I did not attend school until that fall."

"Ahh, yes, I am familiar with the school. My nieces and nephews attend there, but they are still in the elementary grades. Are you Catholic, then?"

"No, no, I am Lutheran. I go to the Trinity Lutheran Church with Aunt Frieda and Uncle Otto. But they decided to send me to the Catholic school after I arrived here."

"Next stop, Race Street!" called the driver from the front of the streetcar.

"My goodness, I didn't realize we were nearly home. This is my stop," Wilhelmina said.

"Yes, it is mine as well. I am surprised we have not met before today, Miss Heinrich. But my work hours recently changed, so perhaps we shall meet again and share another pleasant ride to work."

"Yes, perhaps so, Mr. Schmidt. It was lovely meeting you. And thank you for speaking with me. I haven't any friends here, and it does get quite lonely at times."

"I am sure it does," he said. He bowed slightly and doffed his hat. "Until we meet again. Pleasant day to you."

"And to you," Wilhelmina said.

Smiling to herself as she walked home, Wilhelmina couldn't hold back the skip in her step. She was happier than she had been in many years. She felt at ease with Mr. Schmidt, and blushing, she hoped to meet him again and get to know him better.

Oh, maybe, just maybe, we will meet for tea or a walk through the park.

Wilhelmina was humming a jaunty tune as she strolled through the door to the apartment.

As she lay in bed that night, Wilhelmina found it impossible to concentrate on the verses she was attempting to read. She set her Bible on the nightstand, threw back the covers, and went to the window, where she sat in her rocking chair and gazed outside. The damp streets glittered beneath the light of the gas lamps lining the sidewalks. From the apartment across the street, shadowy figures moved behind thin curtains hanging at the windows, yet the windows of the street-level stores were opaque. The rain clouds had moved out, leaving behind a sky dotted with thousands of flickering stars.

As she rocked, Wilhelmina recalled her conversation with Mr. Schmidt and smiled. She daydreamed about meeting him again and becoming friends. As she had told him on the ride home, she had not made any friends in the two years since arriving in America. Once outgoing and full of life, Wilhelmina had withdrawn inside herself after losing her infant son. Once she fully recovered from the birth, she went to church every Sunday with her aunt and uncle. When she wasn't helping Frieda with the household chores or nursing their neighbors, she spent the remainder of her time alone in her room, praying or reading the Bible.

She often went into confession with Pastor Bergmann, repenting and seeking absolution for the sin she was sure she had committed with Dr. Konig. She grew her hair back to shoulder length, pulling into a bun at the nape of her neck while she worked. She sewed more dresses, raising the necklines and lowering the hemlines, despite the current fashion she had once embraced. The rebellious teenager transformed into a pious, reverent, and meek young woman who spoke only when spoken to, obeyed the wishes of her uncle, and never expressed her own opinions.

At the Old St. Mary's parish school, Wilhelmina studied diligently and never contradicted the nuns. While some of her fellow students were the subjects of unwavering discipline, Wilhelmina was pleasant and agreeable. She flinched each time the nuns inflicted cruel punishments on her classmates, their hands bruised and bleeding from the striking ruler. The school promoted a high level of academics—and emphasized discipline, obedience, and respect.

Until that day on the streetcar, Wilhelmina kept to herself and never spoke to anyone. Perhaps it was the shock of the headline she read—"World War Over"—that made her drop her defenses and speak with Mr. Schmidt. Perhaps it was two years of isolation and loneliness making her long to talk with someone close to her own age. She wasn't sure what it was about him, but he made her come out of her shell that day, and her only wish was to see him again.

Wilhelmina got her wish—she and Mr. Schmidt shared streetcar rides to and from work nearly every day for the next two weeks, parting every morning for their separate work areas at the factory. During their rides, she told him about her childhood in Germany, carefully omitting anything about her rebellious teen years and becoming pregnant. He spoke fondly of his own childhood in Mühlhausen with his sisters, who doted on him shamelessly. He was the youngest of three children and, he regretted to say, was quite spoiled. Like her own parents, his were strict disciplinarians but often softened their punishments when it came to their son. He was an obedient child but, he admitted, had become defiant during his teen years. His admission tempted Wilhelmina to confess her own disobedience, but she remained silent.

"I grew up Catholic," he told her one morning in early January, "but I do not agree with their views on Biblical authority, so I left the church when I turned eighteen. My parents were very disappointed in me, and many arguments ensued between us, until they eventually stopped trying to bring me 'back into the fold,' as they would say."

"I have always been Lutheran myself," she replied, "so I am not knowledgeable about the tenets of the Catholic church."

"Let me try to explain," he said. "You see, Catholics believe there are three sources of authority: scripture, tradition, and magisterium. I see you are still confused. Scripture is obvious. Tradition in the Catholic church refers to the teachings handed down through the ages since the Apostles and magisterium represents the teaching authority of the Catholic church, which is led by bishops, cardinals, and the Pope."

Wilhelmina nodded.

"So, by comparison, the Lutherans believe that scripture alone holds the authority, and they do not recognize the Pope's authority in the same manner as Catholics."

"I see now. Thank you," she said. "Have you attended any church since you left Catholicism?"

"No, no, I have not, but I must be honest with you, I have considered finding a new church home. In fact, I have been studying the Lutheran faith for quite some time and am quite interested, but I just have not been compelled to find a church." He looked into Wilhelmina's eyes, smiled, and said, "But perhaps I have found a reason to do so now."

Wilhelmina averted her eyes, lowering her head as her cheeks reddened. Clearing her throat and straightening her shoulders, she said, "Oh, I do hope so. I find such comfort in the teachings of our church. You must come to worship with us soon."

"Perhaps I will, Miss Heinrich. Perhaps I will. Ahh, I see we are nearing our stop. Thank you for another pleasant ride to work. I trust we shall meet this evening?"

Wilhelmina rose from her seat as the streetcar came to a stop and said, "Yes, of course. I look forward to seeing you. I do hope you have a good day, Mr. Schmidt."

He led the way down the aisle, exiting first, and held his hand out to guide Wilhelmina down the steps onto the sidewalk. They walked in silence to the factory, where Mr. Schmidt touched her elbow before they parted ways.

"Miss Heinrich, if I may ask …"

"Yes, Mr. Schmidt?"

"We have shared streetcars every morning and evening for a few weeks, and I believe we are becoming friends. May I be so bold as to call you by your given name?"

"Oh, yes, Mr. Schmidt! I would like that very much indeed!"

"And you, Miss Wilhelmina, must call me Oskar."

"I will, Mr. Schm … I mean, Oskar. Thank you and have a good day."

"You as well, Wilhelmina."

She practically bounced into the packaging department entrance, her steps light and airy. Wilhelmina often found herself lost in thought that day, distracted from doing her work. She failed to apply labels to several packages and, shaking her head to clear the fog, had to retrieve them to correct her mistake. Nonetheless, her smile never faltered, and she was overjoyed to see Oskar waiting for her on the sidewalk at the end of the day.

During their ride home, Oskar posed a question to Wilhelmina, one she had been dreaming about since the day they met. "Wilhelmina, I have a question for you, if I may," he said.

"Of course, Oskar."

"I would like to call on you at home and perhaps take a stroll through the park. May I do so?"

Wilhelmina swallowed and licked her lips as she planned her response. "I would be very pleased to receive you, Oskar. I must, however, speak with my aunt and uncle on the matter first. Uncle Otto works nights at the factory, so I will not see him until tomorrow. But I will speak with him and let you know on Monday, if that is acceptable."

"Yes, yes, I understand. I will do my best to be patient."

They spent the remainder of the ride in conversation about music and books, but Wilhelmina barely heard a word Oskar said. She was so elated that it was all she could do to keep from leaping from her seat.

That night she told Aunt Frieda about Oskar asking to call on her. Wilhelmina had already confided in her aunt that she and Oskar had met on the streetcar and were becoming friends, but Otto was unaware of the relationship. Frieda was glad to see her niece coming out of her shell and encouraged her continued friendship with Oskar.

Together, they planned how to approach Otto about the situation. Both feared he would deny Oskar's request, and they prayed together that the conversation over the weekend would go well.

But the conversation with Otto never happened. Still dark outside when he arrived home from work the next morning, he was met by the sweet, fragrant smell of coffee brewing when he walked through the door, but he was in no condition to drink it—or to eat the breakfast Frieda was busy making in the kitchen. Otto staggered to the living room, removed his coat, letting it drop to the floor, and sunk into the loveseat. He covered himself with the blanket hanging from the back of the loveseat and laid his head on the arm, curling into a fetal position.

Frieda turned off the fire on the stove and peered into the living room. It wasn't like Otto to not call out a greeting or kiss her cheek whenever he arrived. Through the doorway, the only thing visible on Otto was the top of his head, so Frieda moved the skillet to an unused burner, and quickly walked into the living room. She dropped to her knees at seeing him, her eyes wide with concern. Sweat poured from Otto's forehead, but he was shivering beneath the blanket, teeth chattering.

"Ach, dear h-husband! You are … are ill!" Frieda's chin quivered. Otto leaned forward as a dry, hacking cough overcame him. His nose was running, and as Frieda felt his forehead, he was burning up.

Frieda ran to the kitchen to retrieve the thermometer and returned to take Otto's temperature. It read 103 degrees. An uncontrollable shudder swept through Frieda as she realized her husband had come down with the Spanish flu. She rushed into the kitchen to prepare a cup of hot lemonade for Otto and then helped him take a few sips before he shook his head to let her know he wanted to sleep.

While he rested, Frieda made a neck wrap for him. She filled spare fabric with rice and an aromatic concoction of lavender, chamomile, peppermint, and rosemary. Frieda then sewed the fabric together and placed it in the coal stove to heat. When Otto awoke, she placed the wrap around his neck to help alleviate the aches and pains.

Otto slept fitfully that day and into the night, often transitioning from chills to fever. He sipped hot lemonade and chicken soup that Frieda and Wilhelmina made, but overall, he ate very little for the next few days. When Otto was no better a week later, Frieda sent Wilhelmina out on a blustery December day to the church to seek help. Wilhelmina raced around the building to the parsonage, banging on doors until finding the pastor. She implored him to call the hospital. Within the hour, an ambulance from Good Samaritan Hospital arrived in front of the tenement building on Race Street to transport Otto to the emergency room. He was admitted upon arrival and placed in a ward with twenty beds, all filled with other patients suffering from the flu.

The Spanish flu epidemic hit Cincinnati in the fall of 1918 and lasted for a few months before significant recovery came about. During those months, schools, churches, movie houses, theaters, and retail business were closed, reopened, and closed again. When businesses were open, their hours were restricted, and the city enforced closures no later than six o'clock every evening. City officials instructed everyone to wear gauze masks, even while at home. Only the critically ill could have visits from their loved ones, who had to follow strict guidelines: they were to wear a mask, be accompanied by a nurse, visitation time was limited, and they would undergo disinfection following their visit.

Hospitals were flooded with patients; over 22,000 residents were infected with the disease, though some physicians reported the number to be over 100,000. On January 5, 1919, the Cincinnati Board of Health officer reported the epidemic was essentially over. Nearly 2,000 residents succumbed to the flu, dying of complications such as pneumonia.

Despite the efforts of the doctors and nurses, Otto contracted pneumonia and died in the early morning hours on Christmas Eve. Frieda took to her bed for days following her husband's death, while Wilhelmina went to work as usual but also took on the household duties of cooking, cleaning, doing the laundry, and shopping for food.

On a frigid, snowy day in January, Frieda, Wilhelmina, Oskar, and a handful of friends and neighbors gathered around Otto's grave at Spring Grove Cemetery. Pastor Bergmann spoke few words, mindful of the freezing mourners. As the group stood in line to board the streetcar home, Wilhelmina's knees buckled beneath her. Oskar, standing next to her, grabbed her elbow to prevent her from falling to the ground, easily lifted her into his arms, and carried her onto the streetcar.

Once home he carried her up the three flights to the apartment. Frieda unlocked and opened the door, stepped inside, and led Oskar down the hall to Wilhelmina's bedroom. He sat her gently on the bed and left the room. Frieda helped her niece remove her wet coat, hat and gloves before removing her dress and helping her into a warm nightgown. Frieda eased Wilhelmina down on the bed and covered her with the blankets.

"I will be back soon with some hot lemonade for you, dear child." Frieda rushed down the hall to the kitchen, finding Oskar standing at the stove already preparing it.

"Ach, you are a kind man, Mr. Schmidt. Thank you so much."

"Not to worry, Mrs. Heinrich. Wilhelmina has been doing too much these past few weeks. I have been watching her as we rode to work every morning and have been quite worried about her."

"It is my fault, I'm afraid. Ach, I've allowed my grief to make me forget about her. I should have known she was becoming ill. Oh, I must go and pray!" Frieda fled into the living room and dropped to her knees beneath the crucifix hanging on the wall and began to pray fervently, rocking back and forth, tears streaming down her face.

As Oskar carried the hot lemonade out of the kitchen and headed to Wilhelmina's room, he slowed his pace as Frieda prayed.

"Please, dear God in Heaven, please do not take her, too. Take me instead."

Oskar continued down the hall and into Wilhelmina's room, then softly closed the door behind him.

CHAPTER SIXTEEN

June 1919

Having only a mild case of the flu, coupled with exhaustion, Wilhelmina recovered within a week's time. Frieda left her niece's bedside only when a neighbor or Oskar could take over. Struggling with her own health, Frieda became frail over the following months, but she had promised Otto she would carry on, and so she did.

Wilhelmina never knew of the many nights before Otto's illness when her aunt and uncle lay in bed talking and promising each other they would care for their niece to ensure she lived righteously. Just days before his death, Frieda told Otto about Oskar. She believed he would be a good match for Wilhelmina. She told her husband how Oskar often prepared meals for her and Wilhelmina while they took turns visiting Otto in the hospital. She found him to be a compassionate, kind man. Unable to speak, Otto merely nodded and gave his wife a small, weak smile.

Following the end of the epidemic, Cincinnati returned to normal operation—grocers and retailers reopened, children returned to school, and entertainment restarted with a flourish. Movie houses and theaters were packed nearly every evening. Music Hall celebrated with a grand re-opening and offered orchestra and ballet performances at half the cost for the entire month of March.

Oskar and Wilhelmina would part on the sidewalk after work, both rush home to change into dress clothes, and meet again outside Wilhelmina's tenement building. They often dined at a nearby restaurant before seeing one of the performances at Music Hall. Spring brought warm, sunny days, and the pair frequently enjoyed the sweet aroma of blooming flowers as they sat on a bench in the park, tossing seeds to the birds.

Even though the Great War had ended the previous fall, German troops were still stationed throughout Germany and France. However, in June, the signing of the Treaty of Versailles imposed significant restrictions on German military capabilities. Many Germans now living in America felt the treaty was too harsh on their homeland and believed the punitive measures imposed by Britain and France would lead to long-lasting resentment and instability. These American Germans experienced mixed feelings at this time— they were disheartened by the Treaty's regulations and yet relieved when they received word about loved ones now returning to their homes.

In her three years in America, Wilhelmina had received no responses to the many letters she wrote to her mother and brothers in Germany. Her aunt and uncle, however, corresponded often with Klaus and Brigitta and passed along the news to their niece. It was her Aunt Frieda who happily told her in late June that her brothers were home, safe and sound. Tears of joy streamed down her face at the news; her prayers had been answered.

In their neighborhood, Oskar and Wilhelmina celebrated Independence Day by watching a parade march down Elm Street and then attending a festival in Eden Park. Oskar carried a large basket filled with fried chicken, German potato salad, and slices of apple pie. Street vendors lined the walkways of the park, selling lemonade and iced tea to quench their thirst. At dark the fireworks lit the night sky as thousands of "oohs" and "aahs" resonated around them.

With the last few exploding bursts of light, Oskar dropped to one knee at Wilhelmina's feet and proposed. She nodded her response, unable to speak, as happy tears flooded her eyes. He took her hand and slipped a ring on her finger. She stared at it, mesmerized by its beauty. The white gold band featured geometric shapes in asymmetrical patterns, crowned by two faceted gemstones—a garnet representing her January birthstone and a sapphire for his September birthday.

In October, Wilhelmina and Oskar were married in the Temple of Love, the gazebo in Mt. Storm Park. Nestled among lush gardens of begonias, camellias and orchards, it overlooked a lake filled with black swans. The sun shone brightly that day as a cool, crisp breeze blew over them. The gazebo was designed by Adolph Strauch of Vienna, who also designed Spring Grove Cemetery, and boasted eight towering white Corinthian columns atop a circular concrete base. Four rows of concrete steps surrounded the gazebo's base, while the columns supported a large dome at the top, encrusted with carved swans and flowers encircling the dome.

Married by Pastor Bergmann, Wilhelmina and Oskar had few witnesses to their nuptials. Frieda stood on the grass alongside their neighbors Marta and Frederich, while Felix Ackerman, a friend of Oskar's, stood a short distance away. The small group returned to Frieda's apartment for punch and cake following the brief ceremony.

Thanks to a gift of a large sum of money from Oskar's parents, he and Wilhelmina spent three nights at the luxurious Palace Hotel in downtown Cincinnati. The eight-story French-inspired hotel stood as the tallest building in the city at that time and featured 300 guest rooms, hydraulic elevators, and electric lights. They dined at some of Cincinnati's finest restaurants, took carriage rides, and walked along the Ohio River at sunset.

On their first night at the Palace, Oskar presented Wilhelmina with a gift while they dined in the hotel restaurant. "Darling, I want you to have this small token of my love. This was my mother's and now it is yours," he said, placing a beautiful package on the table in front of his bride.

Wilhelmina peeled away the paper, lips turning up, and gasped at the intricate music box nestled inside. She turned it over in her hands, eyeing every detail. A brass clasp glistened against the dark wood, and a quaint church, surrounded by figurines of children, decorated the top of the box. Wilhelmina lifted the lid, overcome with emotion as a German folk song began to play.

A few weeks after they married, Wilhelmina left Kahn's to work in the laundry room of Good Samaritan Hospital. Her primary tasks were to launder and neatly fold the bed linens, towels, patient gowns, and the doctors' and nurses' gowns and caps. She then delivered them to patient wards and staff storage closets throughout the hospital. The work was much less grueling than at Kahn's and the hours shorter, allowing her to arrive home in time to prepare supper for Frieda, Oskar and herself.

Wilhelmina and Oskar shared a loving relationship; he was gentle and compassionate, and she was determined to be a good wife to him. They faithfully attended worship services at the Lutheran church and spent time with a few couples in their neighborhood, going to plays or concerts or at home playing gin rummy.

Wilhelmina was finally happy—happier than she had ever been.

Wilhelmina and Frieda worked diligently side by side in the small kitchen, preparing Oskar's favorite meal. The March winds danced through the streets of the neighborhood, a playful yet persistent companion, tugging at scarves and lifting men's Ulster coats. Inside the apartment the atmosphere was warm and cheerful as the two women cooked the schnitzel and sauerkraut. While Frieda kept a close eye on the stove, Wilhelmina expertly spread coconut-pecan frosting on the German chocolate cake she had made that morning. Both women hummed happily while they worked and smiled at each other frequently. They shared a secret—one which Wilhelmina would reveal to her husband after supper.

"Sweetheart," she began later that evening as she placed a slice of cake on the table in front of Oskar, "I have something I need to discuss with you."

Oskar took a bite of the cake and smiled. "Mmm …" he moaned. "Delicious." Wilhelmina waited patiently, her hands folded together in her lap, while he swallowed. Oskar wiped his mouth and gazed at Wilhelmina. "Go ahead, dear. I am listening."

"Well"—she cleared her throat—"I … I am with child."

Oskar coughed as he choked down another bite of cake. "You are … are … what?"

"I am pregnant, sweetheart. I saw the doctor today." Wilhelmina wrung her hands together, gaze dropping, for fear of upsetting Oskar.

"Darling Mina," he said as he rose from his chair, "you are … are … pregnant?"

Wilhelmina nodded.

Oskar lifted his wife from her chair and threw his arms around her into a tight embrace. He whispered into her shoulder length hair, "My darling. Oh, my Dear Mina, this is wonderful news!"

She stepped back, searching his eyes. "You are … You are pleased, then?" she said, barely above a whisper.

"Oh, yes, my sweet, my darling. Yes, I am overjoyed! A child!" He grinned, exposing beautiful white teeth, and his eyes crinkled with laughter as he hugged Wilhelmina again. "Well, this certainly is a red-letter day, my dear!"

"What do you mean, sweetheart?"

"I received a promotion at work today. I am now the Meat Processing Supervisor. And it comes with an increase in wages, too! Oh yes, indeed a red-letter day, my sweet Mina!"

Wilhelmina's pregnancy was an easy one, not fraught with morning sickness as her first had been. But as the months went by, she was reminded that she had never told Oskar about her first child. She spoke at length about it with Frieda, who advised her to keep it to herself. "After all," Frieda had said, "after all this time, he might not take kindly to learning about that child now." So, Wilhelmina kept her dark secret hidden from the man she loved with all her heart—and her guilt grew daily.

Halfway through her fifth month, the three of them left the tenement building and moved into a rented row house five blocks away on Madison Street. The two-story brick building offered much more room for their growing family, with a small dining room, living room with a fireplace, and galley kitchen on the first floor; three bedrooms and a roomy bathroom completed the second level of the home.

Wilhelmina left her job at the hospital when she began to show in mid-July. She spent the next three months sewing and crocheting baby clothes. She and Frieda scrubbed the walls and floors of the third bedroom, hung curtains at the window, and carefully folded the freshly ironed crib sheets. Oskar brought in a crib and small chest of drawers one Saturday afternoon, which he painted white before placing them in the room. A few weeks later he showed up with a used rocking chair, which he also painted white, and sat it near the crib. The room was complete and ready for the new baby.

An Indian summer prevailed in Ohio that fall, and on an especially warm, sunny day in October 1920, Albert Klaus Schmidt was born at Good Samaritan Hospital, named for Wilhelmina's dead brother and her father. The delivery, like Wilhelmina's pregnancy, had been easy, and Albert was born soon after Wilhelmina arrived at the hospital. Albert was a healthy, strong, and happy baby. He rarely cried, only wailing when he was hungry. Frieda held him often, humming softly until he fell asleep. Wilhelmina gazed into her son's glimmering green eyes and discovered an ability to love she had never known. And Oskar beamed with pride whenever friends would call on them to get a peek at baby Albert.

Just after ringing in the new year, Wilhelmina returned to work in the laundry room at Good Samaritan Hospital, but with Oskar's new wages, she was able to reduce her hours to only five a day, Monday through Friday. Frieda remained at home, no longer nursing friends and neighbors, and cared for Albert while his parents were at work.

Wilhelmina felt stronger than ever since coming to America and was grateful for the time she was able to spend with her son. She purchased a baby carriage in March and, as the days began to grow mild with the onslaught of spring, she took Albert for many walks through the neighborhood and into Washington Park. Shortly after his first birthday, he loved to toddle after the birds and ducks in the park, throwing them seeds or breadcrumbs, and laughing gaily. Albert was a happy, affectionate child, and he endeared himself to everyone who stopped to fuss over him.

Life in the house on Madison Street was pleasant and joyful for the little family of four. Past debts were paid, and they lived comfortably during those first few years after Albert was born. Frieda gained weight and returned to the health she had once enjoyed with Otto. But tragedy struck in November 1923, just two weeks after Albert's third birthday.

Frieda lay motionless on the kitchen floor with Albert crouched beside her, rivers of tears running down his chubby cheeks as he wailed. Wilhelmina opened the front door to the house and, hearing her son's sobs, sprinted toward the sound. She came to a sudden halt when she reached the kitchen, her hands flying to her mouth to muffle the scream. But, as she took in the sight of her aunt sprawled on the floor, her lifeless eyes open, the scream did indeed come from Wilhelmina.

She quickly lifted her son into her arms and sped out of the house, searching up and down the street for a neighbor. Seeing no one she knew, she began knocking on doors until, finally, someone answered.

"Please," she said, breathless, "I need a telephone. We don't have one. Please, it is an emergency."

The elderly woman peering around the door nodded and said, "Ach, yes, come in. You are Mrs. Schmidt, correct?"

Wilhelmina fought back tears and nodded at the woman. "Yes, yes, I live three doors down. I am sorry, we have not met."

"Ach, 'tis all right, dear. My husband and I have only just moved in. There, on the table, is the telephone. You have an emergency, you say?"

"Yes, yes, it is my aunt. She has fallen in the kitchen and …" Wilhelmina's voice cracked, and she fell silent.

"Please, use the telephone, dear."

Wilhelmina picked up the receiver and waited for the operator to come on the line.

"Operator," the woman droned. "How may I help you?"

"Please, I need an ambulance. Emergency!" Wilhelmina cried.

"What is your address, ma'am?"

"I live at … at"—Wilhelmina's gazed blankly at the wall, thoughts scrambling, tying to recall her address—"at 219 Madison Street. In the Over-the-Rhine district. Please, hurry. My aunt has fallen and … and … I don't know if she is alive!"

Wilhelmina's breath became rapid as she struggled to breathe.

"Remain calm, ma'am. I will send an ambulance right away," said the operator.

Wilhelmina dropped the receiver, sending it crashing to the floor beside the table. The elderly woman drew near, patting her on the back and guiding her to the door.

"There, there, dear. You must breathe. Take your time," she said soothingly. "I will walk with you back to your house."

"Th-Th-Thank you."

Terrified to walk into the kitchen where Frieda lay cold, Wilhelmina plopped down on a chair near the front door. Albert sat on the floor, sobbing, and she handed him a toy left on the coffee table earlier that day. The elderly woman sat on the sofa. Albert's storm of sobs gradually subsided to a mere whimper as he played with the toy. A knock came from the door, and the women went to answer it. Two men in white coats entered the house. They began to ask her questions, but Wilhelmina could only hear snippets, everything moving in slow motion.

She followed the two men farther into the house but could not bring herself to step beyond the dining room, over the threshold to the kitchen. She heard the words "heart seizure" and "coronary," but it was as though they floated to her ears, faint echoes coming from the bottom of a deep well. The last thing Wilhelmina remembered was the men rolling a stretcher through the room and out the front door, her aunt's still body covered by a white sheet.

Frieda was dead.

Frieda was laid to rest four days later beside her husband Otto at Spring Grove Cemetery. Mourners came to the house, quietly whispering in small groups, while Wilhelmina sat with a plate on her lap, picking at the food they had brought. She was relieved when the last of their friends left that evening, leaving her alone with Oskar and Albert.

Oskar sank onto the couch next to his wife and wrapped his arms around her lovingly. She dropped her head onto his shoulder and bawled. Albert sat on the floor, playing with a toy and staring at his mother, tugging at his ears as he tried to understand why Mama was crying. He stood up and walked to the kitchen, calling out for "Fweeda."

"Oh, Oskar, I can't take it. Please put Albert to bed. I can't bear to hear him calling for her."

Oskar picked up his son and carried him upstairs. He gave him a bath, brushed his teeth, and tucked him into bed. He retrieved a book from the dresser and sat down in the rocking chair. Oskar read to Albert until the tot's eyes grew heavy and he drifted off to sleep.

As Oskar pulled Albert's bedroom door closed, Wilhelmina climbed the stairs, her steps gradual and deliberate. Her breath was labored as she steadily raised one foot, then the other. Oskar rushed to meet her, supported her elbow, and helped her ascend the rest of the way to the landing. He led her to the bathroom where he ran a hot bath for her, adding a few drops of lavender oil. He helped Wilhelmina undress and step into the water.

"Just relax a while, dear," he told her. "I will turn out the lights downstairs and be back to check on you straight away."

Visions of Frieda's face as she lay on the cold kitchen floor haunted Wilhelmina's dreams that night … and nearly every night for the next few weeks. The hospital had recently instituted sick days and vacation time for their employees, and they permitted Wilhelmina to take two weeks off before returning to work. She welcomed the respite, spending her days holding Albert and reading to him.

A thin, weak Wilhelmina returned to work in early December. She and Oskar had formally introduced themselves to the neighbor who had helped Wilhelmina on that awful day. Mr. and Mrs. Bauer agreed to care for Albert while Wilhelmina and Oskar were at work, only charging a minimal fee. With no children of their own, they welcomed the Schmidts into their lives with enthusiasm, compassion, and love.

They would often watch Albert in the Schmidt home, rather than taking him to their house; Mrs. Bauer would surprise them with supper already prepared and staying warm on the stove or in the oven. Wilhelmina was hesitant at first to get close to the Bauers, but her heartache began melting away, and they gradually became friends. Wilhelmina missed the closeness she had developed with her Aunt Frieda, but Mrs. Bauer—who Wilhelmina was now calling Karin—proved to be someone she could trust. It was easy for Wilhelmina to confide in Karin, and they enjoyed many of the same things—walks in the park, crocheting or knitting, sewing, and playing with Albert.

Wilhelmina wrote often to her mother, telling her about Oskar and Albert and her life in America. *"I have come to understand the error of my ways when I was living at home with you, dear Mama, and I sincerely apologize for the agony I know now I must have put you through. Oskar, Albert, and I worship every Sunday at the Lutheran Parish nearby, and we have made friends with a few couples near our ages. I am very close with Mr. and Mrs. Bauer, who take care of Albert while I am away at work. They are very sweet people, faithful Lutherans also, and we often study the Scriptures together and pray. I am happy here, Mama, but I miss you and Papa and my brothers tremendously. I pray daily that you will write to me. I love you, Mama."*

Still, Wilhelmina's letters went unanswered.

Wilhelmina was busy stacking gowns in the third-floor doctors' linen closet and did not hear the door open behind her. She gasped, startled by the sound of a man's voice.

"Excuse me, miss," he said, "I am in need of one of those gowns and cap."

"Of course," she said without turning around. "What size gown do you need?"

"A large will do, thank you."

She rifled through the gowns until she found the size he needed, reached to a higher shelf and grabbed a cap, and then turned to hand the items to the man. She took a step toward him and stopped suddenly. Something about him was familiar, but she couldn't determine what it was.

The man stepped closer to Wilhelmina, took the clothes, and turned to leave. His hand was on the doorknob when he slowly turned back to face her.

"Anya?" he said.

Anya. Where have I heard that name before?

Wilhelmina's skin crawled, and she shivered. There was something about this man—she knew him, but for the life of her, she could not put a name to the face. He was tall and handsome, with a straight nose, high cheeks, and a prominent chin. His trimmed hair was peppered with silver streaks. Thickly framed glasses rested on the bridge of his nose, shielding his steel blue eyes.

Steel blue eyes. Oh ... my ... God!

Recognition seeped in, and Wilhelmina began to shake. She intended to run, but her feet were frozen to the ground, and she could not move her legs.

"Anya, is that you?" he asked again. "No, it can't be y ... Wait ... Wait a moment. I know who you are. You are ... Is it possible?" Like Wilhelmina's eyes at this moment, his widened in disbelief. "Yes, it *is* you. It is ... Wilhelmina?"

"Doc-Doctor Konig?" Her voice was tremulous and soft, almost too quiet to hear.

"Yes, but I am known here as Doctor King." His eyes dashed around the small space, as if unsure of what to do or say.

Wilhelmina nervously fiddled with her necklace and, clutching too hard, she broke the chain and the necklace dropped from her hand. The silver cross hanging from the chain caught a ray of light from the overhead bulb and glittered as it fell to the floor.

"I-I must ... must go. Please excuse me," she whimpered.

Dr. Konig—now calling himself King—opened the door and stood to one side, allowing Wilhelmina to rush out of the closet. In her haste to flee, she did not realize—or perhaps did not care—that her precious cross now lay on the white tile floor of the linen closet. She ran as fast as she could to the stairs and down four flights to the basement, not stopping until she reached the safety of the laundry room. There, finding herself completely alone, she doubled over, trying to catch her breath.

"Mrs. Schmidt are you all right?" said Sylvia, another laundry room employee, as she walked into the room.

Wilhelmina shot up and turned to face Sylvia. Panting, she said, "I-I'm not feeling well. I-I just need a minute."

"You don't look well at all. Perhaps you should talk with Mr. Burns about leaving early," Sylvia said.

"Yes ... Yes, I'll do that. Thank you."

Wilhelmina left the room and headed down the hall to the supervisor's office. He, too, saw right away that Wilhelmina did not appear well—she was very pale and shaking—and sent her home. She retrieved her coat and purse from the women's locker room and, slipping the coat over her shoulders, stepped through the staff entrance.

Outside, an unusually warm March sun was melting the snow on the sidewalks and streets, transforming it from a sparkling blanket of pristine white to a brown, messy slush. Wilhelmina had left her boots in her locker, and not daring to return inside, she picked her way through the footprints of others to the streetcars two blocks away.

As she rode the short distance home, her mind raced back to what happened in the linen closet. She closed her eyes, trying to erase the image of his face, his voice, the feel of his fingers as they briefly touched hers when she gave him the gown. She began to pray and, instinctively, reached to caress the cross hanging around her neck—except, it wasn't there! Her eyes flew open and darted around the streetcar, searching for the necklace. *Oh, please, let it be here!*

By the time she turned onto her street, Wilhelmina remembered the chain of her necklace breaking as she stood face-to-face with Dr. King and realized she must have dropped it. She had never expected to see him again, that man who had defiled her, brought shame on her and on her family. She was relieved to find that Karin and Albert were not in the house when she walked through the door. She sped up the stairs to the bathroom to wash her face with cool water, hoping to bring some color back to her ashen cheeks. She unpinned the bun at the nape of her neck, her blond locks falling to her shoulders, and gently brushed her hair while studying her reflection in the mirror. Wilhelmina saw remorse in her eyes—remorse she thought long gone.

In her bedroom, she removed her hospital uniform—a full, white apron and simple button up dress—and hung them in the wardrobe. She donned a knee-length house dress and sweater and headed downstairs to start dinner for her family.

For the next few weeks, Wilhelmina teetered on a precipice between fear and guilt. At home she was withdrawn and quiet, certain the tears swimming along her eyelids would spill over and down her face if she spoke. She picked at her food and found no joy in her reading. She would play with Albert as usual, but her smiles when he did something silly were forced. At work she was paranoid, peering around every corner and glancing behind her as she walked down hallways. She begged her fellow employee, Sylvia, to stock the third-floor doctors' linen closet for fear of running into Dr. King again.

∽𝕾

"Okay, son, let's try again," Oskar said gently. "Don't worry, I'll hold on."

Heart pounding in his chest, Albert climbed onto the bicycle as his father steadied it, placed his feet on the pedals, and looked up at his father.

"Ready now?" Oskar said.

Albert nodded and began to pedal the bicycle while Oskar held onto the seat and walked alongside.

"You're doing great, son. Now, don't move the front wheel so much. Keep it steady."

They traveled a short distance, gaining speed along the park pathway, until Albert found his balance and Oskar released his hold on the seat. Albert pedaled and pedaled and, glancing behind him, realized his father had let go.

"I'm doing it, Papa. I'm doing it!" Albert shouted, a wide grin on his face. "Look, Papa!"

"I see you, son!" Oskar panted as he jogged to catch up. "Now slow your pedaling down. That's good. Now, slowly begin to brake. You remember I showed you how?"

"Yes, Papa." Albert's speed slowed to a crawl, and he pushed back on the pedals, coming to a full stop.

"Good, son! Now just drop your feet to the ground!" Oskar ran to Albert and reached out to steady him. "You did it. I knew you could!"

Albert flicked the kickstand down and turned to his father, laughing and jumping up and down. "Oh, Papa, I did it! I can ride my bike now!"

The two hugged and laughed as people passed by them, all smiling appreciatively at the tender moment between father and son. As they walked home, Oskar talked with his son about safety while riding the bike.

"Be sure to stay on the sidewalk, son," he said. "At least until you improve and are more confident. Your mother and I will let you know when you are ready to ride in the street. Until then, though, you only ride if one of us is outside with you. Do you understand?"

"Yes, Papa," Albert replied. "Papa, can I ask you something?"

"It's '*may* I ask,' son, but yes, you may. What is it?"

"Why is Mama sad? She doesn't laugh and never reads me a bedtime story anymore. Is Mama mad at me?"

Oskar licked his lips and sighed. "No, son, Mama is not mad at you. You are a good boy, and Mama loves you very much. I think something may have happened at Mama's work, but I cannot say for sure."

They walked in silence the rest of the way home, Oskar thinking about his wife, wondering why she had been so sad of late. She had always been so happy, smiling and laughing. She found joy in every moment of the day, whether she was cooking, cleaning the house, reading her Bible, or playing with Albert. Wilhelmina never raised her voice, never disagreed with Oskar, and never shed a tear. Oskar began to fear the worst—perhaps his beautiful wife was ill.

No, please dear God in Heaven, do not let her be ill. I cannot live without my dear Mina.

Oskar quickened his steps, so much so that little Albert had to run alongside the bike to keep up with his father. Intent on finding Wilhelmina to talk with her, Oskar didn't notice the new shiny blue Packard 126 sedan parked at the curb. Lost in his thoughts, he bumped into the man standing on the sidewalk.

"Ach," Oskar said, "I am so sorry. I was not paying attention!"

"Quite all right, sir," said the man. "I wonder if you can help me. I am trying to find someone I work with, but I do not know which house is hers."

"Yes, yes, I live here," Oskar said, pointing to his front door as Albert hid behind his father's legs. "This shy little boy here is my son, Albert. I am Oskar Schmidt."

"Pleased to meet you, Mr. Schmidt. I am Dr. King. I work at Good Samaritan Hospital and one of the workers lost this necklace." He held the chain in the air, the silver cross glinting in the bright sunlight.

"Ach, yes, that is my wife's necklace. I'm sure she will be very happy to have it back. Thank you so much, Dr. King!" Oskar took the bicycle and leaned it against the house, Albert following close behind him. He stepped onto the front stoop, unlocked and opened the door, and said, "She is doing the grocery shopping right now, but she should return soon. Please, come in. Would you like some lemonade?"

"Yes, thank you. That sounds lovely," Dr. King said as he followed Oskar inside.

As they drank their lemonade and waited for Wilhelmina to arrive, Oskar and Dr. King sat on the small sofa while Albert played with his toys on the floor. They talked about their previous lives in Germany—although Dr. King did not mention knowing Wilhelmina or that he had practiced medicine in Munich. They compared stories of their journeys to America: Oskar had traveled in third class on the SS Hellig Olav in 1917, while Dr. King arrived in America in December 1915 via the SS United States passenger ship, where he enjoyed a luxurious first-class stateroom. Deep in conversation about their experiences, Oskar and Dr. King did not hear Wilhelmina come through the back door.

As she unpacked the bags, Wilhelmina began to hum a light, upbeat tune. The warm spring day seemed to permeate her very soul, making her smile for the first time in weeks. She glanced past the dining room, spotting Albert on the living room floor playing with his toys as his father talked to him—

But Oskar was not talking to Albert! There was another voice, a man's voice. Familiar. *Who is that?*

Wilhelmina skirted around the small dining room table and headed into the living room, stopping mid-stride at the doorway. She straightened her spine as her muscles went rigid and her cheeks

144 | Lori Bridges-Hahn

flushed with heat. Subconsciously, she touched her chest, heart racing beneath her fingertips, and she shuffled back a step or two. *It can't be! Why is he HERE?*

In that same moment, Dr. King's gaze drifted over Wilhelmina as she stood frozen in place. Oskar turned toward his wife standing at the threshold unmoving, her cheeks fading from a deep crimson to ghostly white.

"Mina!" he said. "You are home. Come in, darling, come in. We have a guest. I believe you know Dr. King? He found your necklace, dear, and has kindly brought it here."

Wilhelmina's hands dropped flaccidly to her sides, jaw going slack, and eyes wide. Still, she could not move. She could not speak.

"Darling, you look absolutely stunned," Oskar said as he rose from the couch and strode to his wife. Taking her by the hand, he led her to the sofa and gestured her to sit next to Dr. King. "I'll make you a nice cool glass of lemonade, darling." He sped off to the kitchen, leaving Wilhelmina once again face-to-face with the man who had forever changed her life.

CHAPTER SEVENTEEN

October 1924

Wilhelmina took to her bed for four days after the encounter with Dr. King … in her own home, no less. She made excuses to Oskar, saying it was her monthly "visitor" that was causing her illness, and he fussed over her with loving tenderness. Albert played quietly in his room during those days. When he ventured into his parents' room, he sat on the bed beside his mother and caressed her face as he told her about learning to ride his bike and meeting a "pretty girl" in the park.

Karin Bauer watched over both Wilhelmina and Albert when Oskar returned to work the following Monday until, finally, Wilhelmina felt well enough mid-week to leave her bed. She remained at home from work that week and tried to occupy her time by caring for Oskar and Albert. But the following Monday came quickly, and slumping her shoulders, she climbed into the streetcar for the ride to work. At the hospital, Mr. Burns allowed her to perform duties in the laundry room; she no longer had to deliver linens and gowns to the various floors, and therefore, her chances of running into Dr. King again were slim.

The months that followed passed smoothly for Wilhelmina; she did not run into the doctor again, and by mid-summer she returned to her normal, happy self. She planted a vegetable and herb garden in the small patch of dirt outside the back door. She took Albert to the park often and began teaching him to read.

Wilhelmina started a sewing circle with the neighborhood women, including Karin Bauer and Marta Wagner. They made homemade date bread, cinnamon bread, or Dutch apple pie to serve with coffee or tea before the women would set about sewing.

Every Sunday after attending church with their families, the three women prepared a hearty meal for Oskar, Albert, Georg Bauer, Friederich Wagner, and themselves. After dinner they would gather around the radio in the small living room and listen to news broadcasts, jazz or classical music, or local variety shows.

In late September, the Schmidts, Wagners and Bauers watched the Oktoberfest parade in their neighborhood before walking to Washington Park, where they enjoyed bratwursts, schnitzel, pretzels, sauerkraut and strudel. While performers danced polkas and waltzes set to German folk music, Oskar grabbed Wilhelmina's hand and danced with her on the grass as Albert clapped and giggled. Oskar and Friederich won the three-legged sack race, and while walking home, they all sang—quite out of tune—Die Gedanken Sind Frie, a song celebrating freedom of thought and individualism.

October brought a cool autumn, transforming the vibrant green trees into a stunning palette of red, orange, gold and purple. The curtains on the windows of the little house on Madison Street fluttered in the breeze while Wilhelmina moved about dusting the tables and sweeping the floors. In the kitchen, she removed a chocolate cake from the oven and set about making the milk chocolate frosting—Albert's request for his fourth birthday.

A few hours later several neighborhood children and their parents filled the house and yard, now decorated with festive streamers, banners, and paper lanterns. Each child wore a different colored cone-shaped hat and joined in the games—Pin the Tail on the Donkey, Musical Chairs, and Topfschlagen, a game in which a child was blindfolded and given a wooden spoon. A cooking pot was placed on the grass, covering a small prize. The child would then crawl around the tiny yard and tap the spoon on the ground, trying to find the pot by listening closely for the sound of the spoon hitting the metal. The adults provided enough items for every child at the party to play the game and win a prize, usually candy or a small toy.

A smile etched on her face, Wilhelmina watched her son play and laugh. She and Oskar held hands and hugged often throughout the party, and their friends commented to each other how they had never seen Wilhelmina happier.

After singing "Happy Birthday" Albert blew out the candles on his cake before the children sat on the grass in a circle while he opened his presents. Wilhelmina carried the cake into the kitchen and was busy cutting it when someone knocked on the front door.

"Oskar," she called through the open window, "there's someone at the front door. Can you see who it is, please?"

"Of course, Mina," he replied as he walked to the back door. He entered the kitchen and strode through the house to the foyer. The sound of the door creaked open in the distance, and Oskar's voice came after. "Yes, may I help you?"

The familiar and unwelcome voice drifted through the house, and like last spring, Wilhelmina froze and couldn't help but listen in on the conversation between Oskar and the man at the front door.

"Hello again, Mr. Schmidt. Oh, I'm sorry, you don't recognize me! Yes, it's this new mustache. I am Doctor King," the man said. "You may remember, I visited here last April to return your wife's necklace."

"Oh, yes, of course, I remember! I'm sorry. We just weren't expecting anyone else today. You see, we are having a party for our son's birthday. You are more than welcome to join us. Please, come in."

"Thank you, Mr. Schmidt," Dr. King said. "Yes, yes, I heard from someone at the hospital that your son is turning four today, and well, I wanted to bring him a little gift."

"Oh, that's very kind of you," Oskar said as the door creaked open wider.

"I just need to get it. Just a moment." he said.

A few moments of silence passed until Oskar said, "Ach, Dr. King, it is too much!"

"No, no, please, allow me to give this to him. I noticed last spring that his bicycle was old and rusted, and well …" Dr. King said. "You see, I have no children. My wife died in childbirth along with our newborn son. It would give me great pleasure to give this to Albert."

"Again, very kind of you, Dr. King. Please come in. The children are in the backyard and Albert is opening his presents now."

Wilhelmina frantically glanced around the kitchen, searching for a place to hide, somewhere to run, but nothing availed itself. She fled to the backyard, squatted next to Albert, and began helping him rip the paper from the boxes. The world shifted, and feeling faint, she dropped to the grass and folded her legs at the knees, feet planted on the ground beneath her. Her hands shook as she took a box from Albert and gave him a forced smile.

"Mina!" cried Oskar. "There you are! Look who's arrived with a present for Albert! Come, darling, come say hello."

Wilhelmina squeezed her eyes shut and swallowed hard before rising to her feet. She leveled her gaze on Oskar as she walked toward him. As she stood next to Oskar, she glanced down at the bicycle being guided by Dr. King, a shiny, new royal blue bicycle with a matching bow on the handlebars. Biting her lip, she slowly raised her eyes to meet his. Wilhelmina blinked rapidly, doing her best to ward off the tears threatening to spill. His icy blue eyes penetrated her soul, sending shivers down her spine. Feeling her knees buckle, she grabbed Oskar's arm to steady herself. She was about to beg Oskar to help her into the house when Albert spotted the bicycle and ran to his parents.

"Mama, Papa," he shouted, "is this for *me*?"

"Yes, Albert, my son, it is," said Oskar. "You won't remember, but this is Dr. King, and he has brought you this present for your birthday. What do you say, son?"

"Thank you, sir!" Albert began jumping up and down excitedly. "May I ride it now, Papa? Please?"

"No, you still have to eat your cake and play more games with your friends. Now, son, don't be sad. You can ride it later. Now, go play with your friends and Mama and I will bring everyone cake." Turning to Dr. King, "Will you stay for cake, Doctor?"

Wilhelmina squeezed Oskar's arm tighter, silently conveying her anguish to her husband. But Oskar was already releasing her hand and taking the bicycle from Dr. King. He guided it to the back porch and leaned it against the house.

Dr. King followed Oskar to the porch and said, "Thank you for the invitation, but I must be on my way to the hospital. I only wanted to stop by to bring the gift and wish Albert a happy birthday." He turned to Wilhelmina and said, "Thank you for allowing my intrusion. I hope to see you at the hospital again sometime. Good day to you both. I will find my own way out." With that, he strode the length of the house and turned the corner.

Wilhelmina rushed past Oskar, up the porch steps, and into the house. She picked up the knife to resume cutting the cake, but her hand still shook, so the knife slipped through her fingers, clanging on the floor at her feet.

"Mina? Are you alright?" Oskar said as he walked into the kitchen. "Why are you shaking so badly, dear?"

"I-I don't know, Oskar," she said weakly. "Perhaps I have overdone it today. I am a bit tired."

"You go outside, sit and rest. I'll take care of the cake."

Wilhelmina tilted her head up to Oskar, sinking into his gaze where the immense love for her sparkled bright. She stood on tiptoe and kissed him on the cheek. "Thank you, darling, you are wonderful. I will send Marta in to help you."

The rest of the afternoon passed by in a blur. Later, while Oskar tucked Albert into bed, Wilhelmina paced the kitchen floor, wringing her hands, trying to slow her breathing. She began washing the dishes, her mind racing with jumbled thoughts. By the time she had dried and put everything away, her mind was made up.

She was going to confront Dr. King once and for all.

On Monday, Wilhelmina took the stack of doctors' gowns from Sylvia and aimed for the stairs. She hesitated for a moment, then slowly made her way up to the third floor. She peered into patient rooms as she traipsed down the long hallway toward the doctors' linen closet, and stopped at the desk for a moment to say "hello" to the nurses. She arrived at the door to the closet and took a deep breath before turning the knob.

Inside she let the door hang open and balanced the gowns with one arm as she reached for the string to turn on the light. She began to stack the gowns on the shelves according to size, deliberately taking her time. Would she see him today? The sound of footsteps resounded off the tile outside the closet, followed by the all-too-familiar voice giving instructions to a nurse. She squared her shoulders and stepped closer to the threshold between the closet and hallway. He glanced up from the clipboard as he handed it to the nurse and stopped talking mid-sentence.

His piercing eyes leveled on Wilhelmina as his mouth formed a crooked smile. Any other woman would have been flattered to be gazed upon by such a handsome man, but not Wilhelmina. Her skin crawled with his cold, calculating stare.

He turned back to the nurse and said, "Continue the same dosage of morphine and I'll check on Mr. Taylor again in two days." The nurse nodded and headed to the desk as Dr. King took a step closer to the closet.

"Hello, Wil ... Mrs. Schmidt. I was hoping we would meet again." His voice was brittle, like ice crackling underfoot.

"Y-Yes. I wanted to have a word with you, if I may."

Dr. King stepped inside the closet, so close that she quickly took three steps back. He closed the door and said, "Of course. What is it you would like to talk about?"

"You ..." she whispered. Wilhelmina licked her lips, swallowed, and said, "You really must not come to my home again. I am ... I am afraid ..."

His eyes flickered as his lips pulled up in that devilish grin. He chuckled softly. "What are you afraid of, Wil ... Mrs. Schmidt?" His voice dripped with disdain, carrying with it an air of superiority.

For a moment Wilhelmina was certain she was looking into the face of the Devil himself. She said a silent prayer, pushed aside her fears, and gathered her courage. If she wanted to be free of her past, she could not back down. She steadied her voice and spoke slowly, "You ... know ... precisely ... what ... I ... am ... talking ... about, Dr. Konig. Or King, I suppose it is. I-I do not want you in my home again. Oskar, my husband, he-he does not know ... Please, you must leave me alone!"

He laughed softly, like the hiss of a snake, menacing and malicious. He stepped closer and pressed his hands against her shoulders, pinning her to the shelves behind. Holding onto her with one hand, he gently caressed her cheek with the other, one finger along her jawline and moving to her lips. He leaned closer, his mouth brushing her ear. "Oh, I *will* visit you again, Wilhelmina," he whispered. "And you will be happy to see me. I remember that day, so many years ago now. I can still see you walking down the hall into the examination room, batting your eyes, swaying your hips, in that lovely gown you wore, as if you *wanted* to tempt me. And tempt me, you did. Do you know what I remember the most?"

Wilhelmina squeezed her eyes shut and shook her head. Dr. King laughed again, not a gleeful laugh but, rather, quiet and sinister.

"I remember the way your body quivered. You were trying to fight it, to fight me, but your body enjoyed what I was doing to you. Yes, Wilhelmina, you liked having me inside you. You know … it is such a shame that I never kissed you," he growled. "I wonder if your lips are as sweet as your nipples."

Wilhelmina jerked, struggling to push away but he held onto her shoulder even tighter. He rubbed his thumb over her breast, causing her nipple to involuntarily harden beneath her dress and brassiere. He cupped her breast and moaned.

"I remember …" he whispered. "Your vagina was so tight, so good. Is it still tight, Anya?"

"I am *not* Anya!" Wilhelmina shouted. "Please, leave me alone!"

Startled by her outburst, Dr. King released his grasp on her shoulder. Wilhelmina seized the opportunity and shoved him away with all her strength. She bolted for the door, swung it open, and ran the length of the hall, down the stairs, to the safety of the laundry room. There she collapsed onto the floor, panting, trying to catch her breath.

Sylvia walked into the room and rushed over, where Wilhelmina sobbed, crumbled on the floor.

"What is it, Mrs. Schmidt? Are you ill?" she asked.

Wilhelmina nodded.

"I'll get Mr. Burns." She ran from the room.

Moments later Wilhelmina's boss, Mr. Burns, gently escorted her into his office and pulled a chair out for her. She sat with her head bowed, wringing her hands, not daring to look at her boss, certain her shame would be written all over her face.

"Mrs. Schmidt," he said, "are you feeling any better?" Wilhelmina shook her head.

"Then, you must go home, Mrs. Schmidt. You have not been yourself for many months now. I am afraid your health is poor, and you must see a doctor. Perhaps you need an extended leave of absence from work. I will complete the necessary papers, but you must promise to see your doctor very soon. Do you understand, Mrs. Schmidt?"

Wilhelmina coughed and nodded her head as she wiped tears from her cheeks. A few days later she saw her physician and was granted by the hospital to take a three-month leave of absence with strict instructions from her doctor to rest and eat well. She told Oskar she was fatigued, perhaps overworked. She never told him what happened with Dr. King that day in the linen closet. And Oskar still did not know that Wilhelmina knew Dr. King in Munich. She vowed to never let her husband know about the son she had born out of wedlock. He would never know of her sin … ever.

By Christmas, Wilhelmina was feeling rested and much healthier. She spent her days playing with Albert, making special meals for her family, and spending time with the ladies of the sewing circle and her friends. She rang in the new year with Oskar and Albert, and after many long discussions with Oskar, she decided she would not return to work at the hospital. Oskar's income was enough to sustain them, and they both decided her health and well-being were the priority.

As they stood on their front stoop on New Year's Eve, clanging pots and pans together, celebrating with their friends, Wilhelmina knew in her heart that 1925 was going to be a much better year. She would never have to come face-to-face with Dr. King again.

The first day of March brought high winds and blizzard-like conditions to Cincinnati. That blustery day, Oskar stamped the snow off his boots on the front stoop before opening the door and stepping inside. He removed his hat and coat, and hung them on the coat tree next to the door before turning to his companion.

"Please, take off your coat. Come in, sit down. We are happy to have you!" Oskar turned away from Dr. King and strode toward the kitchen. "Mina, I am home. And we have a guest for dinner! Come and say hello, dear."

Wilhelmina gave the stew a stir, set down the spoon, and turned down the draft control to lower the flame on the burner. She wiped her hands on her apron and pushed a stray lock of hair away from her face as she turned to leave the kitchen.

"Coming, honey. I am so glad you are home on time tonight. Dinner is just ab—" Wilhelmina halted abruptly as a wave of shock washed over her. *No, no, NO*, she thought. *It just can't be!*

"There you are," Oskar said with a smile. "You remember Dr. King, I'm sure. Did you know he lives just a few blocks from here? We ran into each other when I got off the streetcar and started talking. He was nice enough to give me a ride home in his car. Come on, dear, sit with us."

Wilhelmina shook her head and stammered, "N-No, the stove."

"Come on, darling, I know you probably lowered the heat before walking away from the stove. You're always so careful about that. Dinner will be fine for a few minutes. Come and sit down."

Wilhelmina inched forward toward the sofa, her body tense as her stomach knotted with anxiety. She sat on the edge of the sofa, as far from Dr. King as she could manage, while Oskar took a seat on the side chair.

"So, as I was saying," he said, oblivious to how pale his wife had become, "Dr. King and I got to talking, and did you know he is a widower? Oh so very sad, his wife died in childbirth—what did you say? About ten years ago? And their son did not survive either. So very sad. And so, he is quite alone, and on such a cold night, I couldn't send him home to a meal of cold cuts. My goodness, something smells wonderful. What are you making for dinner, darling?"

"Yes, it does indeed smell delicious, Mrs. Schmidt," Dr. Konig said as he stared intently at Wilhelmina.

"Umm … it is …" Wilhelmina's voice wobbled as she spoke. "I made an eintopf … err, stew … from the leftover roast from last night, and, oh my, the Kaiser rolls are in the oven!" She rose quickly to her feet and said, "I must see to them!" She skirted around Oskar's chair and fled to the kitchen.

Oskar laughed heartily and said, "You must forgive my wife, Dr. King. She is quite a perfectionist when it comes to the meals she prepares for us. I am sure you will be well fed and find the food to your satisfaction."

"Oh, yes, I am sure. I so rarely have a hot meal these days, being alone, as you know," said Dr. King. "And, please, I believe we now know one another well enough to use our given names. Please, call me Johann."

"Yes, yes, I agree, Dr. K ... I mean, Johann. And you may call me Oskar. My wife's name is Wilhelmina, and you already know our son's name. Oh, even as I speak, there he is now! Come, Albert, say hello to Dr. King."

"Hewwo," Albert said. He descended the stairs and walked into the living room, sticking his arm out straight in front of him to shake Dr. King's hand. "Ni ... Nice to see you."

Johann chuckled and shook Albert's small hand. "And it's nice to see you as well, Albert.

"Ahem," Wilhelmina cleared her throat as she stood in the doorway. "I am sor ... sorry to interrupt but din-dinner is ready. Could you help me carry the dishes to the table, Oskar?"

"Oh yes, of course, dear. Albert, please show Dr. King to the table and then come to the kitchen to wash your hands."

"Yes, Papa," Albert said as he took Dr. King's hand and led him to the small dining room.

Wilhelmina was quiet during dinner, toying with her food and rarely looking up. Oskar and Johann engaged in friendly conversation at the table, both complimenting Wilhelmina often on her cooking. She smiled at Oskar when he thanked her for another tasty meal and merely glanced at Johann, afraid to meet his gaze for more than a moment.

When everyone finished eating, Albert helped his mother carry some of the dishes to the kitchen (only the bread plates and silverware) while Oskar and Johann took seats in the living room and continued their conversation. They chatted about Germany and the war and about life in America. Both men laughed from time to time in the living room. Wilhelmina cringed. It was obvious her husband had taken a liking to Johann, much to her dismay.

Johann told Oskar he had practiced medicine in obstetrics and gynecology when he lived in Germany, but after the death of his wife and unborn son, he lost his passion for the field. When he arrived in America, he decided to switch to general surgery and took the necessary courses at the University of Cincinnati School of Medicine, followed by a three-year residency. He began working at the Good Samaritan Hospital in 1923.

Albert trotted into the room from the kitchen and tugged at his father's shirt sleeve. "Papa?" he said.

"Yes, son?"

"Mama wants to know if you and Dr. King would like coffee with your strudel."

"I do, son. Johann, would you like coffee also?"

"Yes, Oskar, that would be lovely. Albert, tell your mama that I would like cream and sugar with mine."

Grinning happily, Albert bounded into the kitchen to tell his mother. Moments later, Wilhelmina carried a tray bearing the pot of coffee, a sugar bowl, a creamer, and three cups on saucers. Three spoons sat beside the cups. She set the tray on the coffee table in front of Johann and turned to Oskar.

"Dear, would you help me bring in the strudel, please?"

"Of course, darling. You will excuse us, Johann?"

"Of course. I will begin pouring the coffee. Oskar, do you take cream and sugar? Wilhelmina?"

"Yes, I take both, one spoonful of sugar, please. Thank you, Johann. And Mina only takes sugar, two spoonsful, I believe."

When Oskar and Wilhelmina left the room to fetch the strudel, Johann turned to Albert and said, "So, Albert, do you have a favorite toy upstairs?"

"Yes, Doc … Doctor King. Would you like to see it?"

"I'd love to. Can you bring it here?"

Albert smiled and said, "Yes! I'll go get it!" He ran up the stairs as fast as his short legs would carry him.

Alone in the living room, Johann poured coffee into one cup and then took a small glass bottle from his jacket pocket. He glanced toward the kitchen and up the stairs, ensuring no one was approaching, and uncapped the bottle. He poured one heaping teaspoon of the white powder from the bottle into the cup of coffee, stirred it, and added sugar and cream. Johann then carefully set the cup on the table in front of Oskar's seat and rested the spoon on the saucer. He then poured another cup and set it on the table at Wilhelmina's seat before pouring his own.

"Here we are, then!" Oskar announced as he entered the room, carrying two small plates with the strudel and forks. Wilhelmina followed close behind and set one plate on the coffee table and took the other to the dining room table. She then returned to the kitchen, retrieved a small glass of milk, and took it to the dining room table.

Albert flew down the stairs with his toy—a two-car wooden train—and sat it on the floor near the coffee table.

"Sweetie, your strudel is on the table," his mother told him. Albert smiled warmly at his mother as he walked to the dining room, where he sat and ate his dessert.

"I've taken the liberty of adding your cream and sugar, Oskar," Johann said. "I poured your coffee, Wilhelmina, but I have not added your sugar. I am sorry."

Wilhelmina lowered her gaze to the floor and whispered, "That is all right. Thank you."

She took her seat at the end of the couch, added two teaspoons of sugar to her cup, and stirred it slowly. The three adults dug into their dessert and drank their coffee in silence for a few moments, until Johann patted his full stomach and leaned back into the sofa.

"I want to thank you both again, so very much," he said. "Dinner was delicious, as was the strudel. Absolutely delicious. You are both generous and made me feel welcome, but it is getting late, and I have an early surgery tomorrow. I really must be going."

Oskar saw Johann to the door and bid him goodbye while Wilhelmina took the tray of dishes to the kitchen. The front door closed with a click, followed by Oskar telling Albert it was time for bed.

"Read to me tonight, Papa. Pweeze?"

"Okay, son. Go brush your teeth and get your pajamas out and I'll be right up," Oskar told him. "Mina," he called, "I'm going to tuck Albert into bed."

She shouted, "Yes, thank you, Oskar!"

Relieved that both Oskar and Albert were heading up the stairs, Wilhelmina didn't hold back. Tears welled in her eyes and flowed down her cheeks as she stood at the sink washing the dishes. Her shoulders sagged and her entire body shook with silent sobs. She fought to regain her composure as she dried the dishes and put them away. Oskar had not come back downstairs, so she locked the back door and turned out the kitchen light. She walked through the dining room, to the living room and to the front door, turning out more lights as she went. Ensuring the front door was also locked, she turned and ascended the stairs.

As she reached the second floor, she paused as retching noises came from the bathroom and, concerned it was Albert, raced to the door and swung it open. But it wasn't her son she found kneeling on the floor at the toilet—it was Oskar. Beads of sweat blanketed his forehead and face as he held his stomach and vomited profusely. He looked up at his wife between the waves of nausea and tried to talk.

"Stomach ... hurts ... so bad," he croaked before vomiting again. He picked up a damp cloth from the floor and wiped his mouth. "And ... I ... the runs. Please ... privacy," he said as he turned away.

She stepped out of the room, shut the door, and paced up and down the hallway. He moaned and cried out in obvious pain for several minutes until she once again heard him retching.

"Oskar, darling, I'm going for help! I'll be back as soon as I can!"

Wilhelmina sped down the stairs, grabbed her coat, and ran out the door onto the stoop. Her feet immediately sank into a thick blanket of snow. It crunched beneath her feet, bitter iciness seeping through her shoes and stockings. Every step was a struggle as she made her way to the end of the block to Karin's house. She frantically banged on the door. The hour was late, and no lights were on inside their house. She knocked harder and shouted for her friends, "Karin! Georg! I need help! Oh, please, open the door!"

Soon a light in the upstairs window glowed, and a moment later the flicker of candlelight reflected on the glass of the first-floor window next to the door. The lock clicked, and the door opened slowly as Georg's shadowy figure came into view.

"Thank God!" she cried. "Georg, please help. Oskar is ... Oskar is ..." She began weeping.

"There, there, Wilhelmina, calm down. Please, come in out of the cold," Georg told her.

She grabbed Georg's arm. "No, there isn't time. Please, you must call for help. Oskar is very sick. He is vomiting and has ... and has ..." Her cheeks flamed red. "Oh dear ... he has the runs, too. He is in much pain. Please, call an ambulance! I must get back to him!"

"Oh, dear, yes, darling. I will call an ambulance right now. You go back home and they will be here soon. Now stop your crying, child. Everything will be all right. I'm sure Oskar just has the influenza and he'll be good as new in a few days. Now go home and wait for the ambulance dear, and I'll send Karin down to stay with Albert."

"Thank you, Georg," she said as she left and trudged back through the snow to her own door. With every step, she told herself, out loud, "He'll be all right. Good as new in a few days. Just the flu. He'll be all right. God will heal him. Please, God, heal my darling Oskar."

CHAPTER EIGHTEEN

Icy rain pelted Wilhelmina and Albert, their many friends, and neighbors as they crowded together beneath umbrellas, shivering in the cold under bleak, gray skies. Albert's sobs resonated across the property, and all those standing close had lowered their heads against his pain. Eyes closed, Wilhelmina squeezed his hand, a strong reminder that she was there. As the pastor addressed the group, his voice echoed as if he spoke through a tunnel, sounding far away yet he stood mere steps from the mourners.

"We gather here today, not only to mourn the loss of our dear brother but to celebrate the promise of eternal life given to us through our Lord and Savior, Jesus Christ," said Pastor Bergmann.

After these words, Wilhelmina heard nothing else until a muffled, heavy thump flooded her ears. The rain slowed to a drizzle as a ghostly quiet enveloped the cemetery. Wilhelmina opened her eyes as her friends threw handfuls of dirt into the grave. The dirt hit the coffin with hollow thuds, rustling as it settled and shifted into place. She glanced down at the yellow rose clutched in her gloved fist, and lifting her head high, she tossed the flower into the hole. In her eyes, it floated in slow motion, drifting between each drop of bone-chilling rain, finally coming to rest on top of the coffin.

One by one, the mourners stepped away from the gravesite, speaking in low whispers as they walked through the wet snow and ice toward the cemetery exit. Friederich lifted Albert into his arms and carried him away as Marta and Karin flanked Wilhelmina, each taking an elbow, and guided her up the knoll to the street. There, a sparkling blue Packard idled outside the gate, waiting to take her and Albert home; Johann King stood next to his car and opened the door for his two passengers.

Oskar had succumbed to his illness and died five days earlier, just three days after he arrived at the hospital. The doctors said it was a severe case of gastroenteritis, which rapidly shut down his organs. Johann heard the news about Oskar's illness and rushed to Wilhelmina's side where she paced the floor outside Oskar's room. Johann stood beside her while she sat close to her husband's bed and prayed for his recovery. Johann drove her to and from the hospital whenever he could so she would not have to take the streetcar. He spoke with Marta and Karin and some of the sewing circle ladies, who prepared food for Wilhelmina and Albert.

Johann rarely left Wilhelmina's side after, only retreating to his home to sleep. The week following Oskar's death was a blur of activity. For Wilhelmina, it was like watching a movie in which she was the star—each event unfolded, not a single one real. Albert often climbed into her lap, weeping quietly as she absently stroked his back.

Wilhelmina was gravely silent during those two weeks, only speaking to Albert to tell him to wash behind his ears or to brush his teeth or to say his prayers at bedtime. She was vaguely aware of the steady stream of people coming and going from her home, sometimes comforting in its own way, sometimes overwhelming. Platters, casserole dishes, and bowls filled with aromatic entrees, vegetables, and desserts lined every available space on the tables and the few counters in the kitchen. The food was probably delicious, but Wilhelmina ate very little and only because someone placed a plate on her lap and watched over her while she nibbled.

Between the many visits, the house fell silent and felt eerily empty. It was during those times that Wilhelmina was the most afraid. When she was around her friends and neighbors—and when Johann King was with her—she buried her fear of him deep inside. When alone, that fear boiled to the surface in fits of panic and tears. She tried, without success, to be grateful that, since Oskar's death, she had never found herself alone with Johann and prayed she never would.

She paced the floors frequently, unable to sit still, as she worried over how she and Albert would live. She would have to return to work, perhaps take in a boarder or live with one of her friends. She had come to love being at home all day, taking care of her family, and the thought of leaving Albert so soon after losing his father terrified her. There wasn't much money in their bank account; she knew it would run out in a matter of weeks. But two weeks after the funeral, Wilhelmina's situation brightened somewhat.

She found a large envelope on her dining room table one evening when she was home alone. Johann had visited earlier that day and played with Albert, who was now spending the night with a friend. Both Karin and Marta had just left to prepare dinner for their husbands. Wilhelmina sat on the sofa and examined the bulky envelope. Her name was neatly printed in the center, and the envelope did not appear to have been sent through the mail. She turned it over, opened the sealed flap, and peered inside. White-knuckled and shaking, Wilhelmina wrapped her fingers around a wad of money held together by a rubber band and pulled it from the envelope. The envelope fluttered to the floor as she stared, open mouthed, at the bills in her hand. Biting her bottom lip, she removed the rubber band and began counting—one hundred dollars, two hundred—over seven hundred dollars! More than enough to pay the rent and buy groceries for five months or longer.

Who left this? she wondered. *Why would someone leave me this much money? Did Karin and Marta collect this from our friends?*

There was no note inside, no indication as to who might have left the envelope. The next day, she questioned her friends about the money—no one seemed to know anything about it. She wanted to return the money, but the Wagners and Bauers implored with her to keep it.

"Dear," Karin said while pouring a cup of tea for Wilhelmina, "you need that money. Someone must care very deeply for you, enough to help you get through the next few months until you can figure out your next steps. Please don't try to give it back. You'll probably never know who left it anyway."

"But, Karin," Wilhelmina said, "it just doesn't seem right. It's too much. I can't possibly think about keeping it!"

"Listen to me carefully," Karin said. "You *can* and *should* keep that money. Put it in your bank. It will get you through summer and when Albert starts school in September, you could go back to work.

Then you could stay here and …" She let out a small sob and dabbed at her dampening eyes with a handkerchief. "You wouldn't have to move away. Dear girl, I would miss you so much! Please keep the money."

Wilhelmina reached across the table and patted Karin's hand. "All right, Karin, all right. Please don't cry. I'll go to the bank tomorrow, and I promise I won't leave here. I don't know what I would do without you and Georg. And Marta and Friederich, either! The four of you are truly a Godsend to me. And you"—her voice cracked as her own tears welled in her eyes— "you are like a mother to me. I love you!"

"There, there, dear. And I love you like a daughter. You are a blessing to me."

The following day, Wilhelmina left Albert with Karin and took the streetcar to the bank, where she deposited most of the money. Afterward, she stopped at the market and bought food and toiletries. She prepared schnitzel and sauerkraut for dinner that night—the first meal she cooked since losing Oskar. She watched her son while he ate. Like her, Albert had become very quiet over the last several weeks, not his usual boisterous, precocious self. Wilhelmina reached across the table and lovingly ran her hand through his shock of blond hair. He sent her a weak smile and continued eating.

As she lay in bed that night, she set out her plan. She would, indeed, return to work as soon as Albert started school. To supplement her income, she would take in sewing for her elderly neighbors and clean for them for a small fee. Her main thought was of Albert and his happiness. She was determined to erase the sadness in his eyes. She vowed to protect him at all costs; he was all she had left of Oskar, the man she had loved so deeply.

She yawned, closed her eyes and whispered to the empty room, "I will take care of you, sweet Albert. I will never let harm come your way. You are my whole world now, and I will see to it you have everything you need to grow up to be as wonderful as your father was. I cherish you, my sweet Albert, and I love …"

She yawned again and drifted off to sleep.

Wilhelmina was busy working in the small patch of grass in her backyard, planting herbs, tomatoes and onions while Albert played with his toy trucks several feet away. She had obtained a Burpee catalog at one of the nearby grocers and ordered the seeds weeks before. Friederich had tilled an area of the yard, so she rose early that May morning, ready to begin planting. She used her spade to dig deep holes, then sprinkled in the seeds, and refilled the hole with dirt. Marta carried a bucket of water from the kitchen, and together, they watered the newly planted seeds.

Satisfied with their work, the two friends pushed off the ground and walked the short distance to where Albert was playing. Wilhelmina had sewn pillows for the two wicker chairs she had received from Marta and Friederich and, her muscles aching, gratefully sank onto one of the chairs and smiled at Marta.

"Thank you for your help today, Marta," she said. "I couldn't have done all this without you or Friederich."

"You are quite welcome, but it was nothing," Marta replied. "I had fun, and now it feels good to sit here and relax. This lemonade is especially good today."

The two sat in silence, sipping their drinks. Basking in the warmth of the sun, Wilhelmina closed her eyes. She rarely smiled these days, but she was adjusting to life without Oskar with the help of her friends and her church. Lost in thought, she jumped in her seat when Albert shouted.

"Hewwo, Doc … Doctor King!" Albert cried.

Wilhelmina sat straight in her chair, her reddened cheeks going pale.

"Well, hello young Albert. Ahh, I see you are playing with your trucks today. Are you having fun?" Johann asked.

"Yes, sir. Will you play with me?"

"Maybe in a few moments, Albert. I want to visit with your mama first."

Albert's smile faded.

"Now, there, Albert, don't be sad," Johann said. "If you don't smile, I won't take you for a ride in my car later."

A wide grin returned to Albert's face as he clapped his hands together. "Weally?" he asked, eyes bright with excitement.

"Yes, Albert, but you have to be good while I talk with your mama."

"I will. I pwomise!"

Johann strode to the ladies and said, "Hello, Mrs. Wagner, Mrs. Schmidt. How are you lovely ladies on this fine spring day?" He flashed a smile which, to anyone else, would have seemed genuine and charming. The hairs on Wilhelmina's arms stood on end, and a shiver traveled down her spine.

"We are doing wonderfully, Dr. King," Marta gushed. Although happy in her marriage with Friederich, she had never been able to hide her infatuation with Johann and often confessed to Wilhelmina that she found him to be very handsome. "Thank you for asking. How are you?"

"Ahh, very well, very well," he said. "And what have you planted?"

Wilhelmina stared at Johann, unable to find her voice. She was thankful that Marta did not notice and continued chatting with him.

"Oh, today, we planted seeds for onions, tomatoes, some basil, garlic, and parsley. Wilhelmina has ordered more seeds, but they haven't arrived yet."

"A worthy endeavor, I'm sure," he said as he turned to Wilhelmina. "And how are you today, Mrs. Schmidt?"

Wilhelmina's eyes leveled with Johann's. "I ..." she began. "I-I am fine. Thank you." She turned her gaze to Albert, hoping to avoid further conversation with Johann. But her worst nightmare came true in the next moment.

"I'm afraid Wilhelmina is a bit tired from all the planting today," Marta said. She stood and said, "I'll refresh your lemonade, Wilhelmina. Would you like a glass, Dr. King?"

"Yes, Mrs. Wagner, that sounds lovely."

Marta picked up the two empty glasses and headed inside, leaving Wilhelmina alone with Johann and Albert, playing a few feet away. Johann knelt next to Albert and asked him about his trucks, often stealing glances at Wilhelmina, who sat rigid in her chair. As the minutes passed, she tapped her toe on the ground and began biting her thumbnail.

I wish Marta would hurry up, she thought. Just then the back door slammed, and Marta appeared on the porch with two glasses of fresh lemonade.

Marta strode to where Wilhelmina sat, handed her one of the glasses, and set the other on the small table between the chairs. But she didn't resume her seat. Instead, she walked to where Albert and Johann were playing with the trucks and knelt down next to them.

Mussing Albert's hair, Marta said, "I've got to go now, little buddy. But don't forget, I'm taking you to the park tomorrow, as long as it doesn't rain."

Albert grinned widely, clapped his hands together, and cried, "Yay! I'll say an extra prayer tonight, Aunt Marta, so we can go to the park!"

Marta laughed as she rose to her feet and faced Wilhelmina. "Sorry, but I do have to go. I can stop by after dinner if you like."

Wilhelmina opened her eyes wide, silently pleading with Marta to stay, knowing it was futile. The glass shook in her hands, causing a small splash of lemonade to land on her apron. She set the glass on the table and quickly stood.

"Oh, dear, look what I've done! I'm sorry, Dr. King, I must tend to this before the stain sets in. I'm sure you underst—"

"No, no, Wilhelmina," Marta interjected. "You stay and visit with Dr. King. Hand me your apron. I've got some washing to do myself, and one more item won't bother me at all. You need to just rest, my friend. Here, let me help you untie the back."

Marta quickly helped her out of the apron, all the while dismissing Wilhelmina's protests. Once she pulled the apron over Wilhelmina's head, she smiled at her friend and gave her a quick hug.

"I'll bring it back later tonight, dear. Now you sit here and relax. I will see you later," Marta said, and turned to head home.

Wilhelmina dropped into her chair, her mind racing. She wanted to grab Albert in her arms and flee into the house, locking Johann out, but he was already striding toward her, blocking her from doing so. He situated himself on the empty chair, picked up his glass of lemonade, and took three large gulps.

"This is quite good, Mrs. Schmidt," he said. "Did you make it yourself?"

"Uh-huh," she muttered, keeping her eye on Albert playing. A cool breeze picked up around them, and Wilhelmina shivered.

"Albert," Johann called, "It's getting a bit chilly out here. Do you know where your mama's sweater is?"

Albert tilted his head and looked up at the sky as if thinking. "Yes … Yes, I think it's on the chair," he said. "Shall I get your sweater, Mama?"

Wilhelmina slowly nodded. "Yes … Yes, son, thank you. Hurry back, now."

Albert ran inside the house, the back door slamming behind him, and Wilhelmina began wringing her hands in her lap. She was completely alone with Johann for the first time since … since that day at the hospital … and she sat paralyzed with fear.

Johann leaned over the arm of his chair and whispered, "Are you using the money I left for you wisely, Anya?"

Anya. Why does he always call me Anya?

"Wha … What do you mean," Wilhelmina squeaked. "It was … It was *you*?"

"Yes, yes, it was I who left the envelope. Answer my question, Anya. Are you using the money wisely?"

Wilhelmina licked her lips, cleared her throat and said, "Y-Yes, I put it in the bank and … and I only use it f-for food and rent. But your gift is too much. You must … You must allow me to give the money back!"

Johann chuckled, that soft chuckle from deep in his throat, the chuckle that sent shivers down Wilhelmina's spine.

"No, no, Anya," he said. "It was not a gift. You may consider it a loan. And I *do* expect repayment, my dear."

"Oh, my, I-I don't think … I don't think I can repay—"

"Oh, dear Anya, I have already decided how I want to be repaid, and it is not the money I desire. No, I have plenty of that. It is *you*," he replied, and chuckled again.

"Wha-What?"

"I intend to marry you, Anya, and you will comply. Do you know why you will do as I wish?"

"N-N-No," she croaked.

"Because if you do not, I will tell your friends about how you seduced me all those years ago in Munich. And … you *did* seduce me, wearing that silky dress that day, swaying your hips as you walked. If you care anything about your precious son, you'll do as I say."

Wilhelmina shot up to her feet and faced Johann, clenching her fists at her side. "And if I don't?" she demanded.

Johann's jaw moved back and forth as he gnashed his teeth. He narrowed his eyes, and a red vein popped out underneath the skin of his neck. He growled at her. "You will be sorry, *Mrs. Schmidt*! Do as I tell you and no harm will come to Albert. If you don't … then his blood will be on *your* hands!"

"No!" she yelled. "You cannot … You wouldn't!"

The back door creaked, and Albert stepped onto the porch. "Mama, I can't find your sweater."

Wilhelmina swallowed hard, tightened her fists, fingernails digging into palms, and took a slow, deep breath. She turned to face her son and called, "It is all right, honey. Our guest is leaving, and Mama is coming inside now. Come get your trucks. It's time for your nap." Turning back to Johann, she said through gritted teeth, "Leave my house."

Without waiting for a response, Wilhelmina picked up the two glasses and sped into the house, followed closely by Albert. As soon as he was safely inside, she slammed the door and locked it. Wilhelmina then ran through the house and locked the front door before peeking out the window. Outside, Johann slipped into his car. He glanced back at the house and nodded in her direction, obviously chuckling.

She quickly drew the curtains closed and followed Albert up the stairs to tuck him in for his afternoon nap. As she was sitting on the bed while he drifted off to sleep, tears streamed down her face and landed in splotches on her dress. She tiptoed out of the room, closed the door behind her, and paced the hallway, biting her nails. What could she do?

Would he really harm Albert? And tell my friends about what happened between us? Oh, dear Heavenly Father, let it not be true! What am I going to do? I'll move from here, that's what. I'll leave

Cincinnati if I must. Oh, but how will I do that? I have no money other than the ... the filthy money he left for me. I was stupid to keep that money! I must speak with Georg and Friderich right away! Oh, Wilhelmina, what are you thinking? You cannot tell them anything. You cannot ever let anyone know what happened between you and ... and that monster. I've got to hide. I've got to find somewhere to go.

CHAPTER NINETEEN

With no job and no foreseeable source of income, Wilhelmina searched for weeks for a new apartment but came up empty. She desperately wanted to get as far away from Johann as possible, but realized she did not know where he lived. She had always assumed his home was near hers, since he often bumped into Oskar or herself at the streetcar stop or in Washington Park. She went to the public library and scanned the city directory but could find no listing for Johann King or Johann Konig.

Meanwhile, Johann continued visiting Wilhelmina, often finding her at the park with Albert or walking home from the market with Marta or Karin. He brought her small gifts—a new garden hoe, thick cushions for the dining room chairs, a bouquet of flowers beautifully arranged in a crystal vase, a book of poetry, and new toys for Albert. Both Marta and Karin commented often on how charming Dr. King was and how he must be smitten with her to visit so often. They admired the way he spoke so easily with Albert, often sitting on the grass to play with him. Johann frequently took Albert for rides in his car, allowing Albert to honk the horn as they circled the block. The neighbors smiled and waved as they drove by, and they were happy to hear Albert's laughter.

Wilhelmina and Albert often shared their meals with Karin and Georg, and many evenings while they were setting the table, Johann appeared at their door, a bottle of wine or flowers in hand. He had developed a friendly rapport with Wilhelmina's friends, and they gladly welcomed him into their homes.

Karin and Marta noticed Wilhelmina's tenseness every time Johann visited her, but they passed it off as shyness and uncertainty about starting a new relationship so soon after Oskar's death. She did not confide in them about Johann, but this did not surprise them.

They had known Wilhelmina long enough to know she was a private person and would tell them things about herself in her own good time.

What her friends didn't know was how Johann terrified her. They didn't know he always managed to corner her alone during those visits, even if for only a moment—long enough to remind her of his demand. He would simply whisper in her ear, "Don't forget, Anya. You will be my wife soon." At the dinner table, he would often comment that in all his years as a physician he had never met a woman as devoted to her child as Wilhelmina. By the end of July, Wilhelmina slept little, or when she did finally close her eyes, her dreams were filled with visions of Albert lying in a coffin. Her entire body shaking, she would awaken, tears flowing down her cheeks.

Jobs were plentiful in Cincinnati that summer, but Wilhelmina found it difficult to find one that suited her or worked with her schedule. Most of the factories wanted her to work nights, but she hesitated to leave Albert with friends overnight as she feared for his safety. Johann almost always visited at suppertime, or after, and rarely throughout the day. Wilhelmina was certain that something awful would happen to Albert if she was not with him at night, so she turned down the few job offers she received.

The money in her bank was dwindling as August approached. Desperate to escape Johann's threats, she even wrote again to her mother and brothers—but as with every letter since leaving Germany, she received no reply.

On a sweltering, sticky day in the middle of August, Wilhelmina and Albert walked home from church accompanied by Karin and Georg, and Marta and Friederich. The ladies waved their fans in front of their faces, the men used their hats as fans, as they chatted. They turned the corner at Music Hall and headed toward the Wagner home where they would prepare and share a meal out on the lawn. Friederich had purchased planks of wood and constructed a long table for the yard, and he and Georg had carried chairs from Wilhelmina's house and the Bauers's house and placed them around the table, which sat beneath two large shade trees. The men covered the table with one of Marta's old tablecloths while the ladies prepared a *wursteplatte* of cold cuts and cheeses and retrieved the potato salad from the ice box.

Wilhelmina spooned a small amount of mustard into a bowl, grabbed a butter knife, and carried them out the back door to the yard. She headed to the house after placing the items on the table, but as she opened the back door, she froze in place, unable to move.

"Dr. King!" said Friederich. "How nice to see you again. I am glad you could join us today."

"I am glad to be here," Johann said. "And I thank you again for invit—"

Wilhelmina heard no more as she ran through the kitchen and up the stairs to the bathroom. She locked the door and sat on the toilet, doubled over, trying to catch her breath. She did not know that Friederich had invited Johann, and now her mind raced for an excuse to leave. She could feign a sudden headache or say that she felt nauseated or—

It was no use. It was Marta's birthday celebration, and she knew she had to stay. She rocked back and forth as she sat calming her nerves until someone rapped lightly on the door.

"Wilhelmina?" Marta said from the other side of the door. "Are you all right, dear?"

"Yes … Yes, Marta. I am fine," Wilhelmina called. "I was overcome by the heat and needed a cool rag. I'll be out in a moment." She went to the sink, turned the cold-water faucet, and searched for a cloth. Finding one on the shelf nearby, she then dampened it with the cool water and dabbed her face and neck.

"All right, dear. We have everything set and are ready to eat. Come down when you are ready. We will wait for you," Marta said. Wilhelmina took several deep breaths as Marta's footsteps faded down the hall.

Calm yourself, Wilhelmina. You can get through this. Not long now and you'll get a job and move away from here, away from him.

Downstairs, she trudged out the door and down the steps to the yard where everyone was taking their seats around the table. She cringed, finding Albert seated on Johann's right, with one empty chair remaining—on Johann's left. She closed her eyes and took another deep breath, willing herself to walk. At the table, she went through the motions of filling her plate, passing bowls and platters, and sipping her lemonade. Albert was monopolizing Johann's attention, for which she was eternally grateful. Her friends engaged in gleeful chatter as they ate; no one noticed how quiet she was. Her silence was not new to them.

The sun blazed down from a cloudless sky, the air thick with humidity, but the trees provided a shady refuge for the small party. The conversation around the table was light and friendly as they discussed the Cincinnati Reds baseball season and the new subway system being constructed downtown.

Wilhelmina had barely touched her food when the birthday cake was brought to the table—a crumb cake (known as Streuselkuchen) made with a yeast dough and a buttery crumb topping—Marta's favorite dessert. The group of friends sang "Happy Birthday," and Marta blew out the candles to everyone's applause.

While Karin cut and served the cake, Marta stood and peered around the table at her friends. "Dear friends," she said, "my heart is as warm as this August day as I look around this table at all of your faces. Darling Wilhelmina and Albert, how I treasure both of you. Dr. King … I'm sorry, Johann." Marta chuckled and cleared her throat. "I keep forgetting you want us to call you by your given name. Dear Karin and Georg, you are like parents to us and to Wilhelmina, and like grandparents to Albert. My precious friends, my family … Friederich and I have something to share with you."

Wilhelmina's head shot up as she gazed at her friend. She placed her fork on the table and folded her hands in her lap. Friederich walked around the table and stood by his wife's side.

Marta continued, "Today I am twenty-eight years old and I … I mean we … we are so excited to let all of you know that—oh, my goodness. We are expecting a child!"

Karin was the first out of her seat. She raced to the end of the table and threw her arms around Marta and then Friederich! Tears welled in her eyes as she hugged and kissed them both. Georg stood behind her, waiting his turn to hug Marta and shake hands with Friederich. Wilhelmina rose slowly from her chair and stood behind it while she waited her turn.

Marta sobbed. "Dear Karin, dear Georg, you know my parents are still in Germany. I hope—I mean—It is our wish that you consider yourselves our child's grandparents also. We would be honored!"

Karin and Georg nodded enthusiastically, once again hugging the parents-to-be. Marta eased from Karin's grasp and turned to Wilhelmina, who stood behind her.

"My dear, friend," Marta said, "perhaps we shall have a daughter for Albert to marry someday." And she laughed as tears streamed down her face.

Wilhelmina laughed and hugged Marta before turning to Friederich and hugging him as well. Albert began jumping up and down next to them and asking, "What's happening, Mama? Why is everyone crying and laughing?"

Marta knelt to face Albert and drew him into her arms, hugging him tightly. "Oh, you dear, sweet boy, I am going to have a baby!"

Albert laughed. Everyone returned to their seats as Johann stood and raised his glass of lemonade.

"A toast, if I may," he said. Everyone raised their glasses, and Johann continued, "To Marta and Friederich, may you have a happy, healthy child that you will treasure for a lifetime. Congratulations. To Marta and Friederich!"

"To Marta and Friederich!" the group shouted in unison.

Everyone took their seats and ate their cake, smiling and laughing between bites. Just as they were about to finish, Johann stood again.

"I hope I am not imposing on this special day," he said. "After all, we are here to honor Marta on her birthday and now, to celebrate their happy news. But I have some news of my own ... or shall I say, I have something of my own to say."

"Please, Johann, go right ahead," Friederich said.

Johann pushed his chair back farther, turned to Wilhelmina, and stuck a hand into the pocket of his slacks. As he knelt to one knee, Wilhelmina's mouth popped open; he held a small box in his hand.

Oh, dear Father, please, no. Don't let him—

Karin gasped from across the table. Wilhelmina glanced at Karin, then at Marta, who were both grinning widely, and brought her gaze back to Johann—her green silently pleading with his blue for him to stop.

"Darling An … Wilhelmina, I think it is no secret that I have grown quite fond of you these last several months. You are a beautiful angel from Heaven, and I adore you. Darling, would you do me the honor of becoming my wife?" He opened the box, revealing a large diamond ring.

Wilhelmina sat silent as a single tear dropped from her eye onto the napkin on her lap. She looked at her friends, one by one, as they clasped their mouths while smiling and nodding their approval. She then leaned over and peered at her son, who was also nodding and sporting the biggest smile of all.

She gazed back at Johann and opened her mouth, but no words came out.

"Lean closer to me, darling," he said, "so I can hear you."

She automatically leaned forward but before she could speak, he whispered in her ear, "Don't forget what I told you, An … Wilhelmina."

Without realizing what she was doing, Wilhelmina moved her head slowly up and down as Johann pulled her wedding set from her finger, and slipped the diamond ring in its place. Her friends clapped and shouted. Someone threw their arms around her—she couldn't remember later if it was Johann or Marta. Or was it Albert? Their faces flitted across her eyes in a blur, their lips brushing her cheek, their arms hugging her tightly. She heard shouts of "congratulations" and "what a perfect day" and "oh, how romantic," but the voices seemed miles away.

She rose stiffly from her chair as someone lifted Albert and handed him to her. He hugged her and squealed, "Mama, is Doc … Doctor King going to be my papa now? Oh, Mama!"

Black spots swam in her vision, and thinking the sun was blinding her, Wilhelmina raised her hand to shield her eyes. Someone said something about a spring wedding, and then a man answered, "Oh no, we will be married right away." Her skin tingled as goosebumps rose all over her body, and she darted her gaze from face to face, each a watery blur.

Then everything went black as someone yelled, "Grab her!"

❧

Johann and Wilhelmina were married less than two weeks later on August 25, 1925, by the mayor of Cincinnati while Albert, Marta, Friederich, Karin and Georg stood nearby in the small courtroom. Afterward, the newly married couple gathered with their friends at Karin and Georg's backyard for cake and punch before they bid goodbye to Albert and left for the train station in Johann's car with Friederich at the wheel.

After a fourteen-hour train ride, Johann and Wilhelmina spent two nights at a luxury hotel overlooking Niagara Falls. Years later Wilhelmina had little recollection of their honeymoon; from the moment the engagement ring touched her finger until she returned home to her son, each day was like a dense fog clouding her memory. Her actions were mechanical, and she focused solely on Albert's safety. Outwardly, she appeared happy and overcome with love for Johann. Inside, she was dying. She had no concern for her own well-being, and during the first few months of her marriage, she ate little and lost weight.

Four days after returning from their honeymoon, Johann moved Wilhelmina and Albert's belongings to his house on Glenmary Drive in the Gaslight District of Clifton Heights, four miles away and a thirty-minute streetcar ride from her closest friends. The sprawling three-story English Tudor rested atop a small hill, accessed by winding stone stairs. Cobblestone walkways and towering white birch trees encircled the mansion, while a lush courtyard boasting aromatic and colorful flowers comprised the back yard. A large carriage house stood several yards away and was accessible from the alley behind the house.

The large wood door led to a foyer with a colossal parlor to the right and an elegant dining room on the left, both with high ceilings. Each room featured stone fireplaces and luxurious, expensive furnishings. Persian rugs covered the gleaming wood floors, silk and velvet drapes hung at the windows from ceiling to floor, and the sofas and chairs in the parlor were covered in silk and brocade. The mahogany tables and chair arms glistened in the sunlight, the intricate carvings on the arms and legs waxed and buffed into brilliance. A glossy black grand piano sat atop an Oriental rug next to the large bay window at the front of the house.

Wilhelmina stared at her surroundings with awe; she had not enjoyed such luxury since leaving Germany. She stood frozen in the foyer, taking in the opulence surrounding her.

The mahogany table in the dining room featured delicate carvings along its entire length and was surrounded by eight thickly cushioned wood chairs with tall, straight backs. A massive China hutch rested along one wall while an equally large buffet stood on the opposite side of the room beneath another bay window.

Crystal chandeliers hung from the ceilings in both rooms and above Wilhelmina's head where she stood in the foyer. Directly in front of her, a sweeping staircase of marble and richly stained wood led to the second floor of the house.

"Well, don't just stand there, Mrs. King," he said, smiling. "Follow me. There is much to show you."

She lifted her valise and followed Johann up the winding staircase, which led them to a long hallway of shiny wood floors. Across from where she stood, a large, stained oak door stood ajar. She glanced inside and spotted black and white tiled floors and an oversized claw-foot bathtub. Two closed doors flanked both sides of the bathroom. Johann turned to his right and tipped his head, indicating for Wilhelmina to follow him.

He opened the door nearest the bathroom to reveal a spacious bedroom with furnishings as luxurious as those Wilhelmina had seen downstairs. The king-sized bed sat on a raised platform, satin curtains hanging from four posts beneath a cream-colored canopy. The posts, headboard and footboard all featured carved flowers and scrollwork, gilded with mother-of-pearl. A large fireplace sat opposite the foot of the bed while a large window across the room faced the courtyard at the back of the house. A massive armoire rested next to the window, a mirrored dresser beside the fireplace, and a roomy end table next to the bed, topped with a delicate lace doily and Tiffany lamp.

"This will be your room, Mrs. King," Johann said. They had been married a mere ten days and he still had not called her by her first name, only calling her "Anya" while having sex. During dinner one evening in Niagara Falls, Wilhelmina had asked him why he kept calling her Anya, and he dismissed her question with a wave of his hand and a mumbled, "I've done no such thing, Mrs. King. You forget yourself." She didn't bring it up again.

As she stood, drinking in the beautiful bedroom, Johann stepped toward the door and said, "My room is on the other side of the bathroom. The room next to yours will be Albert's, and the room at the other end of the hall will be for guests. There are two rooms on the third floor that are unoccupied. The stairs to the third floor are located just off the kitchen, as those rooms were originally meant for household staff.

"You will, of course, ensure that all rooms are cleaned. This means dusting the furniture daily, the carpets and drapes will be cleaned regularly, and the floors must glisten. You will launder the bed linens once a week. There are spare linens in each room."

As he droned on about her duties, Wilhelmina tilted her head. Had he married her to gain a housemaid, or did he, indeed, love her? This love, if that's what you called it, in no way resembled the love Oskar had shown toward her. A sharp twinge coursed through her chest as she thought about Oskar. She yearned for his gentle demeanor, his tender affection. She missed the love she had locked safely away in her heart for him. Now, her heart was empty. She felt nothing for this man who was now her husband. Nothing except fear and contempt.

"Mrs. King!" Johann shouted. "You must pay attention. There is much for you to learn and much to do to maintain this household." Wilhelmina stood straight and nodded. "Now, follow me to the kitchen, Mrs. King."

At the bottom of the stairs, Johann led Wilhelmina down a hallway where a butler pantry was accessed to the right of the back door, and to the left, the largest kitchen she had ever seen in her life. She barely heard Johann's instructions to prepare three hearty meals every day, wash, dry, and put away the dishes after every meal, and do all the shopping.

Johann opened a bank account for her and would deposit money into it each week to cover the household expenses—food, utilities, and the mortgage payment—and gave her enough cash each week to ride the streetcar to and from Albert's new school or the market and to do the shopping. She would not have access to Johann's car, and as he told her one evening, he would not teach her how to drive.

Albert started kindergarten at the St. Francis Seraph School located in their former neighborhood. Rooted in Franciscan values, the school focused on character development, morals, and overall well-being. Albert was a quick learner, obeyed the nuns and priests, and played with the other children. Johann forced Wilhelmina to leave the Lutheran church and convert to Catholicism, and the three of them attended Mass every Sunday morning at the St. Francis Seraph Church. Occasionally, when Johann was not needed at the hospital, the family attended the weekday morning masses as well. Wilhelmina did not care for the teachings of the Catholic church and attempted to discuss the matter with her husband. Whenever she brought it up, he would silence her by raising his hand, then say, "Have you forgotten what I said I would do if you disobey me?"

At home, like his mother, Albert was quiet and reserved. Johann was a strict stepfather and ruled his household with an iron fist. The child was made to always be quiet, and whenever Johann was home, Albert could only play in his room. Wilhelmina was expected to remain home all day, performing the chores, only venturing out to do the grocery shopping or to escort Albert to and from school.

During those excursions to the school, Wilhelmina sought out her friends in Over-the-Rhine. She now had a telephone in her new home, so she would call Karin and arrange to meet her and Marta once a week. But during the winter months, Karin became quite ill and Marta was nearing the end of her pregnancy, so they were unable to continue their meetings.

In January, Johann began calling the house several times a day to remind Wilhelmina of the duties he assigned her for that day and to ensure she was at home. One evening after Albert went to bed, Johann confronted Wilhelmina—he had not reached her by phone that day—and, after much yelling between the two, gave her a new rule: she was no longer permitted to leave the house. He had hired a nanny to take Albert to and from school and do all the shopping. During their argument, Johann grabbed his wife by the wrist and dragged her up the stairs to the empty third floor.

"Mrs. Henry will be here at six tomorrow morning," he said, "and this will be her room. You will clean it thoroughly and put clean sheets and blankets on the bed. Open the radiator so the room will be warm by morning. You will also have Albert dressed and fed by seven so Mrs. Henry can take him to school. You will *not* leave this house ever again. *Do you understand me?*" he said firmly, teeth clenching.

Johann's grip on Wilhelmina's wrist had tightened, and wincing in pain, she nodded.

"I cannot hear you, woman! I asked you a question—now *answer me!*" he shouted.

"Y-Y-Yes, I un-understand," she whimpered. "But … there's no t-time, Johann. I cannot possibly fin—"

"Silence! You have your orders. I want this room ready by tomorrow morning, even if it means you work all night. Now, do I have to *once again* remind you of what I will do? You don't want your precious Albert to be harmed, do you?" he snarled.

Tears flooded her eyes, and she sobbed, "N-N-No, sir."

"That's better. Now get to work."

Johann turned on his heel and took a step toward the door. Looking over his shoulder, he growled, "And cut that damn hair! You are too old to wear it that long. It must be no longer than an inch below your chin!" He stormed out of the room, leaving Wilhelmina shaking where she stood, hugging herself, trying to quiet her sobs.

The doorbell rang promptly at six the next morning, and wearing a soiled apron and her hair falling from its bun, Wilhelmina opened the door to a middle-aged, stout woman in a threadbare coat and gloves. She held a valise in one hand and an umbrella in the other, a brown handbag hanging from her bent elbow.

"Mrs. King, I presume," she said, and pursed her lips.

"Yes … Yes, please come in out of the cold," Wilhelmina said. "May I take your coat?"

"No, thank you. I prefer to keep all my things in my room. If you'll kindly show me the way, I'll deposit these and be on my way with your son."

It was obvious to Wilhelmina from the very start that Mrs. Henry was rigid and businesslike and would likely not become her confidant. Disappointed, she closed the door and led Mrs. Henry to the kitchen and up the stairs to the third floor.

An hour later Wilhelmina helped Albert with his coat and galoshes and hugged him goodbye while Mrs. Henry stood near the door, tapping her toe.

"Pardon my saying so, Mrs., but the boy will grow up to be a namby-pamby if you continue coddling him that way."

Wilhelmina rose to her full height, albeit she was still four inches shorter than Mrs. Henry, and said, "I *do* mind you saying so, Mrs. Henry, and I'll thank you to keep your opinions on my relationship with *my* son to yourself."

Mrs. Henry snorted, grabbed Albert's hand, and left the house. When she returned a few hours later, after dropping Albert at school and doing the grocery shopping, she stowed the groceries in the cabinets and new electric refrigerator. She then made herself a cold cut sandwich, poured a glass of milk, and sat at the small table in the center of the room. Mrs. Henry finished her lunch, rose from her chair, placed the dirty dishes in the sink, and left the kitchen.

In the utility room off the back porch, Wilhelmina loaded clothes into the washing machine. Clean sheets and towels were already drying on the rope tied between two pegs. Wiping a damp lock of hair from her face, she turned to leave the room, and spotted Mrs. Henry in the doorway.

"Dr. King has instructed me to accompany you to the beauty salon. Please ready yourself. Your appointment is in one hour."

Wilhelmina let out an exasperated sigh, the sound escaping her lips like a deflated balloon, betraying her sheer exhaustion and frustration. "He said nothing to me about it, and I was about to put a cake in the oven."

"I have my orders, Mrs."

Defeated, Wilhelmina climbed the stairs to the bathroom, ran a soapy cloth over her face and under her arms, and donned her bathrobe. In her bedroom, she put on a clean dress and brushed her long hair, staring blankly at her reflection in the mirror.

It was late afternoon by the time Wilhelmina and Mrs. Henry returned home. Wilhelmina rushed to the kitchen to make the rye bread and dessert for that night's dinner before chopping the vegetables for the stew. She worked quickly, painfully aware that Johann would be home by six o'clock—not leaving her much time to have everything hot and on the table upon his arrival.

Wilhelmina didn't see Mrs. Henry again until the woman silently walked into the kitchen at dinnertime, helped herself to a plate of food from the pots and pans, and sat at the table. The loaf of rye bread cooled on a rack on the counter while a cake baked in the oven, filling the kitchen with the warm, sweet aroma of apples, butter, sugar and cinnamon.

Mrs. Henry did not offer to help Wilhelmina set the dining room table or spoon the food into the serving dishes. In fact, Mrs. Henry did not speak to Wilhelmina whatsoever.

Johann seemed to be in good spirits over dinner that night as he recounted stories of his day at the hospital while he and Wilhelmina sat at opposite ends of the long table. Albert had already eaten and was upstairs taking his bath. He was never permitted to take his meals in the dining room or with the adults—one of Johann's many rules. Not once did Johann comment on her new haircut. Not once did he complement her cooking.

Wilhelmina listened intently to her husband, feigning interest in hopes of keeping him in a good mood. When he had finished another story and took a bite of the apple cake, she cleared her throat. His steel eyes flicked up from his plate, aiming down the table to where she sat.

"Johann," she began, her voice barely above a whisper.

"Speak up, Mrs. King. I cannot hear you."

She swallowed and began again, "Johann, may I have a word with you about Mrs. Henry?"

Johann placed his fork on the table with a bang, sighed heavily, and narrowed his lips into a thin slash. "If you must," he said.

"Well, it's just that," she said, "it's just that she is not very friendly. She criticized me for hugging Albert this morning and hasn't said a word to me since. She doesn't help with any of the chores, and—"

"Stop right there, Mrs. King," he growled. "Mrs. Henry was not hired as a maid or housekeeper. Her duties are to take Albert to and from school and go to the market. Your duties have been clearly defined, and as you know, you are not to leave this house unless accompanied by Mrs. Henry or myself. Now, that is final. I trust we will not have this discussion again, Mrs. King?"

Wilhelmina fought back hot tears and nodded. She stared at her half-eaten cake and rose from her chair.

"I'll start the dishes now. Your cigar and paper are ready for you in the sitting room," she said.

After several trips to and from the kitchen with the dishes, Wilhelmina finally settled at the sink and began washing, allowing her tears to flow freely. When she finished drying and putting everything away, she scanned the room to be sure it was spotless and flopped onto one of the metal chairs at the table, resting her head on her arms and sobbing. It was several minutes before she realized she had not gone upstairs to tuck Albert into bed, and she shot up from her chair.

Upstairs, she found her son sitting on his bed, already in his pajamas, holding his story book.

"Mama," he cried, "read to me?"

"Yes, love, of course," she said. She sat on the edge of the bed, took the book, and began reading his favorite story, *Jack and the Beanstalk*. As she read, she wished she could find a magic bean of her own, which would transport her and Albert away from this awful place, away from the monster who controlled every move she made.

Her prayers that night were the same as every night from the moment she married Johann. "Please, Dear Heavenly Father, if it is Your will, take us from this place. Take us away from that horrible man. Please deliver us from this nightmare."

But Wilhelmina was not delivered from her misery. In fact, her living nightmare would only become worse.

CHAPTER TWENTY

October 1929

BLACK TUESDAY
Billions Lost in Wall Street Stock Crash

The newspaper headlines throughout America were ominous—unprecedented sales of stock prompted the first crash on a Thursday in late October, with another the next day. Yet another plunge occurred the following Tuesday. Americans stormed their banks and financial institutions, demanding withdrawal of their money. On Black Tuesday, as it was being dubbed, investors traded nearly 16,000,000 shares of stock in a single day, resulting in billions of dollars lost.

Much speculation surrounded the cause of the crash; some blamed it on the rapid rise of the stock market during the 1920s. Others believed a decline in production, rising unemployment, and excessive debt contributed to the troubled economy. In the months following, public panic led to widespread bank runs with thousands of customers simultaneously withdrawing their funds. These sudden withdrawals caused banks to run out of money and face failure.

Many families lost their homes and livelihoods, some reaching poverty levels and homelessness. Southern states were hit hard the following year by a dust bowl, prompting thousands to migrate west in search of work and better living conditions. With money scarce for millions, people turned to bartering goods and services. Some took on odd jobs, from selling fruits and vegetables on street corners to doing laundry for wealthier families. Many planted their own gardens to reduce grocery costs.

Charitable organizations set up soup kitchens and breadlines, and those hit hardest by the Depression stood in line for hours for a free meal. Neighbor helped neighbor, sharing food, clothing and other necessities. Despite their hardships, community spirit was strong, and people relied on one another for support.

Wilhelmina and Johann were not exempt from the effects of the falling economy, and by early 1930, had to cut back on their personal spending. Cincinnati area hospitals, including Good Samaritan, faced financial difficulties and increased demand for services. They were forced to reduce staff salaries, including the surgeons, who had to work with limited resources in overcrowded conditions.

Johann instructed his wife to reduce the amount of food she prepared for each meal and discontinue making a dessert every day. He hired a young man to prepare an area of the backyard and allowed Wilhelmina to plant a vegetable garden. She grew onions, cabbage, tomatoes, potatoes, and herbs.

Johann parked his car in the carriage house and stored the keys, along with their money, in the safe he kept locked in his bedroom, the streetcar now his mode of transportation to and from the hospital. He gave strict orders to Mrs. Henry to buy less expensive cuts of meat and discontinue the purchase of unnecessary items like beer or wine. At night they reduced the lighting throughout the household and burned candles instead. Johann and Wilhelmina had often spent every evening after dinner in the parlor as he read the newspaper and she sewed, but the reduced lighting made these leisurely tasks difficult. He would often excuse himself quite early and head to bed, leaving Wilhelmina alone with her thoughts in the dimly lit room.

She still prayed daily for an escape from her prison, and although she was unhappy and her marriage loveless, she never lost her faith. She read the Bible as much as daylight would allow and often recited the many parables and stories to Albert. The family still attended Sunday Mass—the only day Johann would use his car—but St. Francis Seraph discontinued the weekday masses during the Depression. Wilhelmina was grateful for this as; even after four years of being Catholic, she still did not believe in all their teachings.

Johann rarely visited his wife after they retired to their separate bedrooms, but when he did, he would quietly walk into her room and slide into the bed next to her. Dreading the moment he climbed on top, Wilhelmina lay stiffly on her back and turned her face to the wall. He took his pleasure from her as she clenched the pillow beneath her head, pain searing through her body from his thrusts. He didn't kiss her, didn't touch her, and never said her name. When he was fully satisfied, he whispered the name "Anya" and rolled away. Johann then silently dressed and returned to his own room down the hall, locking his bedroom door behind him. This was the routine once or twice a month for the duration of their marriage.

∽

The first Thanksgiving and Christmas following the Great Crash held no joy for Americans … and certainly not for Wilhelmina. She had lost all contact with her friends, and Johann had no family in America, so the holidays floated by just as any other day. The house did not bustle with the activity Wilhelmina had come to know since living with her aunt and uncle—there were no special meals prepared, no friends gathering around the fireplace, no apple or pumpkin pies baking in the oven. The house stood bereft of holiday decorations, and at Christmas, no presents were exchanged.

On New Year's Eve, St. Francis Seraph Church opened their doors for Mass as its parishioners genuflected and prayed for better days. But January brought bitter cold temperatures to Cincinnati, causing more hardship than ever. Warm coats and gloves were difficult to find, much less affordable, and many contracted frostbite and respiratory illnesses. The harsh weather conditions contributed to numerous deaths, primarily from pneumonia, especially among the elderly and those without adequate shelter.

One evening at dinner, just as Wilhelmina rose from her chair, Johann raised a hand and cleared his throat. "Mrs. King," he said, "please sit back down. I would like a word with you."

Wilhelmina set the plates on the table and sank into her seat, hands poised in her lap, gaze wary.

"As you know, we have had to greatly reduce our spending these past few months, and I do not anticipate a recovery any time in the foreseeable future. Therefore, we must find other means of earning money to cover our expenses. Yes, yes, before you speak, I know you have taken in sewing, but it is not nearly enough for our needs. I have come to a decision. Now listen closely."

"Yes, Johann," Wilhelmina whispered.

"I have determined it in our best interest to take on a boarder and have interviewed numerous gentlemen and selected one who needs a warm room and home cooked meals. I have rented the second room on the third floor to Mr. Parker. Your duties will now include cleaning his room, cooking his meals and laundering his clothes. He is elderly, so you will be required to take his meals to his room. He will not dine in the kitchen or here in the dining room. Do you understand so far?"

Heat rose to Wilhelmina's cheeks as she squirmed in her seat and fiddled with the cross hanging from her neck. She focused on her lap, merely nodding.

"Very well, then," Johann said. "Further, Mr. Parker's breakfasts will consist of eggs and toast, or a piece of fruit—no bacon, sausage, or ham. He will drink coffee or tea, one cup only. For lunch, he will take a cold cut sandwich and one pickle spear. Now as for his dinners—pay close attention, Mrs. King—his dinners will be soup every night and one slice of bread, nothing more. He has been ailing and cannot stomach the same foods we eat. Are you following this, Mrs. King?"

Wilhelmina raised her head and gazed at Johann. "Yes, Johann, I understand."

"Now, this is the most important part for you to remember, Mrs. King. I have purchased an additional set of canisters and marked them accordingly as they are to be used only for any boarder we have in the house. Mrs. Henry will purchase sugar, flour, coffee, and tea to fill those canisters. You will use these for the meals you prepare for Mr. Parker. They will be kept in the pantry. When you prepare meals for our household, you will use the items in the canisters on the kitchen counter. Do not ever mix the two or use the wrong items. Mrs. Henry will also purchase other food items, such as canned goods, for the boarders and she will clearly mark them when she puts them on the pantry shelves. Is this clear, Mrs. King?"

She tilted her head slightly and furrowed her eyebrows. "I … Yes, well, I understand the instructions, Johan, but I do not understand why—"

Johann slapped his hand on the table. His voice raised higher and higher as he said, "Do not worry about why you are given these instructions. It is quite important that you follow them without fail. Do I have your word on this?"

Wringing her hands together in her lap, out of Johann's sight, Wilhelmina nodded and said, "Yes, Johann, I understand, and I will do as you say."

"Very well," he said.

"Johann, one question, if I may," said Wilhelmina.

"If you must."

"Who will collect Mr. Parker's rent?"

"Leave that to me, Mrs. King. Mr. Parker will pay room and board to me, and this will cover the cost of the food bought for his consumption. You only need to perform the duties I have given to you. Now, if you will excuse me, I believe I will retire to the parlor to read. Good night, Mrs. King."

"Good night, Johann," she replied as she stood.

Jacob Parker moved into the Glenmary Drive house on a dismal, snowy afternoon in late January 1930. A balding, rotund man, he burst into the house behind Johann and stamped his damp shoes on the wood floor. Wilhelmina's heart sank as the puddles grew beneath Mr. Parker's feet, and she mentally added the need to mop the floor to her long list of duties.

"Mrs. King," Johann said, "may I present Mr. Parker. Mr. Parker, this is Mrs. King."

Mr. Parker bowed his head, gave Wilhelmina a weak smile, and nearly doubled over in a fit of wheezing and coughing.

"Pardon me"—Mr. Parker coughed into a stained handkerchief—"forgive me. I have not been well."

"I understand, Mr. Parker. Allow me to show you to your room. I trust you can manage the stairs?"

Mr. Parker looked up at the winding staircase and hesitated.

"Oh, please forgive me," Wilhelmina said. "We will use the stairs off the kitchen. They lead to your room on the third floor. Please, allow me to carry your valise."

Wilhelmina took the valise from Mr. Parker and led him down the hall to the back of the house, into the kitchen, and up the stairs. She showed him the small bathroom he would share with Mrs. Henry and then opened the door to his room. Though sparsely furnished with a twin-size bed, rocking chair, nightstand and lamp, a small armoire and chest of drawers, the room was warm and cozy.

"I hope this room suits you, Mr. Parker. I am sorry we cannot offer you a larger one," Wilhelmina said.

"No, no, Mrs. King, this is fine. Just fine. Thank you. Now if you do not mind, I am quite tired. I believe I'll take a nap. What time shall I expect dinner?" Mr. Parker took the valise from Wilhelmina, his other hand resting on the doorknob.

"I will bring your dinner to you at five, if that is agreeable, Mr. Parker."

"Yes, yes, that will do. Thank you," he replied and shut the door.

Wilhelmina descended the stairs to the kitchen and began preparing pea soup for Mr. Parker's dinner, and sauerbraten made with pork—which had been marinading for several days—for Johann, Mrs. Henry, Albert and herself. She set about dicing onions, carrots, and celery and tossed them into a large pot of water on the stove. She added minced garlic, parsley, and bay leaves from the garden. She then retrieved the split peas from the refrigerator where they were soaking in water and poured them into the pot. She set the burner to a medium flame and walked across the hall to the butler's pantry to retrieve the ham bone she had saved from two nights ago, which she then added to the pot of soup.

Once she was sure the flame was not too high, she turned to the table where several washed potatoes were drying, which would be transformed into potato dumplings and served with the sauerbraten. Wilhelmina opened the previous day's newspaper and began peeling the potatoes, leaving the peels on the paper. Satisfied she had peeled enough potatoes, she dropped half of them into another pot and added water, then set it on the stove to bring to a boil. She then grated the remaining potatoes and put them in a large bowl. Using a cheesecloth, Wilhelmina squeezed out the extra water from the grated potatoes and poured the water down the sink. While the potatoes continued boiling on the stove, she measured out flour, salt, and black pepper.

Once the potatoes on the stove were soft, she drained the pot and began mashing them. She then added them to the bowl of grated potatoes, and stirred in the flour, salt, pepper, and eggs. Carefully,

Wilhelmina formed the mixture into numerous small balls, added a few pinches of breadcrumbs she had set aside earlier, and laid them on a large baking sheet. She covered the sheet with cheesecloth, and stowed it inside the refrigerator to cook later.

Wilhelmina glanced at the pendulum clock on the wall and removed her apron before heading up the stairs to the bathroom. Albert would be home from school soon. She washed her face and brushed her hair. In her room, she smoothed her dress, placed earrings on her lobes, and peered into the mirror.

What's happened to you, Wilhelmina? Where has your joy gone?

She was in the kitchen moments later, tasting the soup, when Albert ran in and threw his arms around her waist and squeezed. Wilhelmina laughed and, setting the spoon on the stove, turned to face her son and return the hug. They both then sat at the table as Mrs. Henry strolled into the room, glanced disapprovingly at Wilhelmina, and headed up the stairs to her room.

Certain Mrs. Henry was out of earshot, Wilhelmina took Albert's small hand and said, "Darling, Albert, did you have a good day at school?"

"Yes, Mama."

"What did you learn today?"

"I learned the times tables today and—"

"The times table? What is that, son?"

"You know, Mama, one times two equals two, or two times four equals eight. I really like mathematics, Mama."

"Oh, yes, yes, multiplication. Good boy. What else did you learn?"

"We learned about the Revo ... Revo ... Revolu ..."

"The Revolutionary War?"

"Yes, Mama, that's it. I can't say it very well yet. And, hmm ... Oh, yes, we learned about Mother Mary and practiced our pen ... penman ... penmanship."

"Good, good. Did you play with your friends today, Albert?"

"Yes, but Hans got in trouble again."

Wilhelmina sighed. "What did he do this time?"

"He was talking in class again. This time, he got Werner in trouble, too. Sister Marguerite slapped Hans's hand with a ruler, and she made both of them stand in corners. Mama, Hans was crying. Does it hurt to get hit with a ruler?"

"Yes, son, it does. That is why you want to always be a good boy in school and do everything the nuns tell you, and if Hans or any other boy tries to get you to do something bad, don't do it. Do you understand?" Wilhelmina was gentle with her son, her voice soft and soothing.

"Yes, Mama. May I play in my room now?"

"Yes, son. Your dinner will be ready soon. I love you."

Albert hugged his mother's neck and said, "I love you, too, Mama."

Mrs. Henry passed through the kitchen promptly at five-thirty that afternoon, walked down the hall, and called up the stairs for Albert.

"Master King!" she yelled. "It is time to wash up for dinner!"

Albert stepped into the hallway, closed his bedroom door, and said, "Yes, ma'am, but, ma'am, I keep telling you my name isn't … isn't King. It's Schmidt."

"Young man, do not be impertinent. Now wash up as you were told and come to the kitchen." Mrs. Henry scowled.

Wilhelmina stood at the stove, steaming not from the heat of the food cooking atop the flames … but from her own anger. She had, without success, mentioned to Johann numerous times about Mrs. Henry calling Albert "Master King," despite her continued efforts to correct the woman. Heat flushed her cheeks as she ladled broth and dumplings onto two nearby plates. She sliced the pork and placed moderate portions on each plate, then set both on the table.

As each thud of Mrs. Henry's footsteps echoed in the hall, Wilhelmina quickly turned back to the stove to avoid making eye contact. Albert bounded into the room a moment later and sat down.

"This smells good, Mama. Thank you for cooking," he said.

"You are welcome, son. Now say your prayers," she said with her back to him.

Mrs. Henry sat stiffly in her chair, fork and knife in hand, while Albert bowed his head and silently prayed. She did not partake in religious rituals, but she knew her place was to wait until her employers—or, in this case, her employer's son—took the first bite.

Wilhelmina turned to look at her son as he ate, then glanced at the clock again. She quickly walked up the stairs to Mr. Parker's room and lightly rapped on his door.

"Mr. Parker, have you finished? May I take your tray now?" she asked through the closed door.

"Yes, yes, Mrs. King, you may enter," he growled.

She opened the door and crossed the room to where he sat in the rocking chair taking his last drink of hot tea. He placed the cup on the saucer and handed it to Wilhelmina. She walked to the nightstand, where the tray held an empty bowl, and set the cup and saucer on it before picking up the tray.

"I'm afraid there is no dessert tonight, Mr. Parker. Mr. King only allows me to make dessert twice a week to save money. There will be dessert on Sunday and again on Wednesday. I do apologize."

"'Tis no matter, Mrs. King. I have had quite enough, thank you." He pushed up slowly from the chair with a groan and stood, waiting for Wilhelmina to depart. In the hallway she balanced the tray on one arm, and as she went to close the door, Mr. Parker sat on the bed and bent over, coughing violently. Her mind drifted back, so many years ago, to the illness she experienced on her travels from Germany to America, and the many who died during the Spanish Flu epidemic, including her Uncle Otto. She said a silent prayer for Mr. Parker, hoping he did not have pneumonia or some other disease that would infect her son, and made a mental note to remind Albert to never bother Mr. Parker.

Downstairs, Wilhelmina set the dishes in the sink and began ladling the dumplings and sauce into a serving dish. She carried the platter of pork to the dining room, returned for the dumplings, and then made another trip to grab the plates and silverware. She meticulously set the table, placing linen napkins on the empty plates, and retrieved two crystal goblets from the China hutch, and set them on the table. She absently smoothed her hair and walked back to the kitchen, where she removed her apron and glanced once again at Albert.

He's such a darling boy. He always eats everything on his plate and never complains. He is so precious to me. Keep him safe, Heavenly Father.

She returned to the dining room and stood behind her chair, waiting until Johann arrived. Moments later the front door opened and closed with a click, and Wilhelmina automatically squared her shoulders and raised her chin as she waited for him to enter the room.

They ate in silence until Johann set down his fork and rose from his chair.

"I'll be in the parlor, Mrs. King. Goodnight to you," he said.

"Goodnight, Johann."

The day ended as usual—Wilhelmina washed and dried the dishes and put them away. She wiped down the tables and countertops and turned out the kitchen light. Her feet dragged on the hallway floor, and she stood at the foot of the stairs, her hand on the newel post, and sighed deeply. She mustered her strength—her energy spent from the day of cleaning, mopping, laundry, and cooking—and climbed the stairs.

At the landing she turned to her right, walked to the second door, and knocked.

"Come in," Albert said.

She opened the door to find her son sprawled on the floor, flat on his stomach, a large book open in front of him.

"Hello, darling. I've come to say goodnight. Did you have your bath and brush your teeth?"

"Yes, Mama."

"Do you have any homework today, son?"

"Yes, Mama. I have to read this chapter about the war," he said, pointing to the book. "And then, I have three math ... mathe ... mathematics problems to solve."

"Do you need any help, honey?"

"No, Mama. I am almost done with my reading, and the problems are easy. I'll be done soon. I promise."

"All right, son. Be a good boy, and don't stay up too late. You still have another day of school before the weekend. Goodnight, sweet boy," she said and knelt to kiss the top of his head.

"Okay, Mama. Goodnight."

Wilhelmina quietly left Albert's room and headed for the bathroom, where she ran a bath and relaxed for a few moments. As she tiptoed to her bedroom, the light from the parlor went out, meaning Johann was heading upstairs. She quickly closed her door, hopped into bed, and turned out her light, praying he would not visit her tonight.

CHAPTER TWENTY-ONE

May 1930

Despite the overwhelming list of chores and the mounting difficulty, Wilhelmina quickly fell into a rhythm and turned the daunting list into a controllable routine. Each day brought a new set of challenges for her, from managing the load of planning and organizing to the physical effort of cleaning, maintaining the home, and cooking separate meals for Mr. Parker and the rest of the household.

Determined to please Johann—and thereby avoid his raging temper—she tackled each chore with her head held high. Her work was exhausting; every muscle in her body ached and she often found herself dozing off to sleep as she read or sewed in the parlor after dinner. Nonetheless, her perseverance shone through, and she was rewarded with fewer arguments from Johann. He treated her with a cool friendliness, albeit lacking in any real warmth or affection.

Mr. Parker coughed much less, hopefully recovering from whatever illness he had when first arriving at the house on Glenmary. He rarely ventured beyond his room, but when he did, he would stroll around the neighborhood or take a streetcar to run his own errands. His diet was meager—he only accepted soups and bread for his lunches and dinners and often ate nothing more than a piece of fruit or toast for breakfast.

As Wilhelmina stood to clear the dinner dishes from the table, Johann wiped his mouth with his napkin and cleared his throat. Wilhelmina hesitated to move; by now she was quite familiar with Johann's "ahem" as his way of letting her know he wanted a word with her. She subconsciously tightened her jaw, back stiffening.

"Mrs. King, I would like a word in private with Mrs. Henry. Please send her to the parlor," he said.

"As you wish, Johann," she replied as the tension faded into relief mixed with a hint of curiosity.

She carried the dishes into the kitchen, and glad to see Mrs. Henry still seated at the table—so she wouldn't have to climb those precarious stairs to the third floor—she said, "Mrs. Henry, Dr. King would like to speak with you right away. He is waiting in the parlor."

Mrs. Henry set her napkin next to the plate, eased up from the table, and sauntered out of the room. Wilhelmina set the dishes in the sink and turned to clear the small table, frowning. Once again, she had to clear Mrs. Henry's dishes.

Oh, I do hope he is going to fire that woman. She never clears her own dishes and never does anything around this house. I would be so happy to be rid of her!

Meanwhile, Johann settled into his chair in the parlor and lit a cigar while he waited for Mrs. Henry. He did not have to wait long, however, as she arrived a moment later.

"You asked to see me, Dr. King?" she said.

"Yes, yes, come in. Have a seat," he said, indicating the opposite chair. "Mrs. King has informed me there are rats in the cellar and, fearing they will infiltrate her kitchen, she has asked to purchase the necessary items to make rat poison. I need you to purchase five pounds of white cornmeal at the market and then go to Hoffman's Pharmacy. The order has already been placed with them by Mrs. King and is waiting under her name. I do not have time to pick up the order myself. Now, I want to be very clear on my next instruction, so please listen carefully."

"Yes, sir," Mrs. Henry replied stiffly.

"Do not give the items to Mrs. King when you return home. I fear she will not mix the ingredients properly, so I will take care of that. Keep the items in your room and I will retrieve them from you after dinner tomorrow night. I will show Mrs. King how to properly mix the ingredients. Always deliver the items directly to me. When I am certain she understands the correct mixture, I will allow her access to the items you pick up for her. Is that clear, Mrs. Henry?"

"Yes, sir, quite clear. Is there a particular time the order will be ready at Hoffman's?"

"After ten in the morning," he said as he handed her a small stack of bills. "Here is the money for the cornmeal and for the order at Hoffman's. All right, then. If you understand my instructions, I will now bid you goodnight."

"Yes, sir. Goodnight, sir," she said, pursing her lips as she stood. She took the money and strode from the room.

The next evening Johann rose from the table before Wilhelmina and left the dining room without a word. She did not know he had gone through the kitchen and up the stairs to Mrs. Henry's room. There he pulled on a pair of surgical gloves and retrieved the items Mrs. Henry had picked up earlier that day—the white cornmeal and several dark bottles of arsenic. He descended the stairs and peered around the doorway into the kitchen. Seeing no one there, he sped through the room, down the hall, and up the stairs to the spare room on the second floor. He stored the items there and closed the door, locking it and pocketing the key. In his room he removed the gloves and stuffed them into his jacket pocket; he would dispose of them at the hospital the next day.

After Wilhelmina finished the dishes, she stood in the doorway to the parlor until she caught Johann's eye.

"Yes, Mrs. King, what is it?" he said.

"I am quite tired tonight, Johann. I believe I will retire early, if that is agreeable with you."

"Yes, yes, that is fine," he said sharply as he folded his arms across his chest.

"Thank you. Well," she muttered, "goodnight then."

"Goodnight."

Johann sat in the parlor reading the newspaper and listened intently for Wilhelmina's footsteps on the floors above his head. He tossed the paper onto the coffee table and walked to the doorway and up the stairs. Standing on the top step, he stared at his wife's bedroom door, and once the light faded inside the room, he made his way down the hall to the spare room. A moment later, he emerged from the room carrying two dark bottles of arsenic in his gloved hands, locked the door behind him, and crept downstairs.

He turned into the pantry, flipped on the light, then located the canister marked "Boarder's Sugar" and opened it. He then uncapped the bottles and poured the entire contents into the sugar. Johann glanced around for a spoon and, not finding one, quickly moved across the hall to the kitchen, removed a spoon from the drawer, and returned to the pantry where he stirred the contents of the sugar canister. He replaced the canister lid, recapped the empty bottles, and shoved them into his pants pocket. He switched off the light as he left the pantry.

Johann carried the spoon to the kitchen and sterilized it with isopropyl alcohol which Wilhelmina stored in one of the cupboards. He then rinsed the spoon with hot water, dried it and returned it to the drawer. He opened the cupboard where Wilhelmina stored the alcohol, a few canned goods, and small jars of herbs and spices. Johann studied the cupboard carefully before pulling the empty bottles from his pocket. He then reached to the back of the cupboard and hid the bottles behind several cans of beans and peas. Chuckling softly, Johann closed the cupboard door and went upstairs to bed, pulling off the gloves as he walked.

Wilhelmina hugged Albert goodbye at the door while Mrs. Henry waited on the front porch and tapped her toe on the concrete.

"If you are a good boy at school today, Albert, I will make your favorite dessert this afternoon," Wilhelmina told him.

"Really, Mama? Streusel?" Albert grinned widely.

"Of course, my dear child. We will celebrate your last day of the fifth grade! Now, run along. You don't want to be late." She hugged him again and whispered, "I love you." Her heart swelling with adoration for her son, Wilhelmina stood at the door, waving, as Albert and Mrs. Henry descended the stone steps and turned left at the sidewalk. When they disappeared around the corner, she went back into the house and headed for the kitchen.

Surprised to find Johann there, she bumped into the doorway jamb. "Ouch! I-I didn't realize you had come downstairs, Johann. I'll get your breakfast right away," she said, rubbing her shoulder.

"Quite all right, Mrs. King," he said. "I know how tired you have been of late and thought I would surprise you by taking Mr. Parker's food to him this morning. I'll get the sugar and finish preparing his coffee while you make his breakfast."

"Thank you, Johann. That is … That is very kind of you," she said. "Last night, he asked for just toast and fruit. I'll get it ready now."

She crossed the room, picked up an apple, banana, and orange, and set them on the counter next to the cutting board. After dropping two slices of bread in the toaster, Wilhelmina began slicing the fruit while Johann went across the hall to the pantry to put sugar in a coffee cup. She had her back to Johann when he returned, so she never saw his gloved hands as he removed a small bottle from his pocket, and she was clueless that he poured the contents into the cup and hid the bottle in the cupboard. Before Wilhelmina could even turn, Johann quickly removed the gloves and pushed them into his pocket.

"The fruit is ready, and I'll butter the toast, Johann," she said as she crossed the room to the refrigerator to grab the butter.

While she buttered the toast, Johann poured coffee into the cup, added a dash of milk, and stirred the liquid. He stepped to the table and placed the cup on the tray. Wilhelmina came up from behind him, and set the fruit and toast beside the cup.

"Thank you for your help," she said, glancing at the clock. "Look at the time, Johann. You must be off to the hospital. I will carry the tray up to Mr. Parker. Have a good day."

"Yes, yes, you are right. I will be late if I do not leave now. Have a good day, Mrs. King," he said and left the room.

As she carried the tray carefully up the steps, she wondered what had put her husband in such a good mood. In the five years since they married, he had never once offered to help with her duties. She quickly dismissed his odd behavior as she left Mr. Parker's room and began attacking the day's chores.

At lunchtime she prepared a sandwich and lemonade for Mr. Parker and trudged up the stairs to his room. The constant going up and down was easily her least favorite part of her many tasks—up and down to deliver breakfast and again to retrieve the tray; up and down twice at lunchtime; up and down twice at dinner. Though just thirty years old, Wilhelmina was beginning to feel the effects of too much work and too little rest. Her body ached, and the skin beneath her eyes was thin and translucent, revealing the dark, sunken hollows that spoke of many sleepless nights.

At the top of the stairs, Mr. Parker's bedroom door stood ajar. Wilhelmina walked to the doorway and looked in—he was not in the room. She laid the tray on the nightstand next to the bed and turned to leave when violent retching came from the bathroom. She walked briskly down the hall and rapped on the door.

"Mr. Parker?" she said. "Are you all right?"

"No … No I am *not* all right, Mrs. King!" he shouted between retches. "I am quite ill. Please, help me get up!"

When opening the door, she found Mr. Parker on his knees, doubled over the toilet. His face was pale, and beads of sweat covered his forehead as he clutched his stomach and vomited again, his body convulsing with each heave. When he was sure he would not vomit again, he wiped his mouth with a cloth and reached for Wilhelmina. She rushed over, helped him to his feet, and supported him down the hallway to his room.

He flopped onto the bed and spotted the tray of food. His face twisted in disgust at the sight of it, as if the thought of eating caused his grimace.

"Please," he groaned, "take that away. I cannot eat."

"Of course, Mr. Parker. I will check on you later. Perhaps some nice chicken soup will do you good this evening."

"Yes, yes, please leave me alone now."

Wilhelmina pursed her lips, and crossing her arms across her stomach, said, "Of course, Mr. Parker." She turned and quickly left the room, shutting the door behind her. *Really! I was only trying to help, and he just rudely dismissed me. I must speak with Johann about this. I do not understand why we must have a boarder in the first place!*

He ate very little of the soup that evening and continued to have spells of vomiting. By morning his skin was red and swollen, and small warts and lesions began to appear. He complained of cramps in his legs and that his fingers and toes tingled. Wilhelmina paced the kitchen that afternoon, the vision of Oskar suffering many of the same symptoms washing over her, filling her with fear.

Mr. Parker's agonizing moans echoed down the stairs and filled every corner of the house. He cried out in pain, begging for someone to help, but Wilhelmina stood frozen in the kitchen, not knowing what to do. Mrs. Henry was at the park with Albert and wouldn't be any help, even if she were home.

Wilhelmina made up her mind; she must call the hospital. She raced into the parlor, picked up the phone and waited for the operator to come on the line.

"Please," Wilhelmina shouted, "I need an ambulance! Please connect me with the hospital! Quickly!"

"Yes, ma'am," droned the operator. "Please hold."

An eternity later, a new voice came on the line, saying, "Good Samaritan Hospital. How may I help you?"

"Please, this is Mrs. King of 14398 Glenmary Drive." Wilhelmina panted. "Please send an ambulance right away. I … We … There is an elderly man living in our home and he is quite ill. Please, hurry."

"Yes, ma'am. We will dispatch an ambulance right away," said the woman, and hung up the line.

Nearly an hour later two uniformed men carried Mr. Parker down the narrow steps to the kitchen, through the hall, and out the front door. They paused for a moment to catch their breath, then picked him up again and headed down the steps to the street where the ambulance waited. It pulled away from the curb, lights flashing and siren blaring, just as Mrs. Henry and Albert rounded the corner to head for home.

"Mama, Mama!" cried Albert as he ran to his mother. "What has happened, Mama?"

"Oh, Albert, Mrs. Henry, I am so worried," she cried. "Mr. Parker is quite ill. He is going to the hospital."

Mrs. Henry clicked her tongue, skirted past Wilhelmina and Albert, and climbed the steps to the house.

"Mama, maybe he will be all right," Albert said. "There, there, Mama, come inside. I'll pour you a glass of lemonade."

"Yes, Albert, let's go inside. You are such a good boy."

"You always take care of *me*, Mama. Now it's my turn to take care of *you*."

The two walked hand in hand into the house. Inside, Wilhelmina told Albert to run upstairs to wash his hands for dinner as she turned into the parlor, the promise of lemonade forgotten. She picked up the phone, once again asked for Good Samaritan Hospital, and when the hospital operator came on the line, she asked to be connected to Dr. Johann King.

Several minutes later Johann came on the line. "Hello? This is Dr. King," he said.

"Johann, it is me, Wilhelmina. Something terrible has happened."

"I was about to head home, Mrs. King. Could this not wait until I arrive?" he said, voice full of annoyance.

"No, no, I'm sorry, Johann, it cannot. Mr. Parker has been quite ill since last night, and today I called for an ambulance. They took him to your hospital. Johann, could you … would you please check on him before coming home? I can keep dinner hot."

"Oh, all right! I'll check on him, but then I'll be home straight away," he said and hung up the phone.

Wilhelmina finished preparing that night's dinner and placed Albert's food on the kitchen table. She then spooned out schnitzel and mashed potatoes for Mrs. Henry and set the plate on the table across from Albert's. Both entered the room simultaneously and sat down to eat while Wilhelmina finished filling serving bowls and platters. She carried the food to the dining room table just as the front door opened and Johann strode into the dining room.

He took his seat and placed his napkin on his lap. Wilhelmina left the room, retrieved two glasses of lemonade, and went back to the dining room. She set Johann's glass on the table, walked to the far end, and took her seat. Johann muttered a prayer and began eating. Wilhelmina sat still in her seat, staring down the long table at her husband.

Johann glanced over and stopped chewing. "You are not eating, Mrs. King," he mumbled.

"Johann, I-I cannot eat a bite until I know"—she squeezed her hands together in her lap— "until I know how Mr. Parker is."

"After dinner, Mrs. King. This is not the place to discuss such matters. Now eat," he ordered.

She managed to eat most of her dinner, cleared the table, and began doing the dishes. Johann stood at the kitchen doorway and said, "Come to the parlor when you are finished here, Mrs. King."

"Of course, Johann. I'll only be a few minutes."

Mrs. Henry left the kitchen and went upstairs to her room, once again without a "thank you" or a "goodnight." Albert jumped up from his chair and helped his mother by drying the dishes and stacking them on the counter for her to put away. When she had finished all the dishes and wiped the stove, counters, and table, she kissed Albert.

"It's time to take your bath, honey. Now run along. I'll be up shortly to tuck you into bed," she told him.

"Yes, Mama," he replied and sped off down the hall.

Wilhelmina placed her towel on the counter and headed for the parlor. She crossed the room and sat on the chair opposite Johann, folding her hands in her lap. She waited silently until Johann spoke.

"Mrs. King, I will need you to gather Mr. Parker's clothes and put them in his valise. You will then need to strip his bed and launder the linens. The third-floor bathroom must be thoroughly scrubbed and sanitized."

"Of course, Johann, but—"

"Mr. Parker has died."

Wilhelmina's jaw dropped open as tears pooled in her eyes.

"Wh ... *What*?"

"I am sorry, Mrs. King, but he has died. He had gastroenteritis. Quite common in a man of his age," Johann said as he lit a cigar.

Her voice barely above a whisper, Wilhelmina said, "Just like Os—"

"That is enough, Mrs. King. Now, you best get started."

"*Tonight?* You want me to do all that *tonight*??" Wilhelmina's eyes widened, and the overflowing tears trickled down her cheeks.

"Of course, tonight. You must rid the room of his germs," he barked. "I will start looking for another suitable boarder tomorrow."

"Please, Johann ..." she said, and swallowed. "Must we have another boarder? It is so much work and—"

"Enough, Mrs. King! Now I will explain this once again, and perhaps this time, you will understand. Our funds have dwindled since the crash, and we need a boarder to help with our household expenses." He held up a hand as Wilhelmina opened her mouth. "And do not question me about the groceries. I have Mrs. Henry buy our food separately from the food consumed by the boarder so that I know how much to charge in room and board. Once again, Mrs. King, none of this is your concern. Your only duty is to maintain this household as I have instructed. I trust you understand?"

"Y-Y-Yes, Johann," she whispered.

"Best get to your work then," he said.

Wilhelmina rose and walked to the kitchen, her shoulders slumped and her feet dragging over the floor. She spent most of the night cleaning Mr. Parker's room, and when she finally finished at three in the morning, she filled the valise with his clothes and set it next to the front door for Johann to remove when he left for the hospital.

Tired as she was, Wilhelmina did not fall asleep right away. She lay in bed, tears streaming down her cheeks and soaking the pillow beneath her head. *Why, oh why, did I ever agree to marry that man? I thought my life would be easier, living in such a luxurious home, but it is not. So tired ... I'm so tired.*

She fell asleep a mere hour before her alarm clock rang and woke her to start yet another monotonous day of exhausting work.

CHAPTER TWENTY-TWO

October 1930

Ernst Müeller moved into the third-floor bedroom in September, and Wilhelmina's brief two-month respite came to an end. Johann lectured her once again about the duties he expected her to perform. He reminded her she was not permitted to leave the house, and Mrs. Henry would continue doing all the shopping and picking up prescriptions and other necessities as directed by Johann.

Mr. Müeller was only a few years younger than Mr. Parker and, at age seventy-two, was in good health. Unlike Mr. Parker, he was a pleasant man who teased Albert and offered his assistance to Wilhelmina. He carried his own tray of food to his bedroom or took his meals in the kitchen. He lugged his own laundry to the first floor and often helped Wilhelmina dry and put away the dishes. Mr. Müeller was careful to lend a hand only when Johann or Mrs. Henry were not at home; he learned early on that Johann ran a strict household and treated his wife as a servant rather than a partner in life.

For Albert's tenth birthday, Mr. Müeller presented him with an electric Lionel train set and helped set it up in Albert's room. The two sat on the floor on many afternoons after Albert arrived home from school and watched the train cars chugging round and round the tracks. He kept an eye on his pocket watch to ensure he was in his own room or in the kitchen when Johann came through the door every evening, ensuring the two would not be caught playing with the train set.

Wilhelmina warmed to Mr. Müeller from the start and enjoyed their conversations in the kitchen while they snapped green beans or peeled potatoes. He made her laugh—something she had not done in a very long time—and her long days of hard work somehow seemed easier. Soon he began calling her "Miss Wilhelmina" and insisted she call him by his first name.

Johann rarely visited Wilhelmina's bed these days, for which she was thankful, but he remained in the parlor long after she retired to her own room. As before, Wilhelmina did not know that Johann was busy adding arsenic to the sugar in the pantry, two bottles at a time. Wilhelmina never noticed her supply of canned goods in the cabinet never seemed to deplete; Johann meticulously restocked the cabinet, ensuring the bottles of arsenic remained well hidden.

Ernst was dressing for bed one evening when a sudden wave of nausea hit him. He raced to the bathroom and began to vomit. Finally feeling somewhat better, he washed his face and walked to the bathroom door when yet another wave hit. He coughed and gagged loudly, and although Mrs. Henry was awake in her room next door and most certainly could hear him, she did not come to check on him. Nearly an hour later, weak and sweating, he made his way back to his room where he slept fitfully.

He did not go to the kitchen the next morning, and when Wilhelmina knocked on his door, a tray of food propped on one arm, he merely groaned from his bed. Wilhelmina set the tray on the floor and cracked open the door. She covered her mouth, stifling a gasp at the sight before her. Ernst was sweating profusely and writhing in bed, holding his stomach. His skin was chalky and dotted with bloody lesions. Wilhelmina started to back away when Ernst raised an arm and reached for her.

"Help … Help me, please," he said breathlessly as he winced with pain. "Call a doctor."

Wilhelmina nodded and sped down the hall to the stairs. She ran as quickly as she could to the first floor, through the kitchen, and to the parlor where, her hands shaking, she lifted the phone to her ear. "Yes, operator," she said, "Please send an ambulance …"

Two hours later the coroner's hearse idled on the street in front of 14398 Glenmary Drive. Michael Wilson, the county coroner, stood on the porch speaking with two police officers. He then walked into the house and found Wilhelmina crying in the parlor.

"Mrs. King?" he said.

She looked up, wiped her eyes, and nodded.

"We are ready to leave. Do you know if Mr. Müeller had any family?"

"No, no, he had no one. His wife died many years ago, and they had no children. He has no other family in America. I-I … He … He only came to live with us a month ago. I'm sorry, I don't know anything more about him."

"Quite all right, Mrs. King. If you like, I can call you once I've completed a more thorough examination at the hospital … to let you know the …" He cleared his throat and continued, "To let you know the cause of death, you see."

"Y-Yes, please. He seemed to be in good health. Y-Yes, please call me. I'll write my number down for you."

"Thank you. I will call you in a few days," he said and left the house.

Wilhelmina lifted the phone receiver to her ear. "Good Samaritan Hospital, please."

The operator paged Johann, but he did not respond, so Wilhelmina left a message for him to call home right away. The phone rang soon after she sat down to eat her lunch, and she ran to the parlor to answer it.

"Mrs. King, why did you call me at the hospital today?" he growled.

"I-I am s-s-sorry, Johann, but it has, it has …" She began to sob loudly.

"For God's sake, woman, calm yourself. What has happened?"

"Mr. Müeller has died. The coroner took him away. Oh, Johann, I did not know what to do!"

Johann sighed heavily on the other end of the phone. "Well, then, since you took care of everything, I fail to understand why you felt it necessary to call me. Must I remind you yet again, Mrs. King, that I am a busy man? Do I need to remind you of your duties? Indeed, do I need to remind you that your disobedience could result in harm to your precious Albert? *Answer me!*" he grumbled.

Wilhelmina choked back another sob. "N-N-N-No, Johann. You are … You are right. I-I-I should not have bothered you."

"Very well, then. Goodbye," he said, and the phone went dead.

A week later, Wilhelmina answered the phone and learned from Mr. Wilson that Ernst Müeller had seemingly died from cardiovascular disease and showed signs of abnormal heart rhythms and "circulatory collapse." Wilhelmina thanked him before hanging up the phone, but did not fully understand the diagnosis.

And she was far too afraid to ask Johann about it.

May 1931

Mrs. Henry stood in the doorway to the parlor one Saturday afternoon and cleared her throat. Johann glanced up at her over the newspaper he was reading, folded it, and placed it on his lap.

"Come in, Mrs. Henry. Please, have a seat," he said. "What can I do for you?"

"Dr. King, I am afraid I must leave your employment," she said, hands clasped on her lap. "Master Albert is nearly eleven now and no longer requires a nanny. And my rheumatism is making it quite difficult for me to climb those stairs these days. And ..."

"Please, go on, Mrs. Henry," Johann said.

"My sister's husband is quite ill, and she has asked if I would come live with them in Cleveland. I have accepted and need to leave as soon as possible. I am sorry for the short notice, Dr. King."

"Quite all right, Mrs. Henry, quite all right. You are quite correct—Albert no longer requires a nanny, and he can make his own way to and from school. I will arrange to have our groceries and other items delivered. You have served my household well, Mrs. Henry, and I thank you. Please, make the necessary arrangements and best of everything to you."

"Thank you, Dr. King. You are most kind," she said.

Mrs. Henry moved out of the house two days after Albert's school term ended, much to Wilhelmina's glee. She would finally be alone with her son and able to spend more time with him, and Albert had already promised his mother to help her around the house over the summer. Johann had brought in a new boarder—Karl Berger—in March, but as with the first boarder, he stayed in his room most of the time, so Wilhelmina was forced once again to lug trays of food up and down the stairs, as well as the bed linens, towels, and Mr. Berger's clothes.

The local grocers delivered food and necessities weekly, and Johann picked up prescriptions from Hoffman's Pharmacy as needed, as well as the supply of arsenic he kept locked in the spare second-floor bedroom. Wilhelmina was still not permitted to leave the house, but she was able to find time to work in her vegetable garden and play in the courtyard behind the house with Albert. Johann began calling the house twice a day to be sure Wilhelmina was home, so whenever outside, she kept a close eye on the time so she'd be ready and waiting. Every day at the same time, she'd patiently sit next to the phone and pick up as soon as it rang. She despised Johann for his controlling ways, but because of her concern for Albert's safety, she kept her mouth shut and did everything Johann demanded.

Mr. Berger was a quiet man; he only spoke to Wilhelmina to thank her for his meals and clean clothes. He often gave her a warm smile but found it unnecessary to carry on a conversation or befriend Wilhelmina or Albert. He broke his silence one sunny afternoon in June.

Standing in the hall outside his bedroom, Mr. Berger shouted, "Someone, help me, please!"

Wilhelmina was busy dusting the furniture in the parlor while Albert sat in the kitchen. When he heard Mr. Berger shouting, he stood at the bottom of the stairs and shouted, "Mr. Berger? Are you all right?"

Mr. Berger moaned loudly, and the sound of his fast-paced footsteps over the floor above followed. Gut-wrenching choking noises came from the upstairs bathroom.

"Mama!" Albert called. "Mama, I think something is wrong with Mr. Berger!"

Wilhelmina dropped the feather duster and ran to the kitchen.

"No, no, no," she cried. "Please, don't let …" Her voice trailed off as she fled up the stairs. She shouted behind her, "Albert, stay where you are!"

She reached the bathroom and found Mr. Berger in the same kneeling position over the toilet she had seen too many times before. He was heaving over the toilet, spewing out the day's meals. The all-too-familiar beads of sweat had formed on his forehead and those ghastly warts already covered his hands. Wilhelmina clutched the cross hanging from her neck and prayed as she watched in horror, unable to move.

Several minutes later, Mr. Berger pushed up from the floor and, spotting Wilhelmina in the doorway, gasped. "Pl-Please, Mrs. King. Close the door. I believe I have the runs now."

Wilhelmina stepped back and shut the door. She turned into the second bedroom—previously occupied by Mrs. Henry—and sat on the edge of the bed. Her foot bounced up and down involuntarily as she wrung her hands and rocked back and forth.

"Please," she whispered. "Please, God, not again. Please let him be all right."

Mr. Berger's condition worsened over the next four days. He could no longer get out of bed, and Wilhelmina found herself emptying pans of vomit and diarrhea several times a day. As she cleaned the pans, waves of nausea coursed through her. Would she succumb to the same disease now infecting Mr. Berger?

On the fifth day, Mr. Berger asked Wilhelmina to call his cousin who lived a few miles away. "Please, Mrs. King," he rasped, "he has a car and will take me to the doctor." He gave his cousin's name, and within the hour his cousin, Victor, helped Mr. Berger to the alley behind the house and into the car.

"I will let you know what the doctor says, Mrs. King," said Victor Berger. "Thank you for all you have done for my cousin."

The call from Victor came two days later—Karl Berger had died of gastroenteritis. "Mrs. King, I will stop by later today to collect Karl's belongings."

The phone fell from Wilhelmina's hand to the floor as she sank into the chair, dizzy and shivering. She was once again faced with telling Johann that another boarder had died.

Johann took the news in stride. He showed no emotion and merely announced he would acquire yet another new boarder.

❧

Albert entered the sixth grade that fall and easily found his way to the streetcar that would deliver him to the St. Francis Seraph School. By November, Johann moved the fourth boarder into the house. Ludwig Klein, sixty-eight, hobbled into the kitchen one evening after dinner and, leaning on his cane, waited patiently for Johann to introduce him. Johann handed Mr. Klein's suitcase to Wilhelmina, and she led the way up the three flights to the bedroom.

While he did not help Wilhelmina with any chores as Mr. Müeller had done, Mr. Klein was pleasant and often took his meals in the kitchen. He helped Albert with his English and science homework but was at a complete loss when Albert ciphered his math problems with ease. He helped Albert cut the cake on his eleventh birthday but did not give the boy a present.

In January, Mr. Klein struggled with a case of bronchitis, which quickly turned into pneumonia. Wilhelmina nursed him for weeks until he was well enough to venture to the kitchen once again. But February brought bitter cold to Cincinnati, and Mr. Klein took a turn for the worse.

In March, he began vomiting and hacking and spent hours in the third-floor bathroom. He took to his bed, complaining of muscle aches and tingling in his toes. Wilhelmina once again paced the floors during the day and slept little at night, racked with worry. Would Mr. Klein fall prey to the same illness that had taken the others?

On a bright, breezy day at the end of March, an ambulance took Mr. Klein to the hospital. He had spent two days vomiting, his skin clammy and ashen, and lesions had developed on his face. Ludwig Klein died on April 2, three days before his sixty-ninth birthday, from apparent gastroenteritis. Johann once again assured Wilhelmina the disease was common for elderly men, and she was not to fret over it.

Johann did not find another boarder until a year later. A cool April rain had just ended, and while Albert and Wilhelmina crouched together on the front porch, sorting rotten tomatoes from good ones, a thin, gray-haired man trudged up the stone stairs from the street and hobbled toward them.

"Hello," he said as he approached. "I am August Weiss. I trust you are Mrs. King?"

Wilhelmina glanced at Albert and pushed up from the ground, extended her hand, and said, "Yes, I am. Please, come in, Mr. Weiss. Albert, please take the suitcase up for me, will you?"

"Yes, Mama," Albert said. He took the case from Mr. Weiss and held the front door open.

As they walked to the back of the house, Wilhelmina told Mr. Weiss what time she would serve his meals and informed him of the days she did the laundering—clothes on Monday, towels on Wednesday, and bed linens on Friday. She told him he could either take his meals in his room or eat in the kitchen with Albert. As they reached the pantry, she showed him the canisters and other food items marked "Boarder" and explained that these were for his consumption alone.

"Dr. King runs the household with efficiency, you see," she explained. "He must keep track of how much you consume so as to know what to charge for your room and board each month."

"Yes, yes, quite understandable," Mr. Weiss said. "He explained it all to me when we met last week."

"Good, good. Here's the kitchen, and the stairs to your room are just over there. Allow me to lead the way," she said as she skirted around him.

After showing Mr. Weiss his room and the bathroom, she told him dinner would be ready at six o'clock and please let her know if he wanted to eat in his room or in the kitchen. He said he would let her know in plenty of time and ushered her out the door, closing it in her face.

As she made her way down the stairs and out to the front porch, she silently repeated the prayer that had become her mantra for eight long years: *I am weary, Lord, and oh, so tired. Please protect my beautiful son and deliver us from this horrible life.*

As the cool days of April faded, Ohio was transformed into the warm, golden embrace of May. The sun rays danced through budding leaves, casting speckled shadows on the ground, while the air filled with cheerful birdsong and the sweet aroma of blooming flowers. The pleasant weather lured Mr. Weiss out to the courtyard to read a book or watch Wilhelmina working in her garden while he sipped fresh lemonade. Though he spoke sparingly, his words ofttimes carried an air of sincerity. He chose his words carefully, frequently redirecting any conversation with Wilhelmina to her life experiences. Soon, though, he began to feel a genuine connection with Wilhelmina and shared glimpses into his own life with her.

Albert formed a bond with Mr. Weiss from the start, however, a bond evident in the way they pored over Albert's mathematics books, solving problems and discussing theorems. Mr. Weiss had been an accountant in Germany before coming to America, and Albert expressed his love for math with the elderly man. The two spent many afternoons after school playing chess, Albert's enthusiasm for learning the game matched by Mr. Weiss's patient guidance. Wilhelmina stole glances at the two, a tender smile forming on her lips.

At the end of the school year, Mr. Weiss appeared in the kitchen with a package under his arm.

"Excuse me, Mrs. King," he said, "is Albert home from school yet?"

"No, he isn't, Mr. Weiss," she replied. "He should be home any moment now. Would you like a glass of lemonade?"

"Yes, that would be lovely. I believe I'll wait for the lad on the front porch."

"All right," she said. "I'll be happy to bring your lemonade to you there."

Mr. Weiss nursed his lemonade while he sat under the shade of the porch roof, waiting for Albert to arrive. Wilhelmina stood at the doorway watching him for a moment, head cocked. The beautifully wrapped package sat on the table next to Mr. Weiss, so obviously curious, Wilhelmina opened the door and stepped outside. "May I join you, Mr. Weiss?" she asked.

"Yes, yes, of course."

They sat in silence while Mr. Weiss rocked in his chair and Wilhelmina fanned herself. Before long, they both looked up as Albert jogged up the steps, two at a time, grinning widely.

"Mama, Mr. Weiss!" he shouted.

"Hello, Albert," Mr. Weiss said. "How was your last day of seventh grade?"

Albert hugged his mother and turned to Mr. Weiss. "It was good. I got mostly A's this year." Turning to Wilhelmina, he said, "I'm sorry, Mama, but I only got a C in religious studies. I will try to do better next year."

"Oh, son, do not worry. I am very proud of you, my boy," she said, her smile emulating the pure joy and adoration she held for her son, eyes crinkling at the corners.

"Albert, come and sit here by me," Mr. Weiss said, indicating a spot on the porch at his feet. "I have a present for you."

Albert glanced at his mother, who nodded, and he flopped down onto the porch. Mr. Weiss handed him the package and Albert carefully removed the bow and ribbon. He then tore at the blue striped paper, revealing a large textbook. Albert turned the book over in his hands to reveal the title, *Essentials of Geometry* by Webster Wells and Walter W. Hart. Albert squealed with delight and jumped to his feet in front of Mr. Weiss.

"Oh, thank you, Mr. Weiss!" he said. "Thank you *so* much!" He then carefully set the book on the small table and threw his arms around Mr. Weiss's neck.

Mr. Weiss chuckled and said, "There, there, son, you are most welcome. There are newer math books available today, but this one will give you additional insights into geometry and help with your class next school year."

Wilhelmina sat in her chair with a hand on her chest, tears forming in her eyes. She smiled at Mr. Weiss and squeaked out a whispered, "Thank you."

After that day, Mr. Weiss ventured outdoors more often and chatted with Wilhelmina while she toiled in her garden or hung laundry out to dry. Wilhelmina began to open up to him and talk about her life as a child in Germany, including her arduous travels to America. She told him about Oskar and the friends she left behind in

Over-the-Rhine. She never discussed her marriage to Johann with Mr. Weiss—and he did not ask.

July brought sweltering days with temperatures soaring above ninety degrees. As dusk approached on one such evening, the sky began to darken ominously, heavy clouds rolling in from the west. The air grew thick and still, a palpable tension building as the first distant rumbles of thunder echoed across the city.

A brilliant flash of lightning split the sky, illuminating the rooftops and casting eerie shadows on the ground. The thunder that followed was a deep, resonant boom, shaking windows and sending a shiver down Wilhelmina's spine as she tore the sheets from the clothesline and raced into the house. The wind picked up, rustling the leaves and sending dust and loose papers skittering down the streets.

As the storm moved closer, the heavens opened, releasing a torrential downpour. Rain hammered against the cobblestone streets, creating rivers that flowed toward the gutters. People hurried to find shelter, feet splashing through puddles as they sought refuge under awnings and in doorways.

The storm raged on with lightning flashing in rapid succession, each bolt followed by a deafening clap of thunder. The rain continued to pour, drenching everything in its path and bringing a much-needed respite from the day's heat. The scent of wet earth filled the air, and the distant sound of car horns mingled with the occasional shout from someone braving the storm.

Safe inside the kitchen, Wilhelmina shook out the damp sheets and began hanging them on the line she had strung across the room. She wiped her wet brow with the back of her hand and turned to the stove to stir the potato soup she had prepared for Mr. Weiss's dinner. Albert was sitting at the table, forming dough into oval balls and placing them on a cookie sheet.

"Albert," she said, "please go upstairs to see if Mr. Weiss is dining down here or in his room tonight."

"Yes, Mama," he said. Albert walked to the sink, washed and dried his hands, and then ran up the steps to the third floor. He reappeared in the doorway moments later and stood, rubbing his hands down the front of his pants, eyes wide with dread.

"Mama ..." he said.

Wilhelmina turned to her son and said, "Oh, goodness! You startled me, son. I did not hear you come down the—what is wrong, son?"

"Mama, it's …" Albert choked back a sob. "It's Mr. Weiss, Mama. He is in the bathroom, and he's really sick."

Oh, dear God, NO!

Wilhelmina lowered the flames on the stove and, pushing past her son, flew up the stairs to the third floor. She stopped short of the bathroom door as the familiar sounds of violent retching reached in her ears. She touched the doorknob and screamed just as a loud clap of thunder reverberated throughout the house. Taking deep breaths, she slowly opened the door and peered inside.

Mr. Weiss was on his knees in front of the toilet, vomiting and sweating profusely. He rocked back and forth between waves of overwhelming nausea and wiped his mouth with a wet cloth. He spotted Wilhelmina at the door and reached for her with swollen hands covered in lesions.

"Please …" he croaked. "Call … Call my … my doctor."

"Who …?" Wilhelmina could not find words and clapped her mouth shut, her body shaking with fear.

"Dr. Burdine … Robert Burdine. Please … hurry." And he vomited again.

Wilhelmina hurried to the parlor and placed the phone call. The doctor arrived within the hour, examined Mr. Weiss, and called for an ambulance. Wilhelmina and Albert listened from the hall outside the parlor. The doctor muttered the words "emergency," "critical," and "gastroenteritis." Wilhelmina's knees buckled, and she put a hand on Albert's shoulder to steady herself. Albert put his arm around his mother's waist and helped her to the kitchen, where she slunk into a chair, her face white as snow.

"Mama?" Albert said. "Mama, should we finish making dinner for … for … Dr. King? Mama … please, Mama, I don't want him to shout at you again."

Wilhelmina shook her head to clear the cobwebs in her mind and gazed blankly at Albert.

"What …?" she said. "Oh, yes, yes, Albert, you are … you're right."

She walked to the stove, raised the heat beneath the sauerbraten, and turned off the flame beneath the pot of soup. She then put the sheet of rolls into the oven and checked the clock. She and Albert then carried the dinner dishes to the dining room and set the table. In the kitchen, she dished out Albert's portion of sauerbraten and removed the rolls from the oven. She placed one on his plate and cut off two slices of butter, adding them to his plate, and carried the butter dish to the dining room.

She was about to head back to the kitchen when the doctor emerged from the parlor.

"Mrs. King, I have an ambulance on the way to take Mr. Weiss to the hospital. He is quite ill. I will be there when he arrives. Thank you for calling me. I will let you know tomorrow how he is doing, if that is all right."

"Mm ... hmm," she mumbled and nodded.

The doctor opened the door just as Johann stepped onto the porch.

"Oh, excuse me, sir! I am most sorry," Dr. Burdine said.

Johann scowled and said, "And my I ask who you are, sir?"

"Yes, yes, I am sorry. I am Dr. Burdine. Your wife called my office. Mr. Weiss is quite ill. An ambulance is on its way here now."

"I see. Well, then, I trust you will be on your way?" Johann's voice was a cold monotone, each word dripping with calculated malice.

"Yes, yes, of course. Good day, sir," said Dr. Burdine.

Johann stepped inside and shut the door without another word to the doctor. Wilhelmina walked quickly to the kitchen and began transferring the food on the stove to the serving dishes. She entered the dining room just as Johann took his seat at the end of the table, and she sighed with relief.

A cloud of tension hung over the table as they ate in silence. Wilhelmina struggled to swallow each bite, terror building with each passing moment. Johann took one last sip of lemonade, wiped his mouth, and rose from his chair. He set the napkin on the table and left the room. Wilhelmina sat rigid in her chair and prayed for Mr. Weiss before she stood and cleared the table, but stopped when she heard a knock at the front door. She stepped into the hallway in time to see

Johann leading two uniformed men toward the kitchen. Moments later, the ambulance carrying Mr. Weiss pulled away from the curb and aimed for the hospital.

Albert helped his mother with the dishes and headed up the stairs to take his nightly bath. Wilhelmina put the last of the dishes away and aimed for the stairs as well but was stopped by Johann calling her name.

"Mrs. King, a word, please," he droned.

She closed her eyes and swallowed. Resting her hand on the wall outside the parlor, she squared her shoulders and stepped toward the doorway. She crossed the room slowly and stood at the end of the sofa.

"Sit, Mrs. King."

She sat on the sofa, as far from Johann as possible, and folded her hands in her lap.

"Mrs. King," he said flatly, "it seems we have acquired yet another ill boarder, does it not?"

"Yes, Johann, it appears so." Wilhelmina dropped her gaze to her lap.

Johann lit a cigar, stood, and paced in front of the fireplace.

"I have just today decided that Mr. Weiss would be our last boarder. Should he return to this house, I will inform him that his stay here will come to an end on August 31."

Wilhelmina's head shot up, her eyes bright with relief.

"Oh, thank you, Johann," she said.

"You are most welcome, Mrs. King. I have noticed your health seems to have declined in the last couple of years. You have lost weight, my dear, and you do not look well. The economy is improving, and I've placed my money in a new bank. I do believe we no longer need the additional income. You will, of course, ensure that Mr. Weiss's clothes are freshly laundered for his departure and then thoroughly clean his room and the bathroom."

"Yes, yes, of course," she replied. Deep inside her, relief flooded in and it was difficult to keep from smiling. *Thank you, dear Heavenly Father. My prayers have been answered!*

"Very well," Johann said. "Goodnight, Mrs. King."

"Goodnight, Johann," she replied and headed upstairs.

Wilhelmina enjoyed a leisurely hot bath as the soft rain pattered against the windows. Finally, the storm began to move out around midnight, the thunder growing fainter and the rain easing to a steady drizzle. The rain left the streets glistening under the gas streetlights, the air cool and fresh in the aftermath.

She slept through the night and woke the next morning with a fresh perspective, eagerly welcoming the day. She hummed as she prepared breakfast for Johann and smiled when she waved goodbye to him at the door. She virtually bounced through the rooms that morning, dusting the furniture and sweeping the floors. She finished her morning chores quickly, and following a light lunch with Albert, she spent the afternoon in the courtyard behind the house weeding her garden and chatting with her son.

Wilhelmina felt happier than she had in months, even years, although she would miss the friendship she was building with Mr. Weiss. She and Albert laughed and talked while she taught him about the various vegetables and herbs she had planted. The afternoon sun blazed down, the temperatures reaching near 100 degrees, so they retreated indoors for a scoop of ice cream. They played checkers at the kitchen table and talked about the new clothes they would need to buy for Albert—he was growing so tall.

The phone rang, and Albert ran down the hall to the parlor, excited to answer the call. He had never been permitted to use the phone before today. He listened intently to the voice on the other end of the line, then gently set the receiver on the table.

"Mama? Mama, the call is for you," he shouted.

Wilhelmina strode into the room, smiling, and said, "Thank you, son. Did you ask who is calling?"

"Yes, Mama. It is that doctor … Doctor Burd …"

She giggled and said, "Doctor Burdine. Thank you, son. You may go to your room and play until it is time for dinner." Albert skipped out of the room and went upstairs.

Wilhelmina placed the receiver against her ear. "Hello? This is Mrs. King," she said.

"Mrs. King, this is Doctor Burdine. I regret to inform you that Mr. Weiss passed this morning. I will be sending someone at the end of the week for his belongings. Can you have them ready by Friday?"

Wilhelmina heard herself saying "Yes, of course" before she dropped the receiver and fainted into the chair.

Johann stayed true to his word and did not seek another boarder after Mr. Weiss's death. Wilhelmina scrubbed both the bathroom and bedroom top to bottom, washed all the linens—including the curtains—and shut the doors on all three rooms on the third floor, hoping to never lay eyes on them again.

With fewer chores to perform, Wilhelmina spent her afternoons with Albert and began eating better. Color returned to her cheeks, and her eyes glimmered. She slept well at night and found time to once again read her Bible, something she had not done in a very long time. She was comforted by the passages and prayed daily, thanking God for His gifts.

Johann was pleasant and talkative at the dinner table and even looked in on Albert as he waited in his room for his mother to tuck him in. After dinner one evening, Johann called Albert from the bottom of the stairs.

"Albert," he shouted, "please come down to the parlor."

Albert stuck his head out his bedroom door and hollered, "Yes, sir!"

Johann waited by the fireplace, cigar in hand, until Albert walked into the room. He turned and said, "Have a seat, son."

Wilhelmina, sitting on the chair, tilted her head toward Johann, curious about him calling Albert "son" for the first time ever. Johann had been so amenable of late that she didn't dare question it and ruin his good mood.

Albert sat on the sofa and placed his hands on his thighs, waiting patiently. Wise beyond his years, he was accustomed to proper behavior and the importance of silent obedience.

"I have a gift for you, Albert, for school, of course," said Johann. "There, on the table. Go ahead, open it!"

Albert looked from Johann to his mother, who smiled and nodded. He picked up the box, nearly dropping it. It was heavier than he expected. He removed the bow and carefully removed the wrapping. His eyes brightened as a wide smile filled his face when he opened the box.

Inside were three novels, all by his favorite authors—*The Adventures of Tom Sawyer* by Mark Twain, *The Call of the Wild* by Jack London, and *Treasure Island* by Robert Louis Stevenson. He lifted the books from the box and gazed at them in awe. He had never received such lovely new books, other than the geometry textbook from Mr. Weiss, and he had certainly not received a gift from his stepfather since ... what seemed like so many years ago.

"Th-Thank you, Doctor King! These are absolutely wonderful. I cannot thank you enough, sir!" Albert rose to his feet and extended his hand to Johann, who grasped it and shook vigorously.

"There, now, boy, don't you think it is time you called me Father? After all, I've been like a father to you for many years now."

Albert swallowed hard and sought his mother's gaze. The smile left her face, but she gave a curt nod to her son. Albert looked at Johann again and said, "Yes, Fa ... Father. Thank you."

"You are welcome. Now, off to bed, son. Goodnight."

"Goodnight, sir ... Father," Albert said. He then hugged Wilhelmina, lifted the books into his arms and left the parlor.

Later Wilhelmina lay on her bed in the dark and thought about the events of the day. Why had Johann's attitude and demeanor suddenly changed in the past few weeks? Maybe it had been the pressures of the stock market crash and his important work as a surgeon that had made him so irascible over the years. A glimmer of hope sparked deep inside, and she smiled to herself. Lost in thought, she didn't hear her door open and close or Johann's soft footsteps as he approached the bed.

He climbed onto the bed and lowered the sheet covering Wilhelmina's body. He caressed her arm, her face, and leaned toward her, then kissed her neck and shoulder. His hands roamed down her waist, over her hips, and to her thighs.

"Take off your nightgown, Wilhelmina," he whispered.

Wilhelmina! He's never called me by name since our wedding day! Could this be a new beginning for us?

Wilhelmina sat up on the bed and raised her hips, pulling her nightgown from under her buttocks and over her head before tossing it to the floor. She eased back, and Johann rolled over her, propping himself on his elbows. He leaned in close, kissed her cheek, her chin, her lips, then lowered his mouth to her neck, her collarbone, and her breast, his tongue swirling around her nipple. She moaned softly as his hands moved over her naked body.

Johann made love to Wilhelmina that night. He was tender and passionate. He kissed her over and over. For the first time since their marriage, Wilhelmina felt pleasure at her husband's ministrations.

"Anya," he groaned, "my beautiful, sweet Anya. My darling, you … mmm … feel so … so … mmm … good." And he shuddered over Wilhelmina. "Beautiful Anya," he whispered and rolled away. He sat up on the bed, pulled on his pajama bottoms and strode out of the room, closing the door behind him.

Johann was in the kitchen the next morning, long before Wilhelmina or Albert awakened, making coffee. He poured the hot liquid into a cup and added cream and sugar. He slipped on a pair of surgical gloves and removed a small dark bottle from his shirt pocket. He tapped the bottle lightly, allowing a miniscule amount of arsenic to fall into the cup. After carefully recapping the bottle, Johann opened the cupboard and hid the bottle behind the canned goods. He reached into his pocket and withdrew the last unopened bottle of arsenic and also hid it in the cupboard. He closed the cupboard door, pocketed the gloves, stirred the liquid in the cup and took a sip. Standing at the counter, Johann drank the entire cup of coffee and set it, along with the spoon, in the sink. He grabbed his suitcoat from the back of the chair and left the house.

As soon as Johann walked through the hospital door, the first wave of nausea hit. He made his way to his office, threw off his suit coat, and headed for the men's room. He vomited for several minutes before the first sign of diarrhea hit and sent painful cramps through his abdomen.

An hour later, Johann walked down the hall to the emergency room and hailed a nurse.

"Yes, Dr. King, what is wrong?" asked the head nurse, Mrs. Jackson.

"I … am … quite ill, nurse. Please, I need to see the attending physician."

"Yes, yes, right away. You do look quite pale, Doctor, and you are sweating. Follow me."

Nurse Jackson led Johann to an empty bed and took his vital signs. She then pulled the curtain around the bed and went in search of the on-duty physician. Within minutes, she returned accompanied by the doctor, who examined Johann. He looked in his eyes, took his temperature again, and pressed on his stomach, causing Johann to cry out in pain.

"Please, doctor," Johann said, "I have to vomit again."

The nurse placed a bedpan on Johann's lap, and he immediately expelled more contents of his stomach into the pan. Feeling better, he pushed the bedpan aside and lay back on the bed.

"How are you feeling now, Dr. King?" asked Dr. Catron.

"Mu-Much better."

"Do you feel up to answering some questions?"

"Yes."

"When was the last time you ate?"

"Dinner last night, around six o'clock."

"And did you have anything for breakfast today, anything at all?"

"Yes, my wife insisted I have a cup of coffee before coming to the hospital."

"I see. You have all the symptoms of gastroenteritis, and yet, these symptoms do not usually dissipate quite so quickly. This leads me to believe you may have food poisoning. I would like to perform a gastric lavage on you, Dr. King."

"Yes, yes, please, pump my stomach. I have never felt so sick in my life. I'm sure that will help, Dr. Catron."

"Very well. Nurse, please prep Dr. King. I will return shortly to perform the procedure."

That afternoon, Dr. Catron knocked on Johann's office door.

"Come in," Johann called. "Ahh, Dr. Catron, please, have a seat. Allow me to thank you once again for coming to my rescue this morning. Your quick thinking certainly saved my life."

"Well, Dr. King, you are quite welcome. Although I'm not sure your life was in grave danger. However, I have sent the contents of your stomach to the lab for testing so we will have a better understanding of what afflicted you."

"Very good, very good," said Johann as he propped his elbows on the desk and interlocked his fingers. "A wise decision, indeed. How soon do you believe you will receive the results?"

"As I'm sure you know, Dr. King, toxicology can sometimes take several weeks, but in this case, I am optimistic that I will receive the test results within a week, if not sooner."

"Very good. And I trust you will share the findings with me?"

"Yes, of course, Dr. King. Well, I must be on my way. Have a good day, Dr. King, and please, do not hesitate to return to the hospital should you feel ill again."

"Of course, Dr. Catron. And thank you again."

Johann waited for ten seemingly long days for the results of the toxicology tests. He carefully scanned the documents while Dr. Catron sat patiently in front of the desk. Johann sighed deeply as he sat back in his chair and laid the papers on the desk.

"Dr. Catron, do you believe these results to be accurate?" he asked.

"Yes, Dr. King, I do. The question now is … how could you have ingested arsenic?"

"I believe I know the answer to that question, Dr. Catron. Do you have time to wait while I make a phone call, or are you expected in the emergency room?"

"No, no, I am off duty and not expected home for a few hours. I have time. May I ask who you will be calling?"

"The police, of course," Johann said as he lifted the receiver and dialed the operator.

CHAPTER TWENTY-THREE

September 20, 1933

Wilhelmina sat on the front porch, whistling a happy tune, as she snapped green beans and waited for Albert to arrive home from school. Johann had not visited her bed since that sultry night in August a few weeks ago, but he had continued to be pleasant and even jovial in her presence. He helped Albert with his homework and played a game of chess with him just the night before.

The sound of an approaching vehicle pulled Wilhelmina's attention away from the beans to the street, where two police cars pulled in to park at the curb in front of the house. Her eyes widened in fear as two officers approached, her breath quickening and heart fluttering.

Please, dear Father, don't let something have happened to my precious boy.

She blinked and rubbed her eyes, as if to be sure she wasn't dreaming.

"How may I help you, officers?" she said, her voice shaking. "Is there a problem?"

One of the officers moved closer to the porch and said, "Are you Mrs. Johann King? Wilhelmina King?"

"Yes, but—"

"We're going to have to ask you to come with us, Mrs. King," he said gruffly.

"I don't understand. What has happened?"

"That will be explained downtown, ma'am. Now if you will please cooperate and come along."

"Yes, yes, but ... I need to put these beans inside first," she said.

"Very well, then," he said and followed her into the house and to the kitchen.

Wilhelmina put the bowl of beans in the refrigerator and turned to the officer. "I still do not understand, sir. Please explain," she begged.

"Ma'am, if you'll just come with us," he said and stepped aside to escort her from the house.

Outside on the porch, another two officers strode closer to Wilhelmina as the first officer took her elbow.

"Ma'am, please turn around," he said as he removed a pair of handcuffs from his belt.

"Wait, please, I don't un—"

"That's enough, ma'am. This will be much easier if you cooperate."

He clapped the cuffs on Wilhelmina's wrists and said, "Mrs. Wilhelmina King, you are under arrest for five counts murder and the attempted murder of your husband, Dr. Johann King."

He and another officer flanked Wilhelmina and led her down the stairs to a waiting police car as she struggled against them. Just before they forced her into the car, Albert came running down the sidewalk toward them.

"Mama! Mama, what is happening?" he shouted.

"Albert! Officer, that is my son. Please ..." She choked on her words, swallowed, and said, "Please let me speak with him."

Wilhelmina climbed into the back seat of the car and turned to her son.

"Son, I-I do not know what is happening. Call Mrs. Wagner. Her number is in the book next to the phone. Call her right away, son." She turned to the officer and said, "Where are you taking me, sir?"

"You are going downtown to the police station, Mrs. King," he said and slammed the door shut.

Albert beat his fists on the door until one of the officers pulled him away and shouted at him to stop. The officers then piled into the car and sped away from the curb, leaving a sobbing Albert standing on the sidewalk. He ran up the steps and into the house, and called Marta Wagner. But no one answered the phone. Karin and Georg had moved out of Ohio just after the stock market crash, and there was no new phone number written in the book. Albert sunk into the chair and covered his face with his hands, crying, until he heard the front door open. He jumped up and sprinted to the foyer. Maybe, just maybe, it had all been a mistake and his mother was home.

Johann, six uniformed police officers and two detectives in brown suits converged on the house, pushing past Albert and scattering throughout the house. Albert followed his stepfather down the hall to the kitchen, where a patrolman was haphazardly tossing items out of the cupboards. Behind him, another patrolman was doing the same in the pantry.

Sergeant Tompkins called from the pantry, "I've found sugar and flour in here!"

The tallest of the two detectives, Detective Barnes, came out of the kitchen, pushed Albert aside, and stood in the doorway to the pantry. Sergeant Tompkins was holding the two canisters, both covered with black dust from the fingerprint kit.

"Bag them and mark them as evidence. They will need to go to the lab," said Detective Barnes. "When you are done bagging them, go to the second floor and help Jones search the bedrooms and bathroom. Daniels, Anderson, and Wright are in the kitchen. I've sent Carr to the third floor with Detective Kilbarger."

"Yes, sir," said Sergeant Tompkins, who bagged the canisters, marked the bags, and set them on the kitchen table. He then walked down the hall and climbed the stairs to the second floor.

Back in the kitchen, Detective Barnes began talking with Johann in a low voice, too soft for Albert to hear.

"Detective Barnes," said Officer Wright, "I believe we've found more evidence."

Detective Barnes cut off his conversation with Johann, strode to the cupboards, and looked inside where the officer was pointing. There, carefully hidden behind cans of peas and corn, stood twelve small, dark bottles, each bearing a label reading "Arsenic" and "Poison." Ten of the bottles were empty; of the two still containing arsenic, one had been opened and recapped. They also extracted a bottle of isopropyl alcohol from the cupboard, which was nearly empty.

"Dust for fingerprints, then bag all of it to go to the lab," instructed Detective Barnes. He turned to resume his conversation with Johann when Detective Kilbarger shouted for Barnes from the third floor.

Detective Barnes climbed the stairs and found Kilbarger in the bathroom, holding a half-empty box of surgical gloves. Detective Barnes scanned the box for a moment and called down the hall for Officer Carr, who was in the boarders' bedroom. Carr bagged the box of gloves and handed it back to Detective Kilbarger.

"Detectives," said Officer Carr, "I searched both bedrooms and found no evidence."

"Very well," said Barnes, and he led the way down the steps back to the kitchen. Officer Carr dropped the bag of surgical gloves on the small table.

"Carr," said Kilbarger, "start boxing all this evidence and then search the parlor. Barnes and I will go up to the second floor."

They found Officer Jones in one of the bedrooms and peered inside. The room was brightly decorated by floral wallpaper, lace drapes, and pastel blankets.

"Find anything, Jones?" said Detective Barnes.

"Nothing in the bedroom next door. That looks to be the kid's room. In here, I did find these," Jones said as he held up a bag containing three bottles of isopropyl alcohol. He cocked his head toward the chest of drawers standing next to the window. "They were under her nightgowns, there in the second drawer."

Sergeant Tompkins appeared in the doorway and said, "Detectives, I've searched the other bedroom. It appears to be the room Dr. King uses. I found no evidence. However, I believe I have found something in the last room at the end of the hall."

"Very good, sergeant. Please lead the way," said Kilbarger.

Detectives Barnes and Kilbarger followed Sergeant Tompkins into the extra bedroom, which was furnished sparsely with a filing cabinet, desk, and chair. Tompkins opened the drawers of the filing cabinet to reveal household files—labeled "property deed," "utilities," and "receipts," among others. He opened the receipts file and rifled through a few pages before extracting three letter-sized pieces of paper—receipts from Hoffman's Pharmacy for orders of arsenic placed by Mrs. Wilhelmina King. He bagged the documents, and all three men returned to the kitchen. Detective Kilbarger set the new bags of evidence on the table, and he and Tompkins went outside, opened the cellar doors, and searched the basement. They found no additional evidence there—including no proof of rats.

Johann left the kitchen and sat in the parlor, smoking a cigar while Officer Carr searched the room. Johann didn't speak to Albert, who sat across from him weeping, too afraid to talk. The house began to grow dark as evening set in. Johann turned on a lamp and read the newspaper, calm, as if nothing out of the ordinary were happening. Officer Carr left the parlor, and Albert stopped crying; his sniffles and growling stomach were the only noises in the room.

"Excuse me, Dr. King," said Detective Barnes from the doorway. "We are finished here."

Johann stood and crossed the room. "Very well, then, thank you. What do I need to do now?" he said.

"Nothing at all. We have your statement. Mrs. King has been arrested and processed. I am returning to the station now and will begin my interrogation. Your wife will be arraigned in court, but at this late hour, it may be morning before that happens. I will know more then."

"Very well, thank you," said Johann.

"You are quite welcome, sir. Is there anything else you need from us? Any assistance with the lad?"

"No, no, we are well, thank you. Albert will have dinner and be off to bed, and he will be at school tomorrow while I am at the hospital. You can reach me there if needed."

"Yes, I will do that. If there's nothing else, then, goodnight, sir."

"Thank you again and goodnight, Detective."

At the station, a physician examined Wilhelmina to ensure she was disease-free before she was fingerprinted and photographed. She was then escorted to a holding cell, where she sat on a cold metal bench for hours, surrounded by prostitutes who also awaited arraignment. When Detective Barnes arrived at the station, an officer unlocked the cell, called Wilhelmina's name, and accompanied her into an interrogation room. She sat slumped in her chair, tears flowing down her cheeks and falling in tiny puddles on the table.

Detective Barnes opened the door to the interrogation room and ushered two people inside—a middle-aged man in a brown suit and a smartly dressed woman in her twenties. The woman carried a stenotype machine, set it on a small table in the corner of the room, and sat.

"Mrs. King, I am Detective Barnes, and this is Detective Kilbarger. We would like to ask you some questions."

Wilhelmina nodded, wiping her eyes. Detective Barnes sat on the opposite side of the table while Detective Kilbarger closed the door, lit a cigarette, and leaned against the wall.

"Good. You must understand that anything you say can and will be used against you in a court of law. Let's begin. Please state your full name and date of birth."

"Wil …" she said and choked back a sob. "Wilhelmina Marie King. I was born on January 10, 1900." She shivered as the clicking sound of metal keys on the machine filled the room.

"Very well. And have you gone by any other names previous to King?"

"Y-Yes. I was … My last name was Schmidt when I was married to Oskar. Before that, my name was Heinrich."

"And how long were you and Oskar Schmidt married?"

"Six years."

"Were you born here in Cincinnati? In America?"

"N-No. I was born in Munich, Germany. I came to America in 1916, here to Cincinnati, and lived with my aunt and uncle."

"And are they still living?"

"N-N-No, they are both dead."

"I see. And how did you meet your husband, Dr. King?"

Wilhelmina shut her eyes, blinking back fresh tears. She was terrified to tell the truth—and terrified not to. *Would Johann tell them the truth about how they met?*

"I-I met Johann—Dr. King—at the hospital where I worked."

"Which hospital, Mrs. King?"

"Good Samaritan. I worked in the laundry room. I was stacking gowns in the doctor's linen closet and bumped into Jo … Dr. King."

"I see. Mrs. King, how did your first husband die?"

"He had bec-become quite ill. I am not sure I can pronounce the word. Severe gastro ... gastroen ... I am sorry, I do not know the word."

"Gastroenteritis?"

"Yes, sir."

"When did he die, Mrs. King?"

"In ... In March 1925."

"And when did you marry Dr. King?"

"In August 1925."

"A very short courtship, indeed, Mrs. King. Can you explain that?"

"I ... We ... I was quite poor, you see, and Oskar left me no money. Johann was so kind to me and my son, Albert. He took care of us after Oskar died. He proposed, and we were married soon after."

"Very well. When did you start taking in boarders at your home, Mrs. King?"

"It was early—I don't remember the month—but it was winter. I believe in early 1930."

"And his name?"

"Mr. Parker. Jacob, I believe."

Detective Barnes's interrogation continued for over two hours as he questioned Wilhelmina about the boarders, how long they lived at the house on Glenmary Drive, and how they died. He asked her about her home life and her marriage to Johann. He was patient and kind with Wilhelmina.

Meanwhile, Detective Kilbarger began pacing the room, circling the table and chain smoking one cigarette after another. He remained silent—until he lost his patience. "All right, that is *enough!*" Detective Kilbarger slammed a fist on the table just inches from Wilhelmina. "Yes, yes, we've heard about your pleasant little life in that mansion, Mrs. King. What I want to know is—*What. Prompted. You. To. Poison. Your. Husband?*"

"P-Poison? I-I-I do not understand. I did not poison my husband!" Wilhelmina began wringing her hands and shrank back from Detective Kilbarger, averting her eyes to her lap.

"No? Then why was Dr. King in the emergency room two weeks ago, very sick and near death? Caused by *arsenic poisoning?*"

"I-I—"

"And can you explain why we found several empty bottles of arsenic in your kitchen cupboards, Mrs. King?"

Wilhelmina vehemently shook her head and opened her mouth to speak. Her voice was lost to her, so she clapped her mouth shut.

"Come now, Mrs. King, surely you can explain those bottles and the half-empty box of surgical gloves found hidden in the third-floor bathroom. The third floor, Mrs. King, that is where your boarders stayed? They used that bathroom, *is that correct?*" He yelled the question.

"Y-Y-Yes, but—"

"Now, let's all calm down, shall we?" Detective Barnes said. "Jim, I believe we have everything we need to schedule an arraignment. The evidence has been sent to the lab, and we'll know more in a few weeks." He turned to Wilhelmina and said, gently, "Mrs. King, we will have to hold you until your arraignment in the morning. At that time, the judge will determine the next steps. Do you have an attorney?"

"An … attorney?" She shook her head and shrugged. "I do not … I do not know."

"Very well. I shall call Dr. King for the name of his attorney, if he has one. If he does not, the court can possibly assign an attorney to you."

Wilhelmina stared at Detective Barnes with glassy eyes. Her mind raced to sort out the jumble of the day's events, and her stomach roiled as the jail matron entered the room and escorted her back to her cell.

The next morning, hands cuffed behind her back, Wilhelmina walked down the long hallway to the courtroom, Detectives Barnes and Kilbarger at her sides, reporters chasing after them firing question after question in her direction. Every step she took seemed mechanical, as if not her own, and dozens of faces blurred around her.

The courtroom doors opened to a racket slamming against Wilhelmina's eardrums, and she took a staggering step back and froze. Detective Barnes squeezed her elbow and prodded her forward to one of the two tables in front of a low wooden barrier. He pulled a chair out and she sat behind the table.

The high ceilings boasted decorative moldings and intricate plasterwork, and the room featured heavy dark wood furniture—the judge's bench, witness stand, and the two tables facing the bench, each with two chairs placed behind them—one which Wilhelmina now occupied. Several rows of wooden benches comprised the public seating area, a wide aisle dividing the two sections in the middle. Tall arched windows, covered in heavy drapes, lined the walls behind the jury box. Heels piercingly clicked on the marble floors as spectators and reporters scrambled to find seats. Directly in front of the judge's bench, a stenotype machine sat atop a small table. A thin, young woman, wearing round shell-framed glasses, sat at the table, hands at the ready on the keys.

Wilhelmina was vaguely aware of a dark-haired man walking toward her and shook her head to clear the fog clouding her mind. She glanced around the room, hoping to spot a friendly face, but saw no one she knew.

"Mrs. King, I am Harold Goetz, attorney-at-law. I have been assigned by the court to represent you," the man said.

Her eyes fixed on his, unblinking gaze empty and distant, as if she were looking through Mr. Goetz rather than at him. Her face remained expressionless, her body rigid. The silence between them grew heavier, the blank stare creating an unsettling atmosphere, as though she were lost in a world far removed from the unfolding events.

"All rise," barked a uniformed man standing near the door adjacent to the judge's bench. "The Court of Common Pleas of Hamilton County is now in session, the Honorable Judge Johnathon Kimble presiding."

The judge, sporting a knee-length black robe, entered the room and took a seat behind the bench.

"Please be seated," said the bailiff, "and come to order."

Feet shuffled on the tiled floors amid the low murmurings of the crowd as they sat.

"Court is now in session," said Judge Kimble. "The matter before us today is the arraignment of Wilhelmina Marie King. The defendant is charged with five counts of first-degree murder and one count of attempted murder of Dr. Johann King, her husband."

Papers rustled and whispers permeated the room, the voices of the onlookers growing in volume until the judge pounded his gavel, eliciting a jump from Wilhelmina.

"Order in the court!" the judge shouted. Once the room yet again grew silent, he continued, "Mrs. King, you are hereby informed of the charges against you. You have the right to remain silent, the right to an attorney, and the right to a fair trial. How do you plead to the charges presented?"

Wilhelmina turned to Mr. Goetz and searched his eyes, her shoulders raising in a silent question. Mr. Goetz rose from his chair and touched Wilhelmina's shoulder, helping her to her feet.

"Your Honor," he said, "my client pleads not guilty to these charges."

"The plea of 'not guilty' is entered into the record. We will now address the matter of bail. You may both be seated," said Judge Kimble. Wilhelmina slumped into her chair while Mr. Goetz remained standing.

The prosecuting attorney rose to his feet behind the table to Wilhelmina's right and said, "Your Honor, given the severity of the charges presented, the State requests that bail be denied."

"Your Honor," said Goetz, "my client has strong ties to the community and has been an upstanding citizen since coming to America over seventeen years ago. She poses no flight risk, and we respectfully request bail to be set at a reasonable amount."

Judge Kimble stroked his chin between his thumb and forefinger for several moments, while Wilhelmina, her attorney, and the entire room of curious onlookers and reporters waited on the edges of their seats.

"After considering the arguments and taking into account the serious nature of the charges, this court orders that bail be denied," said the judge. "The next court date is set for two months from now, on November 6, for a preliminary hearing. Is there anything further from either side?"

Mr. Goetz and the prosecutor simultaneously replied, "No, Your Honor."

"Very well," said the judge. "The defendant will remain in custody at the Hamilton County Jail. This court is adjourned."

Wilhelmina jumped in her seat again as the gavel slammed onto the sounding block. She was then escorted by the detectives to the Hamilton County Jail, where she was issued a plain brown, button-up dress, blankets and pillow, toothbrush, a bar of soap and bottle of shampoo, and two towels. The jail matron introduced herself to Wilhelmina as Mrs. Flick and led her to a cell with a single cot, a small table and chair, and a wash basin affixed to the wall.

Wilhelmina turned to Mrs. Flick and said, "Please, ma'am, would it be all right for me to have a Bible?"

Mrs. Flick—a stout, gray-haired woman—pursed her lips as she closed the cell door. "I will request one be delivered to you from the chaplaincy. Change into the dress. I will return shortly to retrieve your personal belongings." she said and turned on her heel and strode down the hall and out of sight.

An hour later Wilhelmina handed her clothes, neatly folded, to Mrs. Flick through the bars of the cell. The single bulb above her head swayed slightly, creating a shimmer of light on the cross hanging around Wilhelmina's neck. Mrs. Flick caught sight of the necklace and put her hand through the bars.

"Oh, please, no," begged Wilhelmina. "Please, I pray with this cross. Please do not take it from me!"

Mrs. Flick withdrew her hand and studied Wilhelmina for a moment. "Very well, then," she said, her voice softening. "You are given four visits per day to the toilets and one shower. The facilities are shared by the inmates, and you will be escorted at the appropriate times. Your meals will be taken in the cafeteria. You will be under close supervision at all times. I suggest you mind your behavior while here."

"Yes, ma'am," Wilhelmina replied.

That night, Wilhelmina received a Bible and read from the book of Job before kneeling to pray. She rose stiffly from her knees and lay on the bed beneath the thin sheet and threadbare blanket. The lights in the ward went out ten minutes later, and terrified of what her future held, Wilhelmina cried herself to sleep.

The next day, guards escorted Wilhelmina to the bathroom where she used the toilet, and bathed herself in a row of open showers, along with ten other women. She donned her clothes quickly, shy about her nudity, and wrapped a towel around her wet hair. She brushed her teeth, and soon the guards led her and the other inmates to the cafeteria. They stood in line while cafeteria staff spooned globs of oatmeal onto their metal trays, then added a piece of stale bread to the tray before handing each prisoner a glass of water. Wilhelmina followed the line until she found a seat at the end of a table surrounded by six other inmates. She sat away from them and ate in silence.

When she rose moments later to stack her tray with the others, a guard approached and said, "Are you Mrs. King? Wilhelmina King?"

"Y-Yes, I am," she answered.

"Follow me," he said.

He led Wilhelmina out the door, and down a series of hallways, to a small room with one chair facing a glass barrier affixed to a small counter. A hole was cut in the middle of the glass, too small for even the thinnest of arms to reach through. She sat down at the counter as the guard closed the door behind her and stood next to it, hands clasped in front of him. A door on the other side of the glass opened and Albert rushed in.

"Mama, oh Mama!" he cried. "What has happened, Mama? I'm so frightened!"

Wilhelmina threw her handcuffed hands up to the glass and, seeing her son's eyes widen in horror, quickly dropped them back to her lap.

"My darling, boy. Oh my, dear, sweet boy," she cried. "I-I do not know, my darling. I … There … Oh how do I tell you these things?"

"Mama, please tell me. I must know. The police … The police … They have been asking me so many questions. Mama, I do not understand."

"I know, my darling. I do not understand either. I'm sure there has been some terrible mistake, some misunderstanding. They say I killed those men and that I tried to kill your stepfather. I do not know how ..." Wilhelmina's voice cracked, and she began to sob.

"Mama, please don't cry. I-I can't take it if you cry."

"All right, my darling. I'll ... I'll ..." she said and coughed. "I will be all right, son. Are you all right at home? Have you been fed? Is he taking you to school?"

"Yes, Mama. Father has been kind. He brought me here to see you, and I'll go to school from here. He said he will speak with the nuns to let them know why I am late. I wanted to see you so much, and he agreed to bring me here."

"Good, good. Now, son, listen very carefully. No matter what you hear, no matter what you may read, please believe that I did not do the things they said. I am innocent, and I am sure I will be home before you know it. Now promise me you will not worry. Promise."

"Yes, Mama, I promise."

"Son, what ... what did the police officers ask you?"

"They ... They asked if I ever saw you make food for those men who used to stay with us. They asked if I ever saw you use the flour or sugar from the pantry."

"I see. And what did you tell them, son?"

"I-I ... Oh, Mama! I am sorry. I told them that you *did* use that sugar and flour only for those men. I'm ... I'm sorry, Mama!" Albert covered his face in his hands and wept.

"No, no, son, it is all right. It is the truth. It will be all right, son. You did nothing wrong."

The officer standing behind Albert said, "Time is up. It is time for you to go."

"Mama, they are making me leave now. I don't know when Father will bring me to see you again. Oh, Mama, I miss you so much!"

"You go now, son and be a good boy. I miss you, too. And Albert?"

"Yes, Mama."

"Pray for me, son. I love you very much."

"I will, Mama. I love you, too."

◦⭗

The next two months crawled like a snail; the hours felt like days and the months like years. At the preliminary hearing, Wilhelmina sat rigid at the table next to Mr. Goetz while he and the prosecuting attorney, Arthur Skidmore, presented their opening statements. Mr. Goetz spoke positively about Wilhelmina. He detailed her treacherous journey as a teenager to America, her demanding work at Kahn's and then the hospital. He talked about her happy life with her first husband and her protective and tender love for her son. Mr. Goetz spoke of Wilhelmina's strong religious faith and described her as a pious, devout woman.

Mr. Skidmore, however, painted a different picture. He labeled Wilhelmina as ruthless and calculating. He claimed she harbored ill will against her father, who had banished her from his home many years ago, and that she exacted her revenge by poisoning five men who served as father figures to her. He then addressed her marriage to Johann, saying she accepted his proposal for his wealth alone. Mr. Skidmore closed his statement by pointing at Wilhelmina while portraying her as a downtrodden woman, unhappy in her life and filled with despair—a woman who methodically murdered elderly men and attempted to murder her own husband.

Wilhelmina watched, as if from a great distance, while the prosecutor presented damning evidence to the court: ten empty bottles and two full bottles of arsenic, empty flour and sugar canisters labeled "Boarder," four bottles of isopropyl alcohol (one nearly empty), a half-empty box of surgical gloves, receipts from Hoffman's Pharmacy bearing her name, and evidence bags with small amounts of the flour and sugar, now clearly labeled as containing enough arsenic to cause death within a matter of days.

Witnesses were called to the stand—Mrs. Henry contemptuously testified she had been instructed to pick up orders at the pharmacy that had been placed by Wilhelmina, under the guise of needing the arsenic to make rat poison. She stated she had never seen nor heard any rats in the basement of the house on Glenmary Drive.

Dr. Burdine and other physicians from the hospital stated their diagnoses could have been incorrect and concurred with one another that symptoms of arsenic poisoning could frequently be misconstrued for gastroenteritis or even cardiovascular disease. Michael Wilson, the county coroner, testified that autopsies were currently being performed, or had already been, on all five victims and results were expected within four to six weeks.

Finally, Johann took the stand, and Wilhelmina shook her head briskly, snapping out of the daze she had been in throughout the hearing. She heard his oath to tell the truth and sat, unbelieving, while he told the court about his wife—a woman who turned a cold shoulder to him soon after their wedding, a woman who refused his love, a woman who ordered her son to stay in his room and would not allow Albert to play in the parlor or take his meals with his mother or Johann.

Johann recounted the events of the day he became ill—she had left a hot pot of coffee on the stove, but she was nowhere to be seen. He downed a cup quickly and left for work, where he became violently ill. He told of making his way to the emergency room, nauseated and dizzy, doubled over in pain, and how his stomach was pumped to save his life. He described his disbelief at learning about the traces of arsenic in his stomach fluids and, heartbroken, he called the police.

Mr. Goetz's only defense was that Wilhelmina consistently claimed her innocence, stating she knew nothing about rats in the basement, had never placed orders with any pharmacy, and did not hide bottles of arsenic in the cupboard. His statements to the court fell flat compared to the evidence presented by the prosecution.

On the third day of the hearing, Wilhelmina once again stood next to Mr. Goetz while Judge Kimble addressed the court.

"Over the past three days," said the judge in a loud, clear voice, "we have heard overwhelming evidence against Wilhelmina King, who stands before you today, accused of murdering five men by means of arsenic poisoning, as well as the attempted murder of her husband, Dr. Johann King. The purpose of this hearing has not been to determine innocence or guilt but, rather, to determine if there is sufficient evidence to send this case to trial. This court believes such evidence has been presented, and it is our decision to proceed to trial."

Wilhelmina's knees buckled, and she dropped onto the chair. Mr. Goetz grabbed her arm and lifted her back to her feet.

"Trial will be set for six weeks from today, December 18, and will commence at ten in the morning. The Honorable Judge Alfred Walling will preside. Mrs. King will remain in custody at the Hamilton County Jail until such a time as her guilt or innocence is determined. Court is adjourned," he said and slammed the gavel down with a bang.

CHAPTER TWENTY-THREE

December 1933

Wilhelmina sat on the cot in her cell, toying with the cross hanging from her neck while she read her Bible. She had asked to take her breakfast in her cell that morning, but she did not eat. The oatmeal and dry toast grew cold on the metal tray while she read. She closed her Bible, laid it on the bed, and went to stand at the basin to brush her teeth. Dull green eyes looked back at her from the cracked mirror as she smoothed her hair, now falling in waves to her shoulders, and checked her dress for lint. She paced in circles from the cot to the basin to the small table and back again, all the while waiting for the guard to take her to the courtroom.

The past several weeks had been difficult for Wilhelmina. She was assigned to work in the jail laundry room; the hours were long and the work exhausting. The room was a sweltering inferno with temperatures soaring well above comfort levels, despite the cold temperatures raging outside the jail walls. The air in the laundry room was thick and oppressive, making breathing difficult. Sweat dripped from every pore on Wilhelmina's skin, soaking through her clothes in a matter of minutes. The industrial washers and dryers roared incessantly, adding to the heat and creating a cacophony that bounced off the concrete walls. The smell of detergent mixed with the stench of inmate sweat made Wilhelmina's stomach lurch daily.

Formerly a picture of vitality and joy—though many years ago—Wilhelmina's once voluptuous figure and radiant smile faded into a shadow of her former self. Her eyes, now sunken and hollow, reflected a sadness taking root in the depths of her soul. The curves of her body, at one time symbolizing her zest for life, had withered away during the past several weeks, leaving her gaunt and frail. Her laugh, once a happy melody, was replaced by silence that spoke volumes of her sorrow.

The tinkle of metal keys rattling against the others woke Wilhelmina from her reverie. Mrs. Flick unlocked the cell door and swung it open. Wilhelmina stood frozen, unable to move, as if cement encased her feet, and she crossed her arms over her body.

"Let's go, Mrs. King," Mrs. Flick said sternly. "We haven't got all day."

"I …" Wilhelmina cleared her throat. "May I take my Bible?"

"Oh, all right, but be quick about it. Court will be starting soon."

Wilhelmina picked up her Bible, stepped outside the cell, and swayed slightly while Mrs. Flick handcuffed her hands in front of her. She gripped her Bible tightly, somehow drawing strength from it. At the end of the hallway, they passed through a door and turned down another hall, where two police officers met them. Mrs. Flick turned around and walked back down the hall, leaving Wilhelmina alone with the officers, who flanked her on each side. They traversed a series of hallways until they reached a bank of elevators. The three stepped inside an elevator and took it to the basement of the building, where an underground tunnel took them from the jail to the courthouse.

Inside the courthouse, they rode another elevator to the third floor and made their way down the wide corridor to the largest courtroom in the building, all the while fending off dozens of reporters from across the country and hundreds of citizens hoping to witness the trial. Folding chairs had been brought in to provide additional seating, but the room was filled, leaving more than one hundred people in the corridor throughout the day.

An officer uncuffed Wilhelmina's hands, and she took her seat next to Mr. Goetz. Mr. Skidmore and another man in a dark suit sat at the table across the narrow aisleway. This courtroom, like the one used for Wilhelmina's preliminary hearing, though much larger, was adorned with mahogany wood, oversized windows behind the jury box, and marble floors. A pair of twenty-four-inch tall, polished brass lamps graced each side of the bench. Reporters took up their positions at six long tables behind the prosecutor. Beyond that, long wood benches filled each side of the aisle, and folding chairs took up every inch of leftover space along the walls and behind the benches.

A gleaming brass railing—known as the "bar"—enclosed the judge's bench, a small witness stand facing the jury box, and the court reporter's desk. Twelve deputy sheriffs, armed with pistols and billy clubs, had taken strategic positions around the courtroom to maintain order. Their eyes darted left to right, hands clasped in front of their bodies.

The trial, dubbed the "largest mass murder in the history of the country," was called to order at ten o'clock in the morning on Monday, December 18, 1933. Judge Walling took his seat and addressed the crowd.

"The courts are yours as you represent the public," he told them, "but I want to be distinctly understood when I say this trial shall not be turned into a circus performance. This is a serious trial in a court of justice. As many as can be seated within the walls of this courtroom will be permitted, only as long as each and every one of you confine yourselves to listening to the evidence presented. At no time will this court permit or tolerate any interferences or disturbances." He cleared his throat, tapping a stack of papers on his desk. "Now, we may proceed with the selection of the jury."

One by one, thirty men and women were questioned over the next two days. Prosecutor Skidmore asked each one if they accepted or opposed the death penalty and whether their verdict would be influenced by the fact the defendant was a woman. Mr. Goetz aimed his questions on determining whether potential jurors were biased against their client—specifically if they bore any prejudice against Germans.

The jury selection ended just after the lunch break on Wednesday—seven women and five men, plus two alternates, had been chosen to determine Wilhelmina's fate. The clerk swore in each member of the jury before the guards ushered them out of the courtroom and to the Hotel Metropole, a few blocks away. There, they were sequestered for the duration of the trial. Court was adjourned until Friday morning, December 22.

◈

Wilhelmina found herself seated at the table in the courtroom on Friday morning, three days before Christmas, following an agonizing two nights of despair. She ate little; the bones of her wrists protruded beneath the lace cuffs of her simple black dress as she clasped her necklace. Her long hair was pulled into a tight bun at the nape of her neck—she had not been to the salon in a number of years and could not maintain the short hairstyle that Johann had once demanded. Her face was wan, and her eyes were surrounded by dark circles.

Judge Walling took his seat and announced, "Ladies and gentlemen, this court is now in session. We are here to address the case of Wilhelmina Marie King, who stands accused of five counts of first-degree murder and one count of attempted first-degree murder. I will now read the State's indictment. 'Mrs. Wilhelmina Marie King has unlawfully, purposefully, and by means of poison killed five men, to be named further herein, as well committed the attempted murder of her husband, one Dr. Johann King. In so doing, Mrs. King has violated the peace and dignity of the State of Ohio. The victims of these crimes shall hereby be named: Mr. Jacob Parker, age seventy-five, died on May 20, 1930; Mr. Ernst Müeller, age seventy-two, died on October 13, 1930; Mr. Karl Berger, age seventy-nine, died on June 1, 1931; Mr. Ludwig Klein, age sixty-eight, died on April 2, 1932; and Mr. August Weiss, age eighty-one, died on July 27, 1933. Additionally, Dr. Johann King suffered a potentially life-threatening illness on September 20, 1933, as the result of poisoning by arsenic.'

"It is the duty of this court to ensure that justice is served and that the proceedings are conducted with the utmost fairness and respect for the law. We will now hear opening statements. Mr. Skidmore, is the prosecution ready to begin?"

Arthur Skidmore stood and said, "Yes, Your Honor." He walked around the table and faced the jury. As before, he presented Wilhelmina in a negative light and declared the State would without a doubt prove she had in fact committed the murders and attempted murder. He told the jury about the undeniable evidence found in her home and that additional evidence—the autopsy results—would be presented during the trial. He paced the floor in front of the jury box, his gaze meeting each of the jurors as he spoke.

After more than an hour, the prosecutor strode to the table, picked up a thick manila folder, and turned to face the jury once again.

"Ladies and gentlemen, you will learn over the coming days of the real reason Mrs. King came to America, and you will fully understand her true nature and the motive for her crimes. Indeed, you will see and hear damning evidence showing that Mrs. King was, in fact, impregnated at the age of fifteen and was banned from her home by her father and sent to America, where she gave birth to a child who she placed in an orphanage. You will see, ladies and gentlemen, that Mrs. King set out to murder those innocent, elderly gentlemen as an act of revenge on her father!"

The jurors gaped at Wilhelmina—twenty-four eyes widening in disbelief—as loud murmurings filled the courtroom.

The judge banged his gavel down hard. "Order! Order in the court!" he yelled. "Please continue, Mr. Skidmore."

"Thank you, Your Honor," said the prosecutor. "Ladies and gentlemen, by the end of this trial, you will also learn the details surrounding the death of Mrs. King's first husband, Mr. Oskar Schmidt, and you will see that he, too, most likely died of arsenic poisoning at the hands of his wife!"

The crowd gasped as Wilhelmina rose quickly from her chair and shouted, "No! It is *not* true!"

"Quiet! I demand order in this courtroom!" said Judge Walling, slamming the gavel loudly. "Mr. Goetz, you will control the defendant, or she will be held in contempt of court and banned from these procedures. Do you understand?"

Mr. Goetz gently pushed Wilhelmina onto her chair as he stood. He turned to Judge Walling and said, "Yes, of course, Your Honor. We beg your forgiveness."

"Prosecution may continue," said Judge Walling.

"Thank you, Your Honor," said Mr. Skidmore. "With the Court's permission, I present to you the evidence that unequivocally demonstrates the defendant's guilt in these heinous crimes. I beg you, members of the jury, to pay close attention as the list is quite long and contains over thirty-two items."

"You may proceed," said the judge.

Skidmore opened the folder in his hand and extracted a stack of papers held together by a staple in the corner.

"Exhibit A: three orders form from Hoffman's Pharmacy for a total of twelve bottles of arsenic, placed by Mrs. Johann King. Exhibit B: a sample of flour found at the defendant's residence, containing lethal amounts of arsenic. Exhibit C: a sample of sugar also found at the defendant's residence and also containing lethal amounts of arsenic. Exhibits D and E: canisters that contained the flour and sugar previously mentioned, which show trace evidence of arsenic. Exhibit F: ten empty bottles of arsenic. Exhibit G: one full bottle of arsenic, unopened. Exhibit H: one mostly full bottle of arsenic, which had been opened and recapped. Exhibit I: one nearly empty bottle of isopropyl alcohol. Exhibit J: three full and unopened bottles of isopropyl alcohol.

"Exhibit K: one box of surgical gloves, half empty. Exhibits L through P: jars of organs of the five victims, removed during recent autopsies. Exhibit Q: a jar of organs removed during a recent autopsy from the body of the late Mr. Oskar Schmidt. Exhibits R through W: reports from the county coroner indicating the autopsy results of the five victims as well as Mr. Schmidt. Exhibits X through CC: physician reports following treatment in the emergency room of Good Samaritan Hospital of the five victims and Mr. Schmidt.

"Exhibit DD: a certificate of the live birth of one male showing the mother as Wilhelmina Marie Heinrich, known today as King. No father's name is included on the certificate. Exhibit EE: records indicating a newborn male arrived at the St. Joseph Orphanage on July 11, 1916, along with the previously mentioned birth certificate. And finally, ladies and gentlemen, Exhibit FF: written testimonial affidavits from each of the police officers who participated in the arrest of Mrs. King and the subsequent search for evidence in this case."

Mr. Skidmore returned the list to the folder and laid it on the prosecution table. He stood by the table, scanning the eyes of every jury member, lingering on each person for a moment. He then moved closer to the jury box and said a few closing words, none of which reached Wilhelmina's ears. She was no longer focused on the things being said by Mr. Skidmore. The mention of the child she lost shook her to the core. She glanced around the room as she clutched the cross necklace, until her gaze fell on two people sitting across the aisle and four rows back.

Johann sat smirking with his arm around Albert's shoulders as the boy covered his face and sobbed into his hands. Wilhelmina did not know until that moment that her son was in the courtroom, and she longed to sweep him into her arms, to assure him that it wasn't true, that they were all lies.

She was so overcome with worry for her son that she never heard Mr. Goetz's own opening statements. After only an hour, Mr. Goetz returned to his seat behind the table. Judge Walling called for a recess until Tuesday, December 26. He would allow the jurors' families to visit at their hotel on Christmas Eve and Christmas Day. Court was adjourned and the guards returned Wilhelmina, handcuffed, to the jail.

The prosecutor, Arthur Skidmore, called his first witness to the stand—Maximillian Hoffman. A gray-haired man of medium height strode to the front of the courtroom, placed his hand on a Bible, and the clerk swore him in. Seated in the cramped witness box, he removed his glasses and wiped his brow with a crisp, white handkerchief. Mr. Skidmore stood a few feet away with an unobstructed view of the jury while he questioned his witness.

"Good morning," he said to no one in particular. "Mr. Hoffman, for the record, please state your name and occupation."

"Yes, sir. Maximillian Hoffman. I am a pharmacist and owner of Hoffman's Pharmacy on Race Street, in the Over-the-Rhine district."

"Thank you, Mr. Hoffman. I would now like to draw your attention, if I may, to Exhibit A," said Mr. Skidmore as he strode to the prosecutor's table and received three sheets of paper from his co-prosecutor, Edward Douglas. He stepped closer to the witness box, handed him the papers and said, "Sir, do you recognize these documents?"

Mr. Hoffman replied, "Yes, of course. They are order forms from my pharmacy."

"Thank you. And could you tell the court the details of these orders?"

"Yes. The first is an order for four bottles of arsenic placed on May 18, 1930. The second is for five bottles of arsenic placed on March 8, 1932, and the last is for three bottles of arsenic placed on May 3, 1933."

"And do any of these forms indicate who placed the orders?"

"Of course. Each order was placed by Mrs. Johann King of 14398 Glenmary Drive."

"And did you personally take these orders from Mrs. King?"

"No, I did not. Each order was called into the pharmacy and one of my employees filled out the forms. I rarely take the calls into the pharmacy myself. Unfortunately, that employee is no longer with the pharmacy. I believe he moved to California a year ago."

"I see. And did Mrs. King pick up these orders herself?"

"No, sir, she did not."

"Please explain."

"The following morning, that is to say, the morning after the first order was placed, I received a phone call from Dr. King. He explained that Mrs. King was under the weather, but he would be sending their nanny—Mrs. Henry, I believe—to pick up the order on Mrs. King's behalf."

"And when did Mrs. Henry pick up the order?"

"She came into the pharmacy that very afternoon. She paid for the order and left right away."

"Did Mrs. Henry also pick up the other two orders in 1932 and 1933?"

"No, sir, she did not. Those orders were delivered directly to Dr. Johann King at Good Samaritan Hospital."

"Thank you, Mr. Hoffman. No further questions."

Mr. Goetz rose from his chair while Mr. Skidmore returned to his seat.

Judge Walling said, "Does defense wish to cross-examine?"

"Yes, Your Honor," said Mr. Goetz. He approached the witness stand and looked around the room before turning back to the pharmacist.

"Mr. Hoffman," he said, "you stated that each order for arsenic was placed by telephone. Is that correct?"

"Yes, sir, it is," said Mr. Hoffman.

"And you personally did not take any of those phone calls, correct?"

"Yes, that is correct."

"You further stated that the employee who took the orders is no longer in your employ and has moved out of state. Correct?"

"Yes, sir, on both accounts."

"Very well," Goetz said and faced the jury. "Let the record show that several attempts have been made by both the prosecutor's office and myself to locate the employee in question, one Brian Fletcher, and that Mr. Fletcher has not been located to date."

"Objection!" cried Mr. Skidmore. "Irrelevant!"

"Your Honor," said Mr. Goetz, "I am merely attempting to establish that Mr. Fletcher may or may not have been the person who personally took the phone calls and completed the order forms, but since he has not been located, he cannot testify to that fact. Therefore, we can only *assume* that Mrs. King placed the phone calls herself."

"I'll allow the question, Mr. Goetz. Objection overruled. Proceed," said Judge Walling.

"Thank you, Your Honor." Goetz turned to the pharmacist and said, "Do you agree, then, Mr. Hoffman, that it is possible Mrs. King did not place the orders herself and quite possibly someone else may have called your pharmacy on her behalf?"

"Yes, yes, I suppose that is possible, but—"

"No more questions," said Goetz and walked to the defendant table. He stood for a moment gazing at Mr. Hoffman before taking his seat.

"Does the prosecution have any further questions?" said Judge Walling.

"Yes, Your Honor, thank you," said Skidmore as he strode to face the pharmacist. "Mr. Hoffman, you have stated that, since you did not personally take the orders for the arsenic and, further, since Mr. Fletcher cannot be located to testify that he did, in fact, take the phone calls, that you believe there is a slight possibility that the orders were not placed directly from Mrs. King. Is that correct?"

"Yes."

"Mr. Hoffman, how accurate are the orders placed with your pharmacy?"

"I do not understand the question."

"I'm sorry. I will rephrase the question. Please tell us in detail about the information gathered by you or your employees when a phone order is received by your pharmacy."

"Yes, of course," said Mr. Hoffman. "When a call comes into the pharmacy, the employee completes the form with the caller's name, the details of the order being placed such as amounts, brand, and so on. The caller's phone number and address are also written on the form. The employee will then repeat the entire order and verify who will be picking up the order. Once that is done, the employee ends the call and writes his or her name on the form and signs it. It is then placed in the basket marked 'Phone Orders.' I, being the pharmacist, then check the various baskets throughout the day for all orders and begin processing them."

"And what does that entail, Mr. Hoffman?"

"I sort the orders based on two factors—first, if they are orders for generic, over-the-counter items, those go in one stack. The second stack is for prescription orders that must be filled by a pharmacist. In this case, me. I then sort each of those stacks according to the day and time they are scheduled to be picked up or delivered. Once that is done, my employees and I begin filling orders and placing completed orders in bins located in the back of the pharmacy."

"Thank you, Mr. Hoffman. No further questions, Your Honor."

"Very well," said the judge. "You may step down, Mr. Hoffman. Mr. Prosecutor, please call your next witness."

"Thank you, Your Honor. The State calls Mrs. Margaret Henry."

Shoes scuffled on the floor behind Wilhelmina as people rose to let Mrs. Henry pass by as she made her way to the aisle. She walked with her nose in the air, hands clasped in front of her waist, her spine straight as if she were carrying a board on her back. After taking her oath, she squeezed into the witness stand and stared straight ahead.

Skidmore approached the stand and smiled at her. "Good morning, Mrs. Henry. Thank you for coming today. I trust your journey from Cleveland was without incident?"

"Yes," she said, her voice strong and calm. "Thank you."

"For the record, please state your full name and occupation."

"Mrs. Margaret Louise Henry. I am retired."

"And what did you do before you retired, Mrs. Henry?"

"I worked as a nanny."

"How many years, ma'am?"

"All totaled, I worked as a nanny for nearly thirty years."

"And before that?"

"Before that, I raised my seven children."

"And who was your last employer?"

"Dr. Johann King."

"And did you come in contact with Dr. King's wife?"

"Yes, occasionally. I took my meals in the kitchen and Mrs. King was there preparing the day's meals or cleaning. I was out of the house quite often doing the shopping or taking young Mr. King to and from school, and I did not consort with Mrs. King."

"Young Mr. King? Are you referring to Mrs. King's son, Albert? Albert Schmidt?"

"Yes, yes, I apologize. I forget he is not Dr. King's son."

"Very well, thank you. And how long were you in the employ of Dr. King?"

"I started working for Dr. King in January 1926 and left in May 1931."

"And why did you leave the King household?"

"I was getting up in years and my rheumatism was quite bothersome. It was difficult to take the stairs to my room several times a day. And my brother-in-law in Cleveland was ill and my sister asked I move in with her. He died a few months later. In addition, Master King ... I mean, Master Schmidt ... was eleven and no longer needed a nanny."

"I see. Mrs. Henry," Skidmore said as he cocked his head, hand on his chin. He turned back to Mrs. Henry and said, "What sort of shopping did you do for the King household?"

"Practically all of it, sir," she said as she shot a glare in Wilhelmina's direction. "Dr. King gave me cash every Sunday evening and throughout the week, I did the grocery shopping, picked up laundry from the dry cleaners, and picked up prescriptions."

"What pharmacy did the Kings use, Mrs. Henry?"

"Hoffman's Pharmacy."

"Mrs. Henry, to the best of your recollection, did you have a private conversation with Dr. King on the evening of May 18, 1930?"

"Yes, sir, I did."

"Can you please tell the court about that conversation?"

"Yes, of course. Dr. King called me into the parlor and told me Mrs. King suspected rats in the basement and had placed an order at Hoffman's Pharmacy for arsenic. She also needed a pound of oatmeal to mix with the arsenic to make poison for the rats. Dr. King gave me several bills and instructed me to pick up the items the next day, saying Mrs. King would not be able to run the errand herself."

"Did Dr. King give you any other instructions?"

"Yes. He was fearful that Mrs. King would not combine the ingredients properly and asked that I keep them out of her reach, in my room, until he could retrieve them when he arrived home the next evening."

"And did he retrieve the oatmeal and arsenic?"

"Yes, he came to the third floor after dinner and I met him outside my room, in the hallway, and handed the items to him. I do not know what he did with them after that. I assumed he took them to Mrs. King and taught her how to make the rat poison."

"Did you ever see Mrs. King make the rat poison or take it to the basement?"

"No sir, I did not."

"Did you ever see or hear any rats in the basement or anywhere on the property?"

"No, sir, I did not."

"Mrs. Henry, were you aware that the pantry at the house on Glenmary Drive stored food items that were kept separate from the household food supplies?"

"Yes, sir. There were separate canisters for coffee, tea, sugar and … and flour, I believe. There were also several canned goods in the pantry."

"And were these items marked in any way?"

"Yes, everything was marked with the word 'boarder' on the container."

"Thank you, Mrs. Henry. Just a couple more questions, if I may."

"Of course."

"You stated you saw Mrs. King prepare meals. Did you witness her preparing the meals for the boarders?"

"I did not remain in the kitchen once I finished my meals, but yes, I saw her prepare separate meals daily. The boarders all ate simple breakfasts, a very light lunch, and soup for dinner. Mrs. King would prepare these meals separately from the other meals."

"Who ate the other meals, Mrs. Henry?"

"I did, as well as the boy, Dr. King and Mrs. King."

"Did Mrs. King use the items from the pantry for the boarders' meals? The ones marked as you previously stated?"

"Yes, she did. She would carry the canisters and canned goods to the kitchen, and then return the canisters to the pantry after adding those ingredients to the food she was preparing."

"Thank you, Mrs. Henry. No further questions, Your Honor," Skidmore said, and took his seat.

"Defense, do you wish to cross examine the witness?"

"Yes, Your Honor." Goetz made his way to the witness stand and faced Mrs. Henry. "Ma'am, did you ever see Mrs. King add arsenic or any other poison to the food items that were marked for the boarders?"

"No, sir I did not."

"Thank you, Mrs. Henry. No further questions, Your Honor."

"Does the prosecution have any further questions?" said the judge.

"No, Your Honor, we do not. Thank you," said Skidmore.

"Very well, then. You may step down, Mrs. Henry," said the judge. "Court will now take a two-hour recess for lunch and recommence at one o'clock this afternoon. Court is in recess."

A guard handcuffed Wilhelmina, and as he led her down the aisle, she caught sight of her two dearest friends—Marta Wagner and Karin Bauer sat on a bench five rows behind the defendant's table. Neither woman met Wilhelmina's gaze, keeping their heads bowed as they each dabbed their eyes with faded handkerchiefs. She passed just feet away from Johann as she was led from the courtroom. His icy stare sent cold shivers down her spine, leaving her feeling exposed and vulnerable. Thank God, Albert was not in the courtroom.

That afternoon five young men took the witness stand and were questioned by the two prosecutors. Still dazed by seeing her friends that morning and rocked by how Johann had glared at her, Wilhelmina did not hear the names of these witnesses, although she vaguely recognized three of them as the ambulance attendants who had come to the house. Each young man took the stand, one by one, and described what they saw when they arrived at 14398 Glenmary Drive.

Jim Smith and Thomas Davis stated they arrived on May 20, 1930, to find a distraught woman, who they now identified as Wilhelmina, who led them up three precarious flights of stairs to the third-floor bathroom. There they both found a rather large man bent over the toilet and vomiting violently.

"The man's skin was white, very white," said Jim. "We weren't sure we would get him to the ambulance before he threw up again. He said his legs were cramping, his fingers and toes tingled, and he had some sort of warts or sores on his skin."

"It took both of us to carry Mr. Parker," explained Thomas. "Jim had to make his way down backward as he held onto Mr. Parker's legs while I had the gentlemen under his arms and was behind him. There was very little light, and Jim almost missed a couple of steps."

Jim Smith and John Baker responded to the second request for an ambulance on October 13, 1930. They climbed the stairs to the third floor, where they found Mr. Müeller dead on the bathroom floor.

John told the co-prosecutor, Edward Douglas, "There was vomit all over the floor around him and in the toilet, and his hands were covered in sores. It looked like they had bled, but were dried up, you know, with scabs. We backed out of the room and went down those steps as fast as we could. Jim used the telephone to call the coroner's office, and once they arrived, we left."

When Ludwig Klein took ill, Mark Catron and Raymond Feltner found him in his bed, sweating profusely, his face mottled with small bleeding lesions.

"He complained of his stomach hurting," Mark testified. "His skin was gray, very pale, and he was clammy."

Raymond added, "He said his entire body ached and his toes tingled."

Mark Catron and John Baker responded to the final call for an ambulance on July 26, 1933, and arrived to find Dr. Burdine examining his patient, August Weiss. They drove the patient to Good Samaritan Hospital where Dr. Burdine met them in the emergency room. They both testified that Mr. Weiss looked "pale" and was "sweating." They described him as having swollen hands covered in lesions and that he had complained of vomiting most of the night.

Mr. Goetz had no questions for any of these witnesses.

At nearly five o'clock that afternoon, a bailiff entered the courtroom and handed a note to Judge Walling.

"As there are no further questions, I believe we will adjourn for today. I have just been informed that a potential blizzard is moving into the area, so everyone needs to get to safety as soon as possible. Additionally, in light of the upcoming holiday, we will reconvene on Thursday, January fourth. Court is adjourned."

CHAPTER TWENTY-FOUR

January 1934

The prediction of a blizzard turned out to be incorrect, with less than six inches of snow falling to the ground the day after court had adjourned. On New Year's Eve, crowds gathered in Fountain Square in downtown Cincinnati as they listened to live music and watched fireworks light up the night sky. Prohibition in full force, speakeasies and underground clubs bustled with patrons enjoying illicit drinks, jazz music, and dancing. Families held parties in their homes and gathered around radios to hear the countdown to midnight.

From her cell, Wilhelmina could hear the broadcast emanating from somewhere down the hall, and she silently prayed for a better year. She had begun to doubt the efforts of Mr. Goetz on her behalf and made a request for a new attorney; her request was denied. She continued to work hard in the jail's laundry room and ate her meals alone in the cafeteria or in her cell. She spoke to no one and kept her nose buried in her Bible. Her faith ever strong, she was certain God would deliver her from her tribulations.

On January 4, Wilhelmina and her escort of guards made their way to the courtroom, which was, as usual, filled beyond capacity by curious onlookers and reporters. Despite the bitter cold outside, hundreds of people left their home to squeeze shoulder-to-shoulder in the hallway, hoping to acquire a seat or overhear someone's testimony each time the doors swung open. Everyone wanted a glimpse of the "beautiful Poisonous Peach." Weeks before, Wilhelmina had read the headline in the newspaper—*Poisonous Peach to Stand Trial*—and asked Mr. Goetz to explain the nickname.

"I'm afraid, Mrs. King," he had said, "it refers to not only the smell of arsenic but also to you personally." He cleared his throat and looked away. "You see, arsenic sometimes smells of peach blossoms and to call you the 'Poisonous Peach' is to say you are dangerous *and* alluring. It implies that you used your beauty to gain the trust of those men before you murdered them."

The judge called court to order, and Victor Berger took the stand. He explained he was Karl Berger's cousin and had been called to the house on Glenmary Drive on May 30, 1931. He found his cousin hugging his stomach in bed, sweating and moaning loudly. He noticed bleeding warts on his cousin's hands.

"Karl could barely talk, but he told me he had been throwing up for a week and asked me to take him to the hospital," said Mr. Berger. "I drove him to Good Samaritan, which was closest to the house, and he was admitted a few hours later."

"And can you tell us, Mr. Berger," asked Mr. Skidmore, "how long did your cousin remain in the hospital?"

"I went to the hospital two days later and was told he had died that morning. They said he had started … having … please forgive me," he said as he glanced at the jurors, "he had severe diarrhea."

"Thank you, Mr. Berger. Please accept our condolences for your loss," said Skidmore.

"Thank you, sir."

"No further questions, Your Honor."

"Does the defense wish to cross examine?"

"Yes, Your Honor," Goetz said as he stood and straightened his jacket. He approached the bench and said, "Mr. Berger, did the hospital staff tell you what had caused your cousin's death?"

"They said it appeared to be gastro … gastro … I am sorry, my memory fails me. I do not remember the word."

"Quite all right," Goetz said and turned to the judge. "If I may, Your Honor?"

"Proceed," said Judge Walling.

"Mr. Berger, could you be referring to gastroenteritis?"

"Objection!" shouted Skidmore, standing to his full height. "Defense is leading the witness!"

"Your Honor, I am merely attempting to help this witness recall the name of the condition which caused his cousin's death. He clearly is having some difficulty remembering the medical term."

"I'll allow it," said the judge. "Overruled."

Skidmore sank into his chair and scribbled something on his notepad.

"Mr. Berger, I will repeat the question so that everyone is clear. Could the hospital staff have used the term 'gastroenteritis' when you asked about the cause of death?"

"Yes, sir, I do believe that is the word," said Mr. Berger.

"Thank you. No further questions, Your Honor."

"You may step down, Mr. Berger," said Judge Walling.

The remainder of the morning flew by with just two witnesses called: Dr. Christopher Kerley and Dr. Brendan Pottinger—the doctors on duty in the emergency room at Good Samaritan Hospital when the victims arrived. Dr. Kerley had treated Mr. Parker and Mr. Klein, while Dr. Pottinger saw Mr. Berger and Mr. Weiss.

Their testimonies were quite similar: all four men arrived by ambulance with warts or lesions on their skin, complaining of aching muscles and tingling fingers or toes. All four men had been vomiting for more than twenty-four hours, one having severe diarrhea as well. All four died within hours or days of arriving at the hospital, all from apparent severe gastroenteritis while Mr. Weiss also suffered with cardiovascular disease.

Both doctors agreed that "It is not unusual for persons of advanced years and declining health to suffer from gastroenteritis and succumb to the illness" and "We did not find it necessary to request an autopsy on any of the victims."

Harold Goetz once again had no questions for these witnesses, and the judge called for a recess for lunch.

That afternoon Dr. Robert Burdine took the stand. Edward Douglas, the co-prosecutor, began the questioning by asking, "Doctor Burdine, please tell us the events, as you recall, of July 26, 1933."

"Yes," Dr. Burdine said, straightening on his chair. "I received a call on that morning from a Mrs. King, who explained that a gentleman residing in her home, Mr. Weiss, was quite ill and had asked her to call me."

"And would that have been Mr. August Weiss?"

"Yes."

"And what time did you receive that phone call, Doctor?"

"I believe it was around four o'clock in the afternoon."

"And what did you do after you hung up from the call?"

"I immediately left my office and drove to Clifton Heights, to the house on ... on ... Glenmary Drive, I believe. Mrs. King let me into the house and showed me up the back stairs to the third floor, to Mr. Weiss's bedroom."

"And what was Mr. Wiess's condition when you arrived?"

"He was tossing and turning in his bed, holding his stomach, and sweating profusely. He complained of pain in his stomach and told me he had been vomiting all day."

"Did your examination show any other symptoms or conditions?"

"I saw that his hands appeared to be quite swollen, and several bloody lesions were forming on the backs."

"Where was Mrs. King while you examined Mr. Weiss?"

"I believe she had gone back downstairs to the kitchen. That is where I found her when I finished with Mr. Weiss."

"And did you speak with her?"

"Yes, I asked to use her phone to call for an ambulance. I told her Mr. Weiss needed to be hospitalized right away."

"And how did she react? What was her behavior?"

"She was quite distraught and appeared to have been crying."

"How so?"

"Her eyes were red and damp, and her face was streaked with tears."

"How long did it take for the ambulance to arrive?"

"About thirty minutes or so, I believe."

"And did you go to the hospital as well?"

"Yes, I arrived moments after Mr. Weiss was taken into the emergency room. Doctor Pottinger was examining him. He and I conferred for several minutes. I explained to him my findings, and we agreed that Mr. Weiss appeared to have a severe case of gastroenteritis."

"I see. And what happened next, Doctor?"

"Mr. Weiss was admitted to the hospital and taken to a room on the fourth floor."

"And what was his condition upon arriving at his room?"

"He was in severe pain and was vomiting regularly, I'd say about every ten to fifteen minutes or so."

"And you left the hospital?"

"Yes, I left him in the capable hands of the nursing staff of the hospital."

"Doctor Burdine, can you tell us which hospital?"

"Yes, yes, it was Good Samaritan Hospital. I do not normally practice at Good Sam, but it is the closest hospital to the residence where Mr. Weiss resided."

"I see. And Doctor, when did you next see Mr. Weiss?"

"I checked on him at seven the following morning."

"What was his condition?"

"He was experiencing respiratory difficulty, that is, he was having trouble breathing. He was going in and out of consciousness. I examined him thoroughly, and it appeared he was also experiencing circulatory collapse."

"And what exactly is that, Doctor?"

"Circulatory collapse is when the body cannot get enough blood to the organs and tissues. This often causes a person to lose consciousness and directly affects the functions of vital organs, such as the kidneys and lungs."

"And what can cause circulatory collapse?"

"It can often be caused by heart disease, a heart attack, severe infection, an allergic reaction, or even dehydration."

"And what would you say was the cause of this … circulatory collapse in Mr. Weiss?"

"My examination showed he suffered from irregular heart rhythms and extreme dehydration, as a result of several hours of vomiting."

"Doctor Burdine, can arsenic poisoning also lead to circulatory collapse?"

"Objection!" shouted Mr. Goetz. "Prosecution is leading the witness."

Wilhelmina stared at him—it was the first time her attorney had called for an objection during the trial.

Mr. Douglas clasped his hands together on the table. "Your Honor, I am merely trying to establish all the possible causes for Mr. Weiss's condition."

"I'll allow it," said Judge Walling. "Objection overruled. Please answer the question, Doctor Burdine."

"Yes," said the doctor, "circulatory collapse can also be a result of arsenic poisoning."

"Thank you, Doctor," said Douglas. "What happened next?"

"Unfortunately, Mr. Weiss's condition had worsened overnight, and we were unable to save him. He died at around nine o'clock in the morning."

"On what date, Doctor, did Mr. Weiss die?"

"July 27, 1933."

"Thank you. And did you request an autopsy of Mr. Weiss's body?"

"No, I did not."

"Why was that?"

"I felt my examination showed enough evidence of heart disease and dehydration, which as I said before, could very well lead to circulatory collapse and even death. I did not feel an autopsy was warranted."

"I see. Doctor Burdine, did you telephone Mrs. King following the death of Mr. Weiss?"

"Yes, I did. I asked if she could have his belongings gathered and I would send someone by in a few days to retrieve them. I told her Mr. Weiss had died."

"And what was her reaction?"

"I heard her whisper 'yes' but then she was no longer on the line. I shouted her name a few times until her son picked up the phone and told me his mother had fainted. I instructed him to dab her face and neck with a cool cloth until she came around."

"I see. And did you remain on the line while he did this?"

"No, I did not. I did tell him to call for an ambulance if his mother did not wake up soon, however. He thanked me and hung up the phone."

"Thank you, Doctor Burdine. No further questions."

Mr. Goetz approached the stand and frowned intently at Doctor Burdine. "Doctor Burdine, please tell the court, again, when you first encountered Mrs. King at her home on July 26, 1933, what was her behavior?"

"Mrs. King was clearly upset. She had been crying. She was pacing the kitchen floor when I returned from examining Mr. Weiss. She was wringing her hands."

"And how did she react when you phoned her the next day to tell her Mr. Weiss had died?"

"I only heard a whispered 'yes' when I asked her to gather Mr. Weiss's belongings, and then she was no longer on the phone."

"Why was that?"

"Her son picked up the phone and told me she had fainted."

"And would you say this is a normal reaction?"

"I am sorry, I do not understand the question."

"I'll rephrase. Mr. Weiss had been a resident in the King home for three months. Would you say it is possible that Mr. Weiss had developed a rapport, a friendship even, with Mrs. King?"

"I would say that is possible, yes."

"And assuming a friendship was formed, would you say Mrs. King's reaction to the news of Mr. Weiss's death was a normal reaction for a woman?"

"Yes, yes, I suppose it was."

"Thank you, Doctor Burdine. No further questions."

Moments later, with another loud bang of the gavel, court was adjourned until the following Monday morning.

"Court is now in session," said Judge Walling. "Mr. Skidmore, please call your first witness."

Patrolman David Brown was called to the stand and sworn in.

"Officer Brown," said Skidmore, "please tell the court the events of September 20, 1933."

"Yes. Detective Barnes called a meeting at the station at one o'clock and informed us we would be proceeding to a house on

Glenmary Drive to gather evidence in a suspected homicide," said Officer Brown.

"Who else was present in the meeting?"

"As I recall, Detective Kilbarger was there, Sergeants Tompkins and Carr, and Officer Lykins. There were four other patrolmen also, if I'm not mistaken. I believe they were Anderson, Wright, Daniels, and Jones."

"Thank you, officer. And what happened when you arrived at the house?"

"I approached the suspect, Mrs. King, and informed her she would have to come to the police station. She seemed confused and began to resist. She then insisted on taking something inside. Let's see … umm … a bowl of green beans, I believe. I followed her into the house, to the kitchen, and then placed her under arrest."

"Did she go with you willingly?"

"For the most part, yes. She struggled against me when I handcuffed her. She calmed down a bit, so I read her rights to her, and escorted her to the police cruiser waiting at the curb."

"What happened then?"

"A young boy ran to us. It was her son. He called her 'Mama' and kept asking what was happening. I helped Mrs. King into the car, and her son started beating his fists on the door until Officer Lykins pulled the boy away. He then ran into the house. The boy, I mean."

"After you placed Mrs. King in the car, did you go back into the house?"

"No. Officer Lykins and I drove Mrs. King to the station downtown and booked her."

"Thank you. No further questions."

Mr. Goetz had no questions for Officer Brown, and the judge instructed him to step down. Officer Lykins was then called to the stand and corroborated his partner's testimony to the letter.

Mr. Skidmore skirted around the prosecution table and approached the bench.

"Your Honor," he said as he glanced at the twelve jurors, "in the interest of time, this Court has received written testimonial affidavits from the officers present during the search for evidence at 14398 Glenmary Drive on September 20, 1933. Those officers have granted permission for Detective Charles Barnes to submit verbal testimony on their behalf. The prosecution hereby would like to call Detective Barnes to the stand."

"Your request is granted, Mr. Skidmore," said Judge Walling. He faced the jury and said, "Exhibit FF is now entered into the record as evidence, comprised of the written testimonial affidavits of Detective Kilbarger, Sergeant Tompkins, Sergeant Carr, and Patrolmen Daniels, Jones, Anderson, and Wright. Mr. Skidmore, you may call your witness."

"Thank you, Your Honor," said Skidmore. "The State calls Detective Charles Barnes to the stand."

Detective Barnes sat sideways in the witness box to accommodate his long legs as Arthur Skidmore paced in front of the jury box.

"Good morning, Detective Barnes," Skidmore said. "I would like to begin by asking how you became aware of possible crimes that took place at 14398 Glenmary Drive."

"Good morning," said Barnes. "I received a phone call on the morning of September 20, 1933, from Dr. Johann King."

"And what did Dr. King tell you?"

"He said he had taken quite ill several days prior, to the point of being seen in the emergency room of the hospital where he worked and having his stomach pumped. He then explained he had documented evidence he had been poisoned by arsenic."

Wilhelmina sucked in air, and glanced around the room, locking eyes with Johann. His lips curled into a sinister grin as he winked at her, his eyes glinting with cold cunning, sending a chill down her spine.

"And what did you do next, Detective Barnes."

"I met with the captain, and we agreed to call a meeting right away. We met at one o'clock, and I briefed the men on the case."

"Please confirm for the Court who was in attendance during this meeting."

"Myself, Captain Hull, Detective Kilbarger, Sergeants Tompkins and Carr, and six patrolmen. They were officers Brown, Lykins, Daniels, Jones, Anderson, and Wright."

"Thank you, Detective. What happened after the briefing?"

"We dispatched Officers Brown and Lykins to the residence to place the suspect under arrest."

"Can you please state for the Court the name of the suspect?"

"Yes. Mrs. Johann King, er, Wilhelmina Marie King."

"Thank you. If you please, Detective, will you now recount for the Court the events that occurred during the investigation at the property."

Everyone in the courtroom sat on the edge of their seats as Detective Barnes described what happened that day in September. He told the Court about arriving on scene at the same time as Dr. King and finding the young boy home alone and crying. He explained in detail how they found each piece of evidence, then carefully bagged and labeled each. He assured Mr. Skidmore—and the jury—that all floors and every room of the house were thoroughly searched.

"Detective Barnes," said Skidmore, "did your search of the house include the basement?"

"Yes, it did."

"Can you tell the Court what you found there?"

"Nothing."

"Nothing? Please explain."

"I personally searched the basement. I went out the back door and found the cellar doors. There was no light down there, so I used my flashlight and found nothing in the basement except cement block walls and a dirt floor."

"Detective, was there any evidence of a rat infestation in the basement?"

"No sir, there was not."

"Thank you, Detective. Your Honor, I have no further questions."

Harold Goetz rose from his chair and approached the witness.

"Detective Barnes, you have provided us with a very detailed account of the events that occurred on September 20, 1933. I have only a few questions for you."

The detective nodded at Mr. Goetz.

"You stated the basement floor was dirt, is that correct?"

"Yes, sir."

"And did you see any evidence of rat droppings in the dirt?"

"No, sir, I did not."

"Were you specifically looking for rat droppings, Detective Barnes?"

"No, no, I was not, but no droppings were evident."

"How large would you say the basement was, Detective?"

"Rather large, probably expanding under the entire house. It's a rather large house. Some would call it a mansion, I suppose."

"So, with only a flashlight in hand, you could see well enough in a dark basement with no windows and a dirt floor to know there were no rat droppings of any kind on top of or beneath the dirt. Is that correct?"

"Well, yes, but I was not specifically looking for rat droppings."

"Detective, when you spoke with Dr. King that morning on the phone, did he explain why he believed his wife had poisoned him with arsenic?"

"Yes, he said he knew she had purchased arsenic because she had complained of hearing rats in the basement."

"And armed with this knowledge, you did not find it necessary to thoroughly search the basement floor for rat droppings?"

"As I said, I saw no immediate evidence of rats in the basement and did not feel a more complete search was necessary."

"Did you see any evidence of human footprints in the dirt of the basement floor?"

"No, sir, I did not."

"I see. Detective, would you say it is safe to say that it *is* possible there were rats in the basement, which would have been discovered upon a more thorough investigation of the dirt floor?"

"Objection! Defense is leading the witness, Your Honor, and making conjecture about the existence of rats in the basement!" cried Mr. Skidmore.

"Mr. Goetz, the witness has already made it clear that he did not feel further investigation in the basement was warranted," said the judge. He turned to the jury and said, "Counsel's last question will be struck from the record. Objection sustained."

"I apologize, Your Honor. I have no further questions."

"If the prosecution has nothing further…" said Judge Walling. Mr. Skidmore shook his head to indicate he had no more questions for the witness. "Very well, court is adjourned and will reconvene on Wednesday at nine-thirty in the morning."

Bang! The sound of the gavel hitting the block bounced off the courtroom walls as the onlookers sat ominously silent.

Chapter Twenty-Five

Every person in the courtroom leaned forward in their seats as their gazes followed six bailiffs, each carrying a large jar covered by a white cloth into the room. The bailiffs placed the jars on two five-foot-long tables positioned in front of the jury box. The air thick with suspense, the room fell eerily quiet, except for the sound of men's shoes tapping on the marble floor as the bailiffs turned and strode out the door behind the onlookers.

Prosecutor Skidmore paced back and forth next to the tables, peering into the eyes of each jury member.

"Ladies and gentlemen," he said, "these jars contain the preserved organs of the victims and have been meticulously examined by the county coroner, Dr. Michael Wilson. You will hear details from Dr. Wilson about the discovery of lethal doses of arsenic found in these organs. Please pay close attention to this line of questioning, as the evidence presented here could very well provide you with the deciding factors in this case."

Skidmore walked to the prosecution table and turned toward the judge. "Your Honor, I would like to call Dr. Michael Wilson to the stand."

From his seat at the back of the room, Dr. Wilson stood and proceeded up the aisle to face the bailiff. After vowing to "tell the truth," he sat on the chair in the witness stand, removed his glasses, and wiped the lenses with a handkerchief. He slipped the glasses back onto his nose and folded his hands on his lap.

Wilhelmina seemed to be the only person in the courtroom not staring intently at the covered jars. With her eyes closed, she was back in time, remembering a day many years ago—she was a little girl in a lacy pink dress, skipping in the grass with her friends. A full grin filled her face when her mother brought the cake out and set it on a table. The other children sang while she made a wish, and she blew out the flames flicking on five candles nestled in the white icing atop the cake. She squealed with delight when her mother sliced the cake to reveal chocolate layers filled with creamy fudge—her favorite flavors!

Loud cries and gasps rippled through the courtroom, bringing Wilhelmina out of her reverie. She stared at the man on the witness stand and wondered, *Why was I thinking about my birthday?* She leaned toward Mr. Goetz and tapped his arm.

"Mr. Goetz," she whispered. "What is the date today?"

"Ma'am, it is January 10, 1934. Now, hush and pay attention," he hissed back.

January 10. My birthday.

Her gaze drifted around the room until landing on the cause of the cries and gasps from a moment ago—the jars stood on the tables, uncovered and labeled with each victim's name, revealing human organs floating in formalin, a mixture of water and formaldehyde. Wilhelmina's gaze settled on the last jar, labeled "Schmidt," and her mouth watered excessively as queasiness settled in. A wave of heat filled her chest as bile rose up her throat. She clasped her hand over her mouth, a bitter, acrid taste coating her throat and tongue, and grabbed the table, swaying in her seat.

The women in the jury box squirmed in their seats, covering their mouths with handkerchiefs. Their eyes darted around the room in search of somewhere else to aim their eyes. One young woman wept openly. The men in the back row sat on the edge of their seats, peering around the heads blocking their view, rapt with curiosity.

"Ladies and gentlemen," Skidmore was saying, "we present to you Exhibits L, M, N, O, P, and Q." He turned to the witness and said, "Dr. Wilson, please state your name and occupation for the Court."

"Dr. Michael Wilson, County Coroner."

"And how long have you served in that capacity?"

"Ten years."

"And what was your occupation prior to that?"

"I was the medical examiner for Hamilton County for twelve years. Prior to that, I was a general medical practitioner for eight years with my own practice."

"Thank you. And where were you educated, Dr. Wilson?"

"Johns Hopkins University in Baltimore, Maryland."

"And when did you graduate, Doctor?

"In 1903."

"How did you rank among your peers?"

"I graduated in the top one percent of my class and received many honors and accolades from the University."

"Very well. Thank you, Doctor." Skidmore traveled back and forth between the jury box and witness stand as he questioned Dr. Wilson. "Sir, please describe for the Court the contents contained in each of the jars before us, labeled as Exhibits L through P."

"Yes, of course. The jars contain large portions of each victim's stomach and liver."

"Thank you. Let's begin with Exhibit L, the preserved organs of the first victim, Mr. Jacob Parker. Please describe for us your findings in these organs."

For the next hour, Dr. Wilson testified that he received orders in October 1933 from the Court of Common Pleas of Hamilton County to have the bodies of Jacob Parker, Ernst Müeller, Karl Berger, Ludwig Klein, and August Weiss exhumed and delivered to the coroner's office. By the middle of November, he had performed all five autopsies and waited for toxicology reports to arrive from the lab. The results arrived in mid-December, just days before Wilhelmina's trial began.

"The stomachs and livers of all five victims revealed lethal levels of arsenic," Dr. Wilson said.

"Please explain for the Court how much arsenic is considered to be a lethal dose." Skidmore turned to face the jury while he waited for Dr. Wilson to respond.

"Typically, seventy to 180 milligrams would be fatal. This is about the size of a pea, or one-eighth of a teaspoon."

"And how much arsenic was found in these five victims?"

"Each victim had in excess of 200 milligrams in their organs."

"Doctor, what happens to a person who ingests this much arsenic in a short period of time?"

"The person would begin sweating, their muscles could ache, their extremities, such as fingers or toes, would tingle. They would experience violent convulsions, vomiting, and diarrhea. Many often develop warts or lesions on the skin."

"How soon would someone die following the onset of these symptoms?"

"Depending on the person's general health condition prior to ingesting arsenic, most would die within hours or days."

"And could you tell the Court, please, if the symptoms of arsenic poisoning, the symptoms you mentioned a moment ago, could be construed as any other medical condition?"

"Yes, in many cases, these symptoms mirror those of a person with gastroenteritis. Gastroenteritis, if severe, can also cause death. In some cases, although not as common, arsenic poisoning can also appear to be heart disease in some patients."

"What kind of heart disease, Doctor?"

"Heart failure, arrhythmia of the heart, and sometimes cardiovascular circulatory collapse."

"Thank you. Doctor Wilson, I would now like to direct your attention to Exhibit Q. Can you please tell the Court what is contained in this particular jar?"

"Yes, of course. That jar, er, Exhibit Q, contains the stomach and liver of one Oskar Schmidt, the defendant's late husband."

"Objection!" cried Mr. Goetz. "Your Honor, the defendant has not been charged with any crime relating to her late husband, Mr. Schmidt. We respectfully request that this piece of so-called evidence be removed from the record and this line of questioning terminated."

"Your Honor," interjected Mr. Skidmore. "While the prosecution fully understands that the defendant has not been accused of a crime against her late husband, Mr. Oskar Schmidt, it is our desire to show to the jury and to the Court that Mr. Schmidt died in 1925 of the effects of gastroenteritis, which as we all now know, is the same condition initially thought to cause the deaths of four of these victims. We are merely attempting to establish the defendant's pattern of behavior."

Judge Walling glanced at Wilhelmina, who stared blankly into his eyes, while he scrunched his brows in thought. "The court finds that the autopsy results of Mr. Oskar Schmidt are relevant to establishing a pattern and are pertinent to the case at hand. The jury may consider this evidence and testimony. Objection overruled."

Mr. Goetz sank into his chair and stared into his lap.

"You may proceed, Mr. Skidmore," said Judge Walling, "but I will remind the jury that the defendant has not been charged with any crime against her late husband, Mr. Oskar Schmidt. This evidence and testimony are submitted for relevance only."

"Thank you, Your Honor. Dr. Wilson, please tell the court how you came into possession of Exhibit Q. Specifically, the body of Mr. Oskar Schmidt."

"About a week after I began the autopsies on the other victims, I received another court order to have Mr. Schmidt's body exhumed from Spring Grove Cemetery and to perform an autopsy."

"And when did you receive his body?"

"Just before Thanksgiving last year. Er, that is, in late November."

"Very well. When did you perform the autopsy?"

"The autopsy was performed on Tuesday, December 5, 1933."

"And when did the results come back into your office?"

"I sent the organs to the lab that same day and requested expedience, given the trial was set to begin in mid-December. The results arrived on Tuesday, December 19 and were submitted to the Court as evidence."

Skidmore picked up another folder from the prosecution table and addressed the jury, "Let the record show, these documents comprise Exhibits R, S, T, U, V, and W and are the documented autopsy results from the five victims and Mr. Oskar Schmidt. Prosecution hereby submits these exhibits as evidence relevant to this case."

He handed the folder to the bailiff and ambled to the witness stand.

"Dr. Wilson, please tell the Court the results of the autopsy you performed on the body of Mr. Oskar Schmidt."

"Mr. Schmidt's stomach and liver contained 104 milligrams of arsenic. My findings were that, while his condition was mistaken for gastroenteritis, he did in fact die from arsenic poisoning."

"And please tell the court, what was your final judgment on the deaths of Messrs. Parker, Müeller, Berger, Klein, and Weiss?"

"It is my opinion that all five of those gentlemen died from arsenic poisoning."

Behind Wilhelmina, the faint sound of pencils scratching on paper, shoes shuffling on the floor, and muted whispers permeated the room as reporters scrambled to take notes and the onlookers muttered to one another.

"Order in the court!" shouted Judge Walling. "Prosecution may continue."

"No further questions, Your Honor," said Skidmore.

"Very well. Does the defense wish to cross examine?"

Goetz stood and said, "No, Your Honor, no questions."

"Very well, Mr. Goetz," said the judge. "I see the hour is late and Court has not taken a recess for lunch. Therefore, if there are no objections, I believe we should adjourn for the day and reconvene on Friday, January 12."

"No objections, Your Honor," said Skidmore and Goetz simultaneously.

"Very well, then. Court is adjourned."

❧

That night, a powerful storm raged across Cincinnati with wind gusts exceeding fifty miles per hour and ominous clouds dropping several inches of ice on every surface, postponing the next court day until the following Monday. In jail, Wilhelmina spent her time alone reading the Bible, praying, and writing letters to Albert and her family in Germany, none of which were answered.

Mr. Goetz visited her only one time, on Sunday afternoon. She continued to claim her innocence and asked if she would be taking the stand during the trial.

"I have not yet decided, Mrs. King," he told her. "I'm not sure it is in your best interest. I believe the prosecution has only one remaining witness to question, though. I will decide after that if I will put you on the stand."

"Do you know who the witness is, Mr. Goetz?"

"Yes, Mrs. King, it is your husband, Dr. King."

"Oh, dear. I am afraid Johann will not testify in my favor. We don't … didn't … exactly have a happy marriage."

"I tend to agree with you, madam. There is one question I must ask before I take my leave of you."

"And that is …?"

"Mrs. King, I want to call your son to the witness stand, and I would like your permission to do so."

"No!" Wilhelmina rose from her chair and paced the cell floor. "N-No, please, do not …"

"Mrs. King, I must be honest with you. The evidence in this case, as presented by the prosecution, is rather damning. I have found it nearly impossible to find witnesses to testify in your favor. I do not believe the outcome of this trial will be a positive one for you. I feel it is of utmost importance to put Albert on the stand. He adores you and will cast you in a much better light."

"Mis-Mister Goetz, must you?" Wilhelmina removed a tattered handkerchief from her pocket and dabbed her moist eyes.

"Yes, madam, I believe I must."

"What … What … other witnesses have you found for me?"

"I will be calling your former hospital supervisor, Mr. Burns, as well as Pastor Bergmann from the Lutheran church you used to attend. Also, Karin Bauer, Marta Wagner, and Friederich Wagner."

"You … You've located the Bauers, then? I was told they moved to Indianapolis in 1930."

"Yes, that is correct, Mrs. King. But I must let you know … Mr. Bauer passed in 1932. Mrs. Bauer returned to Ohio and is now living with the Wagners."

"Oh, dear. Georg dead? He was always so helpful, so kind. Please, Mr. Goetz, will you deliver a letter to Karin … Mrs. Bauer … for me? And to Mrs. Wagner?"

"Yes, yes, Mrs. King, I will do so. I will stop by tomorrow morning before you are taken to the courthouse. Have your letters ready by then. I must be on my way, Mrs. King. We will talk more about calling Albert to testify after we hear Dr. King's testimony tomorrow. Good day, madam."

Wilhelmina slept fitfully that night, her sleep flooded by a nightmare of Albert crying while on the witness stand. In the hazy depths of the dream, she ran for him to take him in her arms, to tell him it would be all right, only to be pulled away by several policemen and returned to her cell. Mist poured in clouding the vision, but when the fog cleared, she found herself standing in the third-floor hallway of the house, watching five men bent over one toilet in the bathroom, all retching violently, spewing bottles marked with a skull and crossbones from their mouths. Each man turned to look at her, their faces decayed with rotting flesh and bone, their skeletal arms stretching out. Their bodies twisted into nothingness, replaced by one man kneeling at the toilet. Oskar faced her and said, "My darling, my dear Mina, why? Why did you do this to me?"

She screamed and bolted upright on her cot. She shielded her eyes from the sunlight pouring through the window of her cell. The bright rays cast a spotlight on her Bible where it rested on the table against the wall. Her breath quick and shallow, Wilhelmina put a hand to her chest, her heart beating wildly underneath. She took a deep breath, held it, and slowly let it out, over and over until she stopped shaking.

Mrs. Flick appeared at her cell door, keys in hand, and said, "You better dress quickly, madam. You have overslept and will be late for court. I'm afraid no breakfast for you today."

It's just as well, thought Wilhelmina. The idea of food repulsed her.

Johann was impeccably outfitted in a tailored suit—navy blue wool double-breasted herringbone jacket, a crisp white shirt, and charcoal gray slacks. The paisley gray tie, featuring a diamond-studded gold tie clip, perfectly matched the folded handkerchief peeking above the hem of the breast pocket. His salt and pepper hair had recently been cut in a tapered fade from his ears to the nape of his neck, his bangs slicked back from his forehead. His hexagonal eyeglasses, resting on the end of his nose, were framed by genuine tortoiseshell, crafted from the shells of hawksbill sea turtles.

Dr. King elicited an air of wealth and dignity as he gracefully strode to the front of the courtroom. He stood tall, his posture arrow straight, his demeanor a mixture of confidence and subtle arrogance, as he placed his left hand on a Bible, raised his right hand, and took the oath. Wilhelmina's gaze narrowed in on him, intense and unwavering. She turned slightly to her left, away from where Johann stood, and crossed her arms over her chest. She pressed her lips into a thin line and sighed heavily as he took his seat at the witness stand.

Arthur Skidmore stood in front of the stand and said, "Good morning. For the record, please state your name and occupation for the court."

"Johann Hermann King, physician. I am a surgeon."

"And where do you work, Dr. King?"

"At Good Samaritan Hospital here in Cincinnati."

"And how long have you worked there?"

"Nearly eighteen years. I began employment as a general surgeon there in March 1916."

"I see. Dr. King, how did you come to know the defendant?"

"I met her at the hospital. I was looking for a gown, a doctor's gown, that is to say. One of the nurses directed me to the doctor's linen closet on the third floor of the hospital. That is where I met Wilhelmina … er … the defendant."

Johann answered each of Mr. Skidmore's questions and told the court about Wilhelmina's broken necklace and how he met Oskar and Albert Schmidt. He talked about befriending Oskar, about bringing toys to Albert, and about the Schmidt family including him in many dinners at their home. A single tear dripped down his cheek when he talked of his shock at learning of Oskar's death.

"I felt sorry for Wilhel … er … the defendant and her son, Albert. They had been so kind to me. She was not wealthy, I knew, and I gave her some money to get her through a few months before she would need to return to work. I visited her often over those few months and became quite fond of her."

"And when did you and the defendant marry?"

"We were married at the end of August 1925."

"Only a few months after the defendant became a widow?"

"Yes, well, it was nearly six months after Mr. Schmidt died. Wilhelmina had talked of returning to Germany, and being fond of her as I said, I did not want to lose the opportunity to make her my wife. I was quite fond of the boy, as well. I proposed, and she accepted."

"Was this your first marriage?

"Yes."

"And how would you describe your marriage, Dr. King?"

"A very happy one in the beginning. Wilhelmina was an excellent choice for a wife. She kept a fine household and her cooking was, well, quite good."

"You said it was happy 'in the beginning.' What changed, Dr. King?"

"Wilhelmina became distant and cool toward me. She insisted on moving into her own bedroom and kept her door locked while she slept. She became afraid to leave the house and refused to take her son to school. She stopped doing the shopping or running the necessary errands to run the household."

"Is this when you hired the nanny? Mrs. Henry, I believe?"

"Yes, it is."

"Was there anything else out of the ordinary about your wife's behavior?"

"She stopped allowing Albert, her son, to take his meals with us in the dining room and instead fed him in the kitchen. She would not allow him to play in the parlor but sent him upstairs to take his bath and prepare for bed every evening as soon as he finished eating." Johann removed his glasses, wiped them with a handkerchief, and returned them to the end of his nose.

"I see," said Skidmore. "Please, proceed."

"She also cut off all ties with her friends ... Mrs. Bauer and Mrs. Wagner. Wilhelmina had seemed to be quite close with them, but soon after we moved into the house on Glenmary Drive, she stopped

visiting them, stopped calling them. She also … ahem, ahem …"
Johann swallowed and cleared his throat again. "I-I am sorry … I
have m-more, but it is … difficult."

"Would you like a glass of water, Dr. King?"

"Yes, please."

A bailiff left the room and returned a moment later with a glass
of water and handed it to Johann. He drank it down quickly and
wiped his mouth with his handkerchief.

"Thank you."

"Please proceed when you are ready, Dr. King. You said there
was something you wanted to add?"

"Y-Yes. You see, Wilhelmina began accusing me of calling her
'Anya.'"

"Why would she do that?"

"I do not know. I have never known anyone named Anya and
have no reason to call her by that name."

"When did the defendant begin making those accusations, Dr.
King?"

"Almost immediately after we were married. She insisted that I
call her by her given name and stop calling her 'Anya.' I assured her
I never used that name with her, but she would not believe me and
would often become quite agitated and argue with me about the
matter. She would become quite angry and storm out of the room."

"I see. Dr. King, when did you decide to bring in a boarder to
your home?"

"Shortly after the Great Crash. I believe the first boarder … a Mr.
Parker … came to us in early 1930."

"And what was your reason for bringing in these boarders?"

"Like many of us, I had suffered some great financial losses and
needed to supplement the household income."

"Dr. King, did you select your boarders yourself, or did the
defendant participate with you in the interviews?"

"Mrs. King … the defendant … met with each of the potential
boarders while I was at the hospital and told me of her findings every
evening at dinner. I allowed her to make the selection herself, as she
would be the one responsible for their meals, etcetera."

"What responsibilities did the defendant have for the boarders?"

"She made their meals, three a day, cleaned their rooms and the bathroom, and did their laundry."

"And did you have the nanny, Mrs. Henry, purchase separate food items to be used for the boarders alone?"

"Yes, I did."

"Please explain."

"In order to determine how much to charge them for board, in addition to the room rental, I needed to keep tabs on how much food and what types of food they consumed. This way, the money I received from them for board was specifically used to purchase their food."

"I see. Quite efficient, I must say."

"Thank you."

Mr. Skidmore questioned Johann for another hour about each of the boarders, how they behaved, whether they interacted with Wilhelmina, and the circumstances surrounding their deaths as Johann knew them. The court then took a two-hour recess for lunch.

Johann returned to the stand when court reconvened. Mr. Skidmore ambled around the table and stood facing the jury. "Dr. King, in your opinion as a doctor of medicine, would you say that your wife's ... the defendant's behavior during your marriage has been out of the ordinary, even bordering psychotic?"

"Yes, I believe she has been teetering on the edge of insanity for quite some time."

"And what has led you to this belief, Doctor?"

"As I said this morning, she accused me of calling her by a name I've never heard of before. She refused to leave the house. She distanced her son away from me, just as we had begun developing a bond. She distanced *herself* away from me and would not afford me my husbandly rights. She complained about the boarders, often saying they were 'curmudgeonly old men' and that she despised them."

"Dr. King, were you aware that your wife, the defendant, had borne a child out of wedlock?"

"Yes, she told me about it shortly before we were married."

"And did she reveal who the father was?"

"She told me she had been a promiscuous teenager, often sneaking out of her parents' home in Munich to attend college parties and flirt with boys. She said the father could have been any one of those boys."

"And did she tell you how she came to be in America?"

"Yes. Her father banished her from his home and sent her to Cincinnati to live with relatives. His brother, I believe, and his brother's wife."

"And did she ever tell you what happened to the child?"

"She said she took the child when he was only a day old to the orphanage."

"Dr. King, did the defendant tell you how old she was when these events took place?"

"She was fifteen when she became pregnant. I believe she was sixteen by the time the child was born."

"Thank you, Dr. King. No further questions."

Wilhelmina's heart raced inside her chest, and she fanned herself as heat flooded her cheeks. She slumped in her chair when Mr. Goetz stated he did not wish to cross-examine Johann, her shoulders drooping with the weight of increasing dread. Tears poured from her eyes, dampening her dress.

"Does the prosecution have any further witnesses or evidence to present to the court," said Judge Walling.

"No, Your Honor, we do not."

"Very well. We will adjourn until next Monday, January 22, at ten o'clock in the morning, at which time the defense will be afforded the opportunity to present its case. If there is nothing further, court is adjourned."

CHAPTER TWENTY-SIX

The next seven days stretched endlessly for Wilhelmina. Neighboring inmates kept their usual chatter to a minimum with only an occasional whisper amongst themselves. No one spoke to her, and no one taunted her as they passed on the way to the showers or the cafeteria. The relentless ticking of a clock echoed off the metal bars of the long row of cells, each second hammering away at Wilhelmina's fragile calm.

The cell walls seemed to close in around her, and the air grew thick, making it difficult to breathe. She lay on her cot, pressing her hands against her heart as it pounded in sync with the clock, a drumbeat of impending doom. The rhythmic *tick, tick, tick* was a cruel reminder that time was slipping away, every second bringing her closer to an unavoidable end.

She couldn't escape it. The sound of the clock drowned out all rational thought, leaving only a maddening fear of what was to come. She asked for and was granted a radio, which she tuned to a local pop station, hoping the rich, velvety tone of Bing Crosby's voice as he crooned "June in January" over the airwaves would silence the never-ending *tick, tick, tick.*

Mrs. Flick appeared at Wilhelmina's cell door on Sunday afternoon, informing her of a visitor. She followed the jail matron down the series of hallways to the visitor's room, where she sat at the counter, looking through the glass to the other room. No other inmates or visitors were around; both rooms were empty except for the guards standing at each door.

The door in the opposite room opened to admit her visitor; Johann sauntered over and took a seat, his eyes piercing Wilhelmina with a cool hatred. She had not spoken to Johann since before her arrest and, seeing him now, she pushed away from the glass and glanced around, desperate to flee. The guard shot a menacing stare in her direction, so she turned in her seat to face Johann, wringing her hands in her lap.

"What … are … you … doing … here?" she said through clenched teeth.

Johann chuckled softly—that familiar devious chuckle she had come to despise.

"My dear, I wanted to know how you are feeling," he said, an evil smile curling his lips, revealing his perfect white teeth. "Albert and I have been so worried about your health."

"I'm sure," Wilhelmina snarled.

Johann leaned closer to the glass and hissed, "Don't be impertinent, Mrs. King."

Wilhelmina leaned as close as she dared, as close as she could stand, and whispered back, "How dare you come here and pretend you even care. Those lies you told … I wonder how you sleep at night."

"Careful, Mrs. King, or I will have to make good on my old promise to you."

"And what promise is that, Johann?"

"Oh, you know very well what I mean. I am surprised you have not asked about your precious Albert. Have you forgotten him so easily?"

"How … dare—"

Johann chuckled again. "Mrs. King, although you have not bothered to ask, your darling boy is fine. He is thriving at school and sleeps well. I have assured him you will be home before we know it, and that makes him happy. Of course … you and I both know you will never come back to my house again, don't we?"

"I don't know what you mean. I am innoc—"

"Spare me, Mrs. King. You have no defense, and you have no evidence to prove your innocence. Rather clever on my part, isn't it, my dear? Yes, it was I who ordered the arsenic, and it was I who put it in the flour and sugar. I was careful to leave no fingerprints so that only yours would be found on the canisters and bottles of arsenic. Did you know I hid the bottles right under your nose?"

"What do you mean?" Wilhelmina snarled.

"I put them in the kitchen cupboard, right behind the cans of peas and carrots." Johann laughed.

"I will tell my attorney it was you. He will listen."

"No, my dear Mrs. King, you are sadly mistaken. You have no evidence to back your statement. Your fingerprints were found all over those canisters. Your name was on those orders for the poison. I am quite certain you will be found guilty, and you will pay for your crimes."

"The only crime I have ever committed was allowing you to touch me—and agreeing to marry you!"

"Ahh, yes, let's talk about that, shall we?"

"About what?"

"Oh, you know, the first time I touched your sweet breasts and thrust inside you."

"I don't want … want to talk about … that."

"You have no choice, Mrs. King. You will listen to me. You see, I remember that day, oh so well. You waltzed into my office like a vixen, swaying those hips of yours. You *wanted* me to touch you, to f—"

"Stop! Please, Johann!"

The guard behind Wilhelmina cleared his throat. "Madam, control yourself or I will return you to your cell."

"I-I'm sorry," she said to the guard, and then glared at Johann. "You have no right to—"

"Stop talking, woman. I came here to tell you something."

"What could you possibly tell me that I want to hear?"

"I just thought you might want to know who Anya was."

"Wh-What?" Wilhelmina shook her head, not believing what he just said.

"Yes, my dear, there was an Anya before you. She was my wife. Would you like to know what happened to my beautiful darling?"

Wilhelmina straightened in her seat and tilted her head up, keeping her eyes fixed on Johann.

"Well, I will tell you. You see, Anya died in childbirth, along with our son. My father poisoned her."

Wilhelmina's mouth dropped open, her eyes widening, as she raised a hand to her throat.

"That's right. He hated her. You see, she was a Jew, and my father hated Jews. He was angry when I married her. She was only half Jew, on her father's side, but that did not matter to my father. He wanted nothing to do with us after we married. You can imagine my surprise when he showed up at our home for dinner, just two days before Anya went into labor."

"Johann, I don't ..."

"Quiet! He pretended to be making amends, excited about the impending birth of his first grandchild. Anya was struggling with her pregnancy at that time, so Father insisted on making her a cup of tea. She and I waited in the parlor while he prepared it. She became quite ill the next day, and the day following that, she went into labor. My son was born dead and Anya ..." Johann's voice cracked as he choked back tears.

"Anya died a few hours later. The autopsy revealed a lethal dose of arsenic in her stomach. The teacup was still in the sink, unwashed. I took it to the police, and sure enough, they found traces of arsenic in it and my father's fingerprints on the cup. He went to prison a year later for her murder. I left Berlin and moved to Munich and that, my dear, is how you and I came to meet."

"Johann, I-I just ... don't understand. Why are you telling me this?"

"You will be taking the witness stand soon, I presume?"

"Mr. Goetz has not yet decided."

"Well, nonetheless, I thought you should know my reasons for killing those men and for allowing you to be accused of the crimes. And I want to make sure you say the right things on the stand, the things that will ensure your guilt. You see, Mrs. King, I not only loathe elderly men, thanks to my aging father who decided killing my wife was much easier than accepting her, but I also came to despise *you*!"

"But ... why?"

Johann laughed out loud. "Why, you ask? Why? Because you destroyed my career, Wilhelmina Heinrich. Yes, *you*! Your father called me after he learned you were pregnant. I nearly lost everything. I lost my practice, my reputation, and my home. I escaped here to America, changed my name, and started over. But not *only* because of that, my dear. You see, I learned you had given birth to a son—my son. Your midwife was an acquaintance of mine. When she started bragging about helping a young girl give birth, I did some investigating. That's when I found out you took him to an orphanage ... and that's when I vowed my revenge on you."

"But it wasn't ... me ... I didn't ..."

"Spare me your feeble explanations, Wilhelmina. You will never convince me you intended to raise my son. But no matter. The jury has heard my testimony, and they know you gave your child away without a single regret. And they believe, without any doubt, that you murdered five—or shall we say six—innocent men?"

"No, Johann, I ..."

"It no longer matters, Wilhelmina. No matter what your Mr. Goetz does over the next few days, it will make no difference. I am certain you will be found guilty of killing those men and, yes, even your own husband! Yes, Wilhelmina, yes, I also killed Oskar. I even poisoned myself, just enough to become ill, and it was I who called the police to have you arrested. All part of my plan."

"You will never get away with this. I'll tell Mr. Goetz. I'll tell the police."

Another chuckle escaped Johann's lips, resonating from deep within his throat. "I am afraid it is too late for that, Wilhelmina. Besides, if you do, you know what I will do. Think of Albert. Think of your son."

"You couldn't. You ... *wouldn't!*"

"No? I suggest you don't test me on this matter, Wilhelmina. Harm will come to your darling boy if you go against me or say anything about this to anyone."

"Oh, you are an evil, evil man, Johann."

"Perhaps. But you are no saint either, are you? And *you* will pay the ultimate price, won't you?"

"I hate you."

"That has been abundantly obvious from the day I first saw you at the hospital, my dear. And it means nothing whatsoever to me." Johann pulled his pocket watch out and checked the time. "I really must be on my way, Mrs. King," he said loud enough for the guards to hear. "But before I go, I have something for you." He set the

Bavarian music box on the counter—the very music box given to her by Oskar so many years ago—and rose to his feet. "I'll give this to the guard … take it with you to the grave, my dear. Good day."

Wilhelmina kept her tears in check all the way back to her cell, where she flung herself onto her cot and sobbed until falling asleep.

Marta and Friederich Wagner each took the stand the next morning, while Karin Bauer and Mr. Burns, Wilhelmina's former hospital supervisor, were not called until Tuesday morning. Court was adjourned both days before lunchtime due to bitterly cold weather.

Her friends described her as a quiet, gentle woman devoted to her husband and son, a woman deeply committed to her religious beliefs. They spoke of her modest behavior, even in the way she dressed, and recalled her staunch dedication to helping her friends and neighbors by cooking, cleaning, or sewing for them. They recalled calling on her at her home, often finding her kneeling in prayer or reading the Bible daily. Marta and Karin both sobbed into their handkerchiefs when Mr. Goetz asked if they believed Wilhelmina killed her own husband, both emphatically shouting "No!" and declaring her faithfulness and deep love for Oskar.

Mr. Burns spoke of Wilhelmina as a hard-working employee who completed her tasks with utmost efficiency. She had rarely called off work or gone home early, other than one or two times when she had taken ill during her shift.

"Mrs. King was an upstanding employee and a kind woman," said Mr. Burns.

Pastor Bergmann testified on Wednesday afternoon when court reconvened. He, too, described Wilhelmina as a devoted wife and mother, deeply rooted in her faith. "She was a good Samaritan, one of the most pious women I've ever met. Mrs. Schmidt … I mean, er, Mrs. King, was deeply rooted in her faith and spread goodwill to everyone she knew. I was sorry to see her leave the church after she remarried."

"Pastor," said Mr. Goetz, "do you know if Mrs. King moved to a different congregation after she married Dr. King?"

"Mrs. Bauer told me that she believed Mrs. Schm ... King ... had begun attending St. Francis Seraph Catholic church with her second husband."

"I see. Thank you. No further questions."

Surprisingly, the prosecution did not cross-examine any of the defense's witnesses, and with no further questions, the judge adjourned court until Friday, January 26.

Wilhelmina leaned toward Mr. Goetz that Friday morning in the courtroom, and whispered, "Will I be taking the stand this morning?"

"No, Mrs. King. I have one more witness to call first." He directed his attention to the judge, who was calling court to order.

"Defense, please call your first witness," said Judge Walling.

"Yes, Your Honor," Goetz said as he stood behind the table next to Wilhelmina. "Defense calls Master Albert Schmidt to the stand."

Wilhelmina grabbed Mr. Goetz' arm and shook her head violently. He leaned down and whispered, "Mrs. King, it is necessary. Please do not make a scene. I must proceed." He pulled Wilhelmina's hand from his arm and strode to the witness stand, where Albert was scooting forward on the chair.

Wilhelmina gazed upon her son, tears brimming her eyelashes. She had not seen him since that day in court just before Christmas. He was dressed in a blue suit and tie, which hung loosely on his body, his sandy hair combed behind his ears. The corners of his mouth lifted into a thin smile as he looked at his mother. Albert's eyes no longer reflected his joyous childhood; they had become murky wells of sorrow.

Mr. Goetz extended his arm toward Albert and shook his hand gently.

"Please do not be nervous, son, and just answer the questions. Do you understand?"

"Yes ..." Albert swallowed hard. "Yes, sir."

"Please state your name, young man."

"Albert Klaus Schmidt."

"And how old are you, Albert?"

"I am thirteen, sir."

"Where do you go to school, Albert?"

"St. Francis Seraph Catholic School."

"Very good. And what are your favorite subjects in school?"

"I like math, history, and science. I want to be an accountant someday."

"Very good, young man, very good. Albert, what is your relationship to the defendant?" Goetz pointed to Wilhelmina.

"That is my mama. M-My mother."

"Thank you. Young man, do you remember your father, Oskar Schmidt?"

"Yes, very well, sir." Albert wiped a tear away from his eye.

"Tell us about your father, Albert."

"Papa was wonderful. He taught me to ride my bike, and he took me to the park a lot."

"Would you say, to the best of your memory, that your father was happy?"

"Papa laughed all the time. He was especially happy when the Bauers or Wagners came to the house. We used to have picnics in the backyard with them. It was fun."

"Do you remember how your father and mother interacted with each other? That is, can you tell us about how they treated each other?"

"Mama and Papa loved each other. They were always holding hands or hugging or"—Albert giggled as his cheeks flushed pink "—kissing."

"Did you ever hear your mother and father argue or have a fight?"

"Never. They were always happy. I never heard either of them raise their voices. Not even when I had done something bad."

"Like what, Albert?"

"I was tossing a ball in the air in the living room and it hit the lamp. The lamp broke."

"How did your parents react when you broke the lamp?"

"Mama said it was 'okay' and she told me to get the broom and pan, and I helped her clean it up. She didn't yell at me."

"Were you punished at all?"

"I wasn't allowed to play with a ball inside the house after that. And … And … I think I didn't get any streusel that night."

The jurors and many onlookers chuckled. Mr. Goetz and Judge Walling both smiled.

"Was that your favorite dessert, Albert?"

"Yes. Mama made the best streusel in the world!"

"Albert, how did you feel when your mother married Dr. King?"

"I … I liked Dr. King. He was kind to me. Gave me presents. And he took care of Mama after … after"—Albert choked and wiped his eyes again "—after Papa died. I guess it was okay. I-I don't really remember."

"That's all right, son. Let's move on. Do you remember Dr. King and your mother bringing in boarders to the house?"

"Yes."

"Did you talk with any of the boarders much?"

"Not really. Most of them stayed in their rooms. Mr. Weiss was really nice, though. He helped me with math and gave me a book on geometry. I really liked Mr. Weiss."

"Albert, I'm going to ask you some difficult questions, but I want to remind you that you are under oath to tell the truth, no matter what. Do you understand?"

"Y-Yes, sir."

"Did you ever see your mother making food for the boarders?"

"Yes, all the time, well, when I wasn't at school, I mean. I didn't see her make their lunch. But I saw her make food for them that we didn't eat."

"What do you mean, Albert?"

"I mean … I mean, she made their food separate from ours. For dinner, they only ate soup. They never had the same food as us."

"Did you ever go into the pantry at your house, Albert?"

"Sometimes, to get something for Mama."

"Did you see canisters and food in the pantry with any words written on them?"

"Y-Yes, I think so."

"Try hard to remember, Albert. What was written on the canisters and food?"

"Umm, I think … the word 'Boarder' was on the canisters. I don't remember anything else. I'm sorry."

"It's quite all right, Albert. Son, did you ever see your mother add anything extra to the canisters of sugar or flour?"

"Extra? N-No, I never saw her do that. I only saw her carrying the canisters to the kitchen to make rolls or put in the soup. Well, I mean, she put the sugar in the soup and sometimes she would make a few rolls for the boarder's dinner. With the flour, I mean."

"I see. Albert, when each of the boarders became ill, how did your mother react?"

"Umm ... I remember she was crying and very upset. She was frightened."

"Did she call for a doctor?"

"Yes, and she would pace the floor until the ambulance arrived. She was very worried about those men."

"All right, son. Thank you. No further questions."

Mr. Skidmore approached the stand and asked just one question.

"Albert, is it possible that your mother could have added something extra to the canisters of sugar and flour when you weren't at home?"

"Objection! Conjecture! The witness cannot testify to events he did not personally witness," said Mr. Goetz.

"Objection sustained. The question will be struck from the record."

"I apologize, Your Honor," said Skidmore. "No questions for this witness."

"Very well, then," said Judge Walling as Albert stepped out of the witness stand and passed by his mother. He glanced at her, smiled, and followed a bailiff from the courtroom.

"Defense, do you have any further witnesses?" asked the judge.

"Yes, Your Honor, but I would like to approach the bench, if I may," said Goetz.

"Very well."

Both Goetz and Skidmore strode to the bench. Judge Walling leaned forward and whispered, "What is it, Mr. Goetz?"

"I will be calling the defendant to the stand, Your Honor, and given the time, I would like to request a short recess until this afternoon."

Judge Walling looked at his watch and said, "Yes, yes, it is after eleven already. I will allow it, if prosecution agrees."

"Prosecution agrees, Your Honor."

"Very well, you may return to your tables." To the entire courtroom, Judge Walling said, "Court will recess for lunch and reconvene here at one o'clock this afternoon."

∾

Harold Goetz stood between the defense and prosecution tables and called his final witness to the stand.

"Defense calls Mrs. Wilhelmina Marie King to the stand, Your Honor," he said, his voice carrying throughout the courtroom with a resonance commanding the attention of everyone present.

The courtroom fell deathly silent as Wilhelmina slowly rose to her feet, her hands clenching a handkerchief and twisting it like a wet washcloth. Her eyes darted around the room, falling on the faces of Marta and Karin … and Johann. Her hands shook with every step she took toward the witness stand, and her shoulders slumped, feet shuffling on the floor as if she were carrying the world on her shoulders like Atlas.

She stood facing a bailiff and placed a hand on a Bible. The handkerchief fell from her right hand as she raised it.

"Wilhelmina Marie King, do you solemnly swear that the testimony you are about to give will be the truth, the whole truth, and nothing but the truth, so help you God?" said the bailiff.

Her voice barely above a whisper, she replied, "I do."

"You may take the stand, Mrs. King," said Judge Walling.

Wilhelmina made her way to the stand and up two steps. She scanned the jurors as she sat, her attention interrupted by the bailiff handing her the forgotten handkerchief. She sent him a weak smile and clutched the handkerchief in her lap.

Mr. Goetz approached the stand and smiled warmly at Wilhelmina.

"For the record, please state your name for the court," he said.

"Wilhelmina Marie King," she squeaked.

"And have you ever gone by any other names?"

"Yes."

"Please tell the court those names."

"My maiden name was Heinrich. And then I became Mrs. Schmidt when I m-married Oskar."

Mr. Goetz spent the first hour asking questions about Wilhelmina's childhood, her home life, her religion. He asked her to recount the gruesome details of her travels to America, how she became ill on the train in Germany, the illness that ran rampant throughout the ship, and the crowded and uncomfortable conditions of being cleared through Immigration on Ellis Island.

"Mrs. King, did you have a child out of wedlock, before you were married to Oskar Schmidt."

Beads of sweat formed on Wilhelmina's forehead as she peered into the eyes of the jurors and back to Mr. Goetz.

"Please answer the question, Mrs. King," said the judge.

"Y-Yes, I did."

"How old were you when the child was born?" said Goetz.

"Six … Sixteen."

"And who is the father of that child, Mrs. King?"

"It … It was …" she caught a glimpse of Johann scowling and cleared her throat. "I-I cannot say."

"Is that because you do not know, Mrs. King, or you do not remember the man's name?"

"I … I was at a party, a university party." Wilhelmina swiped a tear flowing down her cheek. "I do not know the boy's name."

"I see. Mrs. King, you stated you traveled alone to America. Why did you come here at such a young age?"

"M-My father was very strict with deeply conservative religious beliefs. He enforced a rigid code of conduct in his household. He was … He … He was ashamed of me."

"You mean when he learned you were pregnant?"

"Y-Yes. He sent me away, sent me here to Cincinnati."

Wilhelmina went on to talk about her life with her aunt and uncle, about her first job at Kahn's meat processing plant, and how she met Oskar.

"Mrs. King, let's go back to before you met Oskar Schmidt, back to the birth of your child. What happened after you delivered the child?"

"I was quite ill. I believe I slept for many hours. When I awoke, the child was gone. My Aunt Frieda told me he had been taken to a wet nurse. But many hours later, the child was still not returned to me, and I questioned her and Uncle Otto about it. They told me Uncle Otto took the child to the orphanage. They said it was my father's decree to do so."

"Mrs. King, we have heard previous testimony that it was you who took the child to the orphanage, of your own free will. Are you denying that testimony?"

"Y-Yes. I did not take my son to an orphanage. He was taken away from me."

"I see. Mrs. King, please describe your marriage to Oskar Schmidt and tell us about your life with him."

Wilhelmina talked for nearly a half-hour about how she met Oskar, how they fell in love, and how happy she was. She grinned widely as she related stories of Albert and how much she loved her son. She recounted tales of dinner dates and going to plays or concerts and time spent in Washington Park playing with Albert.

"We were happy, very happy. I-I was dev ..." She choked back a sob. "I was devastated when Oskar died."

"Mrs. King, why did you remarry only six months after Mr. Schmidt died?"

"Doctor ... Johann ... was kind to me. He stayed by my side much of the time following the funeral and brought food and toys for Albert. He gave me money so that I would not have to find a job until the fall when Albert entered kindergarten. He visited me every day and ... and ... he said he had developed quite a fondness for me. My closest friends were there when Johann proposed."

"Who were those friends, Mrs. King?"

"Marta and Friederich ... er ... Mr. and Mrs. Wagner, I mean. And ... And Karin and Georg ... Bauer."

"And were your friends happy when you accepted Dr. King's proposal?"

"Yes."

"And how did Albert react, Mrs. King?"

"He was happy, also. He and Johann got on quite well."

"Were you happy in your new marriage, Mrs. King?"

"I … We …" Wilhelmina looked toward the audience and found Johann staring at her, expression stern, his eyes like shards of ice sending daggers into her heart, silently warning her to choose her words carefully. "Yes, we were happy in the beginning."

"In the beginning. What changed, Mrs. King?"

"We … We moved away from my home, from my friends, to … to the house on Glenmary Drive. I was isolated there, too far away to visit my friends. I missed them. I suppose I was lonely."

"Did you move out of the bedroom you shared with Dr. King?"

"N … I mean"—Wilhelmina took a deep breath—"Y-Yes, I did."

"Why did you do that?"

"I was sad. Nothing made me happy anymore. Nothing except … except Albert."

"Mrs. King, do you believe your husband, Dr. King, called you by another name, a name not your own?"

"Y-Yes, I … Yes, he did."

"And what did he call you?"

"He called me 'Anya.' He never used my given name. Most of the time, he called me 'Mrs. King,' but occasionally, he would call me 'Anya.'"

"And do you know who this 'Anya' was?"

"N-No, I do not."

"When did he call you 'Anya,' Mrs. King, specifically?"

"Err, when … umm, when we were alone … in … in the bedroom." Wilhelmina's cheeks flushed a bright red.

"Mrs. King, what was your relationship with each of the boarders living in your home?"

"I … Mr. Parker kept to himself and rarely came out of his room. He spoke very little to me. Mr. Berger was kind, but he was a quiet man. He also stayed in his room most of the time. Mr. Müeller was friendly and spoke with me … and with Albert … quite often. But"— she licked her lips—"Mr. Klein and Mr. Weiss, they were both pleasant gentlemen. Mr. Klein helped Albert with his homework … English and science, I believe. Mr. Weiss … dear Mr. Weiss … We became friends. He gave Albert a book, a math book of some kind. He was very kind, very kind."

"Mrs. King, did you purchase several bottles of arsenic from Hoffman's Pharmacy … or from any other pharmacy?"

"No, sir, I did not."

"Did you see or hear rats in the basement or any other part of the house on Glenmary Drive?"

"No, I did not."

"One last question, Mrs. King. Did you kill Messrs. Parker, Müeller, Berger, Klein, and Weiss?"

Wilhelmina let out a cry and covered her face in her hands. "No!" She sobbed. She raised her head and looked over to the jury box. "No, I did *not*!"

"Thank you, Mrs. King. No further questions, Your Honor."

"Does prosecution wish to cross examine the witness?" said the judge.

Arthur Skidmore stood and ambled toward the stand. "Yes, Your Honor."

He stared at Wilhelmina for several moments before turning to face the jury. With his back to Wilhelmina, he said, "Mrs. King, you described yourself as having an innocent childhood, one with deeply rooted religious practices, is that correct?"

"Yes."

"And yet, at just fifteen years old, you committed fornication and became pregnant, *is that correct?*" he shouted as he turned, facing her.

"Y-Yes, but I have sought forgiveness for—"

"Mrs. King, your testimony today has directly contradicted previous testimony heard by this court from your husband, Dr. Johann King. Specifically, we have already heard from him on three matters—one, that you told him you willingly gave up your illegitimate son and took him to an orphanage in 1916; two, that he never called you 'Anya' or any name other than your own; and three, that you did in fact complain of rats and asked to purchase the necessary items to concoct rat poison, specifically, arsenic and oatmeal.

"Mrs. King, I ask you now, are you saying Dr. King lied to this court?"

Wringing her hands, Wilhelmina licked her lips and said, "I-I … do …" She threw her face into her hands and sobbed violently, unable to speak.

"Mrs. King, your reaction to my question seems to indicate that it is *you* and not Dr. King who has been lying to this court. What do you have to say about that?"

"I…" She found Johann's icy stare and sunk deeper into the chair, fingering the cross hanging from her neck. Picking at the collar of her dress, she said between sobs, "I … am … sorry … I did not tell … th-the truth."

"And if you have not told the truth about these trivial matters, Mrs. King, *how is this court, this jury, expected to believe you are telling the truth when you say you did not kill those five gentlemen and, yes, perhaps even your own husband, Oskar Schmidt?*" Skidmore said in a strong voice.

"Objection! Counsel is badgering the witness!" cried Mr. Goetz.

"I will remind the court and Mrs. King that lying while under oath is a criminal act of perjury that can and will result in penalties. Mrs. King has admitted to lying to this court. Therefore, objection is overruled. Members of the jury, you are to disregard Mrs. King's previous false testimony and consider only the true testimony of Dr. Johann King in your deliberations. Mrs. King, I will remind you that any further false statements will be met with serious legal consequences. Do you understand?"

"Y-Yes, Your Honor."

"Proceed, Mr. Skidmore."

"No further questions, Your Honor. Prosecution rests."

"Defense, do you have any further evidence to present or any additional witnesses to question?"

"No, Your Honor, we do not. Defense rests."

"Very well. Court will adjourn for the day and reconvene to hear closing arguments on Monday, January 29, at ten in the morning. If there is nothing further, court is hereby adjourned."

CHAPTER TWENTY-SEVEN

January 29, 1934

Thousands of people braved temperatures below freezing that Monday morning, forming a long, winding line outside the courthouse that stretched around the block. Locals and out-of-towners alike buzzed with curious anticipation, each hoping to secure one of the limited seats inside the courtroom to hear the closing statements of the murder trial now famous across the nation. Some had stood for hours, bundled in blankets and sipping from thermoses of hot coffee, determined to witness what would likely be the trial's final day and Wilhelmina's fate determined. A mixture of excitement and tension charged the air, all speculating on the unfolding drama the day would bring.

Twenty bailiffs emerged from the courthouse and distributed numbered pieces of paper to every person waiting for the doors to open. As the bailiffs meandered around the block, they informed the crowds, "The numbers will be drawn randomly at nine o'clock and any person holding one of those numbers will be permitted a seat inside the courtroom for the first session. If a recess is taken, all persons seated inside the courtroom will be escorted out and new numbers will be drawn. Persons holding *those* numbers will then be allowed inside the courtroom for the second session. Admission into the courtroom will continue in this manner until the trial ends, regardless of when that occurs. After the first group is seated inside the courtroom, anyone remaining outside will be permitted to come indoors and wait in the hallway."

The bailiffs ushered 300 hopeful people inside at nine-fifteen and escorted them to courtroom. They took their seats on the benches behind the press tables and in the folding chairs scattered around the perimeter of the room. The remaining hopefuls were then allowed inside the courthouse and made their way to the third-floor hallway, where they stood shoulder-to-shoulder, engaging in muffled conversations.

Wilhelmina stepped off the elevator, flanked by two police officers, and moved through the dense crowd, her eyes fixed straight ahead, seemingly oblivious to the sea of faces staring as she passed. The onlookers parted like the Red Sea, their whispers a low, buzzing murmur penetrating the air. Some pointed while others gasped, but Wilhelmina's expression remained unreadable, a mask of cold determination. She appeared calm, even serene, while a storm of emotions raged beneath the surface.

The doors opened and every eye followed Wilhelmina as she strode up the aisle to the defense table. Mr. Goetz entered the room shortly after, followed by the prosecution team of Arthur Skidmore and Edward Douglas. No one made a sound or moved, the tension palpable as if the very walls held their breath. The only sound breaking the silence was the sharp tap-tap-tap of heels striking the polished floor. Within moments, Judge Walling entered the courtroom, called for the jury to enter, and proclaimed court in session. As she eased down into her chair, Wilhelmina caught sight of Johann seated three rows behind the prosecution table, his arm draped casually around Albert's shoulder. Albert was pale and wide-eyed, his expression blank, as if fighting the urge to seek out his mother.

Mr. Douglas addressed the jury, striding back and forth in front of them, for nearly an hour. He reminded them of the suspect's "promiscuous behavior" during her teen years and her sin of fornication and resulting pregnancy. He painted a picture of a woman with a vendetta against the father who banished her from home, a cold, calculating woman skilled in the art of deception. He described her as a woman who "presented the outward appearance of piety and devotion while she harbored a dark, vengeful heart, ultimately leading her down a path of murder."

As Mr. Douglas took his seat behind the prosecution table, Arthur Skidmore approached the jury box with slow, deliberate steps, studying each face as he drew closer to the jurors. He spent nearly two hours reviewing every piece of evidence in the case, reminding the jurors of every gruesome detail of the autopsies and pointing to the organs within the jars on the floor across the room. He vividly described each victim's harrowing ordeal, emphasizing the violent vomiting and relentless diarrhea that underscored the "gravity of the crime." He reminded them of Dr. King's own illness and proof he, too, had been poisoned by arsenic.

"Ladies and gentlemen of the jury," Skidmore said, "throughout this trial you have seen compelling evidence that the defendant is responsible for the tragic deaths of Jacob Parker, Ernst Müeller, Karl Berger, Ludwig Klein and August Weiss. But there is another individual, Oskar Schmidt, the defendant's first husband, who also died under eerily similar circumstances. While Mr. Schmidt is not part of this indictment, his death cannot be ignored.

"The similarities between these cases are striking and significant. All of these victims suffered the same fatal illnesses, all inflicted in the same manner—by arsenic poisoning. This pattern is not a coincidence. It is a clear indication of the defendant's modus operandi. It shows a deliberate and calculated approach to committing these heinous acts.

"By considering the evidence related to Mr. Schmidt, you can see a broader picture of the defendant's actions and intent. This additional context supports the prosecution's argument that the defendant's actions were not isolated incidents but part of a larger, more sinister pattern.

"We ask you to consider this pattern as you deliberate. It reinforces the prosecution's case and underscores the need for justice for these six victims. The evidence is clear, and the defendant must be held accountable for her actions."

Skidmore strode across the room toward the jars of organs on the floor, causing every head and every eye to follow his movements—directing every eye in the room toward the diseased organs. He then ambled past the defendant's table and gazed at Wilhelmina for several beats before returning to the jury box.

"Ladies and gentlemen, prosecution has shown you a cold-blooded, sly woman," he said, pointing to Wilhelmina. "No other woman, especially one claiming deep religious beliefs as she has, could have sat in this courtroom for the past five weeks hearing such damning testimony with *no show of emotion on her part*! Wilhelmina Marie King is a heartless woman who despised her father for dismissing her from his home, and she exacted her revenge by killing five, nay even six, innocent men.

"I ask you, ladies and gentlemen of the jury, consider the evidence in this case, consider the witness statements, and consider the defendant herself. Do we believe she is the upstanding, pious woman she presents herself to be? Or is there a deeper evil lurking within? It is up to you to decide her fate. It is up to you to deliver a verdict that upholds justice for the victims, for their loved ones, for all of Cincinnati, and for the State of Ohio."

He stood facing the jurors, his hands resting on the jury box, and looked at each face one by one, into each set of eyes, before he turned and took his seat.

Judge Walling said, "We will now recess for two hours and reconvene at two-forty-five this afternoon to hear the closing statements from the defense."

That afternoon Harold Goetz delivered his closing arguments in less than an hour, leaving every person in the courtroom in a tense silence as he merely reiterated his belief that the "prosecution has failed to prove guilt beyond a reasonable doubt" and has "only presented circumstantial evidence to this court."

He said, "I remind you, ladies and gentlemen of the jury, that no fingerprints were found on the bottles of arsenic or the bottles of isopropyl alcohol, both of which are key pieces of evidence in this case. May I also remind you that we received no real proof that Mrs. King personally called Hoffman's Pharmacy to place orders for arsenic. Her name merely appearing on the order forms only provides us with supposition that she placed those orders herself. We lack the testimony of the employee who took the orders and the employee who could tell us whether or not he received phone calls from Mrs. King."

Goetz walked to the middle of the room and stood close to Wilhelmina, close enough that every juror would have a clear view of her as they watched and listened.

"Ladies and gentlemen, allow me to remind you of the defendant's deep love for her late husband, Oskar Schmidt, and their son, Albert, who is just thirteen years of age. She told this court of many happy times with her family, of her devotion to her faith and her church. Yes, she was not without sin. Yes, she was promiscuous as a young girl, but ladies and gentlemen, can any of us say we are perfect? Indeed, has there ever been but only one perfect human in the history of mankind, Jesus Christ Himself? We are not here to judge the defendant based on her youth or her personality. We are here to judge her based on the facts alone. And the facts in this case do not clearly show that Mrs. Wilhelmina King is guilty!

"Esteemed jurors, God tempers with justice and mercy," he said, tears in his eyes. "I ask you to do what is right in this matter. Return Mrs. King to the son she loves so deeply, so affectionately. Grant her freedom so she can return to her son and take care of him."

Wilhelmina dabbed at her eyes with her twisted handkerchief and let out a loud sob. Many of the jurors were openly touched by Mr. Goetz' statement. Four of the women cast their eyes to the floor; three of the men wiped tears from their eyes.

Goetz continued, "You are going to hear Mr. Skidmore demand the death penalty. It is within your power to end the life of Wilhelmina Marie King. It is in your power to give her mercy, and indeed, it is in your power to free her and return her to her loving son. I ask you to send Mrs. King home to Albert. Give him the opportunity in life he deserves."

After Goetz took his seat, Judge Walling asked, "Does the prosecution have any counterarguments?"

"Yes, we do," said Mr. Douglas as he rose from his seat. "Ladies and gentlemen, you heard defense counsel remind you that no fingerprints were found on the bottles of arsenic or isopropyl alcohol. Allow me to remind you that surgical gloves were found at the defendant's home, making it quite logical that the defendant wore the gloves when she handled those bottles.

"You may be asking yourselves why fingerprints were found on the canisters. My answer is simple: would it not appear unusual for the defendant to wear surgical gloves when preparing meals?"

Several of the onlookers, and even a few jurors, chuckled softly.

"Ladies and gentlemen," Mr. Douglas continued, "you also heard Mr. Goetz say that no real proof was presented indicating that the defendant personally called the pharmacy and placed the orders for arsenic. May I remind you, however, that Mr. Hoffman's own testimony showed that he had strict regulations in place for whenever an order was taken over the phone. Regulations which included clearly indicating the name of the person calling to place such orders. Ladies and gentlemen, we have the orders filed as evidence which clearly show the name of the person placing three orders for a total of twelve bottles of arsenic as 'Mrs. Johann King' and we fully understand that this is, in fact, the defendant."

Douglas sat, and Arthur Skidmore stood, walked to the jury box, and paced before it. "Ladies and gentlemen, yes, it is true that I will ask you to return a verdict of guilty and recommend the death penalty for Mrs. Wilhelmina King. As you deliberate, keep in mind the dreadful nature of the crimes, the terrible suffering of the victims, the cold-blooded method by which they died. It is true, you have three choices in this matter. One, you can return a verdict of not guilty and free the defendant. Two, you can return a verdict of guilty with mercy, meaning the defendant will receive a sentence of life imprisonment. Or three, return a verdict of guilty with no mercy, meaning you recommend the defendant be sentenced to death. As you deliberate this case and reach your decision, consider the depth of the crimes. I urge you to match the penalty with the crimes, ladies and gentlemen."

Skidmore slowly walked away and took his place behind the prosecution's table next to his partner.

Judge Walling gazed around the room, studying the faces of the attorneys and jurors, and of Wilhelmina. The courtroom was still, like a windless summer night, until he cleared his throat and said, "Ladies and gentlemen of the jury, you have heard all the evidence and the arguments of counsel. It is now your duty to deliberate upon the evidence and reach a verdict. You must consider all the evidence presented and apply the law as I have instructed you. Remember, the burden of proof rests with the prosecution, and the defendant is presumed innocent until proven guilty beyond a reasonable doubt.

Your verdict must be unanimous. Please retire to the jury room and begin your deliberations."

Amid low whispers from the onlookers, the jury shuffled out of the box and through the door next to the bench. Wilhelmina sat rigid in her chair, tears streaming down her cheeks and falling into her lap.

Two days later, the jail matron, Mrs. Flick, opened Wilhelmina's cell door. The jury was in, the verdict reached.

CHAPTER TWENTY-EIGHT

January 31, 1934

Hundreds once again crammed the courtroom beyond normal capacity while thousands of people crowded the hallways and lobby. Reporters sat at their tables, pencils at the ready, waiting to record the jury's decision.

Wilhelmina was dressed in a lovely light blue dress with a lace collar and cuffs. Her silver cross gleamed beneath the chandeliers and wall sconces about the room. She had brushed her golden hair to a shine, recently cut by the jail staff, and it once again hung in soft waves to her chin. Seated next to Mr. Goetz, Wilhelmina fingered her cross with one hand and gripped her Bible with the other.

The crowd relaxed into an eerie quiet when Judge Walling entered the room and called the court to order. He settled into his chair and directed everyone to be seated.

"Ladies and gentlemen of the jury," he said, "have you reached a verdict?"

The foreman stood, clutching a folded piece of paper, and said, "Yes, Your Honor, we have."

"Please hand the verdict to the bailiff," said the Judge. When he received the paper from the bailiff, Judge Walling opened it, read through it quickly, and handed it back to the bailiff, who then returned it to the foreman. "Mr. Foreman, please read the verdict aloud for the court."

"Yes, Your Honor," said the foreman as he unfolded the paper and cleared his throat. "We, the jury in the case of the State of Ohio versus Wilhelmina Marie King, do hereby find the defendant guilty of five counts of first-degree murder by arsenic poisoning and one count of attempted murder by arsenic poisoning."

Wilhelmina's knees buckled, and Mr. Goetz grabbed her arm to steady her. A sharp, high-pitched cry echoed from the back of the room. Albert's scream escalated into a frantic wail, leaving a chilling silence in its wake. Heart-wrenching sobs saturated the room, mingled with the sounds of noses being blown into handkerchiefs and feet scuffling against the floor, creating a symphony of sorrow that quickly swelled into overwhelming grief.

"Order in the court!" yelled Judge Walling. "*Order!*"

The noise gradually faded into gentle sniffles.

"Ladies and gentlemen of the jury, you have found the defendant guilty of the charges against her. Have you reached a recommendation for sentencing?"

"Yes, Your Honor, we have," said the foreman.

"What say you?" said the judge.

"Your Honor, we, the jury, have reached a unanimous decision and recommend the defendant be sentenced to death."

The crowd erupted in a cacophony of cries and renewed sobs. Wilhelmina stood with her head held high, her back straight, and her eyes dry.

"Thank you, Mr. Foreman," said Judge Walling. He turned to Wilhelmina. "Wilhelmina Marie King, you have been found guilty in this court of five counts of first-degree murder and one count of attempted murder. A jury of your peers has further recommended the death penalty. Do you understand these findings?"

Mr. Goetz squeezed Wilhelmina's elbow. She nodded and whispered, "Yes, Your Honor."

"Please speak up so the court may hear you, Mrs. King."

Wilhelmina cleared her throat and said loudly, "Yes, Your Honor!"

"After careful consideration of the evidence presented, the jury has recommended the death penalty. Taking into account the severity of the crimes and the aggravating factors, and having found no sufficient mitigating circumstances, the court hereby sentences you to imprisonment at the Ohio Reformatory for Women while you await execution. When a date has been set for such execution, you will be transferred to the Ohio Penitentiary where you will be put to death by the electric chair. Defense may file an appeal in this matter while you are imprisoned, and you will be informed of the court's decision."

Wilhelmina stared at the judge while he spoke. When he paused for a moment, she glanced to the back of the courtroom. Johann was dragging Albert down the aisle toward the doors. Her son's face was red and streaked with tears as he struggled against Johann, his arms outstretched to his mother. The doors closed behind him, leaving Wilhelmina with the memory of her son's distress.

Judge Walling continued, "On behalf of the Court of Common Pleas for the State of Ohio, we thank you, the jury, for your participation and careful deliberation in this case. You are hereby dismissed. The case of the State of Ohio vs. Wilhelmina Marie King is hereby closed. Court is adjourned."

The men and women of the jury rose from their seats and strode out of the room, some wiping tears from their faces.

The final BANG of the gavel rang through Wilhelmina's ears and haunted her sleep for weeks.

Two days later, Wilhelmina rode in the back of a police car to the Ohio Reformatory for Women in Marysville, Ohio, over two hours away, where she shared a cell with three other inmates. She met her imprisonment with a quiet repose—keeping to herself, completing the work she was assigned in the cafeteria without complaint, and spending her waking hours praying or reading the Bible.

Her cell provided no room to move around and was sparsely furnished with two bunk beds, one small table resting against the wall between the beds, and one chair. The mattresses were thin and worn, the pillows lay flat, the sheets had faded, and the blankets were threadbare. A single incandescent bulb hung from the ceiling, emitting a faint yellow glow in the middle of the cell and casting oddly shaped shadows on the concrete floor and walls.

Her cellmates jeered her whenever she opened her Bible or knelt on the floor, deep in prayer. Her faith gave her strength to ignore their taunts, allowing her to keep her emotions in check. Yet every morning as she stood under the tepid shower, her tears flowed freely.

She wrote letters to Albert, Marta, Karin, and her mother, but received no replies. In September, she opened a letter from her defense attorney, Harold Goetz, and read his disheartening words:

> Mrs. King,
>
> I have decided not to file an appeal in your case as I do not believe it is in your best interest. I am convinced the outcome would be the same and I do not want to subject you to a repeat of the horrific scrutiny you have already experienced.
>
> It is with regret that I inform you that your husband, Dr. King, has allowed the house on Glenmary Drive to fall into foreclosure with the bank and has abandoned the property. It appears he took your son to the St. Joseph Orphanage immediately following your trial, and Albert will remain there until he is of age. I am afraid Dr. King has left the country with no forwarding address. I believe he may be in Switzerland but cannot find any record of a Johann King on any sailing ships abroad.
>
> I advise you to obey the guards and the superintendent, do everything you are told and, most of all, pray. Only God can deliver you from purgatory and you would be wise to seek His forgiveness.
>
> I will write again when I have been advised of your date of execution.
>
> May God have mercy on your soul.
>
> Regards,
> Harold K. Goetz
> Attorney-at-Law

In March 1935, Wilhelmina was transferred to the Ohio Penitentiary in Columbus where she was placed in a cell on death row while she awaited execution. Equipped with a wash basin and toilet, her cell was a stark contrast to the luxurious surroundings of her childhood home, and to the home on Glenmary Drive. Every morning in the shower room, Wilhelmina washed under the watchful eye of her guard. Every day, she took her meals alone in her cell. Every day, she sunk deeper within herself.

On the third day, she was ordered to clean her cell. She knelt on the cold, hard floor, gripping a stiff-bristled scrub brush. The wooden handle was worn from countless uses, and the bristles were rough and unyielding. Dipping the brush into a bucket of soapy water, Wilhelmina then began to scrub the concrete walls.

The walls were rough and pitted, stained with the grime and residue from years of confinement. As she worked the brush in circular motions, the bristles scraped against the concrete, dislodging dirt and filth. The soapy water ran down the walls in grimy rivulets, pooling on the floor around Wilhelmina's feet.

Each stroke took effort, her weakened muscles straining with the repetitive motion. The smell of the soap mixed with the musty odor of the cell created an almost suffocating atmosphere. Sweat beaded on her forehead, dripping down her face, as she continued to scrub, determined to remove the layers of dirt.

When she finished with the walls, Wilhelmina eased down on her knees and scrubbed the floor, using the same circular motions as before. The grime on the floor was relentless, only shifting from one spot to another with each sweep of the brush. Wilhelmina leaned back and sighed at the sorry sight.

Last, she turned her attention to the toilet, a soiled enamel-coated cast iron fixture on the wall. She dipped the same scrub brush, now even more worn and filthy, into the murky bucket of dark and foul-smelling water. As Wilhelmina began to scrub the toilet, the bristles scraped against the stained surface, dislodging a layer of filth. She moved the brush in vigorous, circular motions, each stroke sending droplets of dirty water splattering onto the floor. With raw and aching hands, Wilhelmina scrubbed the floor a second time, driven by the necessity of the task.

The work was monotonous and exhausting, but it provided Wilhelmina with a rare moment of focus and purpose. As the walls and floor gradually lightened, and the bare concrete beneath finally shined through, a tiny shred of accomplishment settled inside Wilhelmina. The clean cell offered a brief respite in an otherwise hopeless existence.

On the first day of June, Wilhelmina received the dreaded news from Harold Goetz. He wrote telling her she would be executed by electrocution on July 10. She sat at the small table, staring blankly at the letter, the words on the paper blurred by the tears pooling in her eyes. Until this moment, she had held out a flicker of hope that her verdict would be appealed after all, and she would find herself home with Albert.

The untouched ground beef patty and mashed potatoes grew cold on the metal tray sitting next to the letter from Mr. Goetz. Behind her, feet shuffled on the corridor floor as inmates returned to their cells. The tinkling of keys as cell doors opened and the clang of metal striking metal as the doors closed evoked a complex mix of emotions. Each sound amplified her sense of isolation and despair, reminding her of her inescapable future. She grew acutely aware of the passage of time and the impending finality of her fate. The noise created a haunting backdrop to her turmoil, a reminder of the life she was about to leave behind.

The dim light above her head flickered and went out, along with the bulbs from the other cells, and Wilhelmina was shrouded in darkness. Her eyelids became heavy, and her chin dropped to her chest as sleep overtook her.

The guard struck his billy club on the cell bars with a sharp, resonant clang, jolting Wilhelmina awake as the sound traveled in a series of diminishing echoes down the corridor. She turned in her chair as the guard shoved a breakfast tray under the bars, the metal scraping the concrete floor as it slid toward her. She groaned as she moved, her neck stiff and aching from the awkward night's sleep. She rose slowly from her chair, each movement sending a sharp twinge down her spine. As she bent to pick up the tray, another sharp pain shot through her back, causing her to wince.

She inched her way to the cot and gingerly sat on the mattress. Elbows on her knees, hands cradling her face, she stared at the tray on the floor with utter disinterest. She slowly worked the kinks out of her neck, then between her shoulder blades, to the small of her back. She stood carefully, holding onto the table, and tried again to retrieve the tray from the floor. Her fingers slid beneath the cold metal as she hooked the tray with her thumb, pulled it closer, and picked it up. Groaning, she laid the tray on top of last night's dinner and went back to the cot, where she slid under the sheet and drifted to sleep.

Wilhelmina slept through the greater part of the next few days and ate little. The letter from Mr. Goetz still sat on the table, the ink smudged with dried tears. Every time she glanced at the table, the words "electrocution" and "July 10" seemed to float off the paper and hover before her eyes.

The cold, gray walls of the prison cell were closing in, or so it seemed, as the clock ticked relentlessly toward dawn on Wednesday, July 10. Wilhelmina sat on the edge of the narrow cot, her hands trembling, as she clutched a worn photograph of Oskar and Albert. Her Bible and the music box sat on the bed next to her. The world outside continued its indifferent march forward, oblivious to the fate that awaited her.

Wilhelmina's mind drifted back to the events that had led her here. The trial had been relatively swift and merciless, the evidence damning. She had been found guilty of poisoning six men, including her husband, crimes she had relentlessly denied. The newspapers had dubbed her "Poisonous Peach," a moniker that haunted her every waking moment—and her sleep.

She had spent much of the night writing letters to her two friends, Marta and Karin, to her mother in Germany, and to Albert. In each, she claimed her innocence but never mentioned the things Johann had told her—that he had been the one to put the poison in the food. She wrote about her undying faith and belief that God would deliver her. She professed her love and devotion to each of them, and she begged their forgiveness.

The door to her cell creaked open, and Warden Ellis stepped in, his face a mask of professional detachment. "It's time," he said softly, his voice barely above a whisper. Wilhelmina nodded, rising to her feet with a dignity that belied her fear. She had spent countless nights preparing for this moment, rehearsing her final words, but now, as the reality of her impending execution loomed, she found herself at a loss.

She picked up the envelopes and offered them to the warden. He nodded and took them.

The sound of her footsteps echoed ominously as she trudged down the dimly lit corridor. The guards flanked her on either side, their expressions unreadable. Wilhelmina's heart pounded in her chest, each beat reminding her of happier days gone by.

The execution chamber was stark and clinical, a blunt contrast to the warmth of the home she had once known. The electric chair stood in the center of the room, a grim symbol of the justice awaiting her. Wilhelmina took a deep breath, scanning the faces of the witnesses, those who gathered to watch her final moments—among them, the stern visage of the judge who had sentenced her, the prosecutor who had built the case against her, and a handful of reporters eager to capture the story for the morning papers. Her defense attorney and none of her friends had come to witness the end of her life.

As the guards strapped her into the chair, Wilhelmina closed her eyes, summoning the strength to face her fate with grace. She thought of Albert, of the life she had once dreamed of giving him, and a single tear slipped down her cheek.

"Do you have any last words?" Warden Ellis asked.

Wilhelmina opened her eyes. "I am innocent," she said, her voice clear and unwavering despite the fear gripping her heart. "I forgive those who have wronged me. I carry the identity of the true murderer to my grave for no reason other than to protect my Albert."

A guard stepped forward, reached into a bucket of water, and drew out a soaked sponge, then placed it on her head. Her gaze never wavered from him as he attached something cold and metallic above the sponge and drew a black hood over her face.

With that, the switch was thrown, and the room filled with a blinding light. Wilhelmina's body convulsed, and then, mercifully, it was over. As life left her body, three sheets of paper fell from her hand and floated to the floor at her feet. The guard picked them up and handed them to Warden Ellis.

The witnesses stared with wide eyes and open mouths until they shuffled from the room in silence, the weight of the ordeal heavy on their shoulders. Outside, dark clouds littered the sky as warm raindrops fell to the ground and dampened the faces of those who had just watched Wilhelmina die.

That afternoon, Warden Ellis stood at his office window, gazing to the yard below, as the guards carried Wilhelmina's body out the door and placed her in the back of a hearse. As the hearse pulled away, Ellis sat at his desk, looking over the last of Wilhelmina's belongings. Struggling with the knowledge that he had just witnessed the first woman to ever be put to death in Ohio, he placed her silver cross necklace in an envelope and sealed it, then placed the envelope, along with her Bible and music box, in a small cardboard box labeled with Wilhelmina's name. He then applied stamps to the envelopes she had given him that morning, already addressed to Marta and Karin, to Albert, and to her mother.

Warden Ellis then picked up the three pieces of crumbled paper and started to place them in the box. His curiosity got the better of him, and hands shaking, he began to read what Wilhelmina had written:

> I write this letter as my final attempt to prove my innocence of the crimes for which I am about to die. Please do not ever give this letter to Dr. Johann King, my husband (or Konig, or whichever name he goes by). If anyone else arrives here at the prison to retrieve my belongings – regardless of how many years that may take – please give them this letter. I take this letter with me to the death chamber in hopes it will be found and safely filed in the warden's office. As I sit here this morning writing this letter, I have no way of knowing if it will ever reach beyond the walls of this prison.
>
> Nonetheless, it is my desire that the truth is known. It is my further desire that my Bible, music box, and cross necklace, which I will leave in my cell, be kept with this letter and given to whoever requests my personal effects.
>
> Under my solemn vow to God in Heaven, I write the truth, the truth I could not reveal before now. I have learned that my husband has likely left the country and has abandoned my son, Albert, leaving him in

an orphanage. For this reason, and this reason alone, I believe my son is safe and will not be harmed by Johann, and I trust in God to keep Albert under His wing.

I am now and have always been innocent of the crimes for which I am being punished. Johann came to my jail cell on the final day of my trial and told me the truth. It was he, not I, who ordered the arsenic. It was he who mixed the poison into the flour and sugar, without my knowledge. And, indeed, it was he who put arsenic into his own coffee, just enough to become ill, so that he would have a reason to call the police. Johann King, also once known as Johann Konig, is the true murderer.

Johann threatened me throughout our entire marriage. He threatened to harm my son, Albert, if I did not obey him. He forbade me from leaving the house. We never shared a bedroom. He kept me away from my dearest friends. My life with him was a living hell, but I persevered by the Grace of God and accepted my fate as punishment for what I had done with him when I was young, resulting in the birth of our son. It was not I, but rather my Uncle Otto who took the child to the orphanage, as he was instructed to do so by my father. I confess that I did try to attract Johann. He was my physician in Germany and went by the name of Konig at the time. But I did not seduce him; he raped me in the examination room. Perhaps I was at fault for dressing as I did that day and flirting with him. I am prepared to accept punishment for my behavior.

Johann also told me about his first wife, Anya, who died in childbirth before I met him. He claimed that his elderly father held a deep hatred for Anya, as she was a Jew. Johann told me his own father poisoned his wife with arsenic just days before she gave birth. She and their son, their only child, both died. I believe this is what prompted Johann's hatred for elderly men and something evil inside him took over his mind,

*causing him to murder those innocent men
... and my darling Oskar.*

*I take this knowledge to my grave and
pray that someday, somehow, the truth
will be revealed, and that Johann Konig/K-
ing will meet his own punishment —
whether while living or in the afterlife.*

*In God's Trust,
Wilhelmina Schmidt*

Warden Ellis folded the letter and added it to the box. He then retrieved a piece of paper and wrote the words, "Do not give the contents of this box to Johann King/Konig. Contents may be given to anyone else who arrives asking for the belongings of Wilhelmina Marie Heinrich Schmidt King." He then glued the paper to the top of the box before putting the box in a cabinet drawer. He closed the drawer, sighed, and left his office.

The next day, Wilhelmina's body was laid in a simple pine casket and buried in Mt. Calvary Cemetery in Columbus in an unmarked grave. She received no visitors, no flowers marking her grave. No one would ever know the location of Wilhelmina's final resting place.

Part 3: Richard

Hard. Strong Ruler.

Chapter Twenty-Nine

December 1984

Richard Palmer sat patiently on an uncomfortable chair facing a large wooden desk while he waited for Mr. Martin, the St. Joseph Orphanage administrator, to return to the room. The orphanage sat in Bond Hill, an older area of town just eight miles northeast of downtown Cincinnati. The main building, constructed in 1856, featured Gothic Revival architecture with mansard roofs, ornate detailing, and pointed arches.

The utilitarian administrative offices sported high ceilings, large windows, and decorative moldings. The scuffed desks in the outer office held telephones and typewriters. Metal filing cabinets were crammed together along the walls. The building had a faint musty odor from the accumulation of dust coating the furniture and the endless volumes of leather-bound books.

The door opened behind Richard. Mr. Martin strode into the room and took a seat behind the desk.

"Mr. Palmer, I have reviewed the file, and I believe it contains the information you seek," said Mr. Martin as he handed a manila folder to Richard. "This is your copy to keep."

Richard grasped the folder and stared at it for a moment. "Thank you, sir," he mumbled. "I appreciate your cooperation."

When he arrived at his apartment an hour later, he walked to the kitchen and dropped the file onto the table. He opened the refrigerator, grabbed a beer, and popped it open. Leaning against the sink, he took two large gulps and stared at the papers, files, and brown envelopes scattered on the table. Richard set the beer on the counter, took two steps towards the table, and dropped down onto the cold metal chair.

Richard had spent the last ten months poring over books from the library, researching genealogy records, locating birth and death certificates, and meeting with lawyers. He shuffled through the stack of documents, reordered them, and laid them back down. He then withdrew documents from each envelope and placed them on the pile of papers. Richard opened another folder, removed the newspaper clippings, and added them to the pile.

Finally, he opened the file folder from the orphanage and read through the information, gritting his teeth. Richard rose from the chair, strolled to his bedroom, and retrieved a cardboard box from the closet. After grabbing another beer, he laid the box on the table with everything else.

He flipped the box lids aside, one by one, and chugged more of the amber liquid courage. His lips curled up in a sinister grin, and he swallowed the last gulp. The box contained the last of the puzzle pieces: a sealed envelope, some sheets of folded paper, a Bible, and a music box. He chuckled as he read the instructions affixed to the top of the box—the very instructions written many years ago by Warden Ellis. Richard tore open the envelope, and a silver cross necklace fell out onto the table.

Richard snatched up the pen and held it tight in his grip, the tip hovering above the legal pad. Memories of his father's stories about life in the orphanage came rushing in, and he gritted his teeth, closing his eyes. He was back there again, back to that cold day in 1980 when he flew to Switzerland and met his grandfather, Johann, as he lay dying in a hospital.

In his last moments of life, Johann informed Richard about finding his son at the orphanage in 1924. "I got out of my car and started to go inside,"—he wheezed and coughed, gasping for breath—"but the hatred in my heart for Wilhelmina was strong and my need for revenge too great. I drove away and never saw my son."

Johann died a week later.

The sun began dipping behind the hillside as the memory faded, and the room became dim, so Richard ambled across the kitchen, rubbing his temples, and flipped the light switch up. After grabbing yet another beer, he dropped back into the chair and took a swig while pondering. What would he do? And could he do it? A slow, easy smirk pulled at his lips, and he picked up the pen and started writing.

- Birth certificate – Unnamed newborn, July 10, 1916
  - Place of birth – Cincinnati, Ohio (no hospital on record)
  - Father – unknown
  - Mother – Wilhelmina Heinrich (immigrant from Munich, Germany)
- Orphanage record – Unnamed newborn baby brought to orphanage on July 11, 1916; named Michael by orphanage staff
- Adoption record – Michael adopted in 1926 by Anthony and Margaret Palmer (my grandparents) and left St. Joseph Orphanage, age 10
- Birth certificate – Michael's name changed to Charles Richard Palmer (my father)
- Letter from Wilhelm Klaus Heinrich II (Wilhelmina's brother) – confirms father of Charles/Michael to be Dr. Johann Konig, gynecologist in Munich, Germany)
- Immigration record – Johann Konig arrived at Ellis Island in December 1915, name listed as 'King'
- Immigration record – Wilhelmina Schmidt arrived at Ellis Island in January 1916
- Real estate record – Property at 14398 Glenmary Drive purchased by Johann King in May 1924
- Marriage record – Oskar Schmidt m. Wilhelmina Heinrich, October 12, 1919
- Birth certificate – Albert Klaus Schmidt, born October 15, 1920
- Death certificate – Oskar Schmidt, March 4, 1925
- Marriage certificate – Johann King m. Wilhelmina Schmidt, August 25, 1925

- Newspaper clippings – Arrest, trial, imprisonment and execution of Wilhelmina Marie (Heinrich Schmidt) King
- Marriage certificate – Albert Schmidt m. Elizabeth Harper, May 9, 1948
- Birth certificate – Charlotte Marie Schmidt, born to Albert and Elizabeth Schmidt
- Letter written by Wilhelmina King and retrieved from the Ohio Penitentiary, along with a Bible, necklace, and music box
- Death certificate – Johann Hermann Konig, February 8, 1980 (age 90), buried at Sihfeld Cemetery, Zurich, Switzerland
- Death certificate – Wilhelmina Marie King (nee Heinrich, f. Schmidt), July 10, 1935; place of burial unknown

Richard then wrote additional notes on the legal pad—

- Charlotte works for City of Hamilton
- Single
- Spends time with a girlfriend (name unknown)
- Shops at Kroger in Fairfield
- Seen with girlfriend at SICSA Pet Adoption event in May 1984

He was ready to set his plan in motion.

February 1985

Richard sat behind the wheel of his car, keeping warm, as he watched Charlotte and her friend enter the bar. He had waited for this day for years, this moment, the day he would waltz into Charlotte's life and change it forever. For the past six months he had followed Charlotte nearly every evening when she left work. He watched from a distance as she shopped for groceries, picked up her dry cleaning, met her friends for dinner or drinks. He followed her to her apartment and studied her shadowy figure moving about inside.

Armed with everything he needed to move forward with his plan, Richard turned off his car and stepped out into the cold. He entered the dimly lit bar and scanned the room, his eyes falling on Charlotte as she let out a boisterous laugh. She turned to take a sip of her drink and glanced at him through the mirror as he removed his coat. Their gazes met for a moment, and he ambled over.

Over the next few months, he purposely bumped into Charlotte in different places—the movie theater, the pet adoption event, and the grocery store. He wormed his way into her life, charming her with his wide smile and good looks. He ingratiated himself to her friends, to her parents, to her co-workers. Everyone who met him was mesmerized by his warmth and good nature.

No one knew there was a psychopath beneath the surface, lying in wait to exact revenge on Charlotte—on her family—for what his father had endured and, yes, for what he had endured as a child. But the evil lurking inside Richard resurfaced when he saw what Charlotte and Mindy had discovered. They knew the truth—most of it, anyway—and now Charlotte must pay for the things her ancestors had done to his family.

CHAPTER THIRTY

October 1990

Charlotte shut the door behind Mindy and slowly turned to face Richard.

"Sit down, Charlotte," Richard growled. "We have some things to discuss."

"Get out of my way, Richard," Charlotte muttered. "I'm leaving."

She sidestepped around him, but he latched onto her upper arm and tugged her back.

"You aren't going anywhere. I said *sit down!*"

Their gazes connected, his ablaze with an intense anger that burned into her skin. She balled her hands into fists at her sides, fighting to quell the resentment within. She wrenched her arm from Richard's hold and stepped away from him.

"Leave me alone!" she yelled and took another step toward the door.

Richard grabbed her from behind, wrapping one arm around her neck and pulling her into his body. He tightened his grip around her throat, and Charlotte instinctively fought against his grasp, trying to break free. Her eyes bulged as she gasped for air, face blanching and the veins in her neck standing out starkly. Her body trembled with fear and helplessness. Charlotte clawed desperately at Richard's arm as the room around her grew dark.

Richard released Charlotte, and she dropped to the floor at his feet. She coughed as she massaged her throat, her mind racing. How could she escape? Richard's hands slid under her arms, and he lifted her to her feet, then guided her by the elbow toward the couch, and spun her around to face him.

"For the last time, I told you to *sit down!*" he yelled as he pushed down on her shoulders, forcing her to sit.

Charlotte rested her elbows on her thighs, holding her head in her hands, not daring to look at Richard as he began to pace the room. The silence lingered, eating away at her nerves, and her stomach lurched. Several minutes passed before Richard sat across from her and spoke.

"Look at me," he snarled. Charlotte raised her head and leveled her eyes on his. She straightened her back, crossing her arms over her body.

"For months ... no, for years," he said with a calm, controlled voice, each word measured and deliberate. "For years, I've tried to control your actions, your behavior. I wanted to determine the right time to let you learn the truth, but you had to go nosing around before I was ready."

"I don't know what you're tal—"

"Shut up! You do *not* get to speak, Charlotte. Not yet. But you *will* listen!" Richard leaned forward and searched her eyes, his gaze slowly sweeping over her face, her long golden hair, her body.

"I remember the first time we met. Do you remember, Charlotte? That night in the bar. Your laugh was infectious. Everyone in the place smiled, some even chuckled. You were so beautiful. Those strange hazel eyes of yours, that beautiful blond hair and your body ... You have a beautiful body. Did you know that?"

Charlotte stared at Richard, keeping her face blank, no emotion, no response.

"Of course, you know it, Charlotte. But your beauty is only skin dip. Do you also remember how rude you were that night? When I first laid eyes on you, for a brief moment, I thought to myself, 'No, Richard, don't do it, don't destroy this woman's life. She's too perfect, too beautiful.' But then you turned your back on me, and I knew right then that destroying you was no longer a choice, but a necessity."

Richard rose from the chair and took a step toward the kitchen. "Would you like something to drink, my dear? Yes, I'm sure you would. I'll be in the other room, and you may think this is your chance to flee, but I wouldn't advise it. I'll find you, Charlotte. I'll hunt you down, and I'll destroy everyone you love who stands in my way. You are an intelligent woman. I would advise you to use your head and *stay put*."

He strode into the kitchen, where he poured two glasses of wine. Richard then extracted a small bottle from his pants pocket, opened it, and sprinkled a few grains of white powder into one of the glasses. He closed the lid tightly and pocketed the bottle, then grabbed the glasses and returned to the living room. He handed one glass to Charlotte and resumed his position on the chair opposite her.

"Drink up, Charlotte. You're going to need the liquid courage." He chuckled and took a sip from his glass. "Now, where was I? Oh, yes, at the bar. But let's fast forward, shall we? You were an easy target, you know. I charmed my way into your heart in record time. You never realized I was controlling you, leading you to develop a curiosity about your grandmother. Then your father had that stroke, and in the few words he was able to say, he incited you into action. That's when I knew my plan was working.

"It was rather amusing the way you would fall asleep almost immediately after settling on the couch to watch television. Sometimes, you would wake up a few hours later and take your sleeping pill and go right back to sleep. Other times, you didn't wake up until morning, just in time to shower and go to work.

"But then you started sleepwalking, as I hoped you would. I almost laughed when I saw you cooking breakfast at three in the morning, sound asleep. And it was even more enjoyable watching you squirm whenever you would tell me about waking up somewhere you had never been before, and I was able to convince you that you had never left this apartment. Yes, I had to hold back my laughter. You really thought you were going insane, and watching you struggle with that thought was a prize I never expected to receive.

"But you, Charlotte, you are a stubborn, determined woman. You weren't satisfied with my explanations and went to see that psychologist. It bothered me at first, but then I realized how perfectly it fit into my plan because it prompted you and Mindy to begin the research into your family." Richard took a long gulp from his glass. "Drink your wine. You've barely touched it."

She took another sip and set the glass down on the table in front of her. "Really, Richard, what is your point to all of this? So what if I researched my family history. My father wanted me to know something, something about my grandmo—"

"Yes, your father. The perfect child, never in trouble, loved beyond measure by his parents, especially his mother, your grandmother. It's just too bad my own father never had that kind of love in his life, isn't it, Charlotte?"

"I have no idea what you're talking about, Richard."

"Oh, but I think you do. I've seen everything you've learned so far. But you still don't have the full story, do you, Charlotte?"

Charlotte forced herself to look into Richard's eyes, her own unwavering and devoid of emotion.

"Tell me what you have found out so far, Charlotte."

"You said you already know."

"Yes, I already know, but I want to hear it *from you*!"

Charlotte cleared her throat and clasped her hands together in her lap, closing her eyes and taking deep breaths. *Calm yourself, Charlotte. Stay focused. Look for an escape.*

She opened her eyes and stared at Richard.

"I'm waiting," he said.

"I-I," she said and licked her lips. "I learned my grandmother, Wilhelmina Heinrich, became pregnant at fifteen. I haven't found out who the father was. She was sent by her father to America, here to Cincinnati, and gave birth, in 1916, to a son. As I understand it, someone took the child within hours of his birth to an orphanage, St. Joseph, I think. I haven't confirmed any of this yet, but I'm plan … *was* planning to schedule a meeting with them. She then met my grandfather, Oskar Schmidt, and they were married and had a son, Albert. My father."

"Go on."

"My grandfather died nearly six years after they were married. Papa was only four when it happened. My grandmother then married a doctor she met at the hospital where she worked, Dr. King. Jo … Johann, I believe."

"What happened to your grandmother, Charlotte? I saw the newspaper articles on the table. I know you know."

"She killed several men."

"Did she? And how did she do that, Charlotte?"

"She poisoned them."

"And how did your grandfather *really* die, Charlotte?"

"That's … That was *never* proven!" Charlotte yelled. "It was only speculation!"

"Come, now, Charlotte. What are the odds your grandmother poisoned what, five men, by arsenic and, even though your grandfather died after suffering the very same symptoms, you don't believe he was also murdered?"

"I-I … don't know."

"And, after your grandmother murdered those men, what happened to her?"

"She was found guilty and sent to prison where … where she … where …"

"Where she was executed. Is that correct?"

"Y-Yes. By electro … electrocution" Charlotte choked out the words as tears rolled down her cheeks. She wiped them from her face, directing her gaze away from Richard.

"And is that everything you know?"

Charlotte faced her husband and whispered, "Yes. That's everything."

"Don't lie to me, Charlotte. I saw Mindy's notes. I saw you reading them. Now tell me what you know."

"I-I know … who you are."

Richard chuckled, a low laugh from deep within, rolling into the air like distant thunder.

"Tell me."

"The baby that … that my grandmother had … before my father was born. He … He … He was your … your … f-father."

"Yes. And that means … your grandmother is m—"

"Also *your* grandmother," Charlotte whispered. She narrowed her eyes at him, bitter resentment boiling within.

"You have so much more to learn, dear Charlotte."

CHAPTER THIRTY-ONE

"Now it's my turn. But you need more wine. Stay where you are. I'll get it."

Charlotte's mind raced while Richard was gone. She focused on the table at the far side of the room where the phone rested. *Can I get to the phone and back to the couch before he comes back?* But she hesitated too long; Richard was striding from the dining room with a full glass of wine in his hand.

He set it on the table in front of her and resumed his seat on the chair.

"Drink, Charlotte. And listen."

"To what?" she said and took a sip of wine.

"I have a story to tell you. It's about a young German doctor, deeply in love with a Jewish woman named Anya. He marries her and they are blissfully happy … until his own elderly father poisons Anya out of his hatred for the Jews and their son dies. She then dies a few days later. The tragedy leads the doctor to develop a deep hatred for his father, which later transfers to all elderly men.

"This is also the story about a teenage girl living in Munich, overly spoiled by her parents. She's not a nice girl. She's coy and flirtatious and, as it turns out, is a patient of the widowed doctor. While it is true that the doctor raped the teenage girl, your grandmother, it is also true that she dressed provocatively that day, with the full intention of appearing alluring to him. I have a letter from her own brother confirming these facts.

"Your grandmother learns she is pregnant, and her father sets out to destroy the doctor's career. His reputation in ruins, the doctor escapes to America and changes his last name and his field of practice. What no one knows is that the good doctor went insane after his wife died, even before he meets Wilhelmina. When he sees her for the first time, she looks so much like his Anya that he thinks it *is* her."

Richard took a sip of his wine and settled back in his chair.

"You already know what happened to your grandmother. She gave birth, and following Wilhelmina's father's instructions, her uncle took the baby to an orphanage. He gave the child no name and no information other than the day of his birth and his mother's name. He was named Michael by the orphanage nuns. Wilhelmina didn't even try to find the baby! That child, my father, lived in horrible conditions at the orphanage. When he was four, he was made to clean the toilets, and many times, the nuns made him clean them three or four times until they were satisfied. He was angry and unruly and often the victim of their punishments. Do you know what nuns did to orphans in those days, Charlotte?"

Charlotte shook her head slowly and took another sip of wine.

"They were beaten with rulers and sticks, sent to their beds with their arms, legs, and knuckles bleeding. My father was no exception. He had to tear some of his own clothes to make bandages. Many nights he was sent to bed with no supper and, on some occasions, no food the entire day. Dad didn't even learn how to read until he was eight years old!"

Richard's eyes flared, and he gnashed his teeth with each word, the anger boiling inside him.

"He was ten when my grandparents adopted him and changed his name. Dad was frail. He only weighed forty-seven pounds, much too small for a boy his age. He stuttered when he talked, which he didn't do very much. His adoptive mother was loving and patient, and he began to heal. Physically, anyway. Emotionally and mentally, though, he was never well."

Richard sipped from his glass, eyeing Charlotte over the rim. "So, Charlotte, you know that your grandmother, Wilhelmina, was my father's mother. Have you figured out who his father was?"

"You said he was her gynecologist."

"Yes, I did. Ahh, but I suppose I neglected to tell you his name. You see, Charlotte, his name was Johann Konig. You only know him as Johann King."

Charlotte's eyes grew wide as realization settled in. Richard chuckled.

"That's right, Charlotte. Dr. Konig changed his name to King, and yes, he did bump into Wilhelmina at Good Samaritan Hospital where they both worked. So now you know you and I share a grandmother. What does that make us, then? Cousins? I'm not really sure, but we *are* related, aren't we, dear?"

Charlotte remained silent, praying for someone, anyone to knock on their door and bring an end to her ordeal. She turned her head away from Richard and wiped a tear from her cheek.

"Spare me your tears, Charlotte. They won't change anything that's happened in the past, and they certainly won't change what's about to happen to you!"

Charlotte flew to her feet and took a step toward Richard. He lurched, rage etched into his face, so Charlotte backed away. Her head began to swim as nausea built. She swayed on her feet and dropped onto the couch, unable to maintain her balance. Covering her mouth, she was terrified she would be sick right then and there. She wrestled with the nausea and fear, and glared up at Richard.

"But, why … Why did you marry me if … if you knew … if you knew we are related?"

Richard chuckled and said, "Because, dear Charlotte, I *wanted* you to find out the truth! I wanted you to learn who the true murderer was!"

Charlotte held her stomach as she began to rock back and forth. She wasn't sure how much longer she could keep her stomach in check … or how much longer she could fight off the overwhelming need to sleep.

"What … What do you mean, the *true* murderer?" Charlotte said.

"You see, my dear, it was my grandfather, Dr. Konig … or King, I suppose … who murdered your grandfather, Oskar, and those five men. Remember I told you he had developed hatred for elderly men. He also hated Wilhelmina's father and Wilhelmina herself. Because of them, he lost his home, his thriving medical practice, and his outstanding reputation in Germany as one of the leading gynecologists of the day. When he saw Wilhelmina at the hospital in Cincinnati, he plotted his revenge on her and on her entire family.

"Johann poisoned Oskar and then married Wilhelmina. After the stock market crash, although he had plenty of riches to his name, he complained of financial stress and brought in a boarder to their house … that old Tudor house on Glenmary. I'm sure you remember it, Charlotte. You woke up there that morning last July."

Charlotte shook her head, trying to clear the fog filling her brain, and remembered that day. She had seen something—*someone*—in the window on the third floor of the house. Her grandmother's ghost.

"Allow me to continue, my dear. My grandfather wasn't vindicated after Oskar's death, nor after the first victim died. He continued to bring boarders in over the next few years, until all in all, he had murdered five elderly, innocent men. He even poisoned himself, just enough to result in a visit to the emergency room. Only when Wilhelmina, now his wife, was arrested, did Johann find satisfaction. He sat at her trial, seemingly a devoted and concerned husband, a protective arm around the shoulders of her son … your own father. He watched as the pieces of evidence were presented, clear of his fingerprints and only bearing hers. Yes, he had planned it all out so perfectly. He killed just enough men for Wilhelmina to be considered a serial killer. He knew she would get the death penalty."

As if he had not a care in the world, Richard eased into the chair and took a sip of his wine. "I went to the prison where Wilhelmina was executed and was given the few belongings she left behind. Would you like to know what they were? Well, I'll tell you anyway. A Bible. That's a laugh! Still pretending to be godly to the very end. I burned that. Also, a silver cross necklace. A letter she wrote the day she was executed. Oh, and a music box. Yes, Charlotte, *the* music box I gave to you before we were married!"

Richard reached into his pocket and pulled the necklace out, dangling it by the chain.

"This is your grandmother's necklace. And the letter she wrote, well, I was planning to leave it where you could find it, but I think telling you about it is much better. Your dear grandmother revealed that it was Johann King who committed the murders, as he himself confessed to her before her trial ended. And I knew it was true because I found my grandfather in Switzerland about ten years ago. He confessed everything to me."

Richard laid the necklace on the table beside his chair, picked up the goblet, and took another sip.

"The best part of this whole story, my dear, is that your own father never told you about his mother. He must have been filled with shame, knowing his mother was a cold-hearted, murderous bitch who killed not only five innocent men, but his own father!"

Charlotte's eyes widened, mouth falling open, but no words escaped.

Richard chuckled. "Did you ever wonder, Charlotte, why you woke up at that abandoned factory?"

"Y-Yes," she whispered.

"That was the old Kahn's meat processing plant. Oskar and Wilhelmina both worked there. It's probably where they met. They both lived in the Over-the-Rhine area at the time. After they married, Wilhelmina found a job in the laundry room of Good Samaritan Hospital, which is another place you woke up. And you now know why the house was significant, don't you? That is where the murders took place—the murders that sent your dear, innocent, pious grandmother to the electric chair!"

Richard gazed at Charlotte for several moments, studying her eyes, her face.

"You went to those places, Charlotte, because I led you there. As soon as you feel asleep, I would whisper suggestions in your ear."

"Like ...w-what?" Charlotte asked.

"Oh, like 'drive to the factory on Spring Grove Avenue,' or 'go to the laundry room of Good Samaritan Hospital,' that sort of suggestion. The best one of all was when I would tell you that you would see the ghost of a blond-haired woman in your dreams. It was all I could do to hold back my laughter every time you described where you had been and what you had seen.

"I followed you every time you left the house, knowing you were asleep. I watched as you walked around the parking lot of the factory, as you went into the hospital, and when you woke up in the rain at the house. I always left right away so I would be home before you."

Charlotte licked her lips, stomach roiling. "Rich ... Richard ... I-I feel ... so sleepy. So ... sick."

He snickered. "Yes, yes, I am sure you do. You see, Charlotte, I put Melatodrol in your drink. You will fall asleep soon, my dear. I've been slipping it to you, in your drinks at dinner or when you sat on the couch to watch television with me. I always gave you just enough to keep you asleep for hours and, as I had hoped, start sleepwalking. You didn't disappoint me, Charlotte."

"How ... How long?" Charlotte croaked.

"Oh, my dear, for years!"

He laughed then, a slow, sinister laugh that crashed against her mind, forcing her to shake the fog away.

"N-No, you ... you ... wouldn't. You didn't!"

"Yes, Charlotte, I did. And, oh I loved the wonderful gift from Mindy. Confused, Charlotte? Yes, your best friend handed me a treasure when she insisted you start researching your family history and learn about your grandmother. When I walked in on you today and saw everything you had discovered, I knew it was time to make you pay for the things your ancestors did to ruin my grandfather and my father. Do you remember our first dinner date? I told you that night my father had died of cancer."

"I remember," Charlotte muttered.

"It was a lie. My father killed himself. Because he could never erase the memories of the orphanage, of the atrocities he suffered as a child. Did you ever wonder why you never met my mother?

"You told me she moved away right after we started dating. I assumed she just didn't want to travel much or come back to Ohio."

"Well, that's not exactly how it was, my dear. Dad was deeply disturbed by the things he endured at the orphanage. By the time he was adopted, he hated the nuns and projected that hatred onto women in general. I never knew why he married Mother because he hated her, too. Dad drank ... a *lot*. He never kept a job because of his drinking. And he beat Mother ... and me. They had an argument on my eleventh birthday. He didn't see me crouched in the corner of the living room while he beat Mother with a baseball bat."

Richard sucked in a breath of air and swallowed hard. Charlotte lifted her gaze just as a lone tear trickled down Richard's cheek.

"He k-killed my mother that night. I ran to her where she lay on the floor, a pool of blood forming under her head. I shook her and screamed at her to wake up. But she didn't move. I looked down at my hands and saw my mother's blood on them and started crying. I heard the bat fall onto the floor and saw my dad going down the hall to their bedroom. I just sat there. I didn't know what to do. A few minutes later, I heard a loud bang."

He took a sip of wine.

"Dad shot himself in the head. I don't remember how long I sat there on the floor next to my mother. I eventually called the police, and I was taken away. First to the same orphanage where my father had lived and then to foster homes. But I was angry and out of control. I fought with the other kids. I even beat up one boy who made me mad. I hit one of my foster mothers and was sent back to the orphanage where I remained until I turned eighteen. No one wanted me in their home. I was completely alone."

"But … But you told me you had a brother and sister," Charlotte said.

"Also a lie, Charlotte. I had to paint a picture for you of a well-adjusted adult who had enjoyed a happy childhood. I had no siblings, and my childhood was far from happy. But I wanted you to fall in love with me, I wanted you to learn about Wilhelmina, and I wanted to destroy you and all that you represented to me."

Richard sipped his wine, gazing into Charlotte's eyes, and smiled sadistically at the horrified expression she couldn't hide.

"Drink your wine, Charlotte. You usually down it like water."

Charlotte instinctively did what Richard told her—she picked up her goblet and took a drink.

"Wh … What … What happened to the kitten you adopted for your mother? If she really was dea—"

"Oh, I killed that stupid cat! Drowned it in the tub, then threw its limp little body into the trash."

"Dear God," Charlotte muttered.

"Allow me to continue, Charlotte. When I was in college, I became obsessed with learning more about my father's childhood. I wanted to know what made him so angry. His anger lived in me, too, and for a while I honestly wanted to be rid of it. I wanted to be happy. I wanted to be normal. But when I learned the truth about Wilhelmina and my grandfather, the rage consumed me. And that's when I vowed to find you and destroy your life … *and* your father's life." Richard laughed.

"What do you mean, my f-father's life?" Charlotte stifled a yawn. *Stay awake, Charlotte. Don't fall asleep!*

"Your father used my pharmacy to fill his blood pressure prescription. I gradually decreased the dosage until the only thing he was taking was a placebo. And then the gifts just kept coming and coming when his doctor found blood clots in his leg and prescribed a blood thinner. I also started decreasing that dosage, so your father wasn't really getting the medication he needed. The combination was enough to cause his stroke. It took some time, but it was all worth it in the end. Rather brilliant on my part, eh?" Richard winked at Charlotte.

Charlotte flew to her feet and stumbled. She stretched out her arms to regain her balance and screamed, "No! You … You … Oh my GOD!" Tears flooded her eyes as she stood next to the couch, her entire body shaking.

"Yes, my dear, I suppose I inherited the evil natures of my father and grandfather. I may even be a psychopath, just like them." Richard laughed again. "It took me over two years to find you, but when I did, I was determined that a vendetta must be waged against your family—against your father, your grandmother, your great-grandfather—everyone who ruined *my* family!"

Another wave of nausea bubbled up from Charlotte's stomach, and the room began to spin. She sunk onto the couch, struggling to keep her eyes open. "Why are you telling me all of this, Richard?" Charlotte yawned. "I'll … I'll … tell the … police." No matter how hard she fought, Charlotte could not ward off the effects of the sleeping pill Richard had put in her wine. Her eyelids grew heavy, fluttering open, fluttering shut.

Somewhere from the eerie darkness, Richard rasped, "It's payback time, Charlotte. Time for you to die."

Mindy sat in her idling car a block from Charlotte's apartment, hands shaking as she picked up the phone from the console between the seats. She dialed the police station and asked for her husband.

Moments later Caleb came on the line and said, "Hey, Min, what's up?"

"Cal-Caleb … please." She bit her trembling lip.

"Okay, something's wrong. Is it one of the kids?"

"N-No, they're with the babysitter. They … They're fine. It's … It's … Charlotte."

"Okay, honey, calm down. Speak slowly. Tell me what's happened. Was there an accident?"

"No … No accident. Caleb, I think Richard is going to hurt Charlotte!"

"What? No, you must be wrong. Richard adores Charlotte!"

"No, Caleb. I-I don't think he does. We were … We were doing more research about Charlotte's grandmother, and he came home, to their apartment, and … and …"

"Take your time, honey. What happened?"

"He saw the newspaper articles we found and the notes I had written down. Caleb, he got … he got *so* angry! I've never seen anyone that angry before. It terrified me. Please, Caleb, can you … can you send …"

"You want me to send a patrol to check on Charlotte?"

"Y-Yes. And … Can you go, too?"

"Yes, yes, honey. Where are you?"

"I'm about a block away, in my car."

"Okay, listen to me. I know you want to help your friend, but it's important that you just go home and wait to hear from me. Do you understand, Mindy?"

"Yes, but—"

"I mean it, Min. If Charlotte really *is* in danger, I don't want you anywhere near there. You could also be hurt. Please do as I ask."

"Okay … but you better call me as soon as you know she's safe!"

"I will. Just go home and be careful. I love you."

"I love you, too, Caleb. Thank you."

Caleb located two officers about to go on patrol and gave them Charlotte's address. He climbed into his car and led the way to the apartment complex.

Muffled voices drifted like feathers to Charlotte's ears. Her eyes shot open, but she quickly shut them against the bright, fluorescent light above. She twisted on the bed, her head groggy, as she struggled to sit up.

"Charlotte!" cried Mindy, seated on a chair next to the bed. "Caleb, get the doctor!"

Charlotte opened her eyes again, slowly this time. Mindy hovered over, her beautiful smile greeting her friend.

"Min … what …?" Charlotte swallowed hard.

"Don't try to talk just yet, Char. We'll explain soon."

The doctor stepped into the room and stood next to the bed, shining a tiny flashlight into Charlotte's eyes. "How are you feeling, Mrs. Palmer?" said Dr. Cox.

"Gr-Groggy," she replied. "And … thirsty."

"We'll get you some water. Can you sit up?"

Charlotte nodded, and the doctor pressed a button on the bed, raising her head until she was in a partially upright position.

"Wh-What happened … to me? My stomach … hurts."

Mindy handed Charlotte a glass of ice water and said, "In a little while, Char. We want to make sure you're all right."

Charlotte sipped the cool water, eyes locked on the doctor.

"It seems you were given a rather large dosage of Melatodrol and nearly overdosed," said Dr. Cox. "Luckily, the police arrived at your apartment in time and called for an ambulance. We had to pump out your stomach. That explains why it is tender. We're going to keep you overnight for observation, but if all goes well, you should be able to return home tomorrow."

Charlotte nodded and drank more water. The doctor left the room, leaving her alone with her friends.

"Please, I need to know …"

Mindy and Caleb glanced at each other. Caleb nodded, and Mindy sat on the chair, taking Charlotte's hand into her own.

"Char, Richard tried to kill you last night. Do you remember what he said to you after I left?"

Charlotte nodded.

"Well, when you're better, you'll need to tell us ... and the police. He was taken into custody."

"But ... how—"

"When I left your apartment, I drove around the corner and called Caleb. He and two other officers came to the apartment—apparently, just in time, too."

"What happened to Rich ... him?"

"Well, like I said, they took him into custody when they found you passed out on the floor. When you get out of here tomorrow, you'll need to go to the station to file charges and answer some questions. I'll be there with you, don't you worry about that."

"Thank ... Thank you, Min. You're the best."

"Yeah, well, I know it." Mindy and Charlotte both laughed.

Charlotte was released the next afternoon, and Mindy took her straight to the Fairfield Police Station. She filled out the necessary paperwork and waited in an interrogation room for the detective. Recounting the events of two days prior, Charlotte backtracked often to explain what led her to research information about her grandmother. She held Mindy's hand, squeezing it tightly to fight back tears that insisted on pooling in her eyes as she talked.

After leaving the station, they went to Charlotte's townhouse, packed most of her clothes and necessary belongings, and wove their way through traffic to Mindy's house. Charlotte unpacked in the guest room and then watched the children while Mindy prepared dinner.

Later Charlotte sat on the edge of her bed staring at one Melatodrol pill, reluctant to swallow it. She eased up, retrieved her pill cutter from her overnight bag, and halved the pill. She took the half-pill with a large gulp of water and climbed into the bed, soon falling into a restful, deep sleep.

Two days later, after retrieving her car from the apartment complex, Charlotte drove to the nursing home where her father lived.

His condition had not improved, and her mother could no longer provide proper care for him. Charlotte walked into her father's room, hugged her mother, and kissed her father's cheek.

"He hasn't been awake much the last several days, Charlotte," her mother told her. "Talk to him, though. He might be able to hear you. I'm going to the cafeteria. Take your time, darling. I love you." Elizabeth kissed her daughter's cheek and left the room, closing the door behind her.

Charlotte settled on the edge of the bed and took Albert's hand. "Papa?" she croaked as she blinked tears away. "Can you hear me, Papa?"

Albert's eyelids fluttered but did not open.

"Papa, I found out the truth. About your mother. About Grandmama."

Albert's hand tightened around Charlotte's, and his fingers twitched in her grip. When she peered into his face again, Albert's eyes were open and gazing at his daughter.

"Papa! Are you awake? Can you hear me?"

Albert's mouth opened slightly, and he grunted, nodding his head.

"Oh, Papa. I love you so!" she said. "Papa, your mother … she was innocent. She didn't kill those men. It was … It was that doctor … Dr. King. Her second husband. Do you remember him, Papa?"

Albert nodded again and blinked his eyes.

"It was him all along. And … And he … he killed your father, too. I'm so sorry, Papa!

Albert squeezed his daughter's hand again.

"Papa, I'm taking everything I found out to the police. I know it's too late to save your mother, but she will be declared innocent. I'll see to it!"

Albert rubbed his lips together and opened his mouth. The door opened behind Charlotte as Elizabeth tiptoed into the room and to the other side of the bed.

"Th-Th-Thank you," he breathed. "Y-You … sss-sss-saved her."

"Oh, Papa, *I'm* the one who needed saving," Charlotte whispered.

Albert shut his eyes as one side of his mouth twitched into a half-smile. His fingers slackened in Charlotte's hand, and he took his final breath.

CHAPTER THIRTY-TWO

March 1992

Richard was arrested and charged with three crimes—attempted murder, embezzlement, and drug theft. He had been skimming funds from the cash registers at the pharmacy and stealing Melatodrol for many years. The prosecution wanted murder added for the death of Charlotte's father, but there was not enough evidence to prove he had tampered with Albert's prescriptions.

Richard's trial lasted less than a week and he was sentenced to fifty years without parole in the Southern Ohio Correctional Facility in Lucasville, Ohio. He would be ninety-two years old at the end of his sentence, but he died in the prison infirmary just after his seventy-fourth birthday, having succumbed to pneumonia.

Charlotte filed for divorce shortly after Richard's arrest and had her name legally changed back to Schmidt. She bought a house just three doors away from Mindy and Caleb, adopted a puppy, and moved her mother into the master suite.

A month after Richard's trial, Charlotte bumped into her old boyfriend, Robert Miller—literally—in the cereal aisle at the grocery store. They agreed to meet for drinks a few days later.

"I have to tell you, Charlotte," Robert said, "the biggest mistake I ever made in my life was cheating on you. And I'm not just saying that now as a way to get into your bed. I really mean it. I owe you a huge apology for that. I can't begin to hope you will ever forgive me."

They talked for hours, reminiscing about the past, recounting stories of their lives after their breakup, and sharing their hopes for the future. When the bartender announced last call, Robert paid the tab and walked Charlotte to her car.

"Charlotte, this has been amazing. I feel like the last several years haven't happened. I never thought I'd see you again, much less have such an enjoyable evening. I hope you'll agree to see me again."

"Tonight was enjoyable, Robert, but ..." she said.

"It's never good when there's a 'but' involved." Robert groaned.

"I'm sorry, Robert, it's just not going to work between us. You're a great guy and your apology seems sincere, but I really can't forget what you did. If tonight had happened seven or eight years ago, I would have buckled and fallen right back into the relationship. But, Robert, I'm better than that now. I'm stronger. And frankly, I don't need you. Tonight was fun, but that's all it was. I'm sorry."

"I'm sorry, too. I wish it could be different, but I suppose I understand. Goodnight, then?"

"Yes, goodnight. I really need to get home to my mother. Thanks for the drinks."

That night, Charlotte snuggled into her bed next to her Sheltie-Collie puppy, Hank, and drifted into a deep, restful sleep without the assistance of her prescription drug. She dreamt of a row of houses standing side-by-side on a narrow street. A young, blond-haired boy rode on a bicycle, and a tall man ran alongside, teaching the boy how to ride. Seated on the stoop in front of one of the houses, a pretty woman with shoulder-length blond hair laughed and clapped while watching the man and boy.

Charlotte kept her gaze directed at her feet as she walked toward the house and peered back up to find the woman gazing right back. The woman waved at Charlotte, gesturing for her to come closer. She stood as Charlotte drew near and pointed to the man and boy, both laughing as they wheeled the bike back to the house. Charlotte glanced at the two, then back to the woman, as an open smile formed on her lips.

"Are ... Are you ...?" Charlotte said, her voice echoing in the dream state.

"Yes, dear, I am your grandmother. And this is your grandfather and your father."

Charlotte's eyes grew wider as she looked at the three of them—Wilhelmina, Oskar and Albert, together again. A light rain began to trickle from the sky, and a faint mist floated from the street. She peered into her grandmother's eyes just as the fog encompassed her.

Before the mist whisked them all away, Wilhelmina smiled at Charlotte and whispered, "Thank you."

Glossary of German Terms

Ach Mein Schatz _____Oh, my Darling
Die Gedanken Sind Frie___German folk song,
                      "Thoughts Are Free"
Du wirst mir fehlin_____I will miss you
Eintopf_____One pot stew made with
                      meats, vegetables and legumes
Guten morgen_____Good morning
Hure_____Whore
Kindchen_____Dear Child
Schwesterlein_____Little Sister
Streuselkuchen_____Crumb Cake
Topfschlagen_____Hit the Pot (a child's game)
Wurstplatte_____Platter of meats and cheeses

A Note from the Author

On December 7, 1938, serial killer Anna Marie Hahn died in the electric chair at Ohio Penitentiary in Columbus, Ohio. She was the first woman in this state to be executed for her crimes. At the end of a month-long trial in 1937, she was found guilty of the murders of several elderly men, whom she poisoned with arsenic. Anna Marie maintained her innocence throughout her trial and subsequent imprisonment. However, just days before her execution, she wrote a letter of confession, stating she did indeed commit the crimes but wrote: "I couldn't have been in my right mind when I did them (*sic*, these terrible things)."[1] Anna Marie's is a fascinating story—one of deceit, a lust for gambling on racehorses, and a desperation for money.

We have not been able to find any information on Anna Marie's husband, Philip Hahn, or her son Oscar following her death and, therefore, have no proof that Philip or Oscar were ancestors of my husband's.

Regardless, it was her story that inspired me to write *Wilhelmina*. I drew from the basic aspects of Anna Marie's crimes to create this work of fiction. I hope you enjoyed it.

[1] Excerpt from *The Goodbye Door* by Diana Britt Franklin

In Appreciation

First and foremost, I owe my deepest gratitude to my mother, Mary (Catron) Bridges, for encouraging me as a child to explore my creativity and commit pen to paper. Mom has been gone since 2009, but her love remains with me.

I would also like to thank my husband, Douglas Hahn, for your constant encouragement and honesty. You have helped me become a better person and a better writer. I love you today, tomorrow, and always.

My sincere appreciation goes to my Beta readers: Douglas Hahn, Becky Raike, Jenn Dibert, and Isobel Rondeau. Your critiques and suggestions helped craft a much better story.

I would be remiss if I did not include a special thanks to my editor, Melissa Rodgers (who not only edited the manuscript, but offered many tips for improving my writing and extended her hand in friendship); my cover designer, Ruth Anna Evans Designs; my formatter, Kari Holloway of KH Formatting; and my dear friend and photographer, Brenda Pottinger.

Lastly, I want to thank my treasured friends for your support, your encouragement, and your love and friendship: Rachel Feltner (my daughter), Aimie Skidmore, Rose Mary Burdine, Kay Goetz, Rosemary Cox, Julie Kilbarger, Christy Kerley, Brenda Pottinger, and Becky Raike. I would be remiss if I did not also mention Lil Flick, who left us before she could read this book. Life would not be nearly as much fun or filled with as much love without all of you.